PENGUIN BOOKS

The Forgotten Summer

Here's what the readers are saying . . .

'A wonderful story full of family drama and myst
Beautiful and rich writing, wonderful nature, and lo
of secrets and intrigue – this book has it all'
This Chick Reads

'I loved this book. I kept snatching a few more pages whenever I could. It has left me wanting to head to warmer climes and take part in the grape and olive harvests. Well I can dream can't I?'
Mumsnet

'Carol will take you away as you become immersed in the unusual life of the Cambon family, where no one is quite who they first seemed to be'
The French Village Diaries

'Her beautifully written prose propels the reader into a sensory haven of fragrant olive groves, rattling cicadas and bejewelled dragonflies . . . Carol Drinkwater is an incredibly talented writer, with a real skill for weaving an engaging story'
The Bookbag

'*The Forgotten Summer* is literary, well researched and hugely satisfying to read. It explores not just love, but searing grief, hatred, deceit, joy and despair, providing a richness of experience for the reader . . . wonderfully atmospheric writing'
Linda's Bookbag

'A beautiful, atmospheric story of loss, family drama and mystery'
Nicola Edwards, *Love Reading*

'I really enjoyed the tense story . . . and the secret? Well let's just say it was not what I was expecting!'
Angie Rhodes, *Love Reading*

'*The Forgotten Summer* instantly transported me to France and a way of life I had seen many times but long forgotten'
Jan Kirkcaldy, *Love Reading*

'Carol Drinkwater has a way of combining love and mystery along with her love of France that the reader cannot help but be totally absorbed by. For me it just doesn't get any better'
Tracy Shephard, *Net Galley*

'An absolutely outstanding book which I couldn't put down until I finished at 4.30 a.m. Look no further for an intelligently written book with twists and turns I hadn't seen coming. Epically excellent. 5*'
Violet Fields, *Net Galley*

ABOUT THE AUTHOR

Carol Drinkwater is a multi-award-winning actress who is best known for her portrayal of Helen Herriot in the BBC series *All Creatures Great and Small.*

Carol is the author of twenty-one books, both fiction and nonfiction, and has achieved bestselling status – over a million copies sold worldwide – with her quartet of memoirs set on her olive farm in the south of France. Carol's fascination with the olive tree extended to a solo Mediterranean journey in search of the tree's mythical status. The resulting bestselling travel books, *The Olive Route* and *The Olive Tree*, have inspired a five-part documentary film series.

Carol's three short stories released as Kindle Singles, *The Girl in Room Fourteen*, *Hotel Paradise* and *A Simple Act of Kindness*, have reached the top of the charts on both sides of the Atlantic.

Twitter @Carol4OliveFarm
www.caroldrinkwater.com
www.facebook.com/olive.farm

The Forgotten Summer

CAROL DRINKWATER

PENGUIN BOOKS

PENGUIN BOOKS

UK | USA | Canada | Ireland | Australia
India | New Zealand | South Africa

Penguin Books is part of the Penguin Random House group of companies whose addresses can be found at global.penguinrandomhouse.com.

First published by Michael Joseph 2016
Published in Penguin Books 2016
008

Set in 11.88/14.13 pt Garamond MT Std
Typeset by Jouve (UK), Milton Keynes
Printed in Great Britain by Clays Ltd, St Ives plc

A CIP catalogue record for this book is available from the British Library

ISBN: 978–1–405–92414–6

www.greenpenguin.co.uk

For Michel, *jusqu'à la fin . . .*

'I almost wish we were butterflies and liv'd but three summer days – three such days with you I could fill with more delight than fifty common years could ever contain.'

– John Keats, *Bright Star: Love Letters and Poems of John Keats to Fanny Brawne*

Oh, je voudrais tant que tu te souviennes
Des jours heureux où nous étions amis
En ce temps-là la vie était plus belle
Et le soleil plus brûlant qu'aujourd'hui.

Les Feuilles Mortes (Autumn Leaves),
Jacques Prévert

PART ONE
Loss

I

September, South of France

A bouquet of succulent flavours was drifting up the stairs from the kitchen, whetting Jane's appetite and urging her to get out of bed. Even at that unearthly hour, her stomach was growling. She and her husband, Luc Cambon, had been awake since before dawn. The difference was that he was up and busy, while she was still idling beneath the bedcovers. Eyes closed, she inhaled the delectable smells of breakfast. Matty – God bless her cotton socks – was cooking up a feast, a healthy Provençal alternative to a fry-up. Eggs, tomatoes, thinly sliced, garden-grown, purple-black aubergines, their own single-estate olive oil, thick slices of boiled ham from the pastor's pigs, fattened on wild chestnuts, home-baked bread, fresh fruit . . . Mmm. A scrumptious repast.

'Lazybones, get out of bed,' Jane mumbled to herself.

She could hear Luc singing softly in the shower. He had already been at his computer for some time. Knees curled up to her chest, eyes closed, she had listened to him firing off emails, writing texts, preparing interviews: work, work, ad infinitum. She had always been in awe of his passion and energy, but if she were honest, there were times when his relentless drive left her feeling inadequate. Her work as a translator was fulfilling and challenging, but she did not bring to it the same level of obsession he brought to his films. Luc had always been so much more single-minded than she.

She yawned loudly, sounding like their dog, threw off the

sheets and perched on the edge of the mattress, rubbing her temples. A mild headache, and her back and pectorals were killing her. The result of lifting and carrying all those baskets the day before, and she had probably downed a glass too many during the grape-pickers' dinner the previous evening.

She rose gingerly – the aches would soon disappear once she was back out in the fields and her muscles had warmed up – and crossed barefoot to open the shutters. These mid-September mornings were blissful: Indian-summer days, warm and golden. There was little to beat the pleasure of being outdoors, away from her laptop and the reams of French text awaiting translation. Terrific exercise and usually fun. However, the previous day, the temperature had crept into the low thirties, higher than forecast, higher than average. Jane, along with the team of hired hands, was hoping that today would be more merciful.

Luc and the estate's gardener-cum-caretaker, Claude Lefèvre, had been debating climate change, and its effects on the crops, in the barn the previous evening. Jean Dupont and Michel Lonsaud, two locals regularly employed by the Cambons, had thrown in their cent's worth too. All four had eventually agreed that viticulture was a great deal less predictable and, hence, more financially precarious than it had been when those farming men were boys growing up here in the South of France.

Jane flung open the French windows. Their bedroom was on the first floor at the rear of the big old Provençal farmhouse. A generously sized corner room, with two sets of glass doors, one facing inland, north towards the mountains, and the other east, across sprawling plots of black-grape-espaliered vineyards. It was a calming yet invigorating landscape, and Jane welcomed dallying there, before the demands of the day flooded in upon her, to absorb the split second of silence that accompanied sunrise. It was as though every living creature was holding its breath, awaiting the sun's appearance from beyond the mountain summits. It never failed to exhilarate her, to burst her banks of gratitude for the gifts life had given her.

She stepped out onto the iron balcony, dewy-damp underfoot, stretching her arms and torso as the sunlight streamed into the room, a hundred glorious fragrances riding on its sheened wave. Pine resin, wild lavender, garden-fresh thyme, rosemary, juniper . . .

Les Cigales' forty-nine hectares of arable grounds were presided over by the eighteenth-century eight-bedroomed manor house. Three storeys high, constructed with blocks of local stone and adorned with slatted wooden shutters, painted to protect against the southern heat, it was the principal residence in a landscape of low-lying vineyards, outbuildings, cottages and fruit groves. Further inland, the estate's gnarled olive trees clamped the rising grounds, like hunched hikers scaling the mountains.

Jane inhaled the crisp air and listened to the cacophony of calls that came with the dawn: the birds' chorus, an assembly of cocks crowing, a distant donkey braying. Soon it would be the pealing of the Angelus bell from the church in the nearby village of Malaz, summoning the faithful to the first of the day's devotions. She shivered. She needed coffee urgently. A strong shot of Matty's fine Arabic brew. 'I definitely drank too much last night.'

'*Chérie*, what are you mumbling about? The bathroom's free. I'm going to grab some breakfast. See you down there. Don't be too long.'

'Righto.' As much as Jane relished the early starts, she would happily have settled for another hour in bed this morning, but she wouldn't let the team down, couldn't disappoint Luc. In fact, she enjoyed mucking in along with everyone else, a witness to Luc's satisfaction at superintending yet another first-rate harvest, and it certainly went some way to keeping his mother quiet. God, *Luc's mother.* Jane loved almost everything about Les Cigales, except Clarisse Cambon.

The sun was rising fast, hitting the flanks of the mauve mountains, the virid acres of sloping vineyards, and bathing the olive groves in a soft flaxen light. Voices called and echoed in the distance. *Les journaliers*, Clarisse's hired hands. They must already be congregating by the tractor, raring to get started, and Luc would not be far behind them, waving, smiling, orchestrating the launch of the day's picking. Judging by the day before, the first gathering day of this vintage, the workers seemed a jovial bunch and the grapes were top quality.

Whatever his professional commitments, Luc always made a point of returning to Les Cigales to preside over the harvest, the *vendange*. It was a tradition, a family ritual, taught to him by his late grandfather. And Jane always accompanied him. It was a lively, social few weeks although, truth to tell, the family business, these days, was little more than a mother and son affair. It had been struggling since the death of Luc's aunt Isabelle, who had been the driving force, the quality control behind the whole enterprise. Clarisse had no head for figures and she was equally negligent with her staff, which left Luc to pick up the pieces.

Now he opened the door, darting back into the room. 'I forgot my phone.' His hair was still damp from his shower. Jane noticed that he hadn't bothered to shave. He was so handsome, charismatic, younger in all senses than his fifty-five years, and still trim in jeans, a black T-shirt and sturdy boots. He had a half-eaten croissant in his hand.

'Aren't you dressed yet? Matty's serving breakfast in the barn across the courtyard. Dan's down there.'

'Dan?'

'He arrived about midnight, shortly after you'd gone to bed. Claude is about to drive the first bunch up in the trailer to the fields.'

Jane picked up the iPhone from Luc's bedside table and handed it to him. 'I'll be five minutes.'

He nodded, took the phone, tapped at its screen, as though expecting a message, cursed silently, then pecked his wife on the cheek.

Jane thought he seemed tense. 'You all right?' she called, as he returned to the open door.

'Of course. Do get a move on, *chérie*, or we'll have to send the tractor back a second time for you, and I need Claude to keep an eye on that Dutch couple. They haven't picked before and quite a few of their loads were bruised yesterday. It baffles me why Clarisse put them on the payroll. "A waste of precious funds", in her own words. Claude spent half of yesterday explaining how to choose and snip the clusters and then, what with keeping an eye on them as –'

'Hey, I know how important the *vendange* is, but it is only grapes, Luc.'

Luc shook his head and smiled. 'Better not let it get to me, eh? Spoil the fun. Hurry up and join us. It gives a bad impression if we turn up late.'

And with that he was gone.

She listened to his feet pounding down the wooden staircase. Something was on her husband's mind. He had been bickering non-stop with Clarisse, edgy about his film, uncharacteristically short-tempered. He usually took such delight in the *vendange*, even when things weren't a hundred per cent. He handled any snags or problems with grace and ease, without fuss. Jane washed hastily, threw on cargo pants, Converse sneakers, T-shirt, scarf and a wool hoodie. She'd lose the outer layers as the sun's heat began to bite and her body to burn with activity.

But what was troubling Luc?

Downstairs, she breezed through the breakfast room. Because it was too clammy to eat indoors at this time of year, even with the fan whizzing at full speed, the room stood still and empty. Silent, save for the ticking clock on the chimney breast. It read ten past six. Heading towards the rear of the house, she noticed that the door to the large pantry was open. There, she caught sight of Matty, shifting produce from one shelf to the next, lining it up like soldiers. Over the years, Matty had grown thickset – a result of her own splendid recipes – but still she moved efficiently in her rope-soled espadrilles.

Eggs, cups of flour for pastry, fresh leafy salads coated in dew, glass jars running over with preserved fruits. A large, sunflower-yellow bowl chock-full of dark sticky figs bleeding juice. Here, a subtle alchemy was practised, all presided over by Mathilde Lefèvre.

Jane veered right to the pantry and the two women greeted one another with a kiss on both cheeks. When Jane had been a girl, visiting Les Cigales with her father, who had been setting up a wine outlet in Britain, Matty had sometimes looked after her and a lasting bond had grown up between them.

'Morning, Matty. Looks like you're planning one of your delicious tarts for lunch.'

'And a quiche or two, Madame Jane,' the housekeeper replied.

'That'll keep the team happy. See you later.'

Outside, Jane swung left onto the stone paving, jogging towards coffee and sustenance. She was intercepted by

Walnut, their Springer Spaniel, who bounded to the courtyard barn ahead of her, tail wagging at the sight of his mistress. Clarisse Cambon, clad even at this hour in broad-brimmed sunhat and oversized dark glasses, was hovering by the open door, smoking.

Damn!

No morning kisses were exchanged between daughter and mother-in-law.

'You're the last,' was Clarisse's salutation as she tossed the stub of her cigarette to the gravel and ground it out with the toe of her Chanel sandal.

'*Bonjour*, Clarisse. I trust you slept well?'

'When do I ever sleep well, with all this responsibility on my shoulders?'

'I'll just grab a coffee.'

'You're too late. Claude has already left with the second load for the fields. Everybody was ready except you. I'm still here because I'm waiting to ferry you up in my car before I go to the winery. Luc needs Claude on the spot. He can't be back and forth just for you.'

'I'll take one of the bicycles.' Jane eased past Clarisse, who was blocking the doorway, intentionally or perhaps not; Jane didn't know. 'After coffee,' she added emphatically. She had been looking forward to tucking into a substantial breakfast to set her up for the day, but in the company of Clarisse her appetite had unexpectedly diminished.

Clarisse followed Jane into the barn. A long wooden table cluttered with the leftovers from the hired hands' meal dominated the space. Platters of fruit, dredged bowls of coffee, jugs, jam-sticky plates. The older woman, queen bee of the establishment, set her walking stick upright against the vast pine-wood dresser and stood rubbing the backs of her hands as though smothering them in cream. Jane helped herself to an apple and slid it into her pocket. She downed her black coffee in a couple of gulps and ignored her mother-in-law, who looked as though she was agitating about something. Was it Jane's punctuality or was Clarisse spoiling for a row about a more serious matter? There was tension in the air, no doubt about it.

'What's Dan doing here? He turned up late yesterday with all his camera equipment.'

Jane didn't reply. She didn't know the answer.

'Has Luc spoken to you about this wretched film he's making?'

Jane shook her head, puzzled. 'He rarely does until he's finished shooting, you know that.'

'I don't understand why he's digging up the past like this. Rooting about, questioning anybody he can get an opinion out of. Why doesn't he leave the bloody dead to rest? What the hell is the point?'

Jane helped herself to a fig.

'You saw the way he rounded on me yesterday, blaming me, making me wrong for employing the Dutch couple. How was I to know they were not up to the job?'

Jane was bemused by Clarisse's leap from one subject to another, not to mention her edgy frame of mind. 'It's only day two, Clarisse. They'll get the hang of it. It's grape-picking, not brain surgery. One basket of fruit was a little squashed, that's all.'

'It was more than one, and what the hell would you know? Luc is mad with me for hiring them. Or mad with me about something. I can't be held responsible for every bloody mishap. I'm not as young as I was. I've had to struggle to keep this place against all odds . . . When Isa and I first came here, Luc was just a small boy. He wouldn't remember how we were despised, and you know why?'

Jane did. She had heard this rant on many previous occasions.

'Because we were colonials from Algeria. We are a French family, French citizens, French passport-holders, but they call us Pieds-Noirs. No one bothered to ask if there was another side to the story.'

'See you later, Clarisse. Have a good day.'

With that, Jane was on her way, haring across the courtyard to the sheds where the bikes were stowed. Walnut panted, hot on her path, relishing the activity. 'Double damn!' The door was locked.

Jane swung on her heels, retraced her steps to the rear of the house, into the kitchen, past the range, and begged Matty's set of keys, which the housekeeper drew out of her pinafore pocket. 'Two seconds and I'll be back with them.'

'*Merci beaucoup*, Jane. I promised Monsieur Luc I'd dust downstairs in his den later this morning. I think he and Monsieur Daniel are intending to work there later.'

Jane stopped in her tracks. 'Surely not.'

Luc had always set aside his professional commitments during the harvest. It was a sacrosanct period, a crucial season for the estate. Their next year's income depended on it. Overseeing the gathering and crushing required experience and skill. As the grapes ripened on the vines, sugar and acid levels increased, diseases set in, tannin levels changed. Luc had always insisted on being there to oversee the work. Dan's arrival, as Matty had suggested, would mean that Luc had shifted his priorities.

She grabbed a bicycle and set off, cutting across a couple of fields before bouncing onto the firm, dusty tracks that fringed the vineyards. The ride inland towards the mountains would take her about twenty minutes. Time alone. Time with nature, overlooking the Mediterranean, on the borders of the Alpes-Maritimes and Var regions. Jane pedalled fast, singing, hoping Luc wouldn't be angry with her for being so late. Walnut charged along at her side, black ears flapping, racing the bike, then slowing to catch his breath, pink tongue hanging loose, chuffed with himself and his energetic start to the day. In the distance, the bells of the village churches were pealing, beckoning the remaining faithful to the first of the morning's weekday masses. Here on the estate, grapes were the religion and Jane, she chuckled to herself, was the pagan.

2

Everyone was at work when Jane and the spaniel skidded to a halt by the northern fields, planted on sloping land and therefore more arduous to pick: feet balanced unevenly on the earth, body leaning all day at an awkward angle. She ditched the bike on the grass fringe and yelled a greeting to anyone within earshot. Her fellow pickers barely noticed her arrival. They appeared to have a good rhythm going. The roll-call was six regulars, Provençal men, who hailed from various villages thereabouts. They were the same half a dozen who signed up every year to lend a hand, grateful for the opportunity to earn a few extra euros from the proprietors of the great estate.

Not that Clarisse Cambon was renowned for her generosity. Quite the reverse. She had been dubbed a 'tight-fisted old bag' years earlier, but needs will when needs must. 'Life in rural France is not what it used to be,' they grumbled during breaks.

'As they have moaned and bitched for the past three decades,' retorted Clarisse to Claude, when the caretaker had begged a small pay increase on behalf of the labourers.

Luc, on the other hand, firmly held that his mother should raise the hourly picking rate by at least a euro. 'The estate's accounts won't suffer unduly,' he begged her. 'Taking care of your employees is an investment.'

'It will bankrupt me. You don't know how hard I struggle to keep this place afloat. If you were here full-time . . .' There was no arguing with her on the subject. As far as

Clarisse was concerned, Luc and Jane should have given up their own lives, their London home, and moved to Les Cigales five years earlier when Aunt Isabelle, Clarisse's sister-in-law, had died.

Working with the temporary local team was Arnaud Lefèvre, a beefy taciturn man in his early forties. Born and reared on the estate, he was one of Claude and Matty's twin sons. He was the bachelor of the two brothers who, like his parents, had been employed full-time at Les Cigales until after Isabelle had died, at which point Clarisse had laid him off.

The foreign hands this year consisted of a pair of Australians, Sandy and Jake – backpackers and sweethearts. They were halfway through a two-year round-the-world trip and were earning their keep as they travelled onwards. Jane had rather taken to them for their lively, irreverent energy. More so than she had to the two other couples. An English pair, Clive and his wife Susie, both in their mid-thirties, who made it a rule, they'd told Jane, to take their annual holidays in September to be in France for the grape-picking. Then there was the Dutch couple, Merel and Olaf, in their late fifties, a rather dull twosome.

Last on board was Dan, who hailed from Paris and was Luc's cameraman, close friend and confidant. Jane caught sight of him and waved but he didn't notice. His camera was locked to his shoulder. He was not picking fruit but filming the activities. Why? Was this to be a scene in Luc's new documentary? Jane had never known Dan drive down for the *vendange.* His presence didn't displease her, though. She had always liked him, had always felt comfortable in his company. He was less driven than Luc, more lighthearted and easy to be with.

She snipped a bunch of grapes off a nearby vine, a musky thick-skinned variety, then sucked a few to quench her thirst and clear her throat after the dusty cycle ride. Seeds and soft inner flesh disappeared, the empty skins she tossed to the ground. Then she grabbed an empty pannier and lunged the length of one of the vine rows where other pickers hadn't yet penetrated, immersing herself in a maze of green leaves and repetitive activity. 'Select a ripe cluster, clip it and place it in the *comporte*, the basket.' She lifted her face, delighting in the warmth of the early sun on her closed eyelids. 'Select a ripe cluster . . .'

Late cicadas woke to the morning and began to rattle their desire, beating into the monotony. A dragonfly swooped by, settling on a neighbouring plant. Jane paused to watch it, fascinated by the slow lift and fall of its royal-blue body against the rich green leaf, its protruding eyes. She was always pleased to see a dragonfly. Luc had taught her many years earlier, when they were both children and she a visitor to the estate, that dragonflies were 'good guys' and she shouldn't be afraid of them or hurt them: they ate the mosquitoes, 'and no one enjoys picking fruit while mozzies and midges constantly attack you and suck your blood'.

Overhead, swallows were swooping and wheeling. The Indian summer must have delayed their departure. Jane smiled as she worked, recalling blissful childhood days she had spent there. Days when she and Luc had lain side by side in the long grass, birdwatching through binoculars, gorging on fresh strawberries nabbed from the greenhouse; when they had roamed the estate together, like a pair of conquerors, and she had grown to inhabit it and love it as though it were her own. Luc had taught Jane not to fear the great outdoors. Little suburban English Jane, afraid of spiders, cowed by the unknown: Luc had opened her eyes to the power of curiosity and possibility. He still did.

*

Mid-morning, Matty came cannonballing along the rutted tracks. The soil was bone dry after the long rainless months of summer and threw up clouds of dust. Wheels bouncing over the earth, she drew to a halt in her ancient Deux Chevaux on a grass verge alongside two fields where a huddle of labourers were picking together. Close by, the Australians were singing as they hauled their baskets. It was a timely arrival: the pickers were beginning to wilt from the physical exertion and escalating heat.

'*On fait la pause casse-croûte*,' yelled Matty, in her thick, throaty Provençal drawl, as she climbed out of the car, hair flying loose from its accustomed bun.

Claude lifted off his hat, a fraying, yellowing Panama, wiped his brow and whooped, '*Quelle femme formidable!* Mine's a beer!'

Laughter rang through the green, earthy corridors. Claude, arm slung over the shoulders of his son, Arnaud, sauntered towards the food, chatting amiably.

The grape-pickers, grateful for the opportunity to pause for twenty minutes and slake their thirst, trudged as one towards the housekeeper's stationary vehicle. The sun was high and was threatening to explode with an intensity that outscored even the previous day. Most of the group were sweating already, but spirits were lively and no one was crabbing.

Matty, in her wraparound pinafore, white ankle socks and espadrilles, stood proudly at the open boot of her car. It revealed neat stacks of fresh baguettes, each stuffed with locally cured ham, tomatoes and goat's cheese from a neighbour's herd. Substantial triangles of quiche lay on metal trays, still warm from the oven. They were layered deep with vegetables pulled by Claude from the kitchen garden. To accompany, flasks of steaming coffee and chilled bottles of a young fruity red – Clarisse would never allow the quality wine to be doled out to the labourers. And, of course, a chilled beer or two for Claude.

'Wow, take a look at this yummy lot!' called Sandy to her partner, Jake.

Luc hung back, waiting for his wife, slipping his hand into Jane's as they followed the rest of the ravenous crew. He had caught the sun, as she supposed she had too. His green eyes, flecked with amber, shone brightly, their colour emphasized by his bronzed skin. Even plastered in sun cream, Jane's lighter tone burned and stung, but it was not an unpleasant sensation. A few more freckles would be the result.

'We've made a better start today,' he remarked, as he bent to pick up a stick.

'Clarisse seemed upset this morning,' Jane ventured.

'She's not happy about me making this film.'

'Why?'

Luc shrugged.

'There must be a reason.'

'She thinks I should stick to nature films. Probing into the past is dangerous, she says.'

'Dangerous in what way? She's so dramatic.'

'Well, there are elements of French-Algerian history that were ugly and the memories are more painful for her than I'd anticipated. Let sleeping dogs lie, is Clarisse's philosophy. Talking of which, where's Walnut?'

'Chasing a rabbit, or that's what he was doing when I last saw him. Walnut! Does the film have a personal element to it then?'

Luc slewed his gaze and whistled for the dog. 'Walnut, *viens içi*!'

'Clarisse mentioned that you're digging into family history.'

Luc dropped to his haunches as the spaniel loped towards

him. 'I asked her about my father. She refused to talk about him.' Luc ruffled the dog's ears and Walnut rose on his hind legs and began licking his master's face, panting contentedly.

'And what? Why are you being evasive?'

'Because I don't like discussing a film until I've nailed down its structure, you know that.'

Luc's reserve, the private part of himself that he was so unwilling to share, sometimes drove Jane to distraction. 'Why doesn't she want to talk about it? You and she, you can be as maddening as each other sometimes.' Jane laughed, but a flash of frustration steeled her mood.

'She's never been comfortable about the fact that she and Aunt Isa were colonials . . .'

'Your whole family were colonials. What's there to be so secretive about? It's not as if they were personally responsible for the French invasion of Algeria!'

'Please, let's drop it, Jane. And . . . maybe this isn't the best moment to mention it, but she's asked if we'll spend Christmas with her again this year.'

Jane stiffened.

Luc stroked his wife's cheek. 'I know how you feel, but what do you say to a rethink?'

Jane was determined not to be browbeaten. Luc and she hadn't spent a Christmas in London since the death of his aunt Isabelle. 'How about we discuss it when the harvest's in and we're not surrounded by people?'

Luc slid his hand to his wife's shoulder, caressed her neck and pulled her towards him. 'Sure.' He grinned. 'Listen, I know you'd rather we had time in our own home, but I hate to see her alone and particularly while she's *fâché* with me.'

'She's never angry with you. She dotes on you. And what about my father? He's alone as well. It's always about Clarisse.'

'Peter's cared for. He's in a home, whereas Clarisse is –'

A pair of black-winged crows passed overhead, cawing noisily. Jane glanced up at them and bit back her thought. 'Let's discuss it later. Not now.'

She and Luc drew up behind the gathered team, who were queuing for or already guzzling coffee, wine and sandwiches.

'Wow, this work sure burns off the calories. Know the best grape diet, anyone? Pick them. I'm tweeting this,' giggled Sandy.

The Dutch couple had settled themselves a little apart to partake of their mid-morning snack. Their plates were stacked high with food. Pale-skinned, rarely vocal, they appeared uncomfortable in this southern climate, at odds with everything that fluttered or lived. Merel had rolled up the sleeves of her shirt and was swatting at her arms, scratching at where she had been bitten. Jane wondered what had possessed them to volunteer for this experience, what might have been their expectations. The plentiful meals?

'I've got some cream in my bag if you need it,' she said to Merel, in an attempt to include them.

Over to the left, Sandy was posing for a selfie. 'Guess who's the new Charlize Theron? *Moi*!' she called. Others chuckled, wolf-whistled.

The Dutch woman shook her head miserably. 'Have tube.' She had placed her baguette sandwich in the dusty grass. Within seconds a column of black ants was intent upon it. Merel let out an angry incomprehensible word and snatched it out of their reach, slapping at the sandwich until it fell to pieces and the ants had crossed onto her arm.

'Well, let me know if you need anything.'

Several conversations were taking place all at once, in English, French and occasionally a few words in Limburgish, a dialect of Dutch Jane had never heard before. It was only spoken in and around Limburg, a fact she had gleaned the evening before over dinner from the monosyllabic Merel, whom she'd had the misfortune to be seated alongside. It might explain why Jane had drunk too much, although she had been sufficiently fascinated to look up the root of the language on the internet before she'd gone to sleep and had discovered that the local people called it Plat, rather than Limburgish, meaning 'Flat', like the regions where it was spoken.

Jake and Sandy were recounting their travel adventures to Dan. The tales seemed to involve a certain amount of high drama and squealing. Dan, who spoke fluent English, was listening politely, laughing appropriately. He was a patient man. It was an essential trait in his line of work and in his partnership with Luc, who was passionate and tireless, relentless, demanding, and obsessive in his quest for quality and truth in his projects.

Jane accepted a coffee from Matty, helped herself to a slice of quiche with courgette, sage leaves and onion, and broke away from the others. She strode by Luc, who was now on his haunches in lively exchange with the local harvesters, all tearing at hunks of bread, ham and cheese. They were a hardy bunch, in moth-eaten fedoras and tight-fitting waistcoats, who stuck together and rarely mixed with the foreigners. They were jumping between the regional Provençal vernacular and French. Both Luc and Jane spoke a little of the language of the troubadours, he more than she, and he always enjoyed exercising his knowledge, and the villagers revelled in listening to him. They had been acquainted with the mistress's son since he was a small boy. Arnaud and his twin brother, Pierre, who was working further west in the Camargue as the *gardien* of a château-estate renowned for its breeding of the famous indigenous horses, had practically grown up with Luc. He was popular with all of them even if, he had told Jane years earlier, there had been much resistance to his family buying into the tight-knit Provençal community, purchasing the most sought-after vineyard-estate for miles.

'They're rich because they've lived off the fat of our African territories,' neighbours growled behind their backs. 'Those Cambons and others of their kind were the cause of our Algerian War of Independence. Eight bloody years and de Gaulle still gave the country back. And who paid for it? We did. Our sons fought as soldiers and the war cost us in taxes.'

The conflicts had almost caused a civil war. When France, at de Gaulle's bidding, returned Algeria in 1962, nine hundred thousand Algerian-born French had fled, to settle in the mother country. A great proportion chose the south because the Mediterranean climate and lifestyle were what they were accustomed to. A small percentage of them were in a position to buy whatever took their fancy and they picked up the market's prime properties while France was teetering towards bankruptcy. The Cambons, Luc's mother and aunt, had been among the privileged elite. But it had taken years for them to be accepted here.

Luc had told Jane that it was not uncommon for French mainlanders, especially in the south, to spit upon the Pieds-Noirs. Verbally, at least. He had described to her the humiliation of market days in Malaz when his mother and aunt had been ignored and no one would serve them; his local schooldays, when the other kids had hectored him, yelling unkind names at him.

Luc's father had died during the escape. His grandparents had chosen to remain in 'the land of their birth'. Once Luc had waved them goodbye, he never saw them again, never heard what became of them. The loss of his father and grandparents had been a heart-wrenching experience for the four-year-old, he had confided to Jane years before they were married, on one of the rare occasions when he had touched upon his past.

It was a complex and sensitive history, and a very different genre of documentary from his previous films, which had all been explorations of nature and the environment.

'*Bonjour, Jane, comment tu vas?*'

Jane swung round from where she was sitting on the grass and lifted a hand to shade her eyes from the sun. In her early-morning haste, she had forgotten to bring a hat.

'*Mon Dieu*, it's been a while.'

'Dan! How lovely to see you. Yes, it's been an age.' She patted the grass and he dropped down beside her, kissing her warmly on both cheeks.

'You are looking *très belle*, as always, but very deep in thought.'

'Oh, nothing of great importance. It's a surprise to find you here for the *vendange*, Dan.'

'Luc's tracked down an ex-soldier living near Marseille who knew his father. He wants to film an interview with him.'

'Couldn't it have waited till after the harvest?'

'He's in his eighties and sounded frail when we spoke to him on the phone. Many of the subjects are Clarisse's generation. I'm all for filming them as soon as we can. This film could break ground, Jane. We're both pretty excited. Modern French history will never be the same again.'

Dan's enthusiasm made Jane a little sad. It hurt that Luc never shared the creative process with her. It was such a significant part of who he was. Only a few minutes earlier, when she had prodded him, he had been cagey, avoiding details.

'Why is Clarisse so set against it?'

‘She was caught up in that colonial nightmare, lost her husband. Luc remembers almost nothing about him. It was the genesis for the film: “Who was my father?” Some of the material he’s uncovering is bound to ruffle feathers . . .’

‘Then why?’

‘It needs to be exposed, Jane, and Luc is determined to see it through, as only Luc can be!’ Dan smiled. ‘He won’t be coerced or silenced by his mother, or anyone else. In fact, we’ll interview her.’

‘Do you think she’ll agree?’

‘Clarisse can’t resist a camera. You ought to know that.’ Daniel threw his head back and burst out laughing. It had a mischievous ring to it. Jane found herself remarking yet again how attractive he was. He was divorced with a young daughter, and she wondered that he had not been snapped up. Or perhaps there was someone. Dan rarely disclosed details of his personal life and she would never encroach upon his privacy by enquiring.

‘Are you guys picking grapes or sunbathing?’ It was Luc. He had already chivvied the paid labour back to the vines and was now waving like a traffic warden to his friend and wife. Dan grinned and jumped to his feet, brushing grass off his jeans. ‘Here comes the boss,’ he teased.

‘Dan, does all this explain why Luc’s rather tense at present?’ Jane asked hastily, before Luc reached them. But Dan either didn’t hear or ignored her.

‘Is my wife keeping you from the fields? Jane, *chérie*, if Dan and I disappear to catch up on some urgent professional matters, will you stay with Claude and keep this harvest moving?’

Jane stared at her husband. Protesting would get her nowhere. Luc had organized his day and, evidently, it included leaving her with this unforeseen responsibility. ‘Of course.' She smiled. 'Sneaky of you not to have mentioned it before, though.'

He leaned forward, pecked her on the cheek and signalled for Claude to return him and Dan, with camera, to the main house, the *bastide*, on the tractor. 'See you for dinner. Don't let them slack, and do remember, darling, it is up to you and Claude to make sure the fruit is out of the fields and at the winery in perfect condition well before sunset. And keep an eye on that Dutch pair.'

With these instructions, Luc and Dan were on their way, deep in animated conversation as they went, leaving Jane feeling that she had just been manoeuvred into a corner.

3

The scorching sun beat down upon the wide-open patchwork of vineyards, shimmering in the heat. Heat poured like molten liquid into the rows of plants, baking the earth, intensifying thirst. By noon, when Matty returned with more provisions, the team was running low on energy.

'Well timed, Matty,' shouted someone.

'And some say there's no such thing as climate change. I never heard of wine-picking being this bloody tiring,' quipped Sandy, but no one was listening. They were sweltering in a late-summer heatwave, but not unhappily so. For most of them this remained an adventure and they allowed themselves to get baked, sweaty and soiled, to wallow in the diversions and attractions of *La France à la campagne.*

Those who drank the house wine crashed out under the trees, snoring away the rest of their lunch break, heads heavy, hats covering faces, mosquitoes zizzing and bombing, flies circling lazily. The others dozed in the shade, read lethargically, swatted at the midges and cradled bottles of mineral water. Walnut, who had stayed with Jane, lay on his back, mottled pink belly exposed, like an upturned beetle.

Where had this day come from?

Claude and his fellow countrymen shook their heads. They rarely exchanged a word: they knew to conserve their energy. They watched the sky, staring into the ball of incandescent fire, as though it were an evil eye.

*

It was close to four in the afternoon when a light wind began to play up, to menace the trees. Leaves, branches, vine stock began gently to quiver. All who knew the southern terrain were aware that it could be the progenitor of fiercer winds, of angry weather, the precursor of a Var mistral. Jane paused, slipped her secateurs into a trouser pocket and stared about her, taking stock. With the unexpected wind came ominous dark clouds, rising above the horizon, from beyond a distant windbreak of tall cypresses, taking form, gathering force, like a fleet of black sailing ships. An armada inching towards enemy shores, ready to open fire.

Jane lifted her eyes skywards, shielding them with her hand against the rays, rubbing the back of her wrist across her brow, sticky with perspiration and dust. No storm or temperamental atmospheric conditions had been forecast. Luc and Clarisse would have postponed the launch of the *vendange* until it had blown itself out, if it had been reported on the *méteo*. They would have been checking for this and checking again.

Several of the foreign pickers were giggling. They were losing concentration. Wine and fatigue. A weather drama promised a bit of excitement to break up the punishing drudge of the day. The villagers looked heavenwards with sombre eyes, lifting off their hats, unfurling their cotton scarves, dabbing at their foreheads. This did not bode well, the wind swirling, like rushing water, in the crowns of the high trees bordering the vineyards. The harvest could be at risk, fruit damaged, if the signs in the sky delivered on their louring threat. And a ruined harvest meant trouble for the estate's already struggling economy, for its profile, for the contracted wine deliveries. Les Cigales, the largest, most powerful domain in the neighbourhood. Not good for the region's *terroir*. Its reputation. It was already a challenge to pick when the days had grown so hot, temperatures soaring: 30°C to 32°C in the fields, meant 35°C on the vines. It shocked the grapes when they arrived at the winery to be crushed and their juice was plunged into vats regulated at 14°C.

Clarisse should have ordered the picking to be done at night, as these hired men on their own smallholdings might have done in the old days. But Clarisse Cambon was not a Provençal. She was a different breed. A woman with a face full of make-up living on the periphery of their lives. Not God-fearing, like their own tidy wives. Full of self-importance. And loose morals, it used to be whispered in the villages. Madame didn't have their feel for the land. Her sister-in-law, though, the spinster, Isabelle, God rest her soul, she had known better. She had learned the business the hard way: out on the land, digging with her own hands.

Luc needed to step in, to be there full-time, take over the show. A man at the helm: that was what was required. It was the only solution if the domain was to survive, and they were to be paid better.

Jane saw their faces, read their unspoken derision. Whatever their silent opinion, she was the boss today. She was Luc's representative. And she would do right by him, make him proud.

'Claude,' she hollered, but couldn't see him. She scanned the long fields, the acres of greenery, flapping at an insect buzzing near her face. She hollered again. She felt disappointed for Claude. He had been working hard for weeks to get the vineyards cleaned up and clear of late-growth weeds. Like every other year, he had removed the bird netting where it had been installed, ready for folk to tramp the dusty tracks between the long rows of wine stock.

'Claude!' And then she spotted him. Large stick in hand, as though he were a shepherd with a crook, he was signalling to her, beckoning her over. She shifted to one side, her close-to-full pannier dripping with black Mourvèdre grapes – a variety used in the mix to enhance the finest of the domain's three rosés – and beat a path between the vines to meet him. Her back was breaking. When this was done and the fruit was at the winery later, she'd drive to the sea for an evening swim and a stroll along the beach. She'd take Walnut. He loved the sea, loved to jump in and out of the gently unfurling waves.

'What do you think?' she called. Jane had never before been handed the responsibility for any decision-making at Les Cigales. Aunt Isabelle had filled that role fearsomely, but she had been dead for five years now. Ever since, Luc had more or less run the show, and Jane was determined not to let him down today. Surprising, though, that he would cede his role in the fields, even for his film.

'It's threatening, but a dog that barks won't necessarily bite. No storm has been forecast.'

'Still, I don't like the feel of it, Claude, do you?'

'Fine. To be on the safe side, we'll load all the full *comportes* onto the trailer and I'll drive them to the vinification plant. Let's get the beauties safely home. Michel, Jean and I will take charge of that. You keep the pickers at the bushes for as long as possible or Madame Clarisse will hit the roof, screaming about having to shell out full whack for short days. Arnaud will stay with you, just in case.'

Jane nodded her agreement. They began to call in the baskets, sending fellow workers as messengers down the rows, calling '*la hutte*', emptying the loads, one semi-packed basket poured into another, rumbling fruit, moving the clipped stock back towards the trailer, ready to shift the hundreds of kilos of black grapes off the land and out of the threat of any wet weather. Jane felt dizzy. Lifting, bending, driving the energy, directing the crew, heaving weights, almost falling over the dog, who stuck at her heels. She felt herself slip from clear thinking almost to a faint, then drag herself back. The wind swooped into the vine bushes, which swayed and gusted around her. Above, the sky was patches of spilled, seeping ink.

'Let's keep the fruit moving,' she yelled. Few if anyone could hear her in the wind. They were at work fulfilling the order, concentrating hard, backs to it, even if they didn't grasp the technical reasons for the sudden change of order, the urgency. Arnaud, heaving crates, knew, though, and he was watching Jane. Mute in his appraisal of her. *The English woman. Better if Luc had married locally.*

It was in the midst of this bustling activity that the screaming broke out. At first, Jane couldn't locate the source. Everyone was moving fast, calling, lining up baskets, shunting them in a chain towards the grass verge, ready for the trailer where Claude was hauling them aboard. And then the scream, followed by another, piercing into the pewter light. The Australian girl, Sandy, gave a yell to her boyfriend, who was way back up the track working with Claude. 'Jake! Jake! Over here!'

The screams had now transformed themselves into a hysterical yelping. Panic was whipping the team. What had happened? Jane was slow in picking up on the cause of the commotion, which seemed to be coming from the distant border of a neighbouring field, until she spotted Merel. Merel, way down the line, who had been hardly visible among the vast green expanse where she had been working, was hurtling towards the stacked baskets, turning in circles as though she were on fire, waving her arms, knocking the panniers onto their sides, flattening, squashing the fruit as she spilled it beneath her lumpen shoes.

Was she having a fit, some kind of seizure?

'Jesus!' Jane began to run, yelling to Claude and Arnaud as she did so. Fruit and baskets were going over like ninepins. Olaf, now at his wife's side, was attempting to calm her, shaking her, yelling at her in Limburgish. Merel screamed something back at him. Directly afterwards he twisted away from her and began beating at the vines with his fists, punishing the plants, causing them to break and buckle, surrendering their unpicked black bunches to the ground.

'What the hell?' Jane kept running, hurtling over fruit and broken baskets.

Jake was on the spot. Sandy, dusty-legged in shorts, was bouncing like a ball, agitated. It was a chaos of bodies shoving and squelching the wasting fruit.

'Merel's been bitten by a snake!' bellowed Jake. 'A fucking great blighter. Got her in the leg. Rose up like a cobra and began hissing at her, then sank its fangs into her calf. There's a couple of them over there. Possibly a nest.'

'Jake, stop yakking and get the anti-poison gel!' cried Sandy, tears and perspiration dampening her cheeks.

Jean Dupont, a local man, along with Arnaud, was now bearing Merel out of the damaged vine rows towards the edge of the field, near the track. Olaf was hopping alongside them, trying to smother his wife's yelling, his great hand, like a sullied cricket glove, over her mouth. Jane brought up the rear, waving to Claude, who was approaching from another direction. A crack of thunder sounded overhead. The crates were everywhere, a few in the trailer but the rest chaotically scattered across the land or upturned, bleeding their juice back into the rust-red soil.

Jane guessed at the species of snake, a Couleuvre Maillée. Scales of brown to olive green, with glassy malevolent eyes and a clubbed head like that of a golf driver; a terrifying presence. They grew to two metres, but they usually kept their distance. It was rare to chance upon one and rarer still that it would attack or bite. Only if aggravated, or woken abruptly from its sleep in the sun. Their bite, though, sunk deep, was venomous.

Merel had been laid flat on the tufted ground alongside the trailer. Her face was blotched red and puffy from crying, as well as the sweltering conditions and exertion. Her expression was frozen in terror as she fought for breath. Her right leg was swelling to an alarming size, white flesh expanding as though it were being inflated. Jake was attempting to administer a gel from his medical kit but every time he touched the perforation, Merel screamed, kicked and yelled. The English couple were standing back, horrified. 'In all our years of grape-picking, we've never seen this before,' remarked mild-mannered Clive, but no one was listening to him.

Fat drops of rain were beginning to splat onto the earth. The sky was tar, a black curtain drawn closed, about to be thrown open.

'We need to get her to a doctor immediately,' said Claude calmly to Jane. 'She could be having an allergic reaction, and she might be asthmatic, which won't help her deal with the venom. She must have trodden right on the snake while it was basking in the shade of the vines, or protecting its young.'

'Better get medical assistance. It looks nasty,' echoed Tomas, one of the villagers.

Jean Dupont was at Merel's side, having gently eased Olaf out of the way. Jean knew every creature that inhabited these hillsides, those that slithered, stung and nested in the verdant plains, buried beneath the *maquis,* hibernating in the arid slopes, and he knew how to live with them. He was, like his compatriots but perhaps more so, in harmony with and born of that soil. 'It's decades since anyone's died of a snake bite in these parts. She'll be right as rain,' he said.

'I'm not risking it. Let's get this vehicle moving. Claude, we'll lay her flat in the trailer and transport her to the main house where she can be cleaned up. Somebody needs to travel with her. Who should I ask?' Jane was looking to Claude for advice.

'Jean Dupont,' Claude responded, without hesitation.

'I'm happy to accompany her, but you need to ring ahead for the doctor.' This was Dupont.

The Provençaux and Jane were conversing with one another in French and occasional phrases of the local vernacular. Fortunately the six foreigners couldn't follow. Even the British who claimed a certain mastery of French were out of their depth.

'My wife is going to be fine, isn't she?' begged Olaf, hovering behind Jane, shaking his big hands nervously as though trying to unhook them.

Jane was nodding reassurance, patting his arm, opening her phone, ringing Luc. She turned her back on the group to talk with him privately. '. . . By the time Claude gets her to the house, the doctor can be there if you call him now.' She was mumbling, softening her tone, eager not to create any further alarm. 'And then we'll need the trailer back here pretty damn fast if we're to save the grapes.'

The greater portion of the day's crop had been lost, damaged beyond repair, Mourvèdre bunches all, the dominant variety in Clarisse's AOC rosé; all that remained would be jettisoned, left to rot back into the soil. A flash downpour of hailstones, not uncommon in that part of France in early autumn and always a threat to the harvests of both grapes and olives, had accompanied the party's return to the house. Jane, on her bicycle, was barraged, as was the poor bedraggled spaniel, who trotted gamely along by her muddied wheels. The others, when the trailer returned for them, accompanying the few salvaged receptacles of fruits, were also pelted by the hail. What remained of the day's yield was a pitiful offering.

Clarisse, working in her office at the winery and waiting to receive the day's take, watched as her precious vintage was unloaded, her red lips taut as wire.

4

By the time Jane cycled into the courtyard at Les Cigales, the light was fading. The hired labourers were in their various dormitories in the converted stable blocks, showering, towelling off, resting aching limbs, pouring beer. The locals, those who weren't staying over, had returned to their villages either on foot or by bicycle. On a normal day, Claude would have given them a lift, but these exceptional circumstances meant the exhausted men had to make their own way home or stay over in one of the barns.

As Jane wheeled the bike back to the shed, voices drifted through open windows. Shrieks of laughter, yells for the shower or booze refills, nonchalance carried on the wind. Quite in contrast to her own heavy heart.

It was too late for a swim, too late to cycle to the beach, too late even if she took the car. There was no time to hurry down the stone steps and dunk herself in the estate's lovely pool, situated two terraces below the main house. The light was fading fast and she was shattered, soaked to the skin, craved soap, scalding water, oblivion. The day could not have been a greater disaster. She parked the bicycle outside the shed and entered the house by the kitchen where she grabbed a towel and rubbed a sad-faced Walnut dry before feeding him and settling him in his basket. No evidence of life, only a casserole bubbling on the range and six freshly baked baguettes on a board on the solid wooden table, alongside a round marble plate settled with a variety of cheeses. Six cloves of rose garlic sat in a saucer ready to spice up one dish or another. Highlights of the evening meal to be served in the stable block. A tradition. Jane lifted the black iron lid with an oven glove. Condensation dribbled, vapour rose. She pushed her face close, felt the damp heat on her flushed cheeks and inhaled. Her stomach rumbled. The mere smell was comforting.

'Pork loin in tawny port with shallots and figs,' announced Matty, stepping in through the back door, wiping her full round face. Perspiration pearls from her exertions and the raised temperature in the kitchen speckled her forehead. A tea-towel was slung over her right shoulder, and she was clutching an oval dish containing sprigs of rosemary. 'And these go in now.'

'You're a genius, Matty. I'm ravenous.'

'Arnaud said you had a rotten day?'

Jane nodded. 'That's an understatement. See you in fifteen minutes.'

'Anything we can do?'

'Replenish the ice cubes in the library, please. I need a drink.'

Jane heard Luc and the doctor's voices as she dragged herself up the stairs in her socks, boots in hand. No mud on Matty's polished woodwork. She longed to call out to Luc but couldn't face the doctor, or being drawn into the conversation.

Luc was in one of the front drawing rooms, the red room, with the village doctor, Monsieur Beauchene. Merel had been administered a sedative and antihistamine, sent to bed and ordered to rest. The ginger-haired medic was promising to call again in the morning.

'Second this week,' Beauchene was confirming. 'She'll be fine. More scared than injured. When she's fit and ready, if

I were you I'd tactfully send them on their way. This territory is not for them. You don't want another accident and the region doesn't want bad press.'

Luc nodded, politely offering the local physician another dram of whisky, then escorting the loquacious fellow to his car. Beauchene was known to enjoy a tipple or two and, in return, usually came armed with an hour's worth of country gossip. Luc's grandfather's Comtoise clock in the hall read twenty past seven when he closed the front door, listening to the engine of Beauchene's Peugeot fire up. He was whacked. The pickers' meal commenced at seven thirty sharp. Matty was punctual with the courses. The harvesting days began at dawn. Early to bed was the example to set.

Showered, perfumed, groomed, Jane was looking forward to a stiff drink before facing the team. Where was Luc? It was his habit to freshen up before the meal. He must still be trapped with that doctor, who never stopped talking. He'd probably join her shortly in the library where the family had, over the years, enjoyed their early-evening aperitifs. After, she'd lend Matty a hand. The dear woman worked her fingers to the bone. Jane made her way back down the stairs to the library. No Luc. She poured herself a generous gin and tonic and was settling down to it in an armchair by the fireside when she noticed Clarisse, still in her work clothes, standing by the window, her back to the room, facing out towards the lawns that flanked the western side of the house. Jane was uncertain whether her mother-in-law had heard her come in or not.

'Clarisse?' she ventured. No response. She spoke a little louder. 'Clarisse, I'm really sorry about the grapes. Clarisse?'

Clarisse spun round with a movement that belied her seventy-eight years, causing Jane almost to drop her drink.

Decades of buttoned-up rancour were about to be unleashed upon the younger woman.

Once the doctor had been waved away, Luc had descended the narrow stone stairs to his studio to shut down the computers. Dan and he had been working there when he'd received Jane's call about the accident. It was from there he now heard the cries of his mother's rage. Few could have mistaken it. He shot up from the cellars and found both women in the library. There stood Clarisse, arm raised, brandishing her knobbed cane as though about to club Jane, who was near the fireplace, shocked, a hand in front of her face to stave off an impending blow.

'What, in God's name – Jane, Maman, what's going on?' Luc closed the door firmly behind him and stepped between them.

Jane retreated deep into a leather armchair. She was clasping her glass, gulping from it as it knocked against her teeth.

'Look at her! Irresponsible and pathetic. Whatever possessed you to think she could lead the team today? She's incapable of decision-making and, besides, when has she ever expressed any commitment to this place?'

'Stop it, Mother. *Arrêtes!* The she you are referring to is Jane, my wife, your daughter-in-law, and she is here, right in front of you. I don't know what's got into you.'

'We have lost the entire day's crop, that's what has got into me. And I have to pay that good-for-nothing lot. Out of what? And for what? For nothing! It could have been avoided. She was negligent. All the burden rests on my shoulders. It always has. I bleed for this place. You could help –'

'We do help!'

'You could do more. You could both do more! You should be living here but *she* keeps you away.'

'Maman, stop this now, do you hear me?' Luc was directly in front of his mother. He took her gently by the shoulders.

'She doesn't want –'

'I said, *silence*, Maman.'

'We were two women and you, a small boy, who built this place. Two women. After your grandparents stayed in Algeria, we had no one. Your father gone. Two women left to fend for ourselves. Have you forgotten?'

'Maman, *arrêtes*.'

Mother and son glared at one another. The air was full of dampened outrage. Betrayal. The old woman was temporarily hushed, belittled by her son's unwillingness to take her side.

Jane grabbed the opportunity to escape. 'I'm going upstairs,' she muttered to Luc.

'Why must you dig up our past, Luc, with this wretched film? Let it be, I beg you,' Clarisse was pleading, as Jane drew the door shut.

Upstairs on the bed, Jane finished her gin, then lay back, closing her eyes, the glass slipping from between her fingers. She had a thumping headache and she was in shock, although such displays of Clarisse's antagonism were not unusual.

Soon after the death of Luc's aunt Isabelle, Clarisse had moved into one of the estate's smaller properties, Le Cottage du Cerisier or Cherry Tree Lodge, offering this manor house, the estate's principal residence, to her son and daughter-in-law. Jane had mistrusted the gift, perceiving it not as a gesture of generosity towards them but as an enticement, a snare. Clarisse was now alone and she wanted her son back at Les Cigales on a permanent basis.

Jane had put her foot down, determined they hang on to their London home. 'We can visit as often as we want, but we have our own lives,' she'd said to Luc. What she didn't voice was the certainty that if they upped sticks and settled at Les Cigales, they would lose their independence entirely. Their universe would be dominated by Clarisse.

Jane and Luc had built their married life in London. They went to the movies two or three times a week, strolled on Hampstead Heath, ate Sunday lunch in one of their local north London pubs. Occasionally, when he wasn't deep in writing a film, he cooked. Tricks he'd learned from Matty, he'd grin. Luc was passionate about music, particularly live performance, and they regularly visited venues such as the 606 Club or the Jazz Café. Theirs was a good life but Clarisse was hell-bent on putting an end to it and she was furious with Jane for resisting her.

Jane loved London. When Luc was away on location, she drove to see her father more frequently and went to the gym. In good weather, she met friends for a cycle or a swim on the Heath, and sometimes a picnic. She had recently taken up Russian evening classes and was thoroughly enjoying the challenge; also, it would add to her linguistic portfolio. At Les Cigales, Clarisse was the mistress, and their lives, hers and Luc's, were never their own. Even the bed upon which Jane was now holed up had belonged to her mother-in-law.

When Luc pushed open the door, sliding stealthily into the shuttered room, Jane was dozing, still fully clothed, sedated by alcohol, tiredness and misery. Tears stained her cheeks. An empty suitcase lay open on the floor. Luc stepped over it, perched beside his wife and stroked her face.

'Hey, my sweet lady, are you all right?'

She opened her eyes, shielded them from the slant of light coming in from the corridor, and stared at him. 'Just about. You look shattered,' she murmured.

He frowned. 'Professional challenges, difficulties. What happened down there?'

'You never share them with me.'

'I don't want to burden you. Tell me what happened.'

'I'm going back to London,' she whispered.

'Don't be silly.'

'I am. I have a new contract. I want to get on with it.'

'You can do it here.'

She shook her head. 'I prefer to go home.'

'Please, Jane. I know she's being crotchety and ghastly, but tomorrow she'll apologize. I will insist. She's old, she's lost and lonely, please forgive her.'

Jane let her eyelids fall shut again. 'I can't go through this another time, Luc. The perpetual insinuation that I'm not good enough for you.'

Luc sighed and ran his fingers through her blonde hair. 'Jane, listen . . .' The sentence died on his lips.

'What?'

He watched her in silence, deliberating. Beyond the room, footsteps crossed the hall downstairs where the clock was chiming eight. He was running late. He should be presiding at the pickers' dinner.

'What?' Jane waited, but he said no more. 'Luc?'

He glanced at his watch.

She thought he looked more troubled than she had ever seen him.

'I wish you'd tell me about your film. Clarisse knows more about it than I do. Sometimes I feel like I'm just an outsider, an appendage.'

'*Chérie*, Clarisse knows about this one because she's part of that history.'

'Is it about your father?'

He sighed. 'I told you, he was the seed, the germination.'

'In what way?'

'Ssh, no more questions tonight, please.' He leaned forward, laid his lips against her cheek, then kissed her on the nose. 'Matty is already serving the main course. I'd better get down there.'

'How's Merel?'

'The swelling's subsiding and she's sleeping. Meanwhile, Olaf is hitting our finest whisky.' Luc smiled, stroking his wife's hair. 'Sometimes I think my mother hasn't got a clue.'

Jane nodded, eyes still closed, her arm resting across Luc's thigh, a hand holding his. 'Sorry about the grapes. I really wanted to do my best for you.'

'Sour grapes,' he jested. 'It wasn't your fault. I shouldn't have thrust the responsibility on you like that at a minute's notice. I sometimes wish though . . .' Luc's thought drifted to silence.

'What do you wish?' Her eyes opened, scanning his.

'We'll talk about it another time. I have to go. You staying or coming?'

'Staying, if you don't mind.'

He shook his head.

'Don't be too long.'

Luc stroked her cheek, deep in thought, observing her. 'Get some sleep. It wasn't your fault, and stop hatching plans to leave. Tomorrow, laptop in the breakfast room, do you hear? Skype your clients, attack your translations. No one will disturb you, and congratulations on the new contract.' He rose from the bed and let go of her hand.

'*Je t'aime*,' she whispered, as he left the room.

The following morning, Luc was up before the birds, as was his habit, harvest time or not. Jane, tangled hair, puffy-eyed, crawled from the bed moments after him, determined that today she would not be the last and she would not be late. She had resolved during her sleepless night to stick it out, but as a menial, an extra hand only. Nothing more. From that morning on, when Luc was ensconced with Dan in his studio, Claude, Jean and Arnaud could take control of the harvest and Jane would obey orders.

When Merel was rested and had been given the all-clear by Dr Beauchene, she and Olaf stayed on to recuperate for two more days and then, at Luc's request, they set off in their Skoda for the Netherlands. No one was too sorry to see them go.

The intense weather eased off and levelled out. Picking became agreeable once more. The team, although depleted, gelled, and the days passed amicably, without further mishaps. Even the dinners proved to be fun. A patched-up harmony prevailed and Jane slogged it out for the duration of the harvest. Claude, with Jean Dupont at his side, aided by Arnaud, delivered the day's yields safely to the vinification plant where they were loaded onto a sorting table, into the destemmer and fed to the crusher. There, they were separated from their skins and seeds ready for the settling process. Les Deux Soeurs' annual vintage was under way. Clarisse had nothing further to gripe about.

Discreetly, Jane negotiated ways to maintain a safe distance from her unforgiving mother-in-law. When they were obliged to engage with one another, the exchanges on both sides were awkward, icy.

Part of Jane, the bruised, humiliated part, would have preferred to pack her bags and flee, but she hung on, for Luc's sake. If she had run, Luc reminded her, the rift between his wife and her mother-in-law would have deepened, never to be healed. If the two women in his life couldn't reach an understanding about the grievances in their past, how were they ever to accept the realities of the present and the future?

'What will it take?' he asked Jane one evening, when they were alone, sipping a nightcap on their bedroom terrace, Walnut snoring alongside them.

Jane, her bare feet resting on Luc's knees, looked out across the valley beyond the olive groves, oyster-lit by a three-quarter moon, to the shadowed outlines of the mauve mountains, the wild hills of the *massif*, and a deep sky pitted with stars. 'To do what?'

'To put this all to rights.'

'It's too late, Luc,' was Jane's response. 'She's set in her ways and she made up her mind about me long ago.'

'And you don't think you've also made up your mind?'

'I said I was sorry for losing the bloody grapes. It was an accident, not even caused by me.'

'Won't you try to make peace with her once more before we leave?'

'As though one day's wreckage could have brought all this about! Luc, I *have* apologized. It suits your mother to vent her frustrations elsewhere and I have always been her target.'

He was at a loss.

After the *vendange* had been completed and the hired hands had gone their separate ways, the preparations for the fermentation of the grapes began in earnest. Whatever Clarisse believed to the contrary, she had no talent for this process. Her role had traditionally been on the commercial side: sales and marketing. Isabelle and, later, Luc had captained the winemaking, but this year Luc was splitting his time. Up at dawn, he and Claude took charge of the removal of the white grape juice from the settling tanks ready for racking. The pressed red grapes, still with their skins, had already begun to ferment, but the vats still required skilled nursing. By late morning, he was in his car en route to Marseille, where Dan was filming interviews. He returned for dinner. Jane spent her days translating a French guide book for a small independent UK publisher. It was her new contract and she was keen to deliver her best. It was an intense period, each lost in their own worlds, and Jane saw little of Luc.

The Cambons were seated together for a cold supper because Luc had arrived back late from Marseille. Little conversation had passed between them when Clarisse announced, with an air of theatrical gloom, that due to the 'missing or damaged' tons of her Mourvèdre variety, there was insufficient fruit to produce more than a quarter of their usual output of the estate's finest and most commercially successful wine.

Jane recognized this as the opening gambit in yet more recrimination. Sensing that Luc was too tired to deal with it, she stepped directly in. 'Clarisse, it's not possible that the spoil of one day's fruit can cause the loss of three-quarters of the estate's potential output.'

Her mother-in-law grudgingly admitted that this particular variety, their best grape, had also suffered from a smaller yield. The wine would be in short supply for this vintage. Her major concern was that previously loyal customers would place their orders elsewhere. 'All my customers will start buying in the Bandol region. They'll order from Domaine Ott, the Château Minuty vineyards or the Sainte Victoire choices.'

Respectfully, Luc reminded his mother that the wines of Les Deux Soeurs were not comparable to those of the grand Provençal estates. 'If those are the châteaux the buyers are after, they would never have been shopping with us in the first place. We're not in the same league. We don't perform at such a level.'

'Well, we ought to!' Clarisse slapped the palm of her hand against the table. Rings and bracelets jangled and Jane was taken aback by the force of the outburst. 'And we damn well could be in that league if you were here permanently to lead the way! Luc, think about it. We hand pick. Our varieties are first class and we use no chemicals. Competing with those Provençal châteaux should be our goal. It was what Isa envisaged. But we have no wine to sell!'

Luc replenished his mother's glass and poured himself and Jane some sparkling water. 'Please don't get so het up. Les Cigales will still be producing eight hundred or more cases of the *cru classé* rosé and there remains stock in the cellar from last year. None of your regulars will go away empty-handed.'

'Cellar's empty. Nothing left. One case only!' Clarisse retaliated and downed her wine. 'I sold a few dozen bottles to a restaurant in Menton, so that's it. All cancelled or undelivered orders will result in a financial shortfall that this domain, *my* domain, cannot sustain. We are broke. End of story.' She served herself another glass of red.

'I'll go through the accounts when I get back from Paris. I doubt we're broke. Which restaurant?'

Clarisse shrugged.

'Try to remember. The stock book clearly states that thirty-three cases are in the cellar.'

'Well, they're not! And the estate taxes are overdue.'

Luc rubbed a hand across his face. He looked shattered, beleaguered, gripped by his internal world, and with every serving of wine Clarisse grew more belligerent.

Silently, Jane counted the days till their return to London.

*

The following evening, while she and Luc were changing for dinner, Jane asked, 'We wouldn't be responsible for bailing her out, would we?'

'Of course not! Please don't build this into more than it is! I've got enough on my plate. She's probably exaggerating.'

'So what's it all about? A ploy to get you to take over the business?'

Luc picked up his phone, scrolling through messages. 'She's upset with me. Listen, I need to make a call.'

'Why would she be?'

Luc pulled a shirt from the wardrobe and tapped out a number while shrugging it on. 'She says she fought to build our reputation and she'll be afraid to live here on her own when the film's released. Engaged, damn it.' He tossed the phone onto the bed.

'So, is it about wheedling a promise out of you to move back? She's so crafty – she won't drop it till she gets her way.'

'Jane, please, be more flexible and less judgemental than she is. The estate is too much for her. Stock figures don't match the quantities in the storerooms. It's a mess. I'll have to meet the accountant and go through the paperwork myself.' Luc sat back on the bed and ran his fingers through his damp hair. A text came in: he drew the phone towards him.

'Do you think her mind's going?'

He shook his head, impatient at the suggestion, tapping out a response to the message. 'She's always been disorganized.'

'What this place needs is another manager.'

'She says we can't afford one.'

'There's always been someone. Even when Dad and I first came here years ago. Antoine Pesaro, remember him? After Isabelle died he walked out, prompted by a row with Clarisse.'

'No, I don't.'

'Of course you do, Luc. The fellow with short legs, always puffing on a pipe. Stop defending her. And who the hell is so important on that phone?'

Luc sighed and placed the mobile on his nightstand.

Jane, dress still not fastened, dropped her hands to her sides, approached her husband and stroked his head. 'Sorry. You're really shattered. Let's get back to London as soon as we can and have a fun week. You need a break.'

'Not possible now. We can spend a couple of days in Paris. I've got several important meetings, but there's the Hopper exhibition at the Grand Palais – you said you wanted to see it. Afterwards, you can continue on home and I'll return here.'

'Here?'

'I've agreed to base myself here while I shoot this film so she won't be alone, even if she resents the work I'm doing. I can keep an eye on everything. Have you noticed how much she's drinking?'

'How long will you be away?'

'I don't know.'

And what about us? Jane bit back her disappointment. The more time Luc dedicated to Les Cigales and his mother, the less remained for her and their marriage. He must have read her thoughts because he added, 'You don't have to leave. It's your choice. There's no reason why you can't hang on. You work well here. The internet is stable. I'll only be in Paris for a few days.'

Jane refrained from pointing out the obvious. 'I've already missed three Russian classes. Can you zip up my dress, please?'

By degrees Luc was being drawn into what Jane perceived as Clarisse's web. He argued that it was his duty to watch over the 'old girl'. Jane could not disagree or fault this sentiment:

she had her ailing father in a care home in Kent to consider, another reason she preferred to remain in England.

From Luc's point of view, Les Cigales suited his work programme better than their UK address. It offered ample space – he had converted the *bastide* cellars into a den with an editing suite – and if he based himself in France, he was entitled to French cinema subsidies. No British government looked so generously on the arts.

And so their debate ran round in circles, as it had since Aunt Isa's death. Back and forth, without resolution. The fact of the matter was that the two women didn't get on. They never had. Or not for years. Not since that hot troubled night of way too long ago . . . But Jane preferred to leave that summer where it belonged. In the past.

Right now, in the present, the proposed 'jolly' scenario of Jane and Clarisse living together, bumping into one another on a daily basis, almost made her blood run cold. If she and Luc opted to live here permanently, Clarisse would rule the roost and Jane would have no voice in her own decision-making. No, she was determined not to give up her independence. On the other hand, she wanted to accommodate Luc, to offer support. It was clear that he was having a rough time, juggling the weight of his commitments. Jane owed it to him, for Heaven's sake.

She took a deep breath. She'd do as he requested. She'd stitch together some kind of truce with his difficult, demanding mother.

5

The third week of October. The days were amber-lit and that particular morning was no exception. It had unfurled like the others preceding it, offering a heat that was benign and enveloping. It welcomed you to the outdoors, to the working life of the land. Five hundred and eighty-eight tons of top-quality picked grapes had been the estate's yield this season. Seven tons an acre was the figure achieved. Not bad at all. Once the fruit was ready for the primary ferment, Luc and Jane could prepare for their departure.

For Luc's sake, Jane took the old estate car, beat a path across the rutted parkland, cutting through the *parcelles* of vines denuded of their fruit, but still lovely with their russet leaves, to seek out her mother-in-law. Clarisse's office was on the ground floor of the building that contained the winery. It had been installed in the spacious stone-walled cellars of a refurbished, nineteenth-century construction. As well as Clarisse's office, it housed a wine-tasting salon and reception room on the ground floor. Packing rooms were on the level above. The winemaking plant was the heart of the vineyard. Jane was unfamiliar with it and its operating life. She rarely found herself on that section of the property, not since the years when she and Luc had climbed trees together up in the olive groves.

Two middle-aged men were in the yard when Jane drew up. She knew them both by sight. They were local labourers, temporary muscle, called in when heavy lifting or sweat work was required. They were rolling carts stacked with empty unlabelled bottles off a trailer. One raised his head, coughed, wiped his blue-veined brow, acknowledged her arrival with a nod as Jane slammed the car door. His eyes followed her as she strode across the gravelled surround.

'*Où est Madame Cambon?*' she called to him. The yard was scruffy with plastic rubbish spilling over from a trio of dustbins forgotten in a corner. Arnaud or Claude should get over here and organize a major clean-up. Had no one else remarked upon it? For visitors who came to taste and purchase, it gave a rather usavoury impression.

The workman pointed her to the rear of the building while his companion never raised his hatted head. Jane nodded her thanks and strode on, hiding her apprehension.

The French windows of Clarisse's office led out onto a path that intersected a bright flower garden, where a round table and six chairs offered the possibility of al fresco coffee or lunch breaks. Inside, a radio was playing softly. Instrumental jazz. On the wall, slightly askew, hung a black-and-white photograph of the young Romy Schneider. Clarisse was hunched over a desk, a cigarette smoking in an old-fashioned ashtray stamped with the Noilly Prat logo. Papers and chaos surrounded her. Heavy tortoiseshell sunglasses held her grey-flecked auburn hair firmly off her face. Unusually, she was without make-up and looked her age. Jane hovered by the half-open door. She opened her mouth to announce her presence but was cut short by a barked 'What do *you* want?'

Her mother-in-law's greeting took the wind out of her sails. '*Bonjour.* May I come in?'

Clarisse was scribbling a list of figures on a scrap of paper as Jane stepped inside and glanced nervously about. This workplace had the air of a temporary trailer office on a building site, rather than anything more permanent. Two folding chairs were leaning against the far side of the desk. Jane hesitated and decided against opening one to sit down. 'Luc and I'll be setting off early on Thursday morning.'

'I am well aware of that. However, my son is coming back and he will remain here for the olive harvest. He has promised that he'll be here to oversee it, and I'm expecting him to stay on for Christmas.'

Jane held her breath. Why was Clarisse's manner always so bloody challenging? 'I thought I'd drop by, say *au revoir* and apologize again for the loss of the grapes. I hope you are reassured it was an accident.'

Clarisse made no response. Then, slowly, deliberately, she placed her fountain pen, which Jane noticed was leaking, on the desk, lifted her head and stared full into Jane's face. There was no warmth, no forgiveness in her gaze.

'I wonder you dare show yourself here. I suppose it was my son who begged you to come. Good-natured but foolish of him to believe that anything you say could make any difference.'

Momentarily knocked off-centre, Jane took a deep breath, steadying herself, determined to keep the exchange civil, to avoid a scene. 'Yes, he did ask me to drop by, but I wouldn't have done so if I hadn't thought we could sort this out.'

'Sort this out? Even you don't believe that!'

'Well, yes, actually –'

'Do you know, Jane? The one regret I have for Luc is that he married you. You, when he had the choice of all women. I said as much at the time and nothing has changed my mind.'

It was an unexpected, brutal attack and threw Jane off-centre. 'Clari–'

'You have no idea of the battle we had to get out of Africa, fleeing a war zone, dead bodies all about us, grief, driving for days on end, not knowing where we'd end up. Two women and a boy, and we struggled, my God, we struggled to make something of this estate, to build the Cambon reputation, to put this place on the viticulture map. Les Deux Soeurs is a label to be proud of, and everything I did, I did for Luc. Everything I've fought for, every last drop of energy I've given to this enterprise, has been for *my son*.' Clarisse hit her desk with a sideways fist to emphasize her point. Jane watched a sheet of paper float to the floor. 'With little help from the local community, I might add. Full of their prejudices and recriminations about who we were and –'

'I don't see what any of this has to –'

'I dreamed that by this stage of my life my son would be running these vineyards alongside me, that we'd be surrounded by a house full of his children, vibrant and talented like their father.'

'Clarisse, stop right now!'

'Grandchildren to carry on the business. To fill this place with noise and play. Instead of which . . . instead of which . . . You are not worthy of my son. You never were.'

Tears stung Jane's eyes. 'Why do you bring this up? If Luc and I have accepted our loss and built a contented life, why can't you? You talk as though I deliberately tried to spite you, to destroy your dreams of happiness.'

'Oh, no, Jane, you'd never "destroy" anyone's "dreams of happiness", would you? How conveniently you've wiped from your memory the damage you caused to others by your resentments and jealousy. The sacrifice I was forced to make.'

Jane felt the knife sink deeper. 'What sacrifice? For God's sake, Clarisse, what are you talking about?'

Clarisse glared at her. 'You simply don't get it, do you?'

'What I get is that you are hell-bent on blaming me. For no real reason. Nothing I have ever done to you deserves this vile attack. What sacrifice are you talking about?' Jane was leaning against Clarisse's desk. Her cheeks were flushed with anger. She had promised herself she would remain calm – she'd do it for Luc – but . . . this was an impossible, insoluble situation. The force of Clarisse's hatred confounded her. 'Surely you're not talking about . . .'

Clarisse picked up her cigarette, dragged on it deeply and then ground it out in the ashtray.

'Clarisse, that was years ago.'

Ignoring Jane, Clarisse retrieved her pen from the desk and made a performance of slipping on her glasses, of concentration, of drawing towards her a cumbersome old-fashioned ledger.

Jane lingered awkwardly, watching the bent head of the matriarch, lost for words, searching for any gesture of generosity to turn this around, for Luc's sake. To redeem even a smidgeon of respect if not affection between them.

'Clarisse, is that the sacrifice?'

Clarisse opened the ledger and ran her finger down lists of figures. She left an inked fingerprint on the page.

'I was fourteen years old. I was shocked and angry –'

The old woman did not lift her head.

'Why can't we let all this go? Move on. Get on with our lives . . .'

Jane waited, but Clarisse continued to ignore her. Eventually, she retreated. 'You've got ink all over your fingers,' she called back. It was a pathetic final blow and she knew it. Outside, she hurried along the pathway, convinced that all hope of any reconciliation had been dashed.

The day before they were due to leave, Jane cycled to the beach, crossing the snaking coast road, the Golden Route, to the horseshoe bay known as the Cove of Illusions, where she perched on the shingle between blood-red rocks and watched the terns and sandpipers. It was the time of year when the migratory species were gathering. Any day now, flocks of swallows and martins would begin their relocation south across the Mediterranean to Africa. It was time to gather their forces and be on their way. 'France is an excellent crossroads for birds on the wing,' Luc had once told her. When she and he were adolescents, he had shown her many fine lookout points, even on his own estate, where they could hide in the rocks and grass and identify the birds. On one or two rare occasions they had spotted or heard overhead small flocks of cranes.

Jane had always been curious as to whether the migrating avians perceived their north or south lands, their breeding or wintering grounds, as home. 'Which do you think?' she had quizzed Luc years earlier.

'Home is within us,' he had replied. 'Algeria was once my home. Now, I am here and France, Les Cigales, is my home. It will always be my home.'

'Why?'

'I feel connected to this place. It has a special energy.'

The post-harvest departure was filled with regret for Jane. Did Luc still regard France as home, rather than London with her, his wife? The conflict with Clarisse had dredged up so much from the past. Insecurities and grief. Clarisse's cruel allusion to the lack of children.

Since her fourteenth year, Jane had never been made welcome at Les Cigales. She knew that Clarisse judged her a poor choice for Luc, but until this recent confrontation it hadn't occurred to her that her mother-in-law still clung to the events of that long-ago summer night, or that she blamed Jane for a 'destruction of her happiness'. Truth to tell, Jane had never equated Clarisse with any potential for happiness.

*

In Paris, Luc and Jane stayed on the Left Bank in a small hotel in rue Saint-Sulpice, steps from the boulevard Saint-Germain and the dusty, cavernous, baroque splendour of Saint-Sulpice *église* where, occasionally, there were evening recitals. Its great organ was classified as National Heritage. This Left Bank quarter was one of their favourites. Here there were cinemas, art-houses, cafés and food markets aplenty. And for Jane, the perfume department at Bon Marché. They had three days, three precious days, on their own, although as Luc was on business Jane spent her daytime hours without him. She was happy enough. She loved Paris. She bought marmalade-orange suede shoes in a narrow little shop in rue Cherche-Midi and a rather elegant green dress in a boutique along the rue de Sèvres. The colours enhanced her blonde hair and skin, lightly tanned from weeks of grape-picking. She wore the frock out to dinner that first evening. They ate at Les Éditeurs, one of Luc's old haunts, and he complimented her on how beautiful she looked.

The evening was light-hearted, affectionate. The subject of Clarisse and the vineyards had been tactfully set aside. Neither could handle any more disputes for the present. Back at the hotel they made love for the first time in a while. Away from the cares of Les Cigales, Jane found Luc more accessible, although he remained burdened with the weight of his film.

She spent an afternoon in the Grand Palais, at the Edward Hopper exhibition. She was thrilled and astonished, particularly by his lesser-known magazine illustrations, and wished that Luc had been at her side to share it with her, to see the range in the artist's work. That second evening they queued in the cold night air to hear jazz at the piano bar of Aux Trois Mailletz, nestled in a cobbled lane behind the Shakespeare & Co bookshop. Autumn leaves were falling. The club's history was as fascinating as its musical line-up and Luc, who had been frequenting the tiny jazz palace since his days at the Sorbonne, had immersed himself in both. Jane had first visited the club when she was eighteen and Luc had introduced her to blues and boogie with Memphis Slim on the keyboards.

On the third morning, Luc drove her to the Gare du Nord to board the Eurostar alone.

'Any idea when you'll be home?' she asked him, as they kissed goodbye.

'Not yet, but you know I'll come as soon as I can. Say hello to your dad for me.'

She nodded. The urgency of their parting caused a rush of need, a softening and momentary panic within her. A desire to spill out all that they had been avoiding during these last days alone together. 'I tried with Clarisse, Luc, honestly, I did.'

'I know, *chérie*. She has too much responsibility, that's the nub of the matter, living there all alone. She needs me . . . needs us. When the film's delivered, you and I will have to make some decisions.'

'About what?'

'London, but' – he lifted his hands to silence any further argument – 'not now, Jane, please, I beg you. I have to get this film wrapped first.'

Jane felt her stomach clench. 'Do you want us to move to Les Cigales? Is that your preference, for us to sell London? If you think that's best then we could . . . could consider renting out Lady Margaret for a while. I'll give it a try at Les Cigales . . .'

'*Chérie, doucement*. Let's discuss it another time, not here as we're parting.' He pressed his fingers against his forehead and temple as though rubbing away a headache. The gesture was uncharacteristically agitated. 'We do need to talk. There's –' The thought was broken by his phone beginning to ring. He slid his hand into his jeans pocket but the call went dead. 'I'll give you a buzz tonight.'

She waited, scanning his face. Suddenly, a fear. 'Talk about what?'

He shook his head, glanced at his watch. The iPhone was going again. 'I'm late for a meeting.' He smiled. 'And I need to touch base with Dan. Don't worry. Please, don't. I'll sort everything out.'

'I don't want Clarisse and her responsibilities to destroy us. I love you, Luc.'

They embraced once more. She felt tension harden his body and clung to him tightly, wanting never to let him go, sniffing his body scent to keep it close to her during his absence. He shuffled himself loose and pecked her left ear. 'I'll call you later.'

She saw in his expression, in those disturbed green eyes, that he was already elsewhere, his thoughts lost to her. A tight knot gripped her throat, shackling speech. She nodded and hurried away, dreading tears.

Was she losing Luc?

Jane rubbed the carriage window with the sleeve of her cardigan. It was starting to rain. She stared out, barely registering the landscape as it slipped from cityscape to graffiti-walled suburbs, accelerating towards rolling acres of farmland populated with church spires and low-lying stone and timber villages. Northern France in late autumn. Leaves were falling; colours were fading. Her heart ached.

After more than twenty years of marriage, Jane had grown accustomed to the separations she and Luc were obliged to endure. It was the nature of his professional life to travel, and for him to immerse himself in his projects, to dedicate himself wholeheartedly to the next film on the horizon, to raise funding single-handed. His was a small, independent business, which meant that he was his own master, but it also meant that he was the sole carrier of the can for both financial and artistic responsibilities. Despite that, they had always found ways to be together. They had squeezed in weekends, stolen days here and there, meeting where they could, and they had turned those occasions into fun and sexy trysts. Right up until the last couple of years, Luc had managed to dedicate parts of his research time as well as the periods between filming to life in London with Jane, but of late a multitude of commitments seemed to be crowding in on them. And she sensed him slowly slipping into worlds where she couldn't reach him.

Should she renounce her life in London, at least for the foreseeable future, to make circumstances easier for Luc? Her modest translation business was operated via her laptop. There was no requirement to meet her clients face to face. Skype or FaceTime were her boardrooms. Hers was the more flexible of their professional lives. She could base herself anywhere. After Isa's death, a move to the South of France had been mooted, but Jane had vehemently stood her ground against it and Clarisse was now repaying her. At whatever cost, the old woman intended to entice her son back to his family home.

Jane's father, Peter, her only remaining blood relative, ailing and widowed, was in a home in Kent. She needed to be close to him and she wanted a married life that was not ruled by her mother-in-law. Was that so unreasonable?

The consequence of putting her foot down was that her marriage was beginning to drift. The extended separations were becoming more frequent. Luc's responsibilities were crowding in on him. Increasing burdens on the two shores of the Channel were alienating them.

We do need to talk.

Jane sat on the train, staring out at the early-November English countryside, the wet Kent afternoon, feeling miserable and sorry for herself.

Talk about what, Luc?

Did he judge her unnecessarily stubborn? Why hadn't she succeeded in finding a way to make peace with Clarisse? Was Jane misguided to stand her ground against her mother-in-law? Luc held them both responsible in equal measure, or he wasn't taking sides. But he didn't know the whole story. She loved Luc deeply, passionately – she always had – but circumstances were driving them apart. Something had to give. Their life together couldn't continue like this.

6

Whenever Jane was in England, she paid a visit to her father at least once a week. There was no consistency about it: she popped in whenever it was convenient or she felt the need to sit at his side. The staff at the care home were flexible and accommodating and it made little difference to Peter. He was no longer able to keep track of dates, times, days of the week. She had been planning to drive down the first weekend after her return, but as she sat gazing out at the increasing rain, she realized the Eurostar was pulling into Ebbsfleet. On a whim, she grabbed her case and disembarked. Ebbsfleet International Station, Kent's rail connection to the continent, was a dreary, forlorn location battered by winds and surrounded by nothing but a vast car park, usually half empty.

Jane rarely had cause to use this alighting point and the matter of onward transport had not crossed her mind when she leaped off the train. She enquired at the ticket desk and was informed that there was a taxi rank outside, but no taxis were available. The glum girl offered the number for a mini-cab service based in Dartford, but when Jane thought through the logistics of the rest of her day, she realized she would still need to get herself with the suitcase to London. In the deserted concourse, she found a lone car-rental company and handed over her credit card.

The journey was swift, the motorway clear. She made the turn-off for Chislehurst and Bromley in forty minutes. Peter's care home was in a tree-lined residential side street, Garden Park Avenue: three substantial Victorian houses had been knocked together and converted into a nursing home with in-house medical facilities for the elderly, offering specialist supervision to those with dementia. It welcomed both private and state-aided patients.

Once the funds from the sale of Jane's parents' modest home had dried up, Peter's care had switched to the state system. Jane had handled the paperwork. It had been smooth, with little fuss. Peter never knew the difference. That he hadn't been obliged to move had eased Jane's heartache.

Three years off his eightieth birthday, Peter had spent the last two in this establishment. The staff came and went. Most were warm-hearted and compassionate. His Alzheimer's had been diagnosed at an early stage so he still enjoyed a certain quality of life.

Jane parked the car in the leafy street, ran through the rain, which had eased off to a soft, steady downpour, into the reception block where she made her arrival known. Frances, with her permed dark hair, a few grey curls, recognized her immediately. 'You're looking well, got yourself a good colour. Been back to France?'

Jane nodded.

'Lucky you.'

'How is he?'

'Been as good as gold. He's in his room. He had a little potter round the garden after his breakfast before the weather turned. After lunch, a little nap. He was asking after you this morning, wondering when you and your mother would be dropping in.'

Frances and Jane shared a look.

'I'll go on up, then. Anything you want taken in to him?'

Frances shook her head. 'No thanks, love, we'll be round with tea in a little bit. I'll ask them to bring yours in first, if you like.'

Upstairs, Jane knocked softly and let herself into the overly warm room. Peter was sitting on the bed, staring out of the window towards a spacious, meticulously maintained back garden. Hanging on the wall above the headboard was a painting of a small fishing boat bobbing offshore. Jane had bought it in Saint-Raphaël and given it to him one Christmas. It was one of the few possessions he hadn't parted with when their family house had been sold and he'd moved in here. On the dressing-table across the room there were three photographs in frames: Jane's parents on their wedding day; Jane, aged eight, with her father in France; and the last was of Luc and Jane, windblown in Positano, after their wedding.

'Hello, Dad, it's me, Janey.'

He didn't turn, didn't respond. Jane thought at first that he hadn't heard her. She closed the door gently and crept across the pale carpet to stand at his shoulder. It was then she saw that tears were rolling down his cheeks. 'Dad? Dad, it's Jane.' He swivelled his head sideways and looked up into her face. There was such sadness in his startling blue eyes that it took her breath away. Jane perched on the foot of the bed with its pink eiderdown, and lifted her arms towards her father. 'Here,' she said. 'What's up? They told me downstairs you've been doing great.'

'I've lost my banjo,' he said. 'I thought it was in the cupboard. The bass is in the car but I promised them I'd do a few numbers on the banjo. They've specially requested some of the old tunes.'

'Dad, Dad . . .'

'It's a retirement party, you see. They like the classics. A bit of Formby.'

It broke her heart to see him so frail, so confused. The weight he had lost. A slight tremor had appeared in his left hand.

'Dad, we're in Garden Park. This is where you live now. You gave me your banjo a while ago. I have it at our flat in Lady Margaret Road, remember? But if you'd like to play it again, I can bring it next time I come.'

Peter frowned, his eyes darting to and fro as though trying to focus, tussling with memories, trying to locate, to drag the images back. He stared at her, bemused. 'Vivienne?'

'No, Dad, it's Jane.' She took his hands in hers and rested them on her lap, and he seemed to relax. 'We're in Bromley,' she said softly, emphatically.

'Jane? Janey. Where's Luc?' he asked eventually, the concerns over his music seemingly dissipated for the time being.

'He's in France. We've been harvesting grapes.' She waited. No reaction. 'I'll bring him along next time he's over. Would you like that?'

Peter nodded and released a long sigh. A slow exhalation. She felt him surrendering, unknotting.

'It's raining so I won't suggest we go for a walk, but I've got a car if you fancy a little drive. We could go to Shoreham.' She was speaking slowly, clearly, as she had been taught to do, counselled by the staff at the home. 'But don't baby-talk him. Don't interrupt him, let him find the words. Only assist him with the thought when he's agitated and the inability to grasp it is upsetting him.'

Peter shook his head, puzzling over what he wanted to do.

'Hey, we can just stay here. Sit and chat, if you'd rather? Frances has promised they'll bring tea soon.'

'*The bells are ringing for me and my gal* . . .' He began to hum and sing the words softly. A ditty Jane had learned from him years earlier. He often did this, broke unexpectedly into song, and it was frequently this tune he began with. Jane had no idea why he chose it – a childhood memory of his own, perhaps? – but it seemed to indicate that he was at peace again, content, his inner self operating out of a world where he could sing endlessly. Music, the composition of his own tunes, had always been his primary love.

Jane encouraged him with the next line, *The birds are singing*, and they were off on one of their sessions, their riffs. Vocal jamming, he used to call it. Although Jane was a singer of little competence, she made up in enthusiasm for what she lacked in skill. She stayed with her father for another couple of hours, and for most of the time they sat on the bed hand in hand, facing the window, looking out towards the oak trees, swaying gently, like the trees in the wind, softly crooning. It was a sanctuary from the real world and calmed Jane's troubled heart.

Alice, the kitchen assistant with Down's syndrome, brought the tea. She beamed at the sight of Jane. She had included a small plate of Rich Tea biscuits, so Jane and Peter paused from their singing to enjoy their snack together. Looking at her father as he dunked his biscuit in his tea, Jane could fool herself that he didn't have a care in the world, and she was relieved, but she knew that his mood, his state of mind, could change in an instant, triggered by nothing that was apparent to her.

She treasured those moments of affection, of proximity, of lucidity, returning to the twosome they had so frequently been when she was a girl. Daddy's girl. Watching him now, his pupils flitting, thinking hard, running through his mental repertoire, she asked herself why it had all turned out this way. If her mother hadn't got sick, hadn't died . . . Had the loss of his wife sparked Peter's dementia? The doctors had assured Jane that the two were quite unrelated. Still, if Jane had not forced her mother to hear the truth, to face facts, everything might have been different. Jane still felt responsible. She still harboured guilt for the damage she had caused. She recalled Clarisse's recent allegation, that she had destroyed others' lives. It wounded her again. But what could she do now? What could she change? It was the past. What was the sense of raking over old mistakes? It only churned up worn-out emotions.

Saying goodbye was always distressing, particularly today when she felt so vulnerable and craved reassurance from the exuberant father who was no longer present. *Au revoir*, then. Leaving him in the home, in the white room that whiffed gently of a not-unpleasant room spray . . . In spite of the staff's kindness, Jane always wanted to make a run for it with Peter at her side, the truant's head buried beneath her raincoat, the pair of them giggling, just like the old days, their travelling summers, heading south into France in his car.

Past happiness. Full of anticipation. Never growing up.

'*Au revoir.* See you soon, Dad.'

'Yes, see you tomorrow, love. Why not bring Jane? She hasn't been to see me for a while. How is she getting on with her studies?'

Jane pondered for a moment, hesitating to say, *I am Jane, Dad, married, no longer a student, and Mum's been dead thirty years.* But he had spilled what remained of his tea, slopped the saucer, made a damp patch on his trouser leg and begun to whimper. She grabbed a flannel from the sink, helped him mop it up, took the cup from him and set it on the tray near the door, calming him as she did so. When he was quiet, she kissed the crown of his head, gave him a heartfelt hug and hurried to the stairs. She couldn't bear to look round, to see the back of his head still with a full mop of hair, to see him staring out of the window, humming or muttering to himself. Frances would send someone to clear away the tea tray.

What Jane wouldn't trade for a magic flick of a switch to bring him back. Flood his brain with memories, past and recent. Even those she was secretly delighted he had forgotten? Yes, if that was the cost, yes, even those.

One day, before long, at some point in the not too distant future, Peter wouldn't recognize his daughter at all any more. He would no longer remember any of his past. All would be deleted, even the music. Perhaps he was the lucky one to have got off scot-free. The taxes of the mind erased. The guilt buried.

Already he appeared to have no residual memories of Les Cigales, not a trace of the night when Jane was fourteen and her world had caved in.

By the time Jane hit the southern edges of central London, dusk was falling and it was rush-hour. A rainy night in London. She was listening to a popular jazz album: *Rainy Night in Georgia* by Randy Crawford, a CD forgotten by a previous renter. The music washed her senses full of the blues. She was recalling her father as a young man, their pioneering summer together in the South of France. Crossing to the continent in search of employment was an intrepid step to take in the early seventies. Had little girl Jane understood just how desperate her father had been when he had first rung the bell at Les Cigales, all that was at stake for them? Not for the first time, she asked herself what she wouldn't give to bring that vigorous young man back to life, to halt the sickness that was eradicating his mind.

She was startled back to reality by the bleating of horns and the impatient jostle in the urban streets around her. London. She was home. Crossing the Thames by Battersea Bridge, nose to tail bumpers, sirens wailing, rain streaming, cabs hooting, wipers whining, red lights shining, fractured, into the overheated car. She loved its messy energy.

Now she craved a hot bath, plenty of scented bubbles,

several glasses of wine and sleep. Her own bed. Own room. Own rhythms. A text message from Luc on her phone. She glanced at it as she progressed tortuously towards the King's Road. *Hope safe arrival? Running from one meeting to next, will call later. Lx.*

After a light dinner she telephoned Luc, but his mobile was on voicemail. She left a message: "I've been thinking, why don't we invite Clarisse to join us here for Christmas? Call me, love you.' Then, on the off-chance, she rang the hotel on the Left Bank where they had spent the last couple of nights together, hoping to find him working on his laptop in the room where they had so recently made love. She was replaying in her head the intimacy of that night together, his nakedness against hers, when the receptionist returned to the phone to inform her that Monsieur Cambon had checked out that afternoon.

She felt herself go cold. 'Are you sure?'

'*Oui, Madame.*'

That was curious. She had understood he was staying one more night in Paris. Surely, if his plans had changed, he would have contacted her. She telephoned the main house at Les Cigales. Matty answered. 'He's still in Paris, Jane, back tomorrow.'

Jane replaced the receiver, feeling edgy. Where was Luc? She poured a glass of wine and sat with a book that she didn't read. Luc didn't call her as his text had promised, and when she dialled his mobile again, it was still on voicemail. Where was he?

7

London, December, seven weeks later

The flat exuded an air of stillness, of expectancy. Every now and again, its polished oak floors creaked and shifted, as though purring with satisfaction. Jane was excited at the prospect of welcoming Luc and Walnut home after such a long separation. The neutral-carpeted stairway, the upstairs landing and bedrooms were perfumed with lavender pot-pourri. In the downstairs open-plan living areas, a mix of dried flowers, orange peel and cinnamon laid out in blue-and-white Chinese porcelain bowls emitted a spicy, woody scent, a satisfying Christmassy aroma. The ground floor was illuminated with candles. Four antique silver candlesticks – a wedding present, a Cambon family heirloom from Isabelle – were blazing on the dining-table while a spangled array of lights flickered and winked on the tall, blue-pine Christmas tree in the sitting room.

Exhausted by all her preparations, the anticipation and the couple of glasses of wine she had enjoyed while decorating the tree, Jane was curled up in a chair by the fire, the second half of the bottle of white Sancerre growing warm on the mahogany table at her side. She had fallen asleep waiting for the arrival of Luc, who was due in off the last Eurotunnel Shuttle. He had called her before he set off from Les Cigales, then a few hours later from the motorway, during a coffee-and-sandwich stop, north of Beaune.

'Are you on your own? I made up the spare room.'

'I'm alone.'

'No Clarisse, then?' Jane fought to conceal her relief. Since her invitation, she had been growing edgy at the prospect of her mother-in-law arriving, like royalty, for her first stay with them in England.

'She wouldn't come. I'm not sure which of you is the more stubborn.' He didn't elaborate.

South of Beaune in the Massif Central, he had skidded to a standstill, gridlocked by a tailback of holiday traffic on a fog-bound highway buried beneath heavy snow. Wipers slapping against minimal visibility.

'Christmas weather, clogged-up roads, it makes for slow-going.' His voice sounded flat, weary, as she listened to his update. He pushes himself too hard, she had observed silently. Luc never let up and the progress on the new film seemed to be consuming his every waking hour. That, and his mother's ceaseless demands. Jane hadn't seen him since their brief sojourn in Paris. Even their phone conversations, when she had managed to reach him, had been strained, as though his mind was everywhere but with her.

'If I put my foot down and the motorway clears, I might just manage the last Shuttle,' he had told her. 'If not, I'll check into a B-and-B somewhere in Calais and board the first one in the morning.'

She glanced at her watch. It was not yet three p.m. 'But, Luc, unless you get really snarled up, you'll easily make the last Shuttle.'

'I have one more brief stop to make outside Paris.'

'Oh, really, what for?'

There was a moment's silence. 'Some paperwork, research material to deliver.'

'Couldn't you have emailed it across?'

Pause.

'Luc?'

'It won't take long.'

'Luc, it's Christmas and I'm longing to see you. It's been too long.'

Silence, save for the long-distance whine of transport and the hooting of horns.

She bit her tongue. 'I promised Dad we'd drive down and pick him up around midday tomorrow. We're taking him out for lunch at the what's-it-called in Halstead, remember?'

'I'm doing my best, *chérie*. I am not trying to avoid being with you.'

Travel delays could mean that Luc would be approaching the outskirts of Paris and its challenging *périphérique* at rush-hour. Rush-hour the night before Christmas Eve. Why did he put himself through so much stress? If only she could understand what was pushing him so relentlessly.

'I know.' She sighed. 'Let me know how you get on.' She was attempting to conceal her disappointment. 'Get here safely, that's the main thing. Don't drive too fast. I love you.'

He always did drive too fast, speeding from A to B, hurtling along country lanes.

'The first Shuttle out seems the most likely scenario. Either way, I'll give you a ring later. I'm looking forward to seeing you. We'll have plenty of time to relax, enjoy the holidays, talk . . .'

'I'm glad we'll be on our own.'

Jane had remained adamant that she wanted Christmas in their own home. Tomorrow they would take Peter for a pub lunch, and once he was delivered back to Garden Park, she and Luc would spend the holidays alone, low-key. He had promised to be with her till after New Year. Tonight, she was preparing duck, and had opened a bottle of Haut Médoc to accompany it. Silver cutlery polished, Wedgwood White dinner service laid for two (with a third set at the ready, in case). Everything special, a celebration.

They deserved it: they had not seen one another for seven weeks, and Jane had been looking forward to this homecoming with almost childlike anticipation. She was determined that this would be their best Christmas together ever.

She opened her eyes, yawned and glanced at the carriage clock on the mantelpiece. It read a quarter to one. It couldn't be. Luc must have missed the last Shuttle after all. Curious that he had not called to forewarn her, as he had promised, or sent a text at least, she picked up her mobile, lying alongside her wine glass, to confirm that she had not slept through his call. If something was amiss, he would have let her know. He always did. He was diligent and caring in such matters.

At that moment the phone's metallic bell burst rudely into the silence. It was the house telephone. Normally it was only care-home calls that came through on the landline. Jane stared at it, as though it were an intruder, a thing not to be trusted, listening to its emphatic ring, before lifting herself from the armchair to answer it.

The care home. It must be. Oh, Lord, something had happened to her father. A fall, or . . . It wouldn't be Luc. He always rang her iPhone.

'Hello?' She could hear the tremor in her voice.

'Jane? It's Clarisse.'

Clarisse! Jane glanced again at her watch, puzzled. It was almost two a.m in France. Why wasn't the old woman in bed? 'What are you doing up at this hour?' They hadn't seen one another since the grape harvest yet there was no pretence at the usual pleasantries.

'You'd better get over here.'

Jane sighed. Her mother-in-law's sense of drama didn't

lessen with age. 'What's the matter, Clarisse?' Was this about not spending Christmas together?

'Something's happened to Luc.'

'To Luc? What makes you say that? He's on his way home – he rang me earlier.'

'I've just received a call from a police officer in Paris, asking for Madame Cambon.'

'What?'

'Evidently he was trying to contact you, and when he understood that I am Luc's mother, not his wife, he clammed up and refused to give me any information. I may have given birth to the boy but because you and Luc are married I am not his next of kin and the fellow simply refused.'

'Has Luc had an accident?' Jane butted in, the first inkling of something wrong beginning to dawn on her. 'Did the officer suggest that?'

'We'd better get off the phone – they'll be trying to reach you. I don't know why you're not here. I can't understand why you insisted on spending Christmas in London and not down here with me.'

'Clarisse, please, concentrate, did the caller mention an accident?' Jane's voice was firm, urgent.

'Luc would have been perfectly happy to stay at Les Cigales. In fact, he would have preferred it. Less stress for him than driving backwards and forwards, and now . . . Oh, God.'

Jane was anxious to hang up. 'Let me find out where he is. I'll ring you back.' She replaced the receiver and took a deep breath, calming herself, gathering her thoughts. The candles on the dining-table were burning low. One flickered and died. Clarisse was an attention-seeker, Jane knew that. She was miffed because they were not going to be with her for the holidays. Jane had to keep her wits about her, be logical, and not get drawn into Clarisse's manipulative game-playing.

Within seconds, there was a knock at the front door. She glanced at her watch. One fifteen. Luc had finally arrived. He'd forgotten his keys. Oh, thank heavens! As she stepped towards the door, the house phone began to ring again. It was bound to be Clarisse. Let it ring. She crossed to the door, unlocked it, arms ready to embrace her husband.

An average-built man with a creased, shadowed face, hollow bone structure, was standing before her beneath the automatic light in the porch, alongside a short woman with cropped blonde hair. The woman was in police uniform, the man in a trilby and brown overcoat, wrapped up in a thick woollen scarf in various shades of green. 'Mrs Cambon?' As he spoke her name he lifted his hat. His breath rose like steam into the cold night air.

'You'd better come in,' Jane muttered, throat dry, heart kicking, after she had glanced at the identity card the officer had held towards her in his gloved hand.

'And this is Police Constable Sally Branch.'

She offered them tea, a Scotch. They shook solemn heads. Both sat without removing their outer garments. There was a cold, sober air about their presence and Jane's gut lurched as she perched on the arm of the chair she had so recently been dozing in.

'We understand that Luc Cambon is your husband.'

Jane nodded, gripped her hands together.

'We're here concerning your husband, Mrs Cambon. I'm sorry to inform you that there has been an accident.'

'Accident?'

'Mr Cambon's car ran off the road, east of Paris.'

'Oh, God. Is Luc all right? Has he been hurt?'

'We received a call from a Detective Inspector Roussel a

little more than an hour ago. He is requesting your presence at the hospital in Paris.'

Jane was confused. 'Luc's in hospital?'

'Mrs Cambon, there is no easy way to break this to you. Your husband's accident . . . I'm afraid the outcome is not good. The French police will need you to identify him.'

'Ident– Oh, God, what are you telling me?'

'I'm sorry to be the bearer of this news, particularly during this season.' He glanced towards the Christmas tree. The table candles had burned out. The room was descending into darkness. 'According to DI Roussel, there was nothing that could be done to save him. His injuries were fatal.'

'Fatal? Luc is –' She couldn't utter the word. A blockage in her throat. Years of loving him, waiting for his return, for Christmas, for . . .

'Mrs Cambon? Mrs Cambon, can you understand what I'm telling you? Your presence will be required in Paris and we're here to assist you with your arrangements.'

'Would you like me to put the kettle on, make you a cup of tea?' This was the woman in uniform, cherub-faced Sally. On her feet, large black shoes, flat, well polished, her expression perplexed, furrowed, attempting to locate the kitchen.

Jane couldn't direct her. She couldn't remember which room abutted this one.

'The first train leaves from St Pancras at six eighteen and arrives at the Gare du Nord at nine forty-seven. We've made you a reservation. Sally will stay here with you tonight and will accompany you to the station in the morning. Or would you prefer we find someone to travel with you to Paris?'

'That won't be necessary.'

'I have your ticket,' said Sally. 'We can call a taxi.'

'If you don't mind, I'd rather be on my own. I appreciate everything you . . .'

No sooner had Jane seen off her after-hours callers, expressing gratitude for their assistance but desperate to be rid of them, close the door, be alone, catch her breath, take on board the magnitude of what had been imparted, than the phone rang again.

'Mrs Cambon?' A male with a French accent. But not Luc.

Jane's legs buckled. 'Yes?'

'Detective Inspector Roussel. I'm speaking from the thirteenth *arrondissement* commissariat. You are the wife of Monsieur Luc Cambon of Lady Margaret Road, London NW5, is that correct?'

'Y-yes.'

'*Bon*. We are very sorry for your loss.'

'Loss?'

Pause.

Jane swung towards the window. Headlights were shining in through the glass, reflections of passing beams hitting the large wall mirror above the fireplace, drawing to a standstill. A car pulling up? Darkness again in the silent street. A door slamming. Footsteps heading this way, then turning elsewhere. Only the flickering light from the flames of the gas fire and the Christmas tree remained.

'You have spoken to my colleagues in London, I understand. They have paid you a visit, furnished you with travel documents. And you understand that your presence will be required here in Paris, *s'il vous plaît, Madame*.'

'Where is Luc, please?' Jane had instinctively switched to French.

Silence.

'Monsieur, I must speak to my husband. Where is he?'

Jane was clutching the receiver tightly. She felt as though she might vomit. 'There has been a mistake, *je suis sûr.*'

'Madame Cambon?'

She was breathing heavily, trying to get a grip. 'Please.'

'Do you have a pen?'

'It cannot be Luc.' She was having difficulty co-ordinating, remaining upright, ordering her thoughts. 'Someone else was at the wheel . . . Not Luc.'

'Madame Cambon, I need you to write down an address, please.'

The phone, held in her right hand, slid from ear to table as she sank onto her haunches on the floor.

'Hello? Madame Cambon? Madame Cambon?' The man's voice called her name one last time and waited. Jane barely registered it. It was Luc she was waiting for across the miles.

When Jane attempted to replay her exchanges with the police, she recalled little of either beyond the words 'accident', 'loss' and the 'need to identify'. Sally, the police constable, had written down in bold clear letters an address, a hospital in Paris, on the Left Bank. A Eurostar ticket had been placed in Jane's hand. Somehow, numbly, after seeing her bad-news messengers out and speaking to Roussel on the phone, she had climbed the stairs, drawn the silk curtains and crumpled, like a leaf, onto her bed. She had curled into a ball on top of the covers where she remained, quaking, fully dressed, for no more than a few minutes.

There had been a mistake, an identity error. Or she had misunderstood. She had foolishly jumped to the worst-case scenario. Clarisse's selfish behaviour always put her on edge, on the defensive. She hadn't been thinking straight. Luc was driving to London to spend Christmas with her. Of course he was. He had said so. They were to be together. She had spoken to him. *Spoken to him.* She leaped from the bed and went in search of her phone, frantically tapping his number.

Luc answered. *'Allô?'*

Indescribable relief. *He was alive.*

'Oh, Luc, Luc. Thank God. It's me. Sorry if I've woken you, but . . . Luc?'

'. . . leave a message after the bleep and I . . .'

8

A few hours later, on Christmas Eve before daybreak, drained from lack of sleep, Jane climbed aboard the first Eurostar leaving St Pancras bound for Paris, Gare du Nord. In spite of the early hour, the train was bouncing with holiday passengers, excited children, noise, ebullience, expensively wrapped gifts, cuddly toys, suitcases jammed precariously one on top of another in the corridors. Twice during the crossing, her mobile rang. On both occasions it was her mother-in-law. On both occasions, Jane let it switch to voice-mail. The police would keep Clarisse informed. Jane had requested it. She could not face his mother now, could not bear to utter the words *Luc is dead.*

She needed to be armed with facts before she went up against Clarisse. Oh, the prospect of it. Undoubtedly, the old woman would hold her responsible. 'This would never have happened if you had been less obstinate and had agreed to join us here for Christmas instead of selfishly dragging the poor man north.'

Which was a fact. Unpalatable, but a fact. And now he was dead.

From the station in bleak rain and impatient traffic, a taxi to the south of the city. Over the river Seine, through narrow streets bunched tight with cafés, whose interiors were harshly lit against the wintry hour, whose exteriors were illuminated to celebrate the season. Early-morning workers, hunched against the wet, leaned against bar counters downing their third or fourth caffeine shot of the day. Proceeding to the thirteenth *arrondissement*, to a tree-lined avenue where the university hospital of Pitié-Salpêtrière was to be found. In Reception, she was greeted by a clutch of men and women who looked as though they had also been up for the best part of the night: two French police officers in uniform, one rather scruffy man dressed in a grey suit, who confirmed that he was Roussel and that they had spoken on the telephone a matter of hours earlier; a surgeon – she didn't catch his name or which branch of surgery he was engaged in; an emergency nurse in her fifties in a starched white coat-dress, parchment-skinned, wiped out; and an elegant dark-haired female in her early thirties, who was introduced to Jane by the surgeon – he spoke English and French with a discernible Lebanese accent – as 'a specialist in post-accident trauma'.

'We called in the resident priest, who was at your husband's side when he passed away. He received the last rites,' the trauma specialist was assuring her.

Encircled by strangers, Jane listened in dazed silence. Luc wasn't religious. He was an atheist. He had witnessed first hand, he'd said on many occasions, the damage perpetrated by faith. Faith was not in his line of thinking.

Was. Already Luc was the past tense.

The group was now moving as one along a corridor. Jane, netted at the centre of them, had no idea to where she was being escorted. A room, a ward, a mortuary, to Luc?

She could barely place one foot in front of the other, her legs were trembling so. Jelly. Jelly legs.

They turned right into a small, square, off-white room, bare except for a narrow bed. It reeked of sulphur, of chemicals, disinfectant. She could not identify the odours, but the composition was acrid. There, on the bed, lay a shape covered with a white sheet. The body, once the sheet had been peeled to chest level by the surgeon, was Luc's.

Jane felt her innards capsize.

Lingering patches of blood besmirched his lined bluish features. One side of his face had suffered burns. His compassionate green eyes, so curious, so caring, so full of passion, were shrouded beneath closed lids. Someone had done a hasty clean-up job. Jane's legs were threatening to collapse beneath her.

She gulped and lifted a hand to her face. 'Oh, Luc . . . no.'

'Madame, please can you confirm if this is your husband, Monsieur Luc Cambon?'

She nodded.

'*Desolé, Madame*, but I need you to tell us *oui* or *non*.'

'*Oui, c'est Luc Cambon. Mon mari*.'

The sight of him, the lifelessness of him, his inanimate features, aggravated by her exhaustion and the fact that she had not seen him for seven weeks, provoked an explosion of tears.

Roussel coughed awkwardly, looking behind him as though for assistance. The others, including the post-trauma specialist in her well-polished black leather stilettos, seemed to have vanished, evaporated. The inspector suggested coffee. And then, as an afterthought, 'Or perhaps you would prefer tea?'

Jane shook her head. He led her to another small room, with pale grey walls and a table dressed with papers, files and a cutting from a recent *Le Monde*, an interview with Luc discussing his upcoming film. Two chairs, one either side of the table. Roussel gestured her to a seat.

'Your French is excellent. Where did you learn to speak our tongue so well?'

'I'm a linguist. I spent time here as a child. My husband is French.'

Roussel stared at her. *Is.* 'May we continue in French?'

She nodded.

There will be formalities, he warned her gently. An autopsy will need to be carried out. There will be papers to sign. Unfortunately, many offices are closing at noon today until the twenty-sixth. Boxing Day, as Jane knew well, was not a public holiday in France.

'The holidays will cause delays. If you wish to return to London, I can arrange for everything . . .'

'I'll find a hotel.'

Was there someone, a relative, offspring, who could be contacted to keep Jane company? To each question, she shook her head. 'Where's Luc's car?'

'Garaged, awaiting police and insurance inspections, then the breaker's yard. It's a write-off.'

'And the dog? Where is our dog?'

The DI furrowed his brow. No dog had been found. 'Breed?'

'A small black-and-white Springer Spaniel. Luc had christened him Walnut – he was always at Luc's side.'

Roussel frowned, checked his notes. 'No dog.'

He must have left Walnut with Clarisse, Jane thought, which was surprising because the dog was so attached to him.

'The accident occurred east of central Paris, near the Vincennes district on a secondary road. The car skidded in heavy rain, veered off the road to the right where there was a slight cant. The bonnet collided full on with the trunk of a tree and concertinaed. The engine burst into flames. He was wearing his safety belt, but . . .'

Jane was still puzzled about where the dog had disappeared to. Luc would not have left the south without Walnut. Surely, then, this was a clear sign, this was proof, that Luc had not been the driver of the vehicle. She was clinging to straws, shredded straws. Her logic was disjointed. She had just identified his body. Her mind was befuddled, short-fusing.

The man across the desk from her was still talking. 'Had Monsieur Cambon been taking any prescription drugs?'

Not that she was aware of.

'When did you last speak to your husband?'

'Yesterday afternoon.'

'Had he been drinking?'

She shook her head.

'And when did you last see him?'

'Nearly seven weeks ago.'

Roussel expressed surprise.

'Most of the required archive material for his new film was here in France, the interviewees . . .'

Roussel instinctively ran his palm across the newspaper cutting, then frowned and scribbled a couple of words on one of the sheets of paper in front of him. He had a red pencil in one hand. It was looped between two fingers, one of which sported a gold wedding ring. Was his wife at home, engaged in frantic preparations for the traditional Christmas Eve family meal this evening? Jane watched his mouth moving, unable to register anything he was saying. He might as well have been blowing bubbles.

She had a throbbing headache. When had that begun? A child was bawling somewhere beyond the walls of the room. A mother visiting a patient with her youngster? The inspector had a trim brown moustache and a light coating of dandruff on the shoulders of his grey jacket. She felt a certain revulsion towards him. Her judgement was irrational and unkind, but it was so. This man was alive, and still talking. Luc was not. He had been silenced.

Luc, her Luc, was dead.

She had been cheated of the rest of her life with Luc.

What lay ahead?

Jane heard the approach of a trolley in the corridor beyond the door, which had been left marginally ajar, the rubber wheels rumbling along the linoleum-tiled floor, empty cups rattling, a woman humming. The tea lady. Was she in an upbeat frame of mind, looking forward to spending Christmas with her husband, her loved ones? Jane lifted a hand to her head and pressed two fingers against her temple where slow, forceful beats were drumming against her skull. The police officer must have forgotten that he had offered her coffee. Might he also have an aspirin? A wave of sickness was rising up from her stomach, like a slick of oil.

Fighting the urge to vomit, to drop her tired head into her arms on the table and give way to weeping, Jane concentrated hard on the activity of the man seated opposite her. He was opening a notebook marked up with small squares. Such paper had been used for arithmetic when she was at school. She would have to break the news to her father in Kent. Her father in Kent. Was it today they were supposed to be taking him out for lunch? He would be waiting for her, looking forward to seeing Luc again. He would have put on his suit, brushed his hair. Their Christmas outing.

DI Roussel was still talking. Had he been talking all this time? He was sketching a plan. A simple infant's image of a thick-trunked tree, a car approaching it, curving arrows, impact. Car hits tree.

Luc's last trajectory.

9

Jane requested a visit to the site of the accident. A Christmas Day pilgrimage. Although she had insisted that she could accomplish this alone in a hire car, if furnished with a detailed map, Roussel had accompanied her. She felt a compulsion to stand on the spot where Luc had last breathed life and she was convinced that Walnut would be lying low somewhere nearby, hungry, traumatized, awaiting the return of his master, and that her presence would bring their beloved pet out of hiding. But she was mistaken. Her calls and hollering on that foggy, frosty, holy morning brought no response. No young spaniel cantered towards her, tail wagging, buoyant at the sight of her.

Few vehicles passed. The cordoned-off section, marking the accident, was an isolated spot, beyond a dangerous bend, which must have been what threw Luc off course, driving too late for too many hours in low visibility. The lower trunk of the plane tree that had interrupted the car's forward thrust was blackened and scored.

Jane could picture the scene, on the winding lane with a hairpin bend. Luc at the wheel, the dog at his side, skidding as he'd taken the corner, spinning out of control. Rotating in the rain, a dance towards death, the collision, combustion. Luc trapped, struggling with his seatbelt, as the engine exploded and the flames rose and roared. She let out a cry. Had he suffered? Please not.

Roussel was standing a pace or two ahead of her with his hands across his chest deep in thought. He swung round to face her. 'You said?'

She shook her head. 'I was . . . was wondering what caused the skid. Was he driving too fast?'

Roussel made a big deal of scanning the ground, the uneven pebbled surface surrounding the scarred old plane tree, before offering his opinion.

'Tiredness, speeding, alcohol, loss of control, but we are looking for a dog, *non*? I think we will have to assume that a passing vehicle found the distressed creature walking in the road and gathered it up, rescuing what they took to be an abandoned pet. Shall we go?'

'But Walnut had been chipped. He was clearly not abandoned. If he had been found and reported, then we would have received a telephone call by now.' She made a mental note to call the canine refuge centre for the South of France, based in Lyon.

Roussel shrugged.

It was spitting rain now, gaining strength, velocity; a sheeting downpour.

'Are you ready?'

She nodded.

'Let's go.'

During the drive back to Paris, the heater was suffocating, blasting hot air, and the slap and drag of the wipers made her want to open the door and jump out to make a run for it.

'I was a fan of your husband's films,' Roussel said eventually. 'My wife enjoyed them too. The photography, the nature, startlingly beautiful. I remember especially the film about the butterflies.'

'The Swallowtail butterflies? That was his first film.'

'Very impressive.'

Jane smiled to herself. Luc was vaguely impatient that many spectators seemed to prefer his first film above the others.

'What would persuade a man whose passion is the environment to turn his hand to a film that is politically, historically so controversial?'

'He wanted to know more about his background. The French colonials in Algeria. He spoke about it in the article on your desk.'

They drove in silence for a kilometre or two.

'Tragic to lose a man so talented.'

'Thank you,' Jane murmured, although she knew she had played no role in Luc's productions, other than occasionally translating the dialogue and narration texts from French or Spanish into English. She smiled silently, a bittersweet memory of how rigorous he had been with her, his attention to detail, but how satisfied when the modest lines she delivered had pleased him. Her 'succinct use of language' had been one of his compliments. 'Essential in film-making.'

'It's Christmas Day.' Roussel sighed, glancing at his watch, rubbing his chin with his hand. He needed a shave.

'And I have taken you from your family. I apologize. Thank you for your time.'

'It's the nature of my work.' He shrugged.

And that was the first time it crossed her dazed and grieving mind that she was in the company of a senior police inspector who had given up his family holiday to escort her to the site of a car accident. She puzzled for a few miles without saying anything, trying to make sense of all that had happened, the moving force that had crushed her life in so few hours.

'What time did the accident occur?'

'Estimation, around nine thirty p.m. A couple in a saloon car en route to Rheims for the holiday called emergency at ten to ten. The fire service was on the scene at four minutes after ten p.m. The ambulance arrived two minutes later.

Your husband was still alive when they found him. He died fifty-seven minutes after reaching the hospital.'

Jane closed her eyes, thinking of Luc here alone, dying. There were no words to describe the depth of her pain. But what of Luc's?

He had telephoned her from somewhere north of Beaune around three in the afternoon. She remembered it clearly because she had confirmed it on her watch. Beaune was probably a little less than three hours south of where the accident had taken place, which meant there were three hours unaccounted for. Had Luc been delayed somewhere? He had mentioned delivering papers en route. Would that have taken three hours or had he visited someone? Where had he spent those missing hours?

'Is there something you haven't told me?' she asked suddenly.

Roussel momentarily took his eyes off the road. 'About the day, the dog, your husband?'

'The accident.' In spite of her tiredness and vulnerability, her hackles rose.

'There are always questions to be answered in a case such as this one. It is fair to assume that your husband was speeding, yes, but as far as we can ascertain there was no alcohol in his system, no drugs. Obviously a full autopsy has yet to be carried out, which will include a toxicology report.'

'Luc didn't drink when he was driving. And he never took drugs.'

'The most probable scenario is an accident, that your husband fell asleep at the wheel. However, the damage to the mechanics of the engine, the car's digital system, its EDR –'

'EDR?'

'Event Data Recorder. The generic term is "mechanical forensics". Fire damage to the EDR is making it impossible for us to access the information relating to the last hour or two of the car's driving history. So, no, Madame Cambon, I am not hiding anything from you. I don't have the answers myself.'

They fell silent.

She took a breath, glanced out at the waterlogged landscape.

'He had confirmed that he was on his way back to London to spend the holidays with you, not elsewhere?'

The question took her by surprise. 'Yes. Where else would he have been going?'

'Did he suffer from depression?'

'Not at all.' Jane almost laughed. 'He was under a great deal of stress but he was vibrant and upbeat by nature.' Surely Roussel wasn't suggesting the possibility of suicide. Ridiculous.

'Do you have a profession?'

'I gained a master's in languages and started up a small translation business some years ago. French, Spanish, English. Working on the internet.'

'It could be operated out of France?'

'Yes, but I prefer to live in London.'

'Really?'

'Inspector, our marriage was a good one. Our separations were due to Luc's professional commitments, nothing else.'

'Also your preference for living in England, *non*?'

'Not every woman follows a man to his homeland. Our marriage, our relationship, bridged two countries. That is not unusual, these days.'

Roussel made no answer, allowing Jane's voice to hang in the air.

'Luc had everything to live for.'

But did he? His behaviour shifts, his absences, threw up doubts. As well, that five-word sentence, *We do need to talk.*

A conversation they would never have.

When they pulled up outside the Hôtel Lutetia, and Jane was stepping out, shielded from the heavy rain by the doorman holding an umbrella for her, Roussel warned her that they would be releasing the news to the press. 'We will offer as little information as possible and won't mention that you are in the city.' He wished her a *bonne soirée* and shot off into the soggy Christmas night before she could thank him again. She had hoped he might suggest a drink before he returned to his family, an hour, even half, of distraction to alleviate the sense of overwhelming grief that was taking hold. Their conversation in the car was swimming round and round in her head, kicking up questions. Roussel had surely not been suggesting suicide.

She walked through to the bar and ordered a large cognac. The place was dingily lit and deserted. She sat on a banquette by the window, looking out at passing people, hunched in raincoats, hurrying through the grey, miry evening. Christmas Day. She telephoned her father. Frances, at Reception, was on duty. Jane explained where she was and why, but requested that she, Jane, impart the news of Luc's death to Peter when she returned. Frances offered condolences and agreed to remain silent on the subject.

It was time to speak to Clarisse. At Jane's request, the police had already been in touch with her to break the news, but she could not postpone her own call any longer. And when she did ring, the woman's reaction was mordant rage.

'I thought you weren't going to bother,' she snapped. She was adamant that Luc had driven off with Walnut perched on the seat at his side.

Clarisse's words were slurred. She had been drinking.

Who could blame her? Jane doubted there was sufficient alcohol in all Paris to achieve the oblivion she craved.

'He'll be buried here, of course, at Les Cigales. You might be his wife, but . . .'

Jane had not given the location of Luc's final resting place any thought. She hadn't got that far. Luc had never expressed any desire to be buried in his family's plot as far as she knew. His father and grandparents had stayed behind in Algeria. There was only dear Aunt Isabelle in the south, in the village of Malaz. If Jane had reflected on the matter at all, she would have taken it for granted that they would have chosen their final resting place alongside one another somewhere in London.

'I think Luc would have wanted to be with me, Clarisse. We hadn't chosen any particular cemetery but –'

'Precisely. So he'll be buried here.'

Jane silently counted to five. 'Clarisse, the last thing I want is for us to wrangle over ownership of Luc's body, but I am his wife and –'

'And I'm his mother. And if you had one ounce of compassion in your stone-cold heart you'd be here now caring for me and helping with the funeral arrangements. He and I discussed the subject at length. There's a Cambon plot waiting for him.'

'And what about me?'

'You're a Cambon too, aren't you, much to my chagrin? Luc will remain with his family. We fought for our stake here. It's my last word on the subject. You join in or you don't. Please yourself.'

Jane lacked the cogency, the resilience, to argue the matter further. She put the phone down without another word and howled herself to sleep beneath the hotel pillows.

10

Jane remained in Paris over the Christmas and New Year holidays. She didn't know what else to do or where to go. Shock had rendered her anchorless. All she clung to was that Luc was in Paris. His corpse was there, frozen in the morgue, yes, but his spirit was everywhere, around every street corner. She saw him in cafés, engrossed in the comment pages of *Le Monde*; deep within musty secondhand-book shops, rooting for out-of-print illustrated nature tomes, beckoning her to come on in; queuing outside cinemas, his gloved hand holding hers, his breath rising in the chilly winter air, laughing, opinionated, inquisitive, elegant, always elegant; surrounded by stacks of books in the library at the Cinémathèque. Paris was the city she thought of as theirs. More so than London, it occurred to her now. It was the city they had spent time in together before they were married, where they had first become lovers and where they had made love for the very last time after their dinner at Les Éditeurs.

Dutifully, she rang Clarisse every day, and every day Clarisse demanded that she fly to the domain and help with the funeral arrangements, but Jane stalled, temporized. She preferred to stick it out in anonymity at the Lutetia, although it was now drab and down-at-heel, much in need of its advertised refurbishment. Still, this time alone was essential – this proximity to what remained of her husband – to grapple with the trauma and loss.

She telephoned Dan, unsure whether he even knew about

the accident. On each occasion she was connected to an answer-machine. '*Je suis absent. Laissez-moi un message . . .*'

'Dan, it's Jane. Please call me. It's urgent.'

On the fourth or fifth attempt, a woman answered. She spoke perfect French with an accent that Jane couldn't pinpoint. Dan was not available, she said. Jane insisted that it was urgent, that she needed to speak to him. The woman explained that Dan was out of the country on a location shoot. He was expected back mid-January. Jane requested his contact number, but could she call him abroad? To impart such bleak news to him at a distance and over the telephone? No, she needed to see him.

'Please tell him Jane Cambon called and ask him to get in touch with me. It's urgent,' she said. 'Tell him to call me when he gets this message.'

'You are Luc's wife?'

She hesitated. 'Yes, I'm Luc's wife.' Not his widow, she thought. No, not yet his widow. 'And you are?'

'Dan's assistant. I popped round to collect his mail. I'm Annabelle's friend.'

'Annabelle? Sorry, who is Annabelle?'

Long pause.

'Hello?'

'I'll pass on your message when Dan calls me.' And the receiver was replaced.

Winter took hold and wrapped its hoary fingers around her. The days she spent tramping the damp, chilly city; the midnight hours nursing gin and tonic in the hotel's gloomy bar, clinking the ice back and forth in the chilled glass. Several of the national papers ran the story of Luc's death. The reportage was discreet, minimal and professional. Jane rejected offers from Roussel to make a rendezvous with the post-accident trauma specialist. She chose to be companionless in the midst of celebrating crowds, tourists packing activity into every minute or taking their time over leisurely meals, letting the hours roll languorously by. Everyone, bar Jane, had a destination, a purpose. She *had* a purpose, though, she realized: she was waiting for Luc; for the release of Luc. In the interim, she pounded the streets, joints aching, in conversation with her departed husband, puzzling how this had come about when she still felt his presence so close to her, within earshot. His shoulder up against hers. Life alongside one another.

He could not be gone. Even a week beyond his death, an insane part of her clung to optimism, to Roussel or possibly a doctor telephoning her: 'This has all been a ghastly error. We apologize, Madame Cambon. Your husband is alive, fit and well.'

Was she losing her senses?

One snow-flaked late-December morning she stepped out of the lobby of the Lutetia, turned right and then right again. Not directionless, marching along the wind-blown rue Saint-Sulpice towards the boulevard Saint-Germain. From Odéon to Saint-Michel, streaming with bedraggled tourists in plastic capes and hoods, she ploughed onwards into the spinning snow, indifferent to it, trudging through squelching slush towards place Maubert. Upon arrival, the market was in full swing despite the keen weather. The indomitable stallholders had rigged up tarpaulins that sealed in the exposed sides of their stalls, protecting their goods. The canvas sheets were flapping against the downpour, making short, sharp, cracking sounds, like the muted gunshots of hunters preying in distant fields. Every stall was adorned with a necklace of coloured bulbs. All were attempting an end-of-year gaiety, the spirit of Réveillon. Two fish stalls, each displaying a prize selection of oysters: Brittany, Saint-Vaast, Marenne-Oléron, Fines de Claire, sizes 3, 4 and 5, and shoals of whole salmon, robust and pink-fleshed.

Was tonight New Year's Eve or was that tomorrow? Jane had lost track of the days. She pulled her phone out of her raincoat pocket to check the date. Her fingers were stinging, red and curled, like the lobster claws on the stalls in front of her. It was the twenty-ninth. Only the twenty-ninth? Still no message from Dan. One from a girlfriend, Lizzie, who had read the news in the *Guardian*. She should call her father, call the home, let Frances know she was still in Paris, wish her father a Happy New Year, not that he knew which year it was.

Desolation and impotence swept through her. The roof had been blown off her world. Luc was gone. What was she doing here? Not shopping, that was for sure. She found herself drawn to a cheese counter, caught a whiff of softly ripening, creamy Brie. Luc loved Brie. Aged and runny beneath its rhino skin, dripping from a torn chunk of fresh baguette. She remembered this stall from all those years back, when she and Luc used to pop out from the studio he rented in rue Frédéric-Sauton. Together, they would buy a baguette, a selection of cheeses and a bottle of inexpensive red Bordeaux from the wine *cave* directly behind the market stalls. In keeping with the season, the wine-seller's window this morning was decked out with blobs of cotton wool glued to the interior glass. Fabricated snowflakes, behind which was a display of champagne bottles. Outside, a blizzard was blowing. The shop had been bought out by the chain Nicolas, she noted now. Back then, it had been an independent enterprise.

After selecting their purchases, before returning to Luc's fourth-floor studio, he and she, his arm around her shoulders, would pause for a coffee at the café on the corner, which was still going strong and packed with shoppers sheltering from the snow. She stood in the sodden, muddied *place*, purchasers with laden bags bustling about her, frozen by the sight of her freckled, plump eighteen-year-old self in a sundress. A long-haired girl with a tortoiseshell hair-slide, laughing shyly, seated opposite the man she was so desperately, speechlessly, in love with. He was smoking, always smoking, and talking animatedly about the script of his film, lost in his ambitions, his aspirations, arms gesticulating. Leaning towards him across the table, she was entranced, intoxicated, thrilled to have found him again.

To be so high on the energy of the other, of the only man she had ever loved.

1984.

Luc's studies were behind him, a first-class master's from the Sorbonne in arts, humanities and social sciences, and he had written his first film. '*The Scarce Swallowtail Butterfly* – remember, Jane, when I took you to see the newly formed butterflies hill-topping, their mating antics?'

Yes, she remembered that summer, that warm extraordinary day with dozens, hundreds of black-and-white beauties fluttering all around them.

'It's the subject of my film. And the dangers that lie in store for such species if we continue to abuse the earth.'

A host of opportunities was opening up for Luc, and he, with his utopian dreams, was intent on grabbing them, on changing the world. While she . . . she had been shambling forwards. What had she dreamed of besides a life alongside Luc? To be his future wife, his partner, to bear his children. Hers had been unremarkable dreams, commonplace. Her horizons were not boundless as were his. She believed herself ordinary, not born to change the world, but she loved him deeply and would have crossed the great white plains to be at his side, to participate in his vision. She had aspired to be Luc's wife and his loyal helping hand. Her gift was for languages and that was the direction she had finally opted for.

One summer only – the summer of 1984, a few months before her nineteenth birthday – she had spent with him in the City of Lights before she had returned to England to begin her own university education.

Luc could never have known how, that summer, when he had telephoned Jane out of the blue and invited her to Paris, he had swept her out of one of the most ghastly periods of her teenage life. The year before, when she had been seventeen, her mother had passed away while her father was absent from home. Peter had been travelling in the South of France, buying stock for his wine business. By then, he had picked up several impressive accounts and was finally earning a decent living for his family. Les Cigales paled beside them; in any case, he no longer paid visits to the Cambon estate. Even so, he was on the road more than he was in Kent, which left Jane alone with her mother to witness the silent passage from skeletal life to expiration.

A mobile phone was an unheard-of device in the early eighties and Jane was unable to make contact with her father. He had rung home, left messages, but Jane had been at her mother's hospice bedside. She had no way of notifying him, of signalling to him how close Vivienne was to the end. Their only child, Jane, bore the burden of the decision-making for the funeral arrangements. Vivienne Sanderson was buried to the strains of prayers recited by her daughter and a clutch of parishioners from their local congregation.

When Peter eventually stepped through the door, Jane blurted out the news to him. 'I hate you,' she had yelled, running at him, ramming her head in his chest, coughing tears, beating at his V-necked pullover. She had blamed him, blamed her father, for his wife's death, for his absences, for his tanned, easy-going manner, for her mother's anguish and disillusionment.

It was the following year Luc learned the news, eleven months after Vivienne's death. As soon as he heard, he had telephoned Jane in Kent.

'I am so sorry about your mother.'

Jane had been tongue-tied. She hadn't seen or spoken to Luc for four years, not since the summer when she was fourteen and Clarisse had banished her from Les Cigales.

Had Clarisse told her son about the showdown? Jane doubted it.

'How are you, Jane?'

The tenderness in his low-pitched voice, rich and resonant, thrilled her. She held the receiver tight against her face, pressing it deep into her cheekbone. Luc had never telephoned her before. During those lonely four years she had dreamed of him and their childhood days together on the estate, wondering what he was up to, how his student life was panning out, how he might have changed. No contact during all that time, and now he was at the other end of the line, *inviting her to Paris.*

She couldn't think what to answer, other than 'Yes.'

YES.

A week later, she arrived at Charles de Gaulle. Luc met her off the RER train that delivered her to Châtelet from the airport. She had gained weight. 'Puppy fat', her teachers and father called it, but it was depression, big-time. Luc saw it. Her demeanour, her awkwardness. Clothes too tight, puckered around her thickened midrift. She knew she looked a sad sight with her tan skirt and kitten-heeled sandals, her gold-blonde hair pinned up in a scraggly bun in an attempt at bouffant.

'How are you bearing up?' He smiled. 'You're looking . . . fighting fit.'

Her gaze remained downcast. She couldn't bear to see the lie in his piercing green eyes. He lifted her bag from her shoulder, took the weight of it, and side by side they rode the Métro, silences broken by polite conversation, to place Maubert. *He regrets inviting me*, her mind yelled over and over. *I look fat and boring and he's so grown-up and handsome. So sexy.*

He presented her with a key to his studio on the fourth floor of a seventeenth-century stone *haute maison* at 20 rue Frédéric-Sauton. 'Your very own key to Paris. Shall I write both our names in the hallway?' he asked. Surely teasing.

She shook her head. It was unnecessary. Who would be dropping by to visit her? With his usual attention to detail and facts, he pointed out to her that the building had been constructed, along with several others, in the narrow *rue* before the Revolution. Number six had been inhabited by Charles Le Brun. The name meant nothing to Jane.

'Painter to the king, Louis XIV, possibly the most highly regarded artist of the seventeenth century.' Luc winked. 'By the way, our President Mittérrand lives two streets away. You've heard of him?'

They ascended the four flights together in the cramped, iron-grilled lift. His proximity, the scent of him, the fall of his hair, grown longer than she remembered, made her catch her breath; she longed for him so, she thought she might faint.

The narrow bed – narrow even by single standards – was a mattress within a wooden fold-down frame hooked into the wall of the studio. Everything was built into the walls. Bookshelves packed tight with heavy tomes on film-making, nature, philosophy, Algeria – his birth land – and Provence, his adopted one. It was a book-lined studio, perfectly tidy, with a minuscule kitchenette squeezed into a corner, two steps beyond the foot of the bed. It consisted of two electric rings, a metal sink and, beneath, a mini-sized fridge that shimmied and hummed relentlessly. The shower, washbasin and loo were closed off by a partition wall, so compact you had to hold your breath to shut the door. And that was it, aside from one square metre of corridor, with a hook to hang a coat, that led to the studio's front door. The entire apartment comprised twenty-one square metres.

And Jane loved it.

'You'll be fine here.'

'It's fabulous, Luc.'

'I'm staying with a friend. I'll be back to take you for dinner, if I may?'

She nodded, placing her bag on the bed.

Jane never met 'the friend'. Luc returned later with a bottle of Moët. They drank the bubbly, hacked at triangles of cheese, talked incessantly into the late night, by which point they had kissed and he stayed in the studio with her, squeezing onto the mattress alongside her, wrapping his limbs about her to stop her slipping to the floor. Luc had taken her virginity. She had given it joyously, energetically, if a little awkwardly in that narrow, springless bed.

They made love again and then again, and they giggled. She ecstatic, tipsy. A laughter that ripped out of her, surfing on rollers of happiness, of unleashed joy. He was reawakening in her the sap of life that coursed through her veins; she had forgotten ever having possessed such a potent energy.

She had been euphoric, slipping discreetly into his studio, his tiny capital-city kingdom, sharing his bed and the few hours of his daily life that were available to her and not dedicated to his career, his future as a film-maker. When she woke in the mornings, he was gone. Off about his day. Fund-raising for his film. Making contacts, meeting commissioning editors at the various television stations.

During the hours he was away from her, she rose late, luxuriating in sheets perfumed by their bodies, their lovemaking, drank mugs of coffee, read, mooched about the streets, staring into the windows of the boutiques, spent her afternoons at the Louvre, pressed by crowds speaking in a confusion of tongues all of which she longed to learn, or the cinema – *The Shining* (no, they had seen that film together, she remembered; Luc had hated it), *The Last Metro*, *Atlantic City*, *Amadeus*. Buried in small art-houses where she would be one of an audience of two or three, Wajda's *Danton* incarnated by a slender charismatic Gérard Depardieu. *Confidentially Yours*: how she had longed for the poise of Fanny Ardant. Her first encounters with the comedies of Eric Rohmer.

Afterwards out into the clear, light summer evenings, birds chirruping in the plane and chestnut trees along the narrow streets, to the food stalls of the sixth *arrondissement*, close to Odéon, where she shopped for wine and provisions for a supper *à deux* that could be prepared on two electric rings. There was no telephone in the studio. She never knew when he would arrive back, but she was always there waiting, with the tiny, crooked-legged table laid. Candlelit. Wine chilled. She, cross-legged on the bed, devouring his books – she had found Raymond Queneau's *Zazie dans le Métro* – or listening to his music: Miles Davis, *Lift to the Scaffold*, Bill Evans, especially Bill Evans. Some days she played the *Time Remembered* LP over and over, 'What Is This Thing Called Love?' Other days she washed up, showered, made coffee, hummed, danced, spun about the studio to tracks by Jackson Browne, King Sunny Adé, Stan Getz: all unfamiliar names to her. Her horizons were widening. She was in a state of rapture, giddy from good sex. And it hit her one morning, suddenly, just like that, that she was in love. The warmth of the emotion rose up from within her, like a flower opening.

She was creeping out of her shell, shedding her grief, getting slimmer and splashing out on lacy underwear. This chrysalis state would have been pure euphoria had she not been bothered by doubt and fear. Fear because she loved this man so deeply and was afraid of losing him again. Doubt that her love could ever be reciprocated.

Her exaltation was crushed one evening when he told her that he would soon be driving south to spend a few weeks of the summer at the estate with his mother and aunt. 'Come with me?'

She shook her head.

'Why not? You don't start university till October. We can swim and read and take a tent and a camera and go hiking up in the Mercantour, make love on top of the mountains. Let's flush the city out of our hair.'

She longed to say yes. 'I couldn't.'

He furrowed his brow. 'They'll be pleased to see you again.'

'No, no, they . . . She won't. Your mother won't welcome me.'

'Why ever not? You and your father were always welcome in our home. My mother looked forward to your visits. Both she and Aunt Isa regarded your father highly. He has an acute understanding of wine commerce.'

Jane bit her lip. 'Luc, your mother and I had an argument. She kicked me out, never to return.' Dare she confide the whole truth?

'That sounds like my hot-tempered mother.' He laughed. 'You mustn't take her seriously.'

'It's better I don't come . . .'

'I don't know why you would hurt yourself with such nonsense, but if I cannot persuade you, then I must go alone.'

Almost three decades later, Jane Cambon, freshly widowed, stood in the snow in place Maubert and gazed along the street to the building where she and Luc had first become lovers. What if she had accompanied Luc on that youthful trip south? Might she and Clarisse have made their peace, ended the feud that had caused so much heartache over the years? But no apology from Clarisse could have erased the loss that young Jane had carried silently in her heart.

11

Slowly, careful not to slip on the settling snow, Jane crossed the boulevard Saint-Germain, drawn one step at a time towards 20 rue Frédéric-Sauton. The door from the street needed no code to access the interior during the day, or that had been the system back in the eighties. She pressed the exterior buzzer and the door swung open, as if by magic. The tiny hallway was barely bigger than a floor mat. It used to be, and still was, where the letterboxes were situated alongside the call buttons for each of the studios and apartments.

Nothing has changed, she thought. *He might still be here leaning over me, checking for post, nuzzling my hair, or upstairs working at the table, waiting for me.*

Luc's studio had been on the fourth floor. CAMBON had been written in his hand in black ink next to the button. A locked glass door gave access to the lift or stairs alongside it. She tried to recall the entry code from all those years earlier, but she could not. In any case, it would have been changed on numerous occasions since.

She closed her eyes and pressed her head against the bank of mailboxes. A melting snowflake slipped from her sodden hair, licking her face, as she evoked those blissful days of innocence. Days she had lived four floors above where she was now standing. The warmth of her memories wrapped themselves around her, threatening to squeeze too tight . . .

During that long-ago midsummer, as they had lain in bed, the windows were always wide open to alleviate the heat and city clamminess. The clatter of cutlery and buzz of conversations rose up from the pavement restaurants and the roar of traffic from along the boulevard Saint-Germain, while above them were half a dozen *poutres*, the dark wooden beams that ran the length of the ceiling. A candle guttered on the table that doubled as Luc's desk, causing elongated shadows to hover and dance on the white walls. Some nights when he was sleeping and she was awake, staring at those black shadows, she had tried not to dwell on who else might have shared this intimate space with him.

To have the power to turn back the clock. To stop the snow, to switch the thermometer to summer, to bring back that time of innocence. To resurrect Luc.

She lifted her hand now and pressed the bell to his flat, listening to the drill-like buzz. It was ringing upstairs in his studio. Their studio.

'*Allô?*' a woman's voice answered.

Jane was startled.

'*Allô? Qui est là?*'

'Sorry, I . . . I pressed the wrong bell.'

The receiver was replaced without a word.

Jane retreated outside, stumbling along rue Frédéric-Sauton, trudging through the sleet towards the river. Horns hooted, drivers cursed as she blundered across quai Montebello towards the cathedral rising up before her, like an apparition from the tide. The bells of Notre-Dame were clanging. It was eleven a.m. She parked herself on a snow-banked bench on the bridge, not minding the fresh flakes settling in her eyes, and gazed, half seeing, at the Seine. What remained for her? Did she possess the guts to get to her feet, her freezing, damp feet, and shuffle the few steps to the iron barrier, clamber over it and propel herself into the water? She stood up and forced herself to the rails, breathing erratically, revving up her courage. Beneath her, the sludge-green currents were gurgling and spinning. A powerful undertow beckoned her. What was to stop her throwing herself into the river? A clumsy belly-flop to nothingness. She wanted to die. Without Luc, her life had no purpose. She had no children to consider. 'Why don't I follow you, my love?'

Close by, a child in a pram squealed and thrust a furry toy to the ground. It landed in the muddied snow at Jane's feet and momentarily drew her attention. She bent and retrieved it: a bedraggled, one-eyed panda, a bare-headed hand-me-down. Jane passed it back to the mother, whose nose was red and who looked worn out but managed a smile. '*Merci*,' she said. '*Bonne année*.'

Jane mumbled an incoherent response. She followed their progress. Mother and infant moving within the shadows of the great Gothic prayer house, with its flying buttresses, and onwards into the cramped cathedral gardens beyond the waterway. Jane watched them, stung and yet touched by their togetherness. If her own child – an unborn boy miscarried at seven months – had survived, would she be less alone now? Luc's son alongside her, to hold her hand.

A pair of robins were pecking amiably at a birdfeeder suspended from one of the leafless forsythia bushes.

He would have been nineteen now. Might he have followed in his father's footsteps, studied at the Sorbonne? She still mourned him, always honoured the anniversary of his departure. He was gone, and now Luc too.

But she was the living, and she must bury her husband.

Before any thoughts of herself, she had to reclaim Luc's body and take him home. It was her duty and her privilege to accompany Luc south and lay him gently to rest where he had always felt connected.

*

Jane made one brief trip by train back to London, to collect a case of clothes. It included a black frock. She sat in her coat in the sitting room of their London flat and sobbed: sobbed at the sight of the wilting Christmas tree, the dried pine needles fallen to the carpet, the red wine left to breathe, the dining-table she would only now clear away and the uncooked duck rotting in the oven.

Before leaving England once more, she made a swift stopover to visit her father. The news of Luc's death barely impacted on his wandering, bemused state, and for once she was grateful.

'I'll be gone a while, Dad,' she warned him. 'The funeral will be in the south.' She hesitated before adding, 'At Les Cigales.' She held her breath. No reaction, no blink of recognition. 'Clarisse, Luc's mother – you remember Clarisse, don't you? She's organizing it.'

Peter frowned. He was struggling for a link.

'But I'll be back to see you at the very first opportunity.'

The mention of Clarisse and the Cambon vineyard estate had not rung any bells. Jane felt an upsurge of relief, though why, after so many years, it should make any difference, she couldn't have explained. Nothing could be altered now. The damage was done. Her mother was gone. Luc was gone. She kissed her father tenderly on the forehead and smiled. Somehow or other, life had to move on.

He nodded. 'See you tomorrow, then, love. Tell Luc I said hello.'

Roussel was surprisingly generous with his advice and time. Still, she badgered him, telephoning daily, nagging at him to resolve whatever was holding up the proceedings.

She rode with him on three occasions to the forensic morgue after he had called her to confirm that the matter had been concluded, only to discover that there was yet another small detail to be 'cleared up'. She always took the opportunity to linger with Luc for a few moments, in spite of the cameras peering down on them, and none of the staff, with their rolled-up sleeves and harassed faces, tried to discourage her. Even so, she dearly wanted this to be over now, for her man to be at peace. He had waited too long in this wretched chilly mortuary reeking of ammonia.

'What is delaying his release?'

'We need to be certain that we have not missed or overlooked anything. The car was burned out. The last hours can't be traced.'

'But what could have been overlooked? I don't understand.'

'We need to be sure that Luc's death was an accident, that the car wasn't tampered with.'

'What on earth are you talking about?'

'Do the letters OAS ring any bells?'

Jane frowned, shook her head.

'Luc never mentioned them to you?'

'No.'

'The Organisation de l'Armée Secrète, founded by members of the French far right. Although not operative today, within nationalist groups they still count many sympathizers.'

'Who are they?'

'The OAS, or the Secret Armed Organization, was established in February 1961 to prevent, by whatever means, Algeria's independence. Its *raison d'être* was to keep Algeria colonized, under French control. Once de Gaulle announced his intention to return the colony to its rightful people, members of the OAS made several attempts on the president's life.'

'Did Luc know about them?'

'They were the subject of his film.'

Jane was stunned. It was so far removed from the film she had understood he was shooting. 'But why would Luc be interested in bringing this to light?'

'Algeria remains a black spot on French history. Your husband never soft-pedalled. Even in his glorious nature films, he pointed out the destruction caused to the environment by pesticides, the underhand practices of chemical companies. Luc believed it was time to expose the darker dealings of the OAS.'

'Yes, but . . . You think his life was threatened?'

'We've found no evidence, but we need to be vigilant.'

Was this what Luc had implied when he'd said, *We do need to talk*? Those occasions when he had constantly checked his telephone, had he been harbouring the knowledge that his life was in danger?

Once the New Year kicked in, the detective inspector put her in touch with a repatriation service, while assuring her that he was on the backs of those in the departments of Autopsy and the Special Securities Services. The financial and logistical matters concerning the coffin's transport were being handled by Luc's friend and legal adviser Robert Piper. Nevertheless, in spite of Roussel's best intentions, it was the second half of January before he rubber-stamped the papers and Luc's body was finally released. Jane signed for his belongings and was handed a copy of the coroner's report in a large brown envelope.

It stated that death had been caused by trauma, a frontal collision. Death from traumatic multi-system injuries, multiple fractures, organ failure brought about by pericardial tamponade, or blood in the pericardium.

No alcohol or drug traces were found in the body.

Carbon-monoxide saturation (nine per cent) in his bloodstream, caused by fire.

Cause of car collision: fatigue, excessive speed.

'So your worries were unfounded? It was an accident,' Jane confirmed, as they bade each other a final farewell.

Roussel rubbed at his chin and nodded. 'Yes, it would appear our fears were unfounded.'

Jane flew south to Les Cigales with Luc's coffin in the aircraft's hold. Relieved as she was to be finally accompanying him to his resting place, she felt assailed by a worrying number of questions, conundrums, enigmas, paramount of which was where Luc had been during those missing hours before his death. And for what reason had he been hiding the film's subject matter from her? Dan had spoken of Luc's father, and of the war veteran in Marseille who had fought with him. Surely that had been the focus of their film? And what of Walnut, vanishing into thin air? The canine refuge centre had offered no information.

None of it added up.

They were coming in to land. She reclipped her seatbelt, glanced out at the sweeping bays of Cannes and Nice and closed her eyes.

It was time to honour Luc's remarkable life, to say *au revoir* to the man she had loved since she was a girl, the man she would never be able to replace.

The answers to her questions would have to wait.

12

Luc was buried in a cemetery on the outskirts of Malaz, a picturesque medieval hilltop village eight kilometres inland and west of Les Cigales. He was entombed in the plot declared by Clarisse to be the Cambon family 'vault', even though the sole Cambon representative already *in situ* was Luc's aunt, Isabelle. White stones and pencil-thin Italian cypresses enclosed the grounds. Jane could not fault its tranquillity and natural beauty. Its position, close to the summit of a hill, boasted a wide view over woodlands of pine, cork oak, mulberry and scrub, all sloping south to the Mediterranean, to a horizon as blue, as meticulously defined, as a Matisse pencil drawing.

In spite of a negative forecast, the rain stayed away and a lukewarm winter sun braved and blessed the ceremony, which included a high, sung mass celebrated by the village *curé*, Père Simon, whom Jane had never met before. This was their housekeeper Matty's parish. The Catholic church, compact in size, was crowded with mourners, many of whom were local farmers and villagers. There were pews packed with faces unknown to Jane. They included an impressive turnout of film-makers, writers, professional friends of Luc's from the arts and media, hundreds of them, most of whom had flown down from Paris for the occasion. Dan was among them, in attendance with his daughter, a pretty fawn-faced girl of six or seven. He was one of the six pallbearers. As soon as she could, Jane wove her way through the crowds to speak to him. They fell into each other's arms and hugged one another tightly. 'I called you several times,' she mumbled, into the collar of his coat.

'I can't believe it,' he whispered. 'I can't believe he's gone.'

The news had reached Dan in eastern Algeria where he had been on location for Luc.

'It was an accident, wasn't it, Dan?'

He squeezed her tighter and she felt his tears brush her cheek.

'Roussel said you were investigating the OAS.'

Dan pulled himself free.

'Were you? Are you in danger too?'

Dan took Jane by the shoulders. 'Luc's gone, the film's been cancelled. Let it rest, Jane, for his sake.'

'You're not intending to complete it?'

Dan shook his head and drew cigarettes from his overcoat pocket. He jiggled the packet agitatedly. 'Not without him, no. I've signed on for a commercial feature, big budget. It's best forgotten.'

'M-Madame Cambon? *B-bonjour, je suis . . .*' A grey-haired man with a mild stutter, a colleague of Luc's from a cinema-funding body in Paris, was at her side. He was flanked by a stately woman in a dark-purple hat, a middle-aged actress who had worked with Wim Wenders, but Jane couldn't find her name. Others were queuing to offer their condolences, lines of people now. Dan released her arm and stepped discreetly away. 'I don't have your mobile number,' she called after him, as he disappeared into the congregation of dark-clad mourners milling about the cemetery in the lukewarm sunlight. He didn't look back; he couldn't have heard her.

Jane had no opportunity to talk to Dan beyond that brief exchange. She spotted him later in the company of an auburn-haired woman. Thirty-something and rather striking. Might the woman be his partner? She also had a child in tow, an adolescent boy, who was sobbing into his mother's overcoat, clinging to her skirt with podgy fingers. There was something in the woman's stricken face – a glance, her profile, her smile, a look in her ultramarine eyes – that Jane found familiar but she couldn't put a finger on it. She felt reasonably confident they had never met before, though the sense of familiarity nagged at her. Eventually, she dismissed it as tiredness and the confusion of her overtaxed mind. Dan was engaged with groups of people for the rest of the day. Jane found no moment to introduce herself to his companion or talk to him further. In the church, with her son, the woman had sat alongside Claude, Matty, Arnaud and Pierre, Arnaud's twin brother, in attendance with his young family.

Le Monde had published an obituary the previous week and a handful of press photographers swelled the throng but kept a respectful distance. To her astonishment, Roussel made an appearance although a discreet one, standing in one of the back pews and hovering metres from the graveside in the shade of a cedar tree.

Afterwards, there was a buffet meal, catered by a local *traiteur*. Matty, who wept ceaselessly throughout the service, would not have been capable of the task. Everything was spread out in the dining room of the main house at Les Cigales. Clarisse, in flamboyant black silk, presided. It was not the send-off Jane would have given her beloved husband: the music, the tone were too formal. She might have been attending the farewell repast of a stranger, but as she had not been present to offer her input, she had no right to criticize.

Robert Piper, who had flown in from England with his

wife, Marjory, and was staying at a small hotel in one of the nearby towns, mentioned in passing that when Jane returned to London 'we need to lunch'. There were one or two matters concerning Luc's affairs that required her urgent attention. 'Call me the moment you're back. It can't wait,' he whispered in her ear, as he pressed against her in an awkward bear hug.

Jane nodded, crushed and rather alarmed by his request. Something in the way he had spoken had sounded ominous and unsettling.

When the last of the attendees had left the house, Jane lingered on outside, listening to echoes, staring at ghosts, waving to the retreating silhouettes of the bereaved: friends, neighbours, strangers, colleagues, well-wishers. What a turnout. Jane was proud. Luc would have been deeply affected.

The sky was darkening to indigo. She had observed Roussel earlier in conversation with Robert Piper and later with Dan, but she herself had not spoken to him except when he offered his condolences among a long line of others, and he must have been one of the first to take his leave. At one point during his conversation with Dan, Roussel had taken out his notebook and jotted something down. Did he attend the funerals of all the victims who landed up in his professional life? Or was he present for some other, more sinister, reason? The case was closed. 'Cause of collision: fatigue, excessive speed.' Had he or his special-services colleagues worried that there might be an incident at the funeral? That OAS sympathizers would put in an appearance? Surely an outlandish possibility. It was more probable that, as a fan of Luc's films, he wanted to show his respect. The subject he was discussing with Dan would most likely have been cinema.

Gravel spun as vehicles reversed, swung about and

disappeared, their headlights searching out the parameters of the impressive tree-lined avenue; voices fading on air that was damp and loamy. The evening appeared to be rising, not falling, a slow-moving steam ascending from the crust of the earth. It was closing in, as though a Mediterranean fret was threatening to envelop them, to seal her in for ever, leaving her incarcerated with Clarisse. Jane shivered. Reluctant to return inside, she wrapped her arms about herself and remained within the enclosed harbour of the porte-cochère, peering into the grizzled dusk long after the last car had disappeared, swallowed by the weather, by the night. Even the wide lane was engulfed in mist.

The metallic sky groaned. The predicted storm was on its way.

Luc's final circuit round the planet?

'Where are you on this turbulent evening, my love?' She spoke the words aloud. Thunder rumbled in response.

What is left when you have lost your childhood friend, your first boyfriend, your only lover in the purest sense and the partner you have been married to for more than twenty years? Jane had always loved Luc. Today her love was as complete, as unreserved, as it had been when she had been secretly smitten by him as a girl, even though he was seven years her senior in the days when seven years felt like an unbridgeable gap, when he had perceived her as nothing more than a skinny English kid, who stayed from time to time in one of the estate cottages or up at the manor house with her father and, on one occasion, also her mother. Jane was the kid Luc had taught to swim, to snorkel, to whom he showed the underground paths down along the cliffs. He had taken her to paddle and wade while collecting sea urchins in the pellucid green waters of the numerous creeks, *les calanques.* He accompanied her on biking trips through the volcanic hill trails, leading the way, igniting the campfires on which they cooked their simple lunches, packed for them by Matty or caught themselves. They had sunbathed in rarely frequented red-rock coves. As well, he had shared with her the best hiding places on his family's substantial estate. A list of sixteen.

And then had come the summer when she had turned fourteen . . . the summer of her first real kiss, of womanly longings. The summer of perfumed evenings . . . the summer when Luc had wished her *au revoir* and headed off for Paris, when she and Clarisse had clashed and everything had been destroyed.

After that summer, the spell had been broken. She and her father had driven away, a hasty retreat. He resigned his contract with Les Cigales, found other sources for wines, and Jane had not visited the estate again until a decade later when she came back as Luc's newly wedded wife.

Gone were those idyllic childhood expeditions, sojourns along the southern shores of France. Her dreams had been extinguished, her hopes shattered.

'*That girl will never set foot on this estate again.*' Clarisse's angry threat.

During the years when Luc was studying at the Sorbonne in Paris and Jane was still at secondary school in England, she had dreamed of him, pined for him. Scents, tastes, sounds had drawn her back over an imaginary bridge to the land of their enchanted days together, her pre-teens.

The lost domain inhabited by Luc.

While her school chums were dating, Jane had passed her teenage years speculating on whether her friend had found someone else, because, for sure, he would find someone, or whether their paths would cross again before too long. She buried her mother and all sexual longings, and grew plump, blemished by acne.

And then he had telephoned and invited her to Paris . . .

'Jane!'

'Yes.'

'Jane! What are you doing out there with the door open, letting the cold in?'

Jane sighed, turning slowly from the rising mist, the flood of her memories and the first drops of rain. 'I'm coming in now, Clarisse.'

After everything, after the ebbs and flow of life's kismets, had it really come to this, that the only one who remained, the only voice left to call her inside out of the cold, was Clarisse?

During those teenage years, her years of estrangement from the estate and Luc, her loathing of Clarisse had burned within her, choking her. She was stuck at home in Kent caring for her ailing mother. Yet she had longed to return to Les Cigales to rediscover Luc, to reclaim their blissful summers in one another's company and to show him that she wanted to give herself to him. What wouldn't she have sacrificed to relive those summers? Summers of escapades, expeditions, discovery, of innocence. Perfumed summers lying idle in the heat, skin dripping and tangy from dips in the sea, a bottle of rosé from the Cambon estate buried at the water's edge in the damp sand, Luc on his stomach at her side, smoking, perusing soggy, salt-stained newsprint while she covertly gazed upon him, lusting after his tanned leanness through partially closed eyes.

That first tender kiss, that briny ripple of pleasure, of desire. Tobacco on his breath. The breeze from the sea blowing their hair, the departure of innocence.

Her last adolescent summer there, full of happiness, exquisite happiness, anguish and longing. The delicious scents of night as he'd sat in her room, reading at her side, with the windows wide open, and she had pressed herself against him.

His hesitancy: 'You are still a child.'

'I'm not a child. I'm fourteen and I love you, Luc. *Je t'aime.*'

He had laughed warmly, not in an unkind way. He had taken her chin in his hand and looked deep into her eyes, his green ones swimming with tenderness. 'What can you know of love, *ma petite amie*?'

'Everything, because I love you.'

A few days later, he had flown to Paris, to return to his studies.

He had not been present on that haunting, life-changing night. The night of *the discovery*. Luc had been far away, absent, ignorant of the screaming rows that ensued and the banishment that succeeded the scene. Early the following morning Jane, with her father, had retreated, driving off into the sweltering day. If Luc had been present, he would have defended her; he would have put a stop to the injustice. He would have called her back. But he had never known, never been told, what had come to pass *that night*. Jane's guilt had kept her silent. She had blamed herself, not for what she'd exposed or for fear of maligning Clarisse's reputation, but because she had forced the knowledge of her discovery onto her own mother. Her adolescent self-righteousness had caused her mother's heartache. And possibly seeded her sickness.

Back home Jane, who had sailed early towards womanhood, had thought that she'd lost Luc, that all hope for her dream of him was doomed.

'Luc Cambon is engaged to be married,' she learned from her widowed father.

Her heart almost stopped. 'What makes you say that?'

'They were gossiping about it at one of the vineyards in the Var. Clarisse Cambon, they said, has been crowing to the world about the sumptuous wedding her son and his fiancée are arranging.'

So it was a fact, incontestable. The pain in her heart swelled, like a river about to burst its floodgates. If only she could find him, put a stop to it, remind him of *her* love. Or was it a fabrication on Clarisse's part, intended to reach Jane's ears?

Her father's wine business – estate wines from the South of France, summer drinking wines – that he had built up from those early days at Les Cigales, scratched out of his garage in Kent into a flourishing affair, began to spiral downwards due to fierce competition in a burgeoning market and an increasing loss of competence. It had not been caused by his dementia – no, that had not yet been diagnosed, not for many years to come – but by grief and a growing incapacity to cope with details, remarked by Jane after the death of her mother. Suave, charming, outgoing Peter had not managed so well after Vivienne's departure. Jane had asked herself whether he might not be suffering from regret as much as grief, for whatever it was that had gone wrong, not worked out between them . . . but this was not a conversation she and her father had ever shared.

On that first evening in Luc's studio in Paris, perched on his matchbox bed, guzzling Moët, bubbles giving her hiccups, emboldening her, as they were hastening towards becoming lovers, she dared broach the subject.

'Engaged to be married, me?' He had laughed. 'My mother fantasizes.'

Her love had lain silent within her, fostering its hope.

*

After Jane had begun her university studies in London, their contact had dwindled to the occasional letter. She had written frequently, ardently and at length. Luc had replied but intermittently and then almost not at all. 'I am filming, working all hours, loving it,' he had scribbled on a card as an apology. His first commission. Little time for anything else. Luc was moving with zeal and confidence towards his bright future, and she had not figured in his vision.

Not at that stage.

Armed with a decent degree in French and Spanish, Jane had found employment as a freelance interpreter. Her life in London was unfolding. Fellow students, work associates were inviting her out for evenings at the pub, dinner parties, dances, clubs, but she accepted infrequently, preferring weekends alone, walks in the park, solo outings to the cinema. Her heart remained with Luc. She tried to forget him, but she couldn't put their brief affair, their enduring childhood friendship, behind her. Serendipitously, she was offered an assignment in Nice at a European health conference. While strolling down at the old port, one sunlit evening after work, she had caught sight of Luc, seated alone in a café reading *Le Monde*, jotting purposefully in a notebook, smoking, an untouched espresso on the table in front of him. She had blurted out his name. He had looked up, locked green eyes with hers, then a frown creased his brow. He was perplexed, hadn't recognized her. She took a step backwards, regretting her cry. He had forgotten her. *Luc had forgotten her.* She had turned on her heels, cut to the heart, ashamed, embarrassed, and almost missed her footing.

'Jane! *Mon Dieu*, it's Jane.' Rising from the table, knocking the cup, spilling the coffee, he had taken hold of her, swung her about, embraced and hugged her, like a sister. My precious little friend, he'd said. '*Ma belle petite Jane.* You've lost weight, cut off your blonde locks. You've flowered into a woman. *Une très belle femme.*'

Luc had also changed. He had matured in different ways. He was quieter, self-contained, more certain of himself, passionate about where he was going, fired, obsessed by his projects. His first film had been well received: it had won a minor award. There was talk of a theatrical release. Now he was at work on his second and the finance was already in place. There was clarity about who he was, what he wanted from his life. Honesty, yes, an open face with clear forgiving eyes, but never garrulous, never a word or thought wasted. A contradiction, perhaps, but Luc, honest, compassionate, full of integrity in his dealings with others, had always withheld a substantial part of himself. And that reticence had advanced, developed over the years.

Beyond that chance encounter in Nice, their friendship rooted, flourished, blossomed, took flight. He came to London to spend weekends with her – lying in bed reading the *Observer*, drinking coffee he'd brought from Paris – or she crossed the Channel to him. A long weekend in New York, two nights in Madrid, a rendezvous in Normandy. Greedy for opportunities, they created dates to be together, making love, listening to music, travelling, dancing, high on a love that had been born almost two decades earlier, a love that had grown up.

They had married when Jane was twenty-five, Luc thirty-two. He had desired a wedding on the estate but Jane had procrastinated and eventually refused, which bemused him. 'Why not?'

'Your mother doesn't approve of me.'

'Such nonsense you talk. Why would you think such a thing?'

'We had a disagreement, I told you.'

'Clarisse argues with everybody. It means nothing. She will be thrilled. She nags me constantly about settling down, grandchildren. I can't wait to break the news to her and Isa.'

'No, Luc, please. Not yet. Let's surprise her. Let's get married secretly and then tell them.'

'But don't we want a reception, family with us? I don't understand.'

'Just us, somewhere special. Then we can rush to the estate and share our happiness with them.'

Eventually, on a warm September day, they celebrated a simple civil affair in a frescoed villa on a hilltop on the outskirts of Rome, where Luc was in the preparatory stages of his film. No family members were present. They honeymooned in Positano, ate oysters on the beach, got drunk on prosecco, and at the first opportunity Luc flew Jane north from Naples to Nice, to the estate where his aunt Isabelle and Clarisse awaited them. The gardener, Claude, had collected them from the airport. Matty was in the hall of the main house, waiting to usher them to their room. She had already prepared the nuptial chamber, the marriage feast: a champagne supper laid out on the terrace for the newlyweds. Lanterns everywhere, it should have been joyous, enchanting.

But this was Jane's first trip to the estate since *that night*.

She was apprehensive and she understood from Clarisse's tight-lipped greeting when she stepped into the hall, for the first time in ten years, that Luc's mother had not forgiven her; neither had she forgotten. It was a begrudging embrace, lacking warmth or a blessing for the exiled fourteen-year-old who had returned as a woman, and as Luc's wife.

That afternoon, Clarisse suggested to her son that they take their horses and go for a ride to inspect the vines and to say *bonjour* to Antoine Pesaro and his team working in the fields. Jane, who had never been entirely comfortable on a horse, opted for a dip in the pool.

It was more than two hours later when Clarisse, still in her jodhpurs and riding boots, strode into the library where Jane was awaiting their return. Her auburn hair was windswept, her cheeks flushed and damp, but in spite of that she looked self-possessed, arresting. Jane, alone, browsing through an illustrated book, rose at her mother-in-law's entry. 'Good ride?' she enquired tremulously.

Clarisse closed the door with a resolute click. 'Luc's taking a shower. So it gives me the opportunity to talk to you.'

'I hope you're happy for us?' Jane butted in. She was edgy, tense and uncertain about being back on the domain, but she was determined to put the past behind them and build a bridge between her and her mother-in-law. She and Luc were married; there was nothing Clarisse could do.

Clarisse folded her arms across her chest. Her cream silk shirt was puddled with perspiration. 'Frankly, and I won't mince my words, I couldn't be more disappointed. My son is a talented, acclaimed artist, and he is a gentle, intelligent soul. He has achieved all that I dreamed of for him, and more. Every one of the young women he has brought home, and there have been many,' Clarisse smiled at Jane's sharp intake of breath, 'has without exception been a cut above you. In style, class and brilliance, not to mention looks. No words can describe my despondency.'

'Clarisse.' Jane sank back into the chair. The book, left open on the armrest, slid and slammed shut on the rug.

'Are you pregnant? Is that the explanation?'

'No.' The word stuck in Jane's throat.

'So why would my son wait till after his wedding ceremony to inform us, *by telephone*, of the "joyous" news?'

Jane shrugged. 'We . . . preferred no fuss,' she stammered.

Clarisse glared at her. 'For Luc's sake, because his happiness is what matters to me above all else, I intend to keep my mouth shut. But I want it to be absolutely clear between you and me, nothing has changed. I told you once to get out of my home and never come back, and I meant it. And now you have married my son out of greed and spite.'

'That's nonsense. Insulting, cruel nonsense. I love Luc with all my heart. And when I'm pregnant, you'll know it. I want his children, lots of them.'

'You don't begin to know the meaning of the word "love". Your love is selfish and self-serving.'

Jane lifted herself from the chair and made for the door, brushing by Clarisse as she did so. Clarisse caught hold of her by the upper arm and held it tightly, red nails sinking into flesh. 'If you cause my son any heartache, I will kill you. And don't think I'm not capable of it.'

Jane shrugged herself free. 'You're insane.' And with that she was out of the door.

That evening, soon after the quartet had settled for supper at the exterior table, jazz crooned by Nina Simone playing through the open windows, the scents of autumn rising richly all around them, Jane, still unnerved by the confrontation with her mother-in-law, had the eerie sensation that someone else was present, someone watching her, surveying her, monitoring the party. She glanced about, listening to the crickets, scanning the fall of light between the trees before she caught sight of a girl of nine or ten standing in the frame of the back door. The child was wearing a crown of wild flowers, rather like a lopsided daisy chain, and striped espadrilles on her feet. Jane smiled, almost laughed, and the girl nodded. Her eyes were wide with wonder at the sight of the rose-coloured illuminations hanging from the trees and the extravagant bouquets and candles adorning the table.

What Jane noticed first about the stranger was her eyes, cornflower blue. The child's thick hair coiled in one bold plait down her right shoulder. She was scruffily attired but striking. No one else seemed to have noticed her as she loitered there, backlit from the kitchen, eagerly devouring the magic of the occasion, hungry to be included, as though she had chanced upon a fine and secret coven.

Who was she?

'Hello,' Jane called softly. 'Are you coming to join us?'

A look of guilty pleasure lit the girl's features and her face broke into a broad grin. She was a cross between an urchin and a princess. Jane's greeting drew the attention of her new relatives at the table, whose conversation fell silent. Intrigued, heads turned.

'What on earth? Be off with you, you little devil!' snapped Clarisse, stubbing out her cigarette with quick stabs as though readying herself for action. 'Matty!'

'Yes, Madame?' The housekeeper came running from the pantry.

'Matty, take that child away at once.'

The trespasser turned on her heels and scooted out of sight. Her eyes were welling with tears, Jane observed. 'Who is she?' Jane asked.

'Annie.'

'Matty's daughter,' said Isabelle.

'I'm very sorry, Madame,' burbled Matty. 'She's been under my feet all afternoon, overexcited at the prospect of seeing Monsieur Luc again. She only wanted to get a glimpse of him and see who else was attending the party.' Matty seemed flustered, quite unlike her placid self. 'I think she was hoping to meet Madame Jane. You know, catch sight of Luc's new wife.'

'Well, go after her, Matty, call her back, let her meet Jane.

Then we can all say hello. I haven't seen little Annie in a long, long while,' cried Luc, amiably. 'How old is she now?'

'She's just turning ten, sir.'

Jane leaped to her feet and hugged Matty forcefully, thrilled for her that she had eventually been blessed with the daughter she had so passionately longed for. Matty, arms hanging like logs, smiled awkwardly, self-effacingly.

Clarisse, who had witnessed the exchange, reiterated her request that Matty call Claude to come and remove the child: 'Take her home immediately and keep her there. This is a private celebration, family only,' she stated crisply. 'Please take better control of your offspring. Her intrusion is unacceptable.'

'Oh, Maman, don't be so harsh,' joshed Luc. 'You're behaving like a Gorgon.'

Isabelle rested her hand across the jewelled fingers of her sister-in-law. 'She's a child, Clarisse, an inquisitive child. You can't blame her for wanting to see Luc again, to know what all the fuss is about. She worships him, you know that.'

'She's a pretty little thing, all decked up in her floral tiara for the party,' laughed Jane.

Clarisse threw a look at Jane as though the intruder's presence or Jane's discovery of her was somehow Jane's fault. 'She needs to learn her place.'

Jane understood the unspoken message: *As you should have done.*

Jane had borne Luc no children to offer her solace now. No offspring to help construct her future, to receive her into their home and bear the load of grieving with her. She had suffered the late miscarriage of their unborn boy and then nothing. After such passion, such ardour, there should have been a child, at least one, a corroboration, manifestation, of the power of their love. Childlessness had been a harsh blow but she and Luc had accepted their situation without rancour. It had not damaged their relationship. Her role within their marriage took on a different personality. She was able to travel with him on assignments, accompany him to locations, occasionally to translate scripts for him, transcribe interviews for his documentaries.

Luc had been wedded to his work. His gruelling shooting schedules, his travels, business trips, his family estate, his mother: all had demanded of him and had contributed to the diminishing of their social life and their time together. With no child to absorb her attention, Jane had turned her energies to starting up her small business, her translation work, in an attempt to build an independent existence, to keep herself occupied when Luc was absent. She had a sufficient number of friends in London. A circle of loyal girlfriends. A few from her university days, another from her time as an interpreter, a long-term chum, Lizzie, from her schooldays, who had already been in touch after reading an obituary.

Their lives . . . Luc's cut short at fifty-five, Jane seven years his junior, still in her forties. What can a woman, a recently widowed woman, creeping towards fifty hope to build of her future when her husband, her only true love, has been taken?

Those same friends would be generous with their condolences now, heartbroken for her. 'When you're feeling up to it, we must meet for lunch.' One or two would invite her to their country houses, their cottages in Norfolk or Dorset, for a night or two, a weekend. 'Poor you, what shocking news. Don't sit alone. Come and visit.' But, in the end, she *was* alone. Jane Cambon, née Sanderson, startlingly, was about to face her future with no one at her side, no dreams on the horizon. Dashed, snatched from her: all her mental pictures of a present and a future that, in her imagination, had always contained Luc.

Only a sick abstracted father to anchor her to her past.

'Jane! Come in and close that door or I'll lock you out!'

'Yes, Clarisse, I'm coming.'

As she stepped back inside, out of the cold night air, she thought back to Luc's funeral, and the woman with Dan who'd looked so familiar. Was she going mad or could that possibly have been Annie? The little girl with the daisy chain on her head all grown-up? Matty's daughter, of course, seated alongside her parents and brothers in the church. Luc had never mentioned that Matty and Claude's girl had married or had a son. But perhaps he had never known.

13

That evening in the main house, with Luc's mother as her sole companion, the mood was stultifying. The spacious room felt stuffy, claustrophobic, and the faded furnishings, once so elegant, were now old-fashioned, the sofas sagging, the chair legs scuffed. Two women locked together in silence, save for the creaking and settling of the old wooden beams and the tap-tap of Clarisse's club-headed walking stick when she struggled to her feet to cross to the kitchen and replenish the ice for her drink – several hefty measures of gin – then back to the dining room. Jane did not rise to help her. She left Clarisse to get on with it.

For decades, the two women had circled one another, quietly blaming each other for their losses. Clarisse held that no girl, and certainly not one from Jane's lowlier background, was good enough for her gifted son ('He inherited his love of the arts from me'), while Jane had her own reasons for her unforgiving stance.

But Clarisse was a fighter. What did she care about Jane's animosity? Even now, seated at the dining-table, no trace of emotion on her still striking features, she passed the evening playing Solitaire. Her clawed arthritic hands were lifting and sliding the cards up and down, snapping them back and forth as she mumbled or – could it be possible on such an occasion? – hummed to herself.

'What a turnout, eh? Nothing less than my Luc deserved, of course.'

Solitaire was a fruitless pastime that irritated Jane who

preferred a book. One lay alongside her on the couch but she had barely turned its cover.

'What are you reading?'

Sometimes Clarisse's questions were uncanny, as though she had access to Jane's innermost thoughts.

'Le Carré.'

'Any good?'

'I haven't really started it. My mind's not on it.'

'What are your plans?'

'Plans?'

'Oh, for Heaven's sake, Jane. Your plans.' Cards tossed to the table, red nails scratching mottled flesh. 'Are you intending to stay here?'

Jane took a breath. 'I'll be leaving the day after tomorrow.'

'Why don't you stay for a bit, keep me company?'

Wary of where this might be leading, Jane got up and crossed to the mantelpiece. 'I must go back.' Matty had laid a fire when she cleared away the leftovers from the funeral meal. Jane reached for the box of matches and struck one. Her hand was trembling.

'It is what Luc hoped for.'

Jane stared into the kindling flames, anger and pain igniting in equal measure within her. Beyond the windows, an explosion of zigzag lightning, followed moments later by the crash of thunder. The storm was gaining momentum and it was approaching. 'What . . . what did Luc hope for?'

'That you and I would make our peace and – who knows? – rebuild the estate, the wine business. Work alongside one another.'

Then he had hoped for too much, Jane yelled inside herself. She did not believe Luc had envisaged any such future. He had certainly never hinted at such a cosy scenario. No, she would not stay. 'There are matters I want to discuss with you,' he had said on more than one occasion, refusing to elucidate.

'Which matters?'

'I prefer they wait till we meet,' had been his response. 'We do need to talk.'

'Let's talk over Christmas.'

He could not have been referring to a working alliance between Jane and her mother-in-law. He would have known, guessed at her refusal.

'It's not possible for me to stay, Clarisse.'

'I think you'll find that there's more here for you than you're aware of. If you stop running away.'

'What do you mean by that?'

'You will need to find it out for yourself.'

The anger was gaining heat. 'Another of your cryptic games?'

'You are cold, Jane, and heartless.'

'Heartless? Last year, I was hopeless and irresponsible. I was incapable of any constructive act, according to you, and, most importantly, I was not good enough for your son. I was the one who single-handedly destroyed your vintage, remember? And now you suggest we run the estate alongside one another, like a pair of old pals. Widows united.'

Clarisse leaned forward, pressing a black-lace bosom growing round with age against the card table, and yanked a packet of Camels towards her. She drew out a cigarette and lit it, dragging on it hard. 'Well, Jane, you are no stranger to acts of destruction, you surely must admit that.'

'Go to Hell, Clarisse.'

'We are both there, my dear.'

'I'm going up to my room. It's been a long day. Would you like me to drive you back to the cottage or are you intending to stay in one of the spare rooms tonight?'

'This was Luc's home, Jane. I offered it to him, and that included you. Mine is down the lane and I have my own transport.'

'Well, then, if you don't mind, I'll say goodnight.'

Jane lay on the cotton coverlet on their double bed, staring at the static fan on the ceiling, tears burning her cheeks. Anger and pain swirled within her. Shoes cast off, stockinged feet, still clad in her black, she was listening to the storm. The wind howled and hissed while the rain stalked and beat against the house. Branches snapped, thudding earthwards, as the gale, the thunder and lightning, gained momentum and whipped beyond the walls, illuminating the room, then thrusting it into darkness. A part of her would have welcomed a brief spell here surrounded by countryside, to quell her emotions. A sojourn of a week or two during which she could remain close to Luc. She wasn't ready to let him go, wasn't capable of it. And the fact that he would be here for ever, far from her, accentuated her loss. Clarisse had won on that score. '*My* Luc'. She had her son for ever at her side. To be close to him, Jane must stay. But her desire to be shot of the memories, the past, the guilt, to begin anew, a life without Luc's mother, the ghosts of his family, was an equally strong pull. She felt the need for a clean slate, even if the decision to move on, to start again elsewhere, contravened Luc's expectations, his instructions from beyond the grave. Plans he had purportedly discussed with his mother, but never with Jane, his wife.

'Give me a sign,' she whispered to him now.

It was after nine the following morning when Jane went downstairs. Nobody was about. Matty had laid the table in the dining room for one and lit the fire. A heated pot of coffee awaited her on the sideboard. She helped herself to scrambled eggs and toast, and chewed her way through the lukewarm food in a mechanical fashion. When had she last eaten? Unable to swallow a morsel, she had played with a fillet of fish at the funeral gathering the previous day. Beyond the rattling windows, the wind was still busy. Rain skittered down the panes. Silence within, save for the long-case clock ticking in the hall and the rain buffeting the glass. The storm had not yet abated, though it was lessening.

From where she sat, alone at the highly polished mahogany dining-table, she could log the damage: lifeless branches and terracotta shards from fallen flowerpots strewn across the dead-of-winter lawn. Claude would have his work cut out clearing up the detritus. Later in the morning, when the thundery weather had passed, if it passed, she would walk up to the village, to Luc. When she returned, she would offer to give Claude a hand outside. Activity to keep herself occupied until it was time for her departure. Back to an empty home.

At close to midday, thankful to be out of doors, to breathe the cool damp air, she stumbled down the long, curving driveway, breasting the force of the wind, hopping over rivulets of rain, runnels through spongy banks of fallen pine needles. Two rows of giant Cedars of Lebanon, interspersed with straight-boled Corsican pines, flanked her path. Their massive arms reached out as though in song. Drips were falling from their rain-soaked branches. They pounded her shoulders, seeped into her hair and lashes: Nature's tears mourning her loss.

Beyond the iron gates, she swung right onto the *route nationale*. Walnut loved this walk, skirting the lower boundaries of Les Cigales, pausing constantly to sniff and wee at the roots of tree trunks. Where was he? She missed him so. Had he been at Luc's side during those three unexplained hours? Had he witnessed Luc's death, tried to save his master? A heroic act sometimes seen in films. Had he fled from the scene of the accident? If he had died with Luc, wouldn't Roussel's team have found traces of him?

The questions never left her alone.

Twenty minutes later, she had entered deep countryside, *la France profonde*, with its long, straight avenue of plane trees. At the second crossroads, she turned right and began to hike the steep gradient towards Malaz. The sharp cry of birds overhead, shifting and fluttering in the boughs of pine and plane trees, seemed to call a warning. Beyond Malaz, the serpentine ascent would be punctuated by stone villages and secret hilltop towns, all the way into the lower Alps, but she was stopping in Malaz. Puffed from the climb, she paused to catch her breath and to enjoy the distant sea views from the outskirts of the village.

Malaz was a community of some six hundred inhabitants. In summer the numbers swelled to upwards of two thousand. Germans, Dutch, Nords and British descended, arriving with carloads of children and instant coffee to occupy the empty homes rented for extortionate sums as holiday lets. In Malaz, properties hugged tightly up against one another in streets that were narrow and tortuous to protect against the mid-year's scorching heat.

But this was late January. The land was drenched and unsettled after the overnight tempest. Branches broken, wind-sweep in the gutters, water streaming southwards, puddles swelling in the sinking uneven pavements or cobbles along root-torn *ruelles* where every façade was painted a different shade of ochre. Mud. Little traffic. No tourists. The sharp, clean air reeked of rotting leaves, of woodsmoke from chimneys. Multi-generational Maralpin families snug in front of open fires and bowls of bubbling *pot au feu*. Secure in their togetherness, relieved of the 'foreigner' for several months to come. She envied them their kinship, their cosy intimacy. She had rarely felt more battered, more lost at sea.

Leaves were falling around Jane's marching feet, the few that had remained on the deciduous trees. She thrust her gloved hands deep into her pockets and hiked on, wondering whether she would ever feel warm again.

The familiarity of Malaz, which was closed for lunch when she reached its cobbled maze, calmed and embraced her. Past happinesses. Today, quartets of men huddled in the only open café playing cards. Black-eyed Arabs, smoking, cradling brightly coloured soft drinks, watched her through the windows, their gaze impenetrable.

Almost all her memories of moments spent here included Luc, even from her very distant past in the early seventies, the first of her childhood summers in this long-ago Gallo-Roman land with Peter, her father. Over on the ferry from Dover together, on an exploratory trip before his first interview at Les Cigales, her father had rented rooms for the pair of them in an *auberge* in Malaz. Les Amis du Château had been the name of the boarding house . . .

14

Early July 1971

Jane and her father dropped their battered cases on the bed.

'Our lucky day, eh, Janey? Only two single rooms left and we've nabbed them.' Father and daughter had walked in off the street, hot and flustered, desperate for a place to stay, and had been given adjoining rooms by one of the middle-aged women who owned the hostelry. 'Les Amis du Château. You know what that means?'

Jane shook her head.

'Friends of the Castle. That'll be us soon, if all goes according to plan. The French call all their big houses castles.'

'Fingers crossed, Dad.'

'We'll move your things into your room later, after our meeting, all right? We've no time to unpack now.' Peter winked and flung off his crumpled shirt, hastily throwing on a paisley one, ironed and neatly folded by his wife, Vivienne, before they'd left Kent. They hurtled back down the stairs without even washing their hands, as Jane's mother would have insisted they do. How dizzy with happiness Jane felt. She was six years old, seven in October, and here she was in a foreign country with her dad doing just as they pleased. It was daft that her mum felt seasick on boats. She was missing all the fun.

Peter dropped the key at Reception and requested confirmation of his directions to Les Cigales while Jane waited outside in the sunshine.

'On holiday?' asked one of the two female proprietors, a bulky salmon-lipped woman.

'Les Cigales? Why would you want to be going there?' interrupted the other.

Peter swiftly outlined the reason for his presence in the neighbourhood.

The women shook their heads. One fingered a silver cross hanging on a chain around her neck. 'Most of us from over this way keep our distance from that place. They're an ungodly pair, those two.'

'Fancy that.' Peter was refolding his map, biting back his amusement.

'Sisters-in-law they are, but we've heard say they're "witches".'

'Witches? Good Lord! I'd better watch my step.'

'They settled here from Algeria after the war, flashing their money. Colonials. Nothing good ever came from that lot.'

'There's a boy too, no father.'

'Younger one claims she's widowed.'

'A widow in her mid-thirties, rather unlikely, I'd say. And the other, the sister-in-law, she's a spinster.'

The women shook their heads gravely as though nothing was to be done about such blatant immorality.

Peter silently dismissed the tittle-tattle. 'We'll see you later.' He scooted outside to his daughter in the blinding heat, and they climbed into his red Ford Cortina shooting brake. He was smiling to himself, pondering the remarks of the old biddies. Witches! Who talks of witches in 1971?

The two females he was about to meet were potential employers. That was all that mattered to him. This was a desperately sought-after opportunity for the Sandersons, a chance for Peter to secure employment from abroad, to learn a new trade and escape the doldrums of Edward Heath's Britain and the redundancy he had been forced to take more than a year earlier.

'On the dole, but resilient' was how he described himself, but his jaunty exterior belied his concerns and he was worn down, depressed by his financial struggles.

Back on the road, the Cortina twisted and turned, descending the country lanes towards the coast. They were running late. Jane was attempting to decipher the directions from the handwritten letter Peter had received a month earlier.

'Left here, now sharp right. Head down the steep hill, it says. Then we should be on the *route nationale* and the entrance is directly off that. Set back, its says.'

'You're a good little reader.' Peter praised her as they slowed, searching for the gates to the vineyard estate, still hoping to be punctual for his first appointment with the proprietors and wine producers, Madame and Madame Cambon. 'If I get this job, you can travel with me every holiday and learn a bit of French. It'll give you a head start at school.'

'Here it is! Look, Les Cigales,' cried Jane, triumphantly.

A pair of imposing iron gates stood open. Peter swung left, and they made a winding ascent up a driveway lined with tall trees that seemed to go on for ever. The air was filled with heavenly scents from unrecognizable climbers in full bloom. A hot silence embraced them.

'Let's hope I get the job . . .' Peter had spoken under his breath as he switched off the engine. In spite of his earlier haste, he stayed put, drumming on the steering-wheel.

Finding nothing after his redundancy, he had returned to his first love: music. A year of playing at weddings and social clubs, scrambling to make ends meet, up till all hours, had caused dissension within his marriage. Then, quite by chance, he had spotted an advertisement in the *Lady*, a posh magazine he'd picked up in the doctor's surgery where he'd been waiting for a prescription for antidepressants.

Back at home, he'd answered the advert.

His handwritten application had received a favourable response:

The United Kingdom is a growing wine market, promising but not yet sophisticated. My sister-in-law and I are looking for the right representative. Please come and meet us at our estate. Cordialement, Clarisse Cambon

'Right, here we go. Deep breath, Jane, and remember, keep smiling.'

The heat beat down upon Jane's back, now glued to the plastic seat. She pushed open the old car's door, slammed it and trod the gravelled courtyard towards steps that led them to a porte-cochère and double-fronted main doors.

'It *is* a castle. It's as big as Buckingham Palace,' she whispered, as her father tugged on the old-fashioned bell-pull. 'I wish Mummy could see it.'

'If all goes well, she will,' was his response. 'Fingers crossed.'

A dog somewhere deep within the bowels of the mansion began to bark. A female voice called sharply in French. The dog fell silent.

Footsteps were approaching. Peter cleared his throat, fiddled with his shirt collar. In his letter to Madame Cambon, he had claimed that he could visualize the future of mass-market wine sales in Britain:

We need to get the bottles into the pubs and the local stores, out to the ordinary people. The message needs to be 'wine to accompany meals and wine as a social drink in place of beer for the blokes and

Dubonnet with ice and lemonade for the ladies'. Wine is a new concept in early seventies Britain but it is set to become the fashion. As your representative, I would guarantee to offload whatever quantity you and I agree upon.

Clarisse Cambon had an avaricious eye to this new market. She was keen to win over the British. '*Les Anglais* who drink warm beer and call Bordeaux wines "claret". They lack sophistication,' she had remarked to her sister-in-law, 'but we can teach them better and make money into the bargain. This man, his letter, he seems to know his business.'

So, here he was, at the front door of this astonishingly swish property, apprehensive and praying for the opportunity to build a new future for himself and his family.

It was Clarisse who opened the door. '*Bonjour, bonjour.* Such long journeys are exhausting, but you are on time. *Très bien. Entrez.*'

Jane was open-mouthed at the lady's appearance, the slenderness of her wrists, one sporting a gold watch that slid and twirled with her every gesture. She had never set eyes on anyone quite so curvaceous yet trim, quite so resplendent. With her curly auburn hair, the lady was as glamorous and self-assured as a film star, not skinny like Twiggy.

Madame Cambon beckoned Jane's father into the hall in a rather flirtatious manner. Jane followed on tiptoe at his heels. She was repeating to herself the words spoken to them at the door, rolling them around her tongue: *trrray bien, entrray.* Sing-songy words with lots of *rrr*s. What did they mean? The interior was cool and dark, hung with gilt-framed oil paintings. It was as grand as a palace. From here, the trio crossed into a burgundy-walled sitting room with high ceilings, a table lamp hanging low, like a wilting tulip, and a slow breeze emanating from a ceiling fan. It was dimly lit, lacking any sunlight, barred behind slatted shutters. It took a moment for Jane to spot the second Madame Cambon, who was in loose beige slacks and a silk shirt and was seated on a high-backed chair, smoking a cigarette. Without rising, she introduced herself as Isabelle Cambon, the older of the two *soeurs*. (More *rrr*s, thought Jane.) She was sipping something fizzy from a tall glass that clinked with ice and lemon.

On a sideboard across the room a record played on a turntable. The Beatles' 'Hey Jude'. Jane was amazed. 'I love this song,' she cried brightly. 'Dad's often singing it, aren't you, Dad? Dad's a musician, bass and guitar, but he gave it up to become a salesman, didn't you, Dad? Mum said we needed a steady income.'

Her father made no response except to clear his throat. There was a moment's awkward silence.

Jane was suddenly conscious of her gaff – 'speaking without being spoken to' – of her untidiness, of how thirsty she was (she'd love a sip of the lady's lemonade), of her sweat-caked dull clothes and her uncombed honey-blonde fringe. These women looked like they lived in a magazine.

Clarisse Cambon smiled down at her with glossy red lips and asked, 'While your father and I talk *bizness*, I think you would like a *deep*, dear, wouldn't you? It will refresh you.'

Jane stared in panic at the lady with her wide coral smile and matching nails, dressed in a neatly ironed frock, big fat pearls and high, strappy shoes. She wished she could understand what was being said to her. If only she could speak French or could decipher the accented English. She glanced uncertainly at her father, who was smiling, clearly beguiled by the company in which he found himself.

A *deep*? Jane's expression begged him to translate.

'Mrs Cambon is offering to let you swim in her pool, Janey. To take a *dip*. Isn't that generous?'

'She's got her own pool?' Jane gazed with wide eyes back at the owner of the castle who, in her green and yellow frock, reminded her of a daffodil, upright and radiant. Daffodil Lady even smelt of flowers, a much heavier, muskier scent than her mother's Yardley's Lavender Water.

Dare she accept? Would it be polite to enjoy herself when they were here on important business?

'*Allez, ma petite*, off you go. Afterwards, our cook will serve us all a delicious *déjeuner*.'

Her father nodded his approval with a blue-eyed wink and Jane rushed off to grab her towel and swimsuit from the black bag in her father's Cortina, waiting out at the front.

Jane was chuffed to pieces with this unexpected opportunity. Poolside, in the shadow of a big-trunked tree, she peeled off her clothes, checking first that no one was about. Even so, before removing any outer garments, she slipped her knickers off first from under her skirt, then hastily pulled on her bathing costume, wriggling the lower half of it into place. Once changed, clothes rolled into a bundle, she slid on her armbands, scrunched her dark-blonde plaits into an elastic band secured in a knot on top of her head, then gingerly picked her way across burning tiles to the water's edge and descended the first two steps. She paused there, before sinking into the first private swimming-pool she had ever set eyes on.

The water was clear and glistening. It tickled and licked her ankles as it rippled. It was azure from the sky's reflection and reminded her of a giant, veined marble that had been rolled flat. The only sounds came from the racket the crickets were making, several fat bees buzzing about a pot of flowers and the splashing of her bare feet against the tiles. The heat wrapped itself about her, like a blanket. Two tall palm trees, one at each corner of the pool's deep end, stood sentry. Beyond them, a pinafore of lawn and then a high stone wall, which, although Jane hadn't known it then, surrounded a fertile vegetable garden. Beyond, the outline of a range of low mauve mountains.

She lifted her head, screwing up her eyes, watching a big black bird flapping overhead, crossing the sky, cawing loudly.

She waded in up to her knees. The water was cool, refreshing. It caressed her while the sun beat down unforgivingly upon her head, reddening her flesh.

'*Bonjour*.'

Jane swung round guiltily and caught sight of a black-haired boy in shorts and bare feet standing in the shadows some distance behind her.

'What are those blue things you're wearing?' Luc stepped from out of the darkness of a deserted dining area to which Jane had paid no attention earlier. She would never have dared change in public and venture into the daylight in her bathing togs if she'd known he was there. The boy seemed very grown-up, much older than she, perhaps twelve or thirteen.

She hadn't known that Luc, secreted behind one of the pillars of the pool's summer kitchen and barbecue area, where he had been reading in the shade, had clocked her arrival and had sat, one eye pressed against a wooden pillar, the other watching her, fascinated by her coconut-milk complexion and puzzled by her plastic water wings.

'I thought everyone could swim,' he mocked, though not unkindly, when she explained the purpose of the 'blue things' wrapped around her upper arms.

'I was born by the sea,' he swaggered. 'I don't ever remember not being able to swim. I can teach you, if you like. Snorkelling too. You are with the English visitor who has come to meet Maman, *n'est-ce pas*? Why are you in my pool?'

Now she grew afraid. This strapping boy, with skin as tanned as a leather satchel, clutching a paperback book, was moving closer, hovering over her on the steps, she half in, half out of the water. How she feared his scorn. Or, worse, that he might sink her head beneath the surface just for the fun of it.

'My name's Luc, by the way. What's yours?'

'Jane Sanderson,' she croaked.

'*Bonjour*, Jane. I'll get my trunks and join you.'

'*Bonjourrr*,' she repeated shyly. It was the first word she had ever uttered in French and she was thrilled to bits with herself.

Luc spoke more than adequate English and, on that day and the sun-drenched days to come, proved himself to be a treasure chest of fascinating curiosities. Barefoot on the beach, agile and swift, camera swinging from his naked torso, he was always delving, scavenging, photographing his finds. Clues, land knowledge, the sea, marine and rock plants, geography . . . questioning, penetrating, examining. She watched him in wonder and admiration. She trailed after him, carving out her own more ponderous path of discovery, or dared to skip along at his side on his constant hunt for sea drift, magical shells, quizzing him with questions.

Sitting side by side, wrapped in towels after their swim on that first morning, he began to feed her the French names for whatever article or subject he was talking to her about. 'Swimming-pool. *La piscine*. We met in *la piscine*.'

'No, we didn't. I was in the pool, not you. Do you live here alone?' she asked him.

'With my mother and aunt. *Avec ma mere et ma tante*.'

'Brothers and sisters?'

'*Non*.'

'Me neither. What about your father?'

Luc took a beat, withdrawing like a snail. She'd touched a tender spot, prodded accidentally. She sensed that, even at her young age. 'He stayed back in Algeria,' he replied cautiously, 'where I was born. My grandparents stayed on too.'

'Where's Algeria?'

'North Africa.'

'You were born in Africa?!'

'And some day I'll go back. I'll build a boat and sail. Just me on the open sea in my boat. And I'll find our farm and my father again.'

Africa! Her new friend was so exotic, unlike anyone else she had ever met, and he swam like a porpoise.

Jane, the bashful English girl, with plaits and canvas sandals, had been utterly bewitched by everything and everyone at Les Cigales – the big house and its vineyard estate, its mistresses in their snazzy clothes, especially Madame Clarisse, gushing yet forbidding. A curious eye-catching bird, she was, clucking and foraging and chivvying.

Back at the *auberge* that evening, father and daughter had dined in the restaurant. The other guests were all northern European tourists, passing through. Jane felt curiously at odds with them, as though she, and perhaps her father also, had been enchanted. She had entered a universe that was magical and fabulous, and would change her for ever. So overwhelmed by wonder was she, by sights beyond her imaginings and most of all by the company of her new friend, Luc, that it left her giddy, and she could barely swallow her fancy food.

'His name is Luc and he's promised to teach me to swim without my water wings.'

'Good girl.'

'I wish Mummy was here to see all this, all those blossoms hanging like jewels in the bushes, the pots of fat flowers and the tall straight trees,' Jane had whispered to her father, 'and to hear me speak the French words Luc's been teaching me. Will we visit the castle again?'

'It seemed to go well,' had been her father's response. 'I understand what they're after and I'm sure I could do it.'

'Fingers crossed, Dad.'

'We'll know tomorrow.'

One of the two proprietors at Les Amis du Château served dinner while the other cooked. Whenever possible, they fussed at the Sandersons' table, greedy, full-breasted, grey-haired scavengers, hungry to peck at the gossip from the great estate. 'How did you get on up there?' The pair of wait-resses tittle-tattled about the Cambons, destroying their reputations in salacious tones, as though nothing gave them greater satisfaction.

'The most unpopular females in the vicinity. Pieds-Noirs is what they are. Born in Africa. African habits.'

'The younger one is a nettled-eyed sorceress.'

'We never see them at mass.'

'Good luck to you.'

Peter was amused, Jane a little frightened but she couldn't have said whether her fears had been sown by the two at the hotel or the two at the big house.

During their return visit to Les Cigales the following morning, Peter was offered the job. Clarisse, striking in a loose magenta shirt, high gold mules and white linen skirt, had led him to the table in the dining room, poured two glasses of chilled white wine and together, watched by Jane, they had signed a one-year contract. 'Next year, we'll take another look.' Clarisse had smiled, her green eyes narrowed, cat-like.

And so began a series of adventures, to and from Les Cigales during long, untroubled summers. Memorable, joyous were those return journeys to England in her father's Cortina shooting brake, packed to the gunwales with cartons of wine to be stored in their garage at home until they were sold, until Peter could afford to open his own off-licence, singing together in perfect harmony, happy as a pair of drunken sailors.

'*The bells are ringin' for me and my gal.* Come on, Janey, sing up.'

'I don't know that one, Dad.'

'Well, what shall we sing, then? You choose the next one.'

'Let's sing one you wrote, Dad.'

Hot, everlasting days.

Peter shared those expeditions with his growing daughter who, in turn, shared her days at 'the castle' with Luc, while Vivienne stayed behind in England.

Until the day she drew her last breath, Vivienne had obstinately preferred England. After much badgering, she had once agreed to spend a few weeks on the Cambon estate. Jane had been nine or ten. By that stage, the Cambon sisters had designated one of their cottages for the Sandersons.

'It is preferable to that local *auberge*,' claimed Clarisse, who described Les Amis du Château as 'down-at-'eel and shady' and the inhabitants of the village 'full of jealousies, with begrudging faces'. However, Vivienne was not comfortable. She could not acclimatize to the hot southern other-land with its mosquitoes and foreigners, or to the grand surroundings and the company of Clarisse and Isabelle who, she was convinced, were sneering at her. She found the atmosphere 'sticky and unpleasant'. She found her husband's two female employers formidable and snobby. She went home and never returned.

The delights and discoveries had belonged exclusively to Jane in the company of Luc or on the road with her father; father and daughter side by side.

Until the night of that awful scene with Clarisse, the summer Jane was fourteen . . .

Peter's business was growing well. The customers were biting. He had his eye on a little shop in Kent. Jane had mistakenly read all this as the reasons for his new-found lightheartedness. She had been too much of a child, too naive or too consumed by her own girlish passions, her developing infatuation for Luc, to read between the lines, to understand the extent, the results of her father's charm, the reason why when they visited they were now welcomed warmly as guests at the manor house, no longer the cottage. Her father, who had dreamed of building himself a modest enterprise, a little something to keep his family secure, to keep himself out of the dole queue, had been seduced.

The voices filtering through the ceiling awakened her. Jane opened her eyes to listen harder. There were bumping and scuffing sounds coming from the level above her room. In earlier centuries, the top storey had been the servants' quarters but, these days, the rooms were ordinarily kept locked. Jane knew this because she had occasionally accompanied Matty when the housekeeper went up to the third floor to give it an airing.

Alone that night, fourteen-year-old Jane, bereft because Luc had returned to Paris to university, crept up the stairs in the darkness, inching her way along the narrow corridor, following the muted voices and laughter coming from behind the closed door of one of the locked rooms. She slid stealthily from door to door, hoping to detect from behind which the sounds were emanating. Ear against the wood, she had located the animation and had listened. Eavesdropping, intrigued, disturbed, flushed with trepidation. With prescience? Her hand reached for the doorknob. Her palm and fingers gripped tightly the cold brass. She turned and paused, heart jumping like a jack-in-the-box, before shoving the sticking door open. There, directly ahead of her, on a single bed, starkly illuminated by an opalescent shaft of moonlight beaming in through an attic window, the bestial vision. Jane had let out a cry, a hard shriek of disgust. One figure instantly disentangled himself, dragging a white sheet with him, hopping across the small room. Nettle-green eyes, those witch's eyes, locked on Jane as she pelted towards the mistress of the house. She grabbed at Clarisse whose hair was a bird's nest, hanging in messy whorls, pulling, tearing at her. Jane's rage was white, blind, as she beat her balled fists against Clarisse's breast. Peter, who had hastily wrapped the sheet about his lower torso, was now disentangling Jane from her.

Jane had flung her father's hands off her. 'Get away from me. I hate you, hate you!' she had screamed, recoiling, slamming the door, thundering down the stairs, shrieking, yelling, feet pounding to her own room where she had locked herself in, fighting her desire to throw up, shutting out the memory of the disgusting vision of her naked father buried in the creamy thighs of Clarisse.

Some sort of a scene ensued overhead. A chaos of footsteps and heated voices, then a bumping on the stairs, followed by a thud, a furious wail of pain and a string of expletives.

Clarisse had fallen down the stairs and, it later turned out, broken her ankle.

Jane had not emerged from her room. She had stayed in the dark on the floor by her bed, stiff-backed, cross-legged, listening to the commotion, with her arms wrapped around herself, weeping and howling, her heart breaking.

Her heart was breaking for the absence of Luc, who had

gone away when she needed him more than ever, but most of all she was crying for the loss of her father. A part of her life was over for ever; it would never be the same again. Her father as idol had been toppled.

Early the following morning, while the doctor was ministering to Clarisse, Jane and her father had slung their belongings into the car and departed. No one had appeared to see them on their way. As Luc was in Paris, Jane was never given the opportunity to say goodbye to him.

That bleak autumn back in England, Jane had been wretchedly miserable. During those ensuing cold winter months, she watched her father take on another persona, become a different man. He was never less than kind to her, his only daughter, his only child, but he grew curt and short-tempered in the home, as though he were carrying a heavy burden. Jane's mother, who knew 'the truth' by then because Jane had forced it upon her, had pined silently. Jane, angry, brokenhearted, churning with teenage angst and irrational emotions, had blamed her mother, blamed her for staying at home, and had spat out her vision of the scene in gory detail, fact by fact.

As the days grew shorter and darker, Vivienne withdrew, crawling further into a silent world of her own. Until, eventually, she was diagnosed. From then on, she disappeared beyond reach. She had inhabited a shrivelled, decreasing universe where only the cancer was alive within her and nothing, no one, could draw her back, not even Jane or Peter.

15

The present

The Malaz church bells were striking three as Jane approached the lychgate. She stepped through onto the paving stones and almost lost her footing. The path was brown with rotting leaves and slippery from the torrential downpour. Luc's grave was to the left at the furthest extreme of the cemetery, dipping beyond the hill's summit.

When Jane reached the hole she found that, not unexpectedly, it had been filled in. It was a hump of sodden soil. Just that. It smelt peaty. She pulled off her gloves, tossed them to the ground and touched the red-brown earth, caressing it. There were small stones mixed in with the recently created mound, but no grass. It looked bald compared to the others around it, bald and swollen. Directly beside Luc's plot was his aunt's with its engraved headstone: 'In loving memory of Isabelle Cambon. Born in Algeria, died in France.'

Such spare language to sum up a life. Jane would want more for Luc. There was nothing yet, of course, no indication of the presence of the rare and gifted soul who had been laid so recently to rest. She would be obliged to discuss the choice of the stone and wording with Clarisse.

Luc's identity lay in the messages that accompanied the drenched bouquets and wreaths. Jane slipped off her raincoat and laid it out on the soft sodden grass, then spread herself on it beside her husband. Except that she wasn't beside him. If she could have lifted up the layers of earth, like bedding, and crawled beneath them to lie close at his side she would have done so. The earth was keeping them apart.

'Will I ever be able to reach you, to touch you again?' she whispered.

The air about her was fragrant with the smoke of fires. 'Can you smell it too?' she asked him. She wanted to talk to him, would give the world to. But there was just silence, save for birds overhead. She reached for several of the notes and cards.

'Shall I read them to you, Luc?' The ink on many had been smudged during the overnight storm and had left flowers destroyed and several messages partially illegible. 'Here, what does this one say? Maybe you can understand it better than I.' She deciphered what she could but only a few meant anything to her until she found one that sent a wave of alarm through her, like an electric shock. It was attached to a bouquet of cream roses browning at the tips of the tight, unopened, unspoiled petals. She stared at the signature, handwritten in black ink, and re-read it. '*Notre cher Luc, nos vies sans toi ne seront plus jamais les mêmes. Nous t'aimerons toujours. A. P. x*'

Our lives without you will never be the same again. We will always love you.

'A. P.' or 'A' and 'P'? 'Our lives . . .' so two mourning friends.

'Did you ever talk to me of A and P, Luc? A. P. I don't remember them.'

Had she been introduced to anyone the day before with those initials? There had been so many, such a crowd of faces, such an onslaught of sympathy. She couldn't recall. Why, of all the condolence cards laid out sopping here, did this one send an arrow of dread through her heart?

A and P?

Jane sat up, shivering without her coat, muddied fingers unconsciously twisting her wedding ring back and forth. More than anything, she longed to reach out and take Luc's hand. To lift it up and hold it between hers, smell his warm flesh, kiss his fingertips as she had so often done during his life when he was sleeping and she had lain awake, watching him. 'I can't recall you ever speaking to me of anyone who fits "A" and "P". Both of whom loved you so deeply.'

The sun was nudging through, sliding the clouds apart, slipping free. It was strong and clear after the wash of rain. She felt a tinge of warmth drift across her face. Was it Luc's hand stroking her, buoying her, easing her knot of pain, reassuring her that he was still at her side, that she had nothing to fear?

Possibly 'A. P.' was shorthand for a more general group? 'Our' as in a group of friends. Clarisse was Luc's sole remaining relative, as far as Jane was aware. Unless there were living relations in Algeria. 'A' and 'P'. Might they have been colleagues, work associates, fellow film-makers who admired his oeuvre and his courage? Who loved him to the extent that their lives would never be the same again?

'As my life will never be the same again, Luc. Why, *why* did you have to go?'

Might Clarisse be able to identify 'A' and 'P' or would she use Jane's ignorance as a point against her, underscoring her vulnerability? No, she would not ask Clarisse. She tucked the card back among the withering flowers and then, as an afterthought, slipped it into her pocket. She would find their identities for herself.

16

London, three weeks later

Jane stared at herself, making a face – tongue out, sunken blue eyes wide – in the mirror in the Ladies at the Wolseley restaurant on Piccadilly. She was paper-thin, pale as milk. A stem, barely a flower. An ambulance, snarled up in the West End traffic beyond the window, was flashing its impatience, its periwinkle light pulsing. It gave her appearance a ghostly hue. She sighed and fussed at the collar of her light-green sweater, delaying her return to the table. She would rather not go through with this meeting, but it couldn't be avoided. Robert Piper had telephoned her the day before, insisting they have lunch, that it couldn't wait another moment. His tone had been short-tempered because she'd been avoiding him, not returning his calls.

She had seen hardly a soul since her return to London, almost three weeks earlier, other than Lizzie, her friend from schooldays: she had taken the train from the south coast to buy Jane tea at Blakes in South Kensington. Lizzie, widow and twice divorcee, an artist of moderate talent who dressed like a hippie from the late sixties, was employed by Hastings Borough Council in the Arts and Museums Department. Jane had done her best to wriggle politely out of the invitation but Lizzie being Lizzie had coerced her and they had spent most of the afternoon struggling through small-talk, sipping endless cups of tea, until Lizzie had started to harry Jane about beginning anew. 'Move to the coast. There's quite a lively dating scene growing up around our way. I've met someone . . .'

Jane felt fragile, spaced out, and so alone in her echoing home, wandering like a phantom from room to room in search of Luc. She was only able to function, as far as she was functioning at all, in isolation, in hibernation, talking to him, trying to resurrect him, rarely answering the phone, working furiously through the black hours of insomnia translating a series of guide books. When she slept, it was on his side of the mattress. She drank her coffee from his favourite mug and she wrapped herself in his sweaters.

It was the middle of February, close to two months since Luc's death. The initial shock of his passing, the explosion in the gut, had settled into a pain that was seeping deep, running through her arteries, always on the lookout for new corners to insinuate itself. Grief was closing her down, paralysing her. Coming out to meet Robert today, as much as she bucked against it, was a step towards pulling herself together and into the daily stream of life.

She took a deep breath and tracked unsteadily to the table where Robert was seated, drinking his way through a bottle of wine. He looked her over, staring into her face, and frowned.

'I won't mince words with you, Jane,' he announced, once they had ordered and the main courses had been served. 'This is the last conversation I want to be having with my friend's widow, but it has to be broached.'

'What is it, Robert?'

'There's no easy way to break this to you, Jane.'

Her eyes were on his face, her pulse racing. She couldn't handle more bad news. 'Oh, Robert, please, just say whatever it is and get it over with.'

'Luc has left his affairs in a lamentable state.'

'Affairs?'

'Finances.'

Jane was taken aback. Luc had been exacting in the accounts he kept. It was she, Jane, who was more extravagant. No, not extravagant, but sloppier about keeping receipts, recording figures. Neither of them had ever been frivolous with money and Luc had earned decently from his films. Hadn't he? In fact, she didn't really know. All his income went through his film company, most reinvested in the next project. They didn't have a house kitty, they shared whatever was available at the time. If they went out for dinner, either might pay, but they rarely ate in expensive restaurants. Luc usually bought the tickets when they went to the cinema or a club because some of those receipts he could claim against his tax. Her own income was modest. She had a little saved for holidays and clothes, a deposit account with close to ten thousand pounds in it, but not much else. Luc paid the mortage on their flat.

'Meaning?'

'He has left debts that total over two hundred thousand sterling. On top of which your mortgage payments have not been met for over six months and there is a high rate of interest accruing on them.'

Jane stared in disbelief at the man opposite her.

'You'll need to make some rather unpalatable decisions and then act fast.'

'But what about his life-insurance policy? Won't that cover the worst of it? Our mortgage, for instance, that'll be cleared, surely.'

'There *is* no policy. Please, Jane, before you start jumping up and down, let me explain.'

Jane felt her heart pound. Her mouth was dry and metallic.

Robert pressed his fingers together. A gesture that brought to mind a childhood rhyme to do with churches and steeples. Jane couldn't recall it now. Her forehead was breaking out in a sweat. She felt sticky and impatient. She had no reason to doubt Robert. She trusted him. He had been more than Luc's lawyer. The pair had been close friends since their university days in Paris where Robert had been studying French and European *droits*, specializing in company and commercial law at the Panthéon-Sorbonne.

'There is a policy, Robert. I'm – I'm sure of it.'

'By the time Luc decided to confide in me about his situation he had already made the decision to cash in his life insurance. I strongly advised him against it. He refused to listen. The funds were sunk into his debts, but they made little real impact. The fact is he was weeks away from bankruptcy.'

Jane sat in the crowded restaurant opposite Robert, staring at her untouched fish: sea bass in a champagne sauce. It had the appeal of custard poured over a bed of cotton wool. Her head was spinning. 'Are you sure?'

He nodded.

'I had no idea . . . not a clue . . . He never talked about it, but you know Luc . . . knew Luc. He was never one to tell the world . . . Jesus.'

'I suspected you weren't aware of what was going on.'

'What do you advise?'

'He remortgaged your London home to release cash but, as I said, the payments are gravely in arrears. The mortgage company has written twice, warning of an impending repossession order.'

'But his death?' Jane felt a treacherous lump rise into her throat. She took a sip from the untouched glass of white wine on the table in front of her. 'Luc's death surely means that the flat is covered by the mortgage insurance.'

'Alas, there was no mortgage protection plan in place.'

She was drowning, sinking beneath the reverberating buzz of conversation, corks being drawn, the clatter of crockery all about her, and there was no seabed. Not only had she lost her beloved husband, it was now looking as though she was about to lose everything they had built together.

'What should I do?'

'I'll speak to the mortgage company and beg a little time. Distraught widow and all that.'

Jane winced at this description of herself.

'I suggest you get the flat on the market and sold as soon as you can. Accept any decent offer. Don't wait, hoping for better. If you do, it will cost you more in the long run. Depending on the usual delays and unforeseen expenses, the sale, once the debts have been cleared, should still leave you with a modest lump sum.'

'A modest lump sum. What does that add up to?'

'Sufficient for a small studio or one-bed somewhere.'

Jane was incredulous. 'Is there no alternative?'

'Unless you have substantial capital tucked away, no. Most of the financial commitments died with Luc but you'll need to cover certain other liabilities. At the very least, the mortgage payment arrears and interest.'

'Totalling?'

'From memory, I'd calculate in the vicinity of a quarter of a million.' He shook his head. 'No, I don't want to pull a figure out of thin air. I'll have to look it up. As I said, some of the debts died with him but certainly not the loan against your property, and there appear to be one or two other commitments. Personally, I think you're far better to cut your losses and begin again.'

Robert made it sound as simple as chopping vegetables.

'But who does he owe these large sums of money to?'

'Banks, loan companies, a couple of which you won't want to cross. They are merciless. I've been sending out letters, assuring them that Luc's estate has every intention of settling its affairs honourably, but these guys are lethal and they're not patient.'

Jane was wrestling with the breadth of this news, struggling to take it on board. 'What was he doing with the money? What could he have been spending it on? Unlike you, we don't own a boat. Well, there's his old family fishing vessel in the South of France but certainly not a state-of-the-art yacht. He wasn't interested in cars, he worked hard, never let up . . . Are there film investment arrears, shortfalls? Can we sell the rights to his films?'

Robert gave a half-hearted shrug that Jane took to mean her guess was as good as his and that he had no magic formula to fix this mess. 'I think the finance on this last film was proving tricky. He was probably funding most of it.'

'And his family estate in France, is that at risk too?'

'I understood from Luc that it belongs to his mother and he owned a share. He wasn't able to use it as collateral. Possibly you might have some claim on his part, but those French Napoleonic laws are sticky to negotiate and I'm not qualified, not *au fait* with the ins and outs of French inheritance matters, to deal with it. However, the likelihood is that anything of the estate he owned would go to Luc's children first, of which there are none and after, back to his mother.'

'He co-owned it with Clarisse,' confirmed Jane. 'He inherited his aunt's half. I don't know who is the proprietor of the wine business, which in any case seems to be floundering, but the land and properties were fifty per cent his. But while Clarisse lives, she has the deciding voice.'

Robert listened, sipping his wine. 'I think she has no alternative but to offer you a home. Luc assured me that, even in the event of his premature death, if the London flat was lost, you would be taken care of. My guess is that, legally speaking, Luc's share reverts to Clarisse, but you're entitled to reside there. I could get one of my Parisian associates, who specializes in family bequests, to dig into it for you. Let me know if you want me to give him a call.'

'Luc never mentioned any of this.'

'The bottom line, the good news, is that the French home and vineyards are in the clear.' Robert smiled, but she caught a fleeting glimpse of pity in his solid features.

'Is there something else, Robert? Something you're not telling me?'

Robert frowned, shook his head.

'I mean, besides assuring you that his wife was not going to be thrown out on the street, what else did Luc tell you? Did he say what all this money was for?'

'Jane,' Robert moved his hand across the table and ineptly patted hers, 'if I knew . . .'

'Surely, as his friend, you must have been concerned. Jesus!' Jane lifted her fingers to her face and choked back tears. How much worse was this going to get? 'There seem to be holes in his life, gaps that I cannot stitch together. Luc, we're talking about Luc. I've known him since I was six and I'm beginning to feel as though I never knew him at all. Every day I relive memories from our past – it's all I do – and I cannot equate them with the man who was taken from me last December. My Luc seems to have disappeared into thin air and I want him back. Oh, Robert . . . I'm so sorry. A and P, do those initials mean anything to you?'

The waiter was at their side, hovering to clear plates. Robert discreetly waved him away. 'Let me get you a brandy.'

'No, thanks.' She rubbed her nose and sniffed. 'Do they? A and P?'

'I don't know what they represent, sorry. Is it an organization or . . . ?'

Jane shook her head.

He waited, but she didn't elucidate. 'I've given you the facts, Jane, much as I would have preferred not to have such a conversation with you, particularly at this time.'

'Did Luc tell you that he'd tried to borrow against Les Cigales?' Jane persisted, suddenly rattled by the wall of secrecy, of dissimulation, corralling her. 'I mean, if he'd tried to raise a loan against his mother's home, he must have been desperate. Desperate . . . but he didn't confide any of it in me.'

'Over Clarisse's dead body, I'd say.' Robert had intended it as a lighthearted riposte, but it fell flat between them, causing an embarrassed silence.

Robert swiftly called for the bill.

They parted at the edge of Green Park with gushing assurances from Robert that both the London and Paris offices of his firm would continue to act gratis for his late friend's estate as a gesture of goodwill. He assured her once more that he would do his best to see her through the crisis with as much dignity and financial win as was possible.

'By the way,' he added, before departing, 'Marje says hello and suggests that when you're more settled you pop down to see us in Chichester for a weekend. We'll take you sailing. Don't let this get you down, Jane.'

Jane nodded her thanks, suspecting that she would never take Marjory up on the offer. And of course it was getting her down. Luc was dead. He was *dead*, for God's sake, and she couldn't string the latter months of his life into a coherent existence.

They embraced.

'Don't hesitate to call me if things get too rough,' he urged. 'Luc was my friend way before he was a client. I miss him too, you know.' She nodded and watched Robert hurry away, fishing for his iPhone in the pocket of his navy-blue Crombie, taking a call as he strode in the direction of Marble Arch.

If things get too rough . . . Just how much rougher could they get?

She walked back towards Piccadilly Circus, past the Ritz and the Wolseley where they had just dined, intending to take the Tube from Leicester Square, and then she decided to wait for a bus to Camden Town and from there walk to her empty flat and the impending nightmare of estate agents. How was she going to survive? Had Robert said almost a quarter of a million or half a million pounds? It made no sense.

How many holes were there left to pick open in one man's life? Where was this trail of deception leading her?

PART TWO
Sowing Seeds
France

I

Jane navigated the driveway cautiously, heart thumping. She parked in the forecourt of the manor house and switched off the engine, but remained in her seat. It was May. Luc had been dead for five months. She was making her first trip back to Les Cigales since his funeral. Her nerves, an eddying anxiety, were rising. First impressions suggested that a great deal had changed since her last sojourn. The house and land appeared to be gently decaying, as though the past was picking away at it, fragmenting the present. Even as she pulled over from the *route nationale* to the parking spot beyond the locked gates, the neglect was signalled. From the road, any passer-by might conclude that the domain had been abandoned. Weeds were growing up alongside and curling themselves around the iron gateposts. The stones of the boundary wall were covered with unsightly ivy. Luc had always insisted that the ivy be kept at bay. It ate its way into everything, he had claimed. His absence was evident even before Jane had crossed the grounds' perimeter.

The parklands were equally unkempt. The grapevines banked close to the driveway, those visible beyond the columns of cedars and pines, had shot up and sprouted into raggedy bushes. It was practice to cut the vines hard back during January and February, before the spring, to allow space for the new trained growth, so that in March the weeds could be more easily cleared away and the soil ploughed. But, as far as she could see, none of the vineyards had been touched. She wondered why not.

As she drew close to the house, a sense of gloom, of weathered darkness, hung like a cloud over the place. How could a building become so transformed in such a short space of time? Did Clarisse never visit the *bastide*? Was she unaware of its deteriorating condition? Was she as strapped for cash as Jane was?

Robert had told her that Luc had been unable to borrow against the estate, but might he have been borrowing from his mother, money that would not now be repaid? Had it left Clarisse, her wine business and the properties, destitute? Or had Luc sunk every penny he earned into this place, and now, without him, there were no more injections of cash? Was Clarisse expecting Jane to contribute, or worse, take full responsibility for the running costs and upkeep of the manor house? Whatever verbal commitments Luc had taken on, promises made to his mother, Jane could not allow herself to be saddled with them. There were so many unanswered questions and concerns. Nothing had been discussed. Clarisse and Jane had barely spoken since she'd left for London. They had engaged in one or two brief, rather brittle phone conversations, which had amounted to chilly exchanges, a charade of keeping in touch. Jane was there now to empty the house of her and Luc's possessions, to visit his grave, make arrangements and decisions for his headstone before departing, to abandon this chapter of her life. And once she had cut her ties here, once her home in London had been sold, what then? She was contemplating doing a little travelling. A solitary widow circumnavigating the globe? Whatever for? She had no idea. She stepped out of the car.

The lawns laid out before the west and east faces of the mansion had recently been mown, but the striking purple bougainvillaea and roses, planted for colour and shade to hang from iron pergolas sunk into the quadrangles of lawn, were running riot. It wasn't an unattractive sight, but it was unexpected. Jane felt sure that neither Claude nor the generously efficient Matty could be held responsible for the unruly state of the grounds. An honourable, trustworthy pair, they would have contributed all that could be expected of them and more, given that, according to Clarisse, they were no longer in the Cambons' full-time employment. 'I have been obliged to cut back their hours. The running costs are crippling me. I am an old lady facing the future here on my own. Drastic measures are called for. I may need to ask them to leave.'

Jane had been incensed by this revelation. The Lefèvres had been a loyal labour force for over forty years. Where else were they to find employment at this stage in their lives?

'You cannot do that to them!' she'd cried.

'It's done. Let the state keep them. I can't.'

This news had hastened Jane's return. As a girl, before Matty's own daughter was born, Jane had been close to the housekeeper. When her father was elsewhere, occupied on wine matters, and Luc was not at home, Matty had cared for Jane and taken her about with her. The affection that had been seeded in Jane's infancy had never paled. Matty had once looked out for her, and now Jane felt an obligation to protect the Lefèvre family.

Two paved pathways fanned out from the forecourt into a horseshoe and wrapped themselves around both sides of the main house, meeting again at the rear, in what had once been known as the 'formal gardens'. These paths were tufted with grass shoots growing vigorously up through the cracks. They had been hastily swept but not weeded. Dried twigs and leaves had been stacked into pyramids set back from the paths, ready to feed bonfires during the cooler autumn days. On both sides and to the rear, the borders had been trimmed. First impressions in this small sector were welcoming, not alarming, but when Jane strolled round to the back of the house, delaying the moment of entering it for a minute or two longer, the growth, a creeping encroachment of time and nature, was upsetting to behold.

What an uninviting spectacle the swimming-pool had become. Its base was carpeted with leaves that had drifted and fallen in throughout the seasons while algae organisms were coating the interior walls with a slimy green film. The water was tainted the same emerald while skeins of ivy had grown up over the pool's stone surround and were drifting on the water's surface. Jane asked herself whether this had not been a deliberate act on Clarisse's part, a punishment for her absence. Or was she too hard on the old woman? It was more likely that the maintenance and costly pool products were beyond the estate's means now. A luxury item. In any case, who would be using it?

Jane loved to swim and Clarisse knew it. Jane loved the gardens too. Clarisse had never been green-fingered and proudly claimed it. Isabelle had been the one who had tended the crops, who had added flair to the displays surrounding the property, the lavish bouquets on the dining-table and in the library.

She recalled the first time she had dunked herself in the pool. Midsummer, baking hot. She had been dusty and fretful, enervated after the long drive from England and awed by her surroundings. Her first encounter with Luc; she had been scared of him. She smiled now at the thought of it. How could she ever have feared him, even back then when he was twice her age? Gentle Luc, whose driving compulsion in life had been to help people, to celebrate the existence of every creature he dug out of rock pools or found living on the land, exploring his childhood fascination to make his fabulous nature films. So unlike his mother. If he were standing here beside her now, what would Luc say of this neglect, of his mother's hard-heartedness towards Claude and Matty? Was his financial mess in some way responsible for all this? Jane had not yet broached the subject of Luc's penury with Clarisse, but if Clarisse was ignorant of the situation, she might be expecting an injection of funds from Jane, from Luc's will. And what fury might be unleashed when she learned that Jane had nothing to contribute? Jane would need to pick her moment carefully.

She passed through into the kitchen garden, with its high stone walls, by its north-facing door. The latch was stiff, in need of oiling and scarred with rust. Ahead lay a jungle of bolted growth, buzzing and fluttering with insect life. Even the cracks between the stones in the walls had been invaded by thick, bristly ferns. In the old days, Jane would have expected to find Claude leaning over a fork, digging, rummaging, humming to himself or chatting with his wife, discussing the health of the plants as though they were old friends. Both of them born of this red earth, married to it. Matty at his side, sometimes with her two sons, the squabbling twins, Arnaud and Pierre, would have been scrutinizing the lusty crops, then singling out the vegetables that took her fancy for her next cooking bonanza.

Jane remembered being left alone, as a girl, with Claude, clutching an empty basket with pride, waiting for instructions. She had watched, fascinated, as Claude clipped off the heavy tomatoes, removing the ripe, sweet fruits from their slender, hirsute stalks. Edging dutifully along the stone path behind him, she proffered the basket as he uprooted a burgundy Lollo Rossa and then a Romaine lettuce, both muddy at the roots. They might have been followed by a handful of pea pods, fresh mint leaves, the golden flowers from the courgette plants. All to be washed clean of soil, he instructed her, at one of the outdoor taps before she delivered them to Matty's pantry in readiness for her lunchtime menu. 'And you wash your hands too, girl.'

'*Bien sûr, Monsieur Claude.*' With what relish she had examined her muddied digits, the dark-red earth packed beneath her nails like dried blood.

'Go on, then, get along with you.'

Such memories made the spectacle before her an even sadder one. If any vegetables were still surviving, they were invisible to Jane's eye, strangled beneath banks of muscly dock and carpets of dandelions the colour of egg yolk, each furry yellow blossom crawling with tiny black insects. White cabbage butterflies fluttered between one bolted legume and the next. The entire expanse had been so ordered and invitingly laid out, especially, she recalled, the circular beds of rosemary, thyme, coriander, rich mauve-and-white-flowering sage in the culinary herbs allotment, the canes of scarlet-flowered runner beans with pendulous green bodies, the dark or striped aubergines, soft raspberries, redcurrants, strawberries, edible marigolds, bold, red-stalked rhubarb – oh, such kaleidoscopes of colour were once on display here. Banquets to gorge herself on when no one was watching, to stuff herself until the seeds and juices had trickled down to dry sticky on her chin, and her stomach had swelled from greed and happiness. Today, it was nothing but a barrage of weeds and wild flowers.

She opened her mouth and took a deep gulp of air. Fresh leafy air. Compost-rich, feracious. Tiny insects floated like spores before her eyes. She heard the humming of bumble bees, honeybees, hornets sating themselves in their fluorescent paradise. Well, at least they're happy, she thought.

What had possessed Clarisse to allow the gardens to run wild like this? Was her grief over the loss of Luc, her only child, paralysing her, as it had Jane?

The espaliered apples, pruned regularly by Claude and Luc and secured to the inner surrounds of this garden's high stone walls were clinging on, more or less. It would take a little time and effort to reattach them. The first job would be to remove the rotting trellis and replace it. Even she could manage that, with a saw and a little assistance. The quartet of fig trees offering shade, one at each of the four corners of this garden – two with wooden benches placed strategically beneath them for digging pauses – had grown tall. Their reach was spreading, blocking out light. They were in need of pruning but they hung heavy with hard oval fruits and promised a fine late-August yield, so best to leave them for now. Jane was reminded of Matty's marvellous fig tarts. A taste from the early days of her childhood. When before or since had she devoured a dessert so flavoursome, so scrumptious? Only when topped with scoops of Matty's homemade mint or lavender ice cream as an accompaniment. Jane should ask her for her recipes, file and catalogue them before it was too late.

Before it was too late . . .

How could all this be the past? Where was the spirit of Luc among such desolation? Was he here somewhere, striding the big open spaces, pushing up through the forests of roots, heartbroken at the dereliction? She longed to be alone with him, flesh to flesh, to hold and stroke him again. Was it pathetic of her to beg the world to stop turning, to arrest time, to rewind, to admit that without Luc she had lost her present and her future?

Feet crunching swiftly on grass-infested, loose-pebbled pathways, Jane slipped out through the garden's southern door. It creaked closed behind her. She reached the uppermost point of the iron-arched staircase. Ahead, there was a flight of stone steps that descended to the lower terraces where rockery and lavender beds had long ago been laid. Those elegant rose-clad arches, whose curving structures Jane had painted apple green one long weekend soon after Clarisse had decamped to Cherry Tree Lodge, when Luc had accepted responsibility for the management of the main house, to alleviate his mother of the burden and Jane, in a spirit of solidarity, had set about refreshing parts of the surrounding gardens: five and a half years on, the arches were flaking and rusty again. No longer entwined with cinnamon-scented climbing roses that, in full blossom, hung like dollops of clotted cream, they were overrun with thorny briars.

And where were the canvas director chairs, ready to unfold and drag to a vanilla- or rosemary-perfumed corner in the shade, where she could settle with a book or her Kindle for an afternoon's tranquillity? Where was the order in the planted pathways? It was all disappearing, lost, wasted by wilderness. Glancing back towards the rear of the house, its walls scaled with strands of browning jasmine, Jane concluded that the heart of the property had gone adrift. It was rudderless. All *joie de vivre* had drained away. Eviscerated, heartbroken.

Gone with Luc.

And there was no dog to skip to greet her, jumping excitedly, tail wagging as it barked its welcome. Walnut. What had become of Walnut? No trace of his remains had been detected in the car. Hairs from his coat had been identified, but there was nothing to prove that they were not several days old. He had vanished into thin air, and his mysterious departure continued to haunt Jane. There were moments when the loss of the animal seemed to fell her more than the loss of her husband. She knew that Luc was dead, she'd finally begun to accept it as the months crawled by, but Walnut's disappearance was one of the enigmas, the conundrums begging explanation. 'A' and 'P': who were they? Those three lost hours in or near Paris, the night after she had been with him when he had checked out of their hotel? Luc's financial calamities, and the vanished dog . . . She had telephoned the central canine refuge in Lyon and three local ones. None had heard of Walnut.

Unanswered questions. So many of them.

'*Madame Cambon! Jane!*'

'Yes?'

'*Bonjour!*'

She swung round and caught sight of Claude in his battered straw Panama and blue overalls, waving to her with both bare arms raised. Her spirits lifted. 'Claude, hello! *Bonjour, bonjour.*'

The gardener, whose shoulders were growing humped, she noticed now, picked up the handles of his wheelbarrow and pushed it across one of the pebbled pathways to greet her. In spite of his advancing years, he was in rude health, as she had always known him, but as he drew close she saw that his grey-lashed eyes were glistening with emotion.

'Welcome home. It's very good to see you again, Madame.'

They exchanged *bises* companionably, but she avoided his direct gaze. It was not out of embarrassment, but the sight of this perennial figure so open with his grief brought back the ghosts of summers past, and those memories cut Jane to the quick. Her own grief was too raw to indulge in his nostalgia, to listen to reminiscences of Luc as a child: the evenings Matty as a teenage girl from the village had cycled over to baby-sit the boy for pocket-money; the adolescent Luc harvesting at Claude's side in the olive groves; Luc at their wedding . . . A roll-call of the years Claude and his country wife had been in the employment of the Cambons and during those years had been instrumental in Luc's development.

Jane had already played audience to a wealth of stories narrated to her before and after the funeral. Memories recounted and shared by the dozens and dozens of faces she could not put names to, whose owners she only vaguely recognized. Somehow, back then, almost six months earlier, numbed by shock, she had managed to play her role, to hold it together, but today she was floundering. As the numbness had begun to thaw, her grief had opened up and it was raw.

She needed time alone, time for her own recollections, to cherish and polish her personal pictures of Luc. Beyond the commiserations and warm-heartedness of others, well-meant as their intentions were, Jane craved seclusion. If she couldn't curl up and die, disappear entirely, then she craved solitude and later, when she was stronger, a compass to guide her forward. She was directionless and might soon be penniless. Luc had left her in dire circumstances. Any day she might receive Robert's call to confirm the sale of their London flat. In some ways now, its release would be a relief, a lessening of financial burdens, closing the door on memories, but what would remain? Nothing. Wilderness, desert, and she was terrified of that trek forwards alone. With Luc's death, the roof had blown off her world and now the walls, their home, were to be removed as well.

She was tired of hearing 'how sorry we are' and 'such a marvellous man'. There was no one, it seemed, who'd had an inkling of the trouble Luc had been in. He had carried the weight of his debts alone. Jane needed to understand what had led him to the financial abyss he had been grappling with and she needed a plan. How was she to rise above the deprivation she was inheriting?

'Madame?'

'Sorry, Claude, what did you say?'

'Are you all right?'

'Yes, yes, I'm fine. What were you saying?'

'Clarisse . . . er, Madame Cambon told us you were on your way. I've been expecting you to telephone, to give us your flight details. It would have been a pleasure to collect you from the airport, and lend a hand with your cases. How are you, Jane?'

'Oh, you know . . . I mean . . . as well as I can be, under the circumstances.'

'Matty and I . . . feel his loss too . . .'

Silence.

'Are you here to stay?'

'No, no, just a day or two. Collecting belongings, you know, and then, then . . .' She took a deep breath and swung her attention elsewhere, eyes welling with cursed tears. She coughed. 'My case is still in the car, Claude, if you would be so kind. I'll go and unlock the house. Thank you.'

'Of course, Madame.' He looked chastened.

Damn it! Her tone had been more brusque, more aloof, than she had intended. She was very fond of the old fellow, very fond. She and he had a history together too. And she had not even enquired after his or Matty's health.

She made her way to the back door, the kitchen entrance, slipped her key into the lock and stepped inside. In spite of the warmth outside, the small pantry felt chilly, unlived-in. The shelves were bare, empty, scrubbed wood. She shivered, pulling her cardigan tightly about her as she made her way tentatively, passing the laundry rooms, the larger pantry, also bare as far as she could see, and through to the breakfast room.

Even the communal spaces reeked of damp, of developing mould, of life having crept away, but in spite of Clarisse's harsh cutbacks, dearest Matty had obviously been into the house and given it a damn good clean. The downstairs areas, at least. The floors, walls, ceilings, even the cracks, all had been cleared of cobwebs and the usual invasion of creepy-crawlies Jane and Luc had encountered whenever they'd returned after an absence, but it was sterile. The house lacked life, activity. It lacked that wonderfully uplifting smell of baking, of warm fresh bread and quiches, of fruits and vegetables picked that morning from the garden, still wearing a light dusting of earth, laid out in the larder on sheets of greaseproof paper, ready to be transformed into salads or soups.

It lacked music. Luc loved music. If he were beside her now, he'd be slipping Brad Mehldau or Amy Winehouse into the CD player. One evening, long ago at the Cobden Club in London, they'd chanced upon a session by the young unknown Amy Winehouse. Jane hadn't been to a music venue since their Trois Mailletz outing the previous autumn. 'Music gives life to everything,' Luc used to say. But since he'd died, she could tolerate only silence. The screaming silence in her head.

In happier years, the breakfast room was where the family had congregated. Once upon a time, in winter and during the olive and grape harvests, when Isabelle had been alive, the house had been stuffed to bursting with guests' laughter and energy. In summer, all meals were taken out of doors in the shade of a magnificent *Magnolia grandiflora*, with its waxy, white flowers, from the southern United States, or at the iron table overhung by a quintet of fig trees, strategically planted to cast neat midday shadows the entire length of the south lawn border.

Jane laid her hand on the wooden refectory table. She stroked its oiled surface with her fingers. Her touch released echoes, reverberations. Uproarious laughter from bygone days. Jazz on the gramophone. Dancing cheek to cheek. This room, this house, was a repository of memories, but not all were untroubled. There had been days when sparks flew, when the cries had been ominous, the discoveries heart-breaking . . . How she had wept, rent by disappointment and shock that night when she had found her father with Clarisse . . .

She withdrew her hand smartly, as though it had been singed, and passed through into the hall, with its low-hanging glass chandelier and the familiar pendulum swing of the pot-bellied grandfather clock. The air gave off a resinous perfume: cedarwood and beeswax furniture polish. There Jane lingered, picturing herself tiptoeing behind her father on that initial visit. Clarisse's musky perfume, the daffodil-yellow dress hugging her curvacious buttocks, conducting them into a world shuttered from sunlight. Clarisse, stroking and lifting the fat pearls hanging about her neck, had welcomed the child Jane and her father with a red-lipped smile.

Predatory.

Jane's thoughts crashed back to the present and she stepped in a clumsy semi-circle, deliberating about which direction to take next, which room to enter. Loss had rendered her indecisive even when faced with the simplest choice. Every step into her future was clouded by vacillation. Four open doors, four uninhabited living areas, excluding the kitchen spaces, awaited her occupation, and she dithered. Rooms in stillness, lying in wait, watchful.

Each, generously proportioned, exuded its history: sunken seats in scruffy sofas now hidden beneath baggy white dust sheets, a used pack of cards stacked and waiting for hands to cut and shuffle it on the card table in the *petit salon*; regiments of books lining the walls of the library, growing dusty behind finger-printed glass; used grates, sooty dampers, a marshmallow-roasting fork forgotten in the hearth. She and Luc had once made love on the carpet in front of that hearth. His naked body crossing the room by firelight . . .

The fading scents, the cold embers of the last fires burned

in these chimneys, which would have been when? The gathering after Luc's funeral?

Had anyone besides Matty walked these floors since? Did Clarisse ever come here? Did she creep through these rooms alone, listening to her own footfall, searching for ghosts while trying to recall music fading beyond earshot? This must be as painful for his mother as it was for Jane. She felt a twinge of sympathy for her.

When Jane had telephoned Clarisse from London, once her flat had been made ready and put on the market, and had tentatively proposed a visit, Clarisse had not been overjoyed. 'I knew you'd call again sooner or later,' had been her bald response. 'It's almost a month since you bothered to pick up the phone, but you're welcome to come whenever you want.' And with that she had replaced the receiver.

Jane asked herself now whether she shouldn't drive up the lane directly and pay a call at Cherry Tree Lodge before she settled her belongings in their bedroom. It was polite to make her arrival known, put on a brave face and suggest they had dinner together that evening. But her heart sank at the prospect. What was there to say to one another? Besides recriminations. Still, it had to be done. Common courtesy. Her mother-in-law was the boss here, after all.

She had almost forgotten Claude and her bags. She stepped towards the front door, unlocking it from the inside. There on the gravelled driveway, hat now folded and stuffed beneath his braces on his left shoulder, Claude had closed the boot of Jane's hire car. Her overnight bag, plus two empty cases ready to be filled with her bits and pieces, were under his arms and at his feet. She left the door wide open and hovered, surrounded by the drawing rooms. Not since she had been a child, visiting for the first time, had the house seemed so daunting, so overwhelming.

Claude jogged on aged legs to the porte-cochère and paused, puffing, dropping the cases at his feet. 'Where do you want these?'

'Thanks, Claude. Just dump them here inside the door. I'll deal with them later.'

Hands free, the old gardener tugged his straw hat from beneath his braces and twisted it in his hands. 'I switched the electricity back on. The fridge is functioning and the house lights, both interior and exterior, are all in order. I replaced several bulbs, and Matty put a baguette, a jug of olive oil and a bag of coffee in the large pantry for you. I picked you a bowl of cherries.' He grinned. 'They're a little underripe but I know that's how you like them. Oh, and I purloined a couple of bottles of estate wine, the finest, from out of the store, too.' He winked. 'I'm sure you'll be in need of a good glass or two and she won't miss them. She's hardly got a clue what's in there any more.' He shook his head.

'That's very thoughtful. Thank you so much, Claude.' She shuffled forward to hug him, then found herself frozen mid-step, arms dangling uselessly.

'Matty also popped in with a spot of dinner for you. She said to tell you it's in a dish in the kitchen and you only need to stick it in the range to heat it. Lamb, and there's one of her apricot and tomato chutneys to go with it. I've left the receipts for all the purchases and the light bulbs on the dresser in there as well. If you need me, you'll have to use your phone. The main one's dead. They've cut the line, disconnected it. Mail is on the dining-table. It does include a fair number of bills, I'm afraid. Anything else?'

'Thank you both for your kindness, Claude. *Merci beaucoup*. Madame Cambon must have overlooked the phone bill.'

'She told us to leave all the bills for you, that you'd be

settling them. Luc always paid the utility bills for this house, she said.'

'Did she?' Jane took a deep breath. Did that include the upkeep of the pool and the maintenance of the gardens? She and Clarisse would need to discuss the arrangements. She wasn't intending to stay. 'I'll sort it out with Clarisse, but I'll settle everything owed to you both later this afternoon, if I may? And if there is any other expenditure, extra hours worked, for example, just add it to the list.'

Jane had somehow delivered the translated manuscripts for three travel guides during her grieving days in London. The extended contract with the publishing house had been a lifeline, a reason to get out of bed, and the funds due in her bank account any day now would see her through this trip, at least.

'Matty's kept the accounts. That's not my department. I never was too good with figures.'

'How is she? How are you both keeping? And the family?'

He dropped his head and worried at his Panama. 'We're trying to keep ourselves active. We're doing just the one day a week here so we're struggling . . . and Madame says she might let us go altogether.'

'Yes, I heard from her.' Pause. 'Is she around?'

'I saw her out and about this morning. She was headed in the direction of her office at the winery.' Claude sighed. 'It's a poor vintage, this one, the worst we've known in quite some years. On top of everything else . . .'

Jane felt a stab of guilt. In spite of her protestations at the time, had the loss of crop on that fateful September day been the worm in the apple for this poor harvest? Was she inadvertently responsible for the laying off of Claude and Matty?

'It's proving tough on the treasury, according to Madame

Cambon. She's struggling to pay us. She's asked us to look elsewhere for employment but . . .' he lowered his gaze '. . . we're not getting any younger, you know. We've lived here all our married lives. Raised the kids here. All three of them. Well, you know all that . . .'

'I'm so sorry,' muttered Jane. 'If there's anything I can do . . .'

Silence. The sound of Claude's heavier breathing. 'Pity you're not staying longer. We could do with you here.'

'Maybe next time.'

'Would you like me to call Madame for you and tell her you've arrived?' He dug into the chest pocket of his overalls, proudly displaying a mobile phone. 'Arnaud bought me this contraption for my birthday. No peace with it. No skulking in the groves.'

'No, that won't be necessary. Thank you. I'll pop down to her myself.'

'Will there be anything else for now?'

'No, thank you.'

'Then I'll be on my way.' He hesitated. 'Madame Jane, my wife and I are both deeply sorry for the lo–'

'*Merci, Claude.* I'll drop by later after I've been to the bank.'

He nodded and touched her lightly on the shoulder. 'It's good to see you here. The old place is, well, it's a bit sorry for itself, these days. We're missing Luc too. Idleness improves nothing and that includes gardens and us old folk.'

Idleness was a killer indeed. Thank God for her own little business. She'd check her bank account later, draw out sufficient funds to cover Claude and Matty's expenditure. But, first, there was Clarisse.

2

Cherry Tree Lodge, Le Cottage du Cerisier, was situated in a magical setting in the middle of what might have been mistaken for nowhere, halfway along a narrow, rutted lane that continued onwards to the north-east boundary of the domain. The house perched at the edge of a copse of holm oak and Mediterranean shrub, a spinney for pheasants when the hunters, led by Arnaud Lefèvre, were prowling the countryside during the season. It was an attractive two-up two-down cottage, and in better condition than most of the other less substantial habitations on the estate. Clarisse had bagged it for herself after Isabelle passed away, at which point she declared the main property 'too rattling' for her requirements.

It had its own patch of flower-filled garden, a tapestry of multi-coloured blooms, few of which Jane could name and none of which were from Clarisse's labours. They grew wild, irrigated by a mountain-fed stream flowing fast at the foot of her backyard.

Less than half a kilometre along this same path, further north, towards the lower Alp ranges, had stood an impressive water mill, constructed in the seventeenth century by the Benedictine monks who had owned these lands and had transformed them from Mediterranean scrubland into lucrative wine and olive oil reserves. All that remained of the mill today were heaps of stones and rubble. In its heyday, it would have been a sight to behold: the great oakwood wheel creaking and grinding, turned by the force of the stream's flow, throwing off whorls of sweet crystal-clear drinking water, snow melt from the Alps. The wheel, according to Luc's calculations, had stood two and a half metres high. Its purpose had been to mechanize the mighty crushing stones that pressed the estate's olives into a thick paste from which was drawn the golden oil. Constructed from stone with oak beams, the mill had lain in ruins, defunct for a century or more. But it was the reason the cottage had been built. Originally, Clarisse's habitation would have been intended as the miller's residence.

Few passed this way. There was no reason to, unless you were visiting Cherry Tree Lodge, as Jane was now. As she drew up, the catkins garlanding the holm oaks glowed a soft moon-yellow, a halo of light shot through with sun, and the splendid ornamental cherry tree that gave the lodge its name, decades old, hanging low over the gated pathway, was in full May flower, a day or two past its glory. Its white blossoms were shedding flurries of drifting petals that quilted the paved stones. Jane lifted the latch on the wooden gate and paused to look out beyond where she had parked, to ingest the farmland view, the far-reaching acres of leafy green vineyards. She stood very still, head thrown back, staring at a blizzard of flowers, inhaling the cherry blossom scent, inhaling the marvellous seclusion, firing up her courage. Nothing but the distant putt of an engine, a tractor or mower, broke the stillness of Clarisse's kingdom, and songbirds trilling in the young green thicket; Luc would have identified each and every one of them. How she longed for the sound of his voice; how she missed his head-thrown-back laughter, his loosely cut long hair, like a black stallion's mane. She reached up to the tree and snapped off the head of a thin branch, breathing in the perfume from the delicately rose-tinted white blossoms.

It was remote here. She had forgotten the extent of its isolation. Was Clarisse at risk in this unpopulated hinterland? Jane couldn't picture how the old woman managed. She suffered from arthritis; she walked with a cane; this was an outback location even for a woman half Clarisse's age. Was she not afraid, living so far from others in the sweeping plain under a wide blue sky, crickets and vines her sole companions?

But nothing scared Clarisse. She was not one to fade away, frail as a winter leaf. She was a fighter, a stayer, and Jane had no desire to run up against her another time. All Jane craved was a dignified departure. A civilized adieu. Her heart was beating fast as she lifted the knocker and rapped it against the door. She had not yet broached the subject of Luc's financial calamities with Clarisse. She had no way of assessing to what extent Clarisse had been implicated or what of the reality the old woman knew.

Had Luc been sinking personal earnings into the family wine business? If the estate was running at a loss and he had felt obliged to chip in, to borrow money to keep this family affair afloat, why had he not shared the situation with his wife?

How could I confide in you, Jane? It would have served no purpose but to aggravate the bad blood that already exists between you two.

Would that have been his reasoning? Jane lowered her head in shame. 'You're right,' she whispered, to the man who was no longer there.

'It's unlocked. Just lift the latch.'

Aside from the day when she and Luc had assisted Clarisse with her move from the *bastide* to the cottage, Jane had never set foot inside her mother-in-law's house. The door opened directly into a sitting room, low-ceilinged, lacking light. In spite of the season it felt chilly. Jane stifled a shudder as she stepped over the threshold and onto a flagstone floor. Clarisse, as extravagantly attired as ever, was seated in an armchair with her legs outstretched and her slippered feet resting on a Moroccan-designed leather pouffe. Her crippled hands were mapped with veins, her fingers with jewellery. Nails manicured, painted. A small wooden table to her right held a sprawling jumble of papers – bank statements, cheque books, bills and a pile of out-of-date film magazines. Alongside the paperwork was a bone china cup and saucer and an empty Scotch glass. Both cup and glass bore the residue of Clarisse's Persian pink lipstick. She was smoking and the room was mildly fuggy. In her lap lay a black Spanish fan.

'I can't say I rate you highly as a daughter-in-law, Jane. You arrived yesterday, I hear from the staff, and you didn't even have the courtesy to drop by. I haven't seen you, indeed barely had a phone conversation with you, since my son's funeral.'

Jane hovered inside the half-open door. 'I arrived this morning, Clarisse, about two hours ago, not yesterday. No one could have told you otherwise. I made it clear when I rang you that I was flying in today. How are you?'

'Close the damn door and come in. There's coffee in the machine. Serve yourself. Or, if you prefer gin, the bottle's by the fridge. I'm resting my legs.'

It was a little late in the day for Jane to drink coffee and certainly too early for gin, but she walked dutifully to the bar that separated the living space from the kitchen on the other side and poured herself a small quantity of black coffee from a percolator, taking her time over the process.

'So what has kept you so busy these last months? My God, I might have believed you were killed in the accident along with Luc for all the attention you've paid me.'

Still with her back to her mother-in-law, stirring the liquid that contained neither milk nor sugar, Jane measured her response. 'Sorry not to have been in touch.' Turning, cup in hand, she rested her weight against the bar.

'For heaven's sake, sit down. Don't stand there, playing it cool, as though you were about to leave the moment you've arrived.'

Jane sighed, obeyed. At all costs, she was determined to avoid an argument, yet Clarisse's hackles were rising.

They sat in silence facing one another.

'So, what's the news?'

'About what?'

'I don't know. You tell me! Have you settled everything? Don't be so fucking tight-lipped. What about the insurers?'

'Which insurers?'

'The car. Luc's policies. Have they paid up? Jesus, Jane, you're hard work.'

Was Clarisse asking because she, the estate, needed money, because she was angling for a share in Luc's assets?

'Luc died without any life or mortgage policies in place. There is nothing to be paid out.'

Clarisse lifted her head, pouting, raising her chin into the air. A habit she had when deep in thought or churning over unexpected information. It exposed the turkey skin of her aged neck. 'What about his car?'

'He had downgraded the policy to third party.'

'*What?*'

'I thought you would have known, but since you don't . . .'

'Known what?'

'Luc's assets amount to nothing, except a rather alarming catalogue of debts.'

'Rubbish! He was always so prudent with money.'

Jane shrugged. 'I was wondering whether he had mentioned his financial problems to you. Was he investing in your wine business?'

Clarisse shook her head. 'He said nothing, but that's hardly surprising. He was never forthcoming. Your wedding is a fine example.'

Jane pushed ahead, ignoring the allusion to their wedding. 'Robert Piper filled me in. Luc had escalating loans. I don't know what the money was used for.'

'I had no idea,' Clarisse whispered. 'How serious is it?'

'I'm obliged to sell our flat.'

'Sell the –'

'It should cover everything, or so Robert has assured me.'

'And then?'

'Robert calculates that when the debts have been cleared, I should be left with sufficient to buy a modest studio or small flat in London. So I shan't be homeless.'

'Is that why you're here?'

'I don't understand.'

'To make some sort of a claim? Are you after money? Because if you are, you're out of luck.'

'My God, Clarisse! You really know how to stick a knife in. I came to clear out my possessions, as I requested on the phone. I'll be out of your life within a couple of days. I'll pay the outstanding bills for the main house, as Luc had agreed with you, up to the present, but beyond this, I can't. I'm sorry, really I am.'

'So you're not planning to stay?'

'You know I'm not.'

A moment's silence. Clarisse dragged on her cigarette, eyes half shut. 'How's your father?'

Jane felt her spine stiffen. This was unexpected. 'He's doing well, under the circumstances. Thank you for asking.'

'Have you told him about Luc?'

'I told him the week after Christmas that Luc had been killed in an accident. I haven't mentioned the rest.'

'You should bring him over here.'

'My father?'

'There's plenty of room on the plantation.' Clarisse frequently referred to Les Cigales as a 'plantation' rather than a domain or an estate, as though insisting she lived in the tropics with a bevy of servants.

'Why would I do that?'

'He could live with you up at the main house. He liked it here. He was happy. He could have played an important role in this estate if . . .'

Jane took a breath, bit her lip.

'You may not like it, but your father was happy here. And he was doing a fine job for our export market and would have gone on doing so, if you . . .'

'He doesn't remember the place now, or you.'

'Nothing of it?'

'Nothing, I'm afraid.' Jane caught the fleeting crease of pain in Clarisse's eyes and couldn't help but relish the minor moment of victory. Then, instantly, she chided herself. Such unkindness was unnecessary. 'It would only confuse and upset him to be moved from where he is. I have explained to him several times about Luc's death. Each visit, once he's connected to who I am, he asks after Luc, but within fifteen minutes he's wanting to know when Luc might see him and I have to go back over the story.'

'What a tragedy. Dear Peter. How he loved to dance, and sing. Do you remember all those evenings when he played his guitar and crooned to us? After you'd gone to bed, we'd dance, dance in the moonlight and then . . . Such a sense of humour he had. No one made me laugh the way your father did.'

Jane lowered her head. 'He still sings.'

'Should I telephone him? Give him a ring, cheer him up?'

'No.'

'Why not?'

'I've just told you, he wouldn't know you.'

'Wouldn't know me, that's rich.' Clarisse rummaged for a handkerchief stuffed up her sleeve, dabbed at her eyes, then pulled out another cigarette, forgetting the one smoking in the ashtray. 'Really rich . . .'

They returned to silence, Jane clinging to self-control. The last person in the world she wished to appear vulnerable in front of was Clarisse, but the memories of Peter out on the terrace singing, embracing Clarisse, had melted her resolve.

'So you're leaving again in a couple of days? I thought I might persuade you to stay on for a while. Keep me company.'

'I have to be available to show the flat until the sale goes through. Once Luc's financial commitments have been resolved, I'll need to look for somewhere to live.'

'The estate agent can show the flat. That's what they're paid for.'

'I need to get on with my life.'

'Leaving me high and dry?'

'That's silly, Clarisse. Obviously we'll stay in touch. I'd better get going.' Jane rose.

'You carry your hate like a little prize, don't you?'

'Please, don't let's rake up the past.'

'Your wretched little jealousies. You've harboured them for years, close against you, like some precious gold locket.'

Jane rubbed her fingers through her hair. Her head was exploding with questions. She didn't want this animosity. She just wanted to fill in the gaps and get on with her life. 'Clarisse, I can't deal with anything but the present right now.'

'My boy is dead and buried. If you hadn't insisted that he drive to London, he'd be here now. Alive!'

Now Jane was fighting for control. 'That is grossly unfair.'

'It's a fact. You just don't want to face it.'

She had readied herself. Even so, Clarisse always knew just when and where to pull the trigger.

'I'm on my own with no one to help me run this place, and once your affairs are sorted and you've paid the "outstanding bills" – thank you kindly – you'll drive off from here, boot laden, and I'll be lucky if I get a fucking Christmas card. You've never cared one jot for me or the sacrifices I made, have you?'

Sacrifices?

Jane lowered herself back into the chair, perched her cup on its saucer on the small table alongside her mother-in-law, nudging papers to make space, and stared at her empty hands clutched in her lap. 'Don't let's begin all this again. We've been there. Not again, Clarisse. Let's part amicably.'

'But that is about the sum total of it, isn't it, Jane?'

In spite of all the years and memories, Clarisse's summation was accurate. All they had in common was Luc. Too much had passed between them, too many sour encounters. 'Our relationship has never been easy. For God's sake, Clarisse, it's too late.'

'And Luc's wishes count for nothing? His dream that we would work together, rebuild the estate . . .'

'He never expressed any such wish to me. I don't believe you.'

'Well, it would seem that there is rather a lot he never mentioned to you.'

Jane was stunned by this remark. 'What are you talking about?'

Did Clarisse have answers? To the identity of A and P? About Luc's missing hours?

'His financial mess, for a start. And the rest.'

'The rest of what?'

Silence.

'What, Clarisse?'

'You couldn't handle it,' she sneered, and took another drag on her cigarette.

'Clarisse, if there is something you know, something you want to tell me . . .'

'There's nothing.'

Jane pursed her lips and waited. She refused to allow herself to be dragged into this game. The old woman didn't know anything.

'I'm only pointing out that my son appears to have been a dark horse, not to have shared his financial worries with his wife.'

Jane ignored this. 'I'd like to clear out Luc's studio while I'm here, unless you have any objection?'

Clarisse shook her head.

'Is there anything in there you would like to keep?'

'I haven't a clue what *is* in there. It was his private space. Film stuff, I suppose. If there's a photo of him, I'll have that.'

'I'll find you one. By the way, I've been looking for his address book. The burgundy leather one. It wasn't in London and I can't find it here. Have you seen it?'

'What would I want with his address book?'

'It must be in the cellars, then.' Jane rose, lifting up her cup. 'Dishwasher?'

'Leave it.'

'I'll rinse it.'

'I said, leave it.'

Jane leaned towards the bar, depositing the cup next to the coffee machine. Back to Clarisse, she asked casually, 'Do the initials A and P mean anything to you?'

Clarisse rubbed her hands over her face and lifted her empty gin glass, twirling it. 'Can you pass over that bottle?'

'It's a little early for gin.'

Clarisse sighed theatrically and pulled herself to her feet. Jane reached for the bottle first.

'Do they, Clarisse?'

'Matty's family, I suppose.'

Jane stood silently, registering this, as her mother-in-law snatched the bottle from her, poured herself a drink and shuffled past her to the kitchen in search of ice.

'I'm going to the village after lunch. Can I collect anything for you?'

The old woman shook her head.

'How about I cook us dinner later?'

'Just go, Jane, cut the bullshit.'

'Very well. I'll drop the house keys down to you before I leave . . . and say *au revoir*.'

'Do what you like.'

She hovered a moment before lifting the latch. This was Luc's mother, no matter their chequered past. Why did it always have to be so ghastly?

Outside, Jane paused by the cherry tree and took a long, deep breath. Arnaud and Pierre. Matty's sons. How completely stupid she had been. How could she have overlooked such an obvious connection?

3

It was a short distance to Malaz, less than five kilometres, a brisk, shaded walk that Jane had always enjoyed, particularly when Walnut had been trotting along with her. That afternoon she took the rented car. She needed cash to reimburse the Lefèvres and she needed to stock up at the *épicerie*, provisions for her short stay, two or three days at the outside. Time to clear out her few possessions, and all of Luc's. The sale of the Kentish Town flat was her priority, but if she could find clues in the cellars to those missing hours, the cause of his debts . . . she might return.

She parked the Peugeot in the central square, opposite the bank. The *place* was decorated with climbing purple clematis, bougainvillaea and rows of vibrant oleanders just coming into bloom in generous-sized tubs, which demarcated the boundary between one café or bar and another. The tables were crammed with casually attired early-season tourists and second-home owners. High-octane chatter, cutlery rattling, lunch being consumed beneath spreading white parasols. This time last year, she and Luc might have been spotted among them, seated at their favourite table in the shade alongside the stone walls of the ruined abbey. Lunch in the square had been a ritual established between Luc and Jane on every summer visit, even before they had taken over the manor house five years earlier. Their first day back at Les Cigales, they were here, accompanying their meal with a bottle of chilled rosé from one of Château Ott's three domains. It was an extravagant choice, the most expensive Provençal pink wine on any restaurant menu, and a high-end competitor to the Cambon range. How she would love to be sitting with him now, enjoying a glass at his side, Walnut spread-eagled at their feet.

Jane switched off the engine but didn't budge, wondering yet again why Luc hadn't shared his financial difficulties with her. She would never have described him as talkative, but then again she wouldn't have judged him to be so guarded, so secretive. Underhand? If he had confided his problems, what might she have done? What could she have done? Well, for starters, they could have settled for a cheaper wine and lunched in the estate garden on baguettes and chunks of cheese. For Heaven's sake, Les Cigales produced plenty of its own very drinkable *cru classé*.

Did he ever turn it over in his mind, come close to requesting her help? When they had lain in bed, curled up against one another in the darkness, during the act of love-making, during those late-night or afternoon moments of intimacy, of tenderness, had there been one fleeting second when he had opened his mouth to divulge the truth, then decided against it? Was it pride or shame or guilt that had made him keep his problems so clandestine? Or was there another, more sinister, explanation? Since his death she had replayed ad infinitum their final few weeks together, here at Les Cigales, in Paris, trawling through the memories, raking over them for clues. Hadn't he attempted to speak to her, then drawn back? She reached out desperately for words, phrases, but it was like trying to pick fruit from the distant heights of a tree. They remained just beyond her grasp. It was useless. Did she recall snippets of conversation, or was hindsight dictating the text? She had rewound the tape so many times now that she had grown confused, lost between actual moments and imagined ones.

The gruelling fact was that it seemed now she would never know. There were so many questions. So few answers. So many sentiments unvoiced. If she could be in his company again, for one brief hour . . . But at least one piece of the puzzle had been resolved. A and P.

She stepped out of the car and crossed the square to the cash machine.

Fumbling for her French bank card, her thoughts still with Luc, she glanced back across the street and caught sight of a man, reddish-haired, standing by the door of a *tabac*, smoking, watching her. She felt sure she had seen his face recently. When he noted her observe him, he crossed the street, striding towards her.

He had been on the same British Airways flight earlier that morning. In the queue behind her at the Heathrow check-in counter. 'Off to Nice on holiday?' he'd asked, grinning and winking.

Now he drew close, calling, '*Bonjour!*' Excruciating accent. 'What a pleasant surprise. Fancy a drink?'

Jane shook her head. '*Merci, non*, no thanks.'

'Why not, if you're on your own?'

Jane swung on her heels and hurried to the car.

'No reason to be rude,' he called after her.

She revved up the engine and pulled out without checking her rear-view mirror. The driver of an open-top BMW speeding up behind her leaned his hand on the horn and left it there. He braked hard. Diners at the restaurants turned. A head in a white baseball cap leaned out of the BMW and swore abuse at Jane in Russian. She riposted with a sweet apology in his native tongue and was delighted by the surprise she caught written across his face.

She had failed to draw out money. She would have to find another branch, for Claude and Matty's sake. Who was that frightful man? For one ghastly second she had thought he might be a representative from a loan company. But after a few kilometres, she talked sense into herself. His presence was a coincidence. Malaz was teeming with tourists. She was too jumpy. Why do certain men presume that if you're a woman on your own you're waiting to get picked up?

She found another cash machine and a florist, and afterwards made her way back to the Malaz cemetery, to Luc's grave. Several small bouquets of marguerite daisies in jars decorated it. Bonne Maman jam jars. Jane lifted up each in turn to see whether they contained a message, but none did. She laid her red roses on the settling earth and sat with her husband for a while in the sunshine. The now-scruffy card that had been left there six months earlier was in her shoulder bag. She had carried it with her everywhere.

Notre cher Luc, nos vies sans toi ne seront plus jamais les mêmes. Nous t'aimerons toujours. A. P. x

Arnaud and Pierre. His boyhood companions from the estate. 'How foolish I was to have worried so.' She pulled the card from the side pocket in her bag, tore it into pieces and slipped the shreds beneath one of the jam jars.

Back at Les Cigales, she took refuge in their bedroom, its planked oak floor smooth beneath her bare feet. The spinning, creaking blades of the overhead fan cut through the walled-in heat. Jane loved this room. Their room. It was tranquil and spacious and full of light, with the two pairs of French windows that reached from ceiling to floor. In midsummer afternoon siestas on the bed or reading, stretched out alongside one another or curled, with each other's stomach as head cushions, it was a haven from the hot sun. Today it gave off a musty smell. Once upon a time, it had been Clarisse's room and occasionally a whiff of her musky perfume or an alien scent on padded coat-hangers reminded Jane of its legitimate proprietor. It felt airless now and a little suffocating.

She crossed to the French windows, barred and shuttered. One set gave onto a small balcony where she and Luc used to enjoy their early-morning coffee. After a fair amount of pushing and shoving, because the frames had expanded in the humidity, the doors and shutters swung open and the room exploded with sunlight, the white muslin curtains fluttering and lifting in the unexpected rush of air. The balcony, with its pretty filigree ironwork, looked out over the gardens and pool, and beyond to the hazy outline of damson-coloured mountains rising out of the silent acres of vineyards, olive groves, apricot and other soft-fruit orchards. It was a picture-postcard setting.

In winter, in the early mornings, from this balcony, she and Luc had listened to the calls of the hunters, led by Arnaud Lefèvre, setting out with their excited dogs to bag unfortunate victims for Matty to deliver stuffed and roasted to the dinner table. On warm, balmy summer evenings, Jane and Luc had drunk their nightcaps there, a late-night glass of wine, occasionally an aged malt for Luc, after house guests had retired to bed. They sat at peace in one another's company, entertained by choruses of frogs croaking in the valley beyond the now-dank pool. In this room they had slept, drugged by the fragrances of the season drifting in through the open windows: mimosa, jasmine, citrus blossom, cherry and apple; all had wafted in to weave their spell, their enchantment. And during all those episodes, all the daily moments of the life they were sharing together, Luc had been harbouring secrets, financial troubles.

For Luc, Les Cigales had always been home, ever since his family had purchased the run-down estate after their flight from Algeria. Even after he had relocated as a film student to Paris and later on to London with Jane, he never stopped describing the vineyard domain as his home. Had the money been required for here, for an investment that even Clarisse was not party to? Or had Clarisse lied?

Jane had come upstairs to unpack her bag, but when she opened the wardrobe, an eighteenth-century country walnut armoire left by Clarisse, the clutter within included piles of Luc's clothes as well as her own. In London, she had cleared out the cupboards and donated everything to a local hospice outlet in the high street. It had been a task for which she had steeled herself, but she had achieved it. Now she had to face it all over again.

Afterwards, the cellars, Luc's studio, with whatever clues to his past they might hold.

4

Luc's workspace was in the *caves* that ran under the manor house. It had been his sanctum. Jane had always respected his need for privacy and had rarely ventured down there. When they were kids hiding from adults they had sometimes secreted themselves in these cellars, armed with homemade biscuits and Matty's lemonade. Luc had loved the subterranean maze. After Isabelle's death, he had spent months converting it into a sprawling, secluded studio. During the renovations, Jane visited only once or twice to encourage his progress. And now here she was, turning the lock in the door that led off from the pantry, bringing a gust of fresh air into his sealed world. Her heart was beating fast. If there were secrets here, clues to his troubles, she had to know them, but now, so close, she almost felt afraid of what she might uncover.

As if to warn her away, she was instantly hit by the rank stench of rotting flesh. A trapped rat or bat, perhaps. Holding her nose, and bending her head so she didn't hit it on the low, sloping ceiling, she descended the steep, narrow stairway. The roughly hewn stone walls were meshed with cobwebs, resinous curtains that brushed against her face as she passed. The broad shaft of daylight that shone from beyond the open door above was lost to her as she reached the basement. One step further and she was in darkness. She tried to recall the geography of the space. Her memory told her this was the first of several low-ceilinged vaults. Murky caverns of limestone beneath which the foundations of the house had been laid. The original cellars had been employed as wine and provisions stores. Silent, sombre, deprived of all natural light.

Where had Luc installed the power switches?

She shuffled forwards into the humidity and gloom, trying not to inhale the stench that burned her nostrils or tread on whatever rodent remains were corroding the air. She was groping with both hands for a switch, cursing herself because there must have been one at the top of the stairs and she should have thought to bring a torch. It was so chilly down here, like a tomb. Luc's tomb.

A ghastly thought crossed her mind. Walnut. Might he have been trapped here for months, starving? Clarisse had sworn that Walnut was in the car when Luc departed, but what if the dog had jumped out at the last moment, hidden himself in his master's world and Luc, running late, had let him be, assured that Matty and Claude would care for him? But Luc had locked the cellar door before he'd left. Still . . .

She shivered, turning circles. It would be easier to return to the top of the stairs. Foolish to grope about in this dank and sombre setting. It was giving her the creeps. She had been bemused by Luc's delight as he and Arnaud, with a couple of local tradesmen, had converted the space to suit his needs, hammering and banging, installing Wi-Fi, telephone, television, computers . . . She had forgotten how easy Arnaud and Luc had been in one another's company.

Her fingers fumbled over plastic, a bank of switches. She flicked at the first. Lights.

Tiers of cupboards and shelves greeted her. Dials, electronic equipment. She stepped slowly, looking about her as she moved through into the second chamber, which resembled a bridge, a control centre in a sunless spacecraft. Beyond, further vaults were furnished as offices with benches. How transformed it was, piled high with documents, film clips, footage, research material. She ran her fingers along the spines of thick tomes on Arab history, France and the Algerian war. There were shelves of books in all shapes and thicknesses, a well-thumbed paperback edition of Rachel Carson's *Silent Spring*. Hefty volumes, textbooks, scripts. Draft one, draft two . . . DVD copies of his earlier, completed, films. Should all this material be donated to a media college, a university or to the CNC, the Centre National du Cinéma, in Paris? As far as Jane was aware, the latter had been the principal funding body for all Luc's films. Had they also been involved in his unfinished Algerian documentary? Robert had suggested difficulties with raising the finance. Why? Because of its subject matter, the OAS? Were the French television companies too nervous to commission and invest in a film that showed a period of France's modern history in a negative light? Dan would know. She wondered where he was now. Off on location somewhere, he'd said, moving forward with his professional life.

This body of work was certainly not for discarding. Collections of rare documents, his research findings, some of it must be. There were agricultural catalogues, nature encyclopaedias, two dictionaries on advanced winemaking for oenologists, a stack of home-movie tapes, dusty, rusted projectors, audio cassettes . . . Jane was blown away by the breadth and quantity of material. The private milieu of a brilliant and creative man. Some of it must go back decades. What future had he intended for it? Who owned the copyright to all this? Presumably Luc had.

Might Robert Piper have instructions?

The rooms, one unfolding into another, were meticulously tidy. Luc had been obsessive about creating order in the world that existed around him. Aside from the settling dust, cobwebs and encroaching insect life, the bugs that had crept in beyond his death and the reek of putrefying flesh, Jane might have been persuaded that her husband had merely gone away for a few days, as his intention had been before Christmas when he had locked up and driven north to be with her in London.

Hand still clutching her nose, inhaling as infrequently as possible, she turned a slow circle, wondering where on earth to start. Then she lowered herself into the leather swivel chair, Luc's chair, placing his bunch of keys on the desk's dusty surface. She had hoped his address book might be there, but it wasn't.

To the left of her was a metal filing cabinet, impressively solid. She leaned in to pull open one of the drawers, but found it locked. She tried the drawers above and below. They, too, were locked. She reached down to the drawers on either side of the desk where she was seated, hoping for keys. They were also secured, inaccessible.

She inspected the collection she had laid out on the desktop. So many Yales, Chubbs, even an old skeleton key, but nothing among them fitted. She lifted the bronze lid to an inkwell. She remembered it from his studio in Paris. It contained nothing but a few paper clips. Inside a small tin box there was a rubber and three pencils. She opened another and found ink cartridges. Nothing. She was trying to remember from the wreckage of the car, his body – her numbed journey to Paris, to the spot where the accident had occurred, east of the city, the identification block, the reclamation of his possessions – if any other keys, apart from these, had been with the cache handed over to her. The ignition key-card had been destroyed with the car, his Chubb lock keys for London she had upstairs. And this bunch: his house keys for Les Cigales, but no others. Logically – and Luc had been logical – the cabinet keys should have been among this collection or somewhere in the studio.

If not, they had to be upstairs in the house, unless he had left them with Claude and Matty. Or Clarisse.

Damn it!

Standing, she bullied at doors, worried at bolts, turned over piles of papers, careful not to disrupt the order. She lifted books, ran her fingers along shelves. Nothing but dust. Every cupboard and storage unit that was lockable had been secured and there were no keys to be found anywhere. For what reason had he been so guarded? Was there something so very serious to hide? She stood and turned a circle, then ran from one vault to the next and back again. Was she just not seeing the blasted keys? It was as though with every step she took to draw closer to her husband, to delve into his clandestine self, he skipped a foot away from her.

Don't do this, Luc. What are you hiding? It's me, Jane.

She was getting frantic. She had to unfasten these cupboards somehow, with a crowbar, if necessary. And even if she found nothing untoward, no explanation for the debts, the gaps in his last days, it was not feasible to leave all Luc's documents, close to thirty years' worth of professional material, to disintegrate. Some of the paperwork might be classified, borrowed or required for archival purposes. But who were his colleagues in the field? Who had been his research assistants? Should she ring Dan again? Aside from a warm but surprisingly noncommittal note tucked into a bereavement card, she had not heard from him. He had not returned her calls. He was away.

What was the meaning of this stupid cloak-and-dagger charade? Impossible that all these cupboards were filled with classified material for Luc's new film. OAS secrets. Was he being blackmailed?

Scenarios whirled through her head, each more outlandish than the last.

Who might have a key? Luc had rarely mentioned any specific researchers or editors. There was no one she could think of to telephone. He didn't even have a personal assistant. Dan had someone. Hadn't Jane, during her stunned days in Paris after Luc's death, spoken to her briefly on the phone? Had she worked for Luc and Dan? Annabelle? Was that her name? No, that wasn't it. Had the girl been employed by Luc's company as a film assistant? Even if she had been, she, like Dan, would have moved on elsewhere by now. There was no company left to employ anyone. It stunned Jane now to realize how little she had enquired about his work. She had accepted years earlier that Luc shut her out from some areas of his life and she had learned to respect that and not pry.

She returned to the bottom of the stairs, the entrance to the studios, and flicked all the switches. Six. Three controlled the lighting. The fourth triggered a ceiling fan. Another a primitive air-conditioning apparatus. And the last? TV, video machines? It didn't seem to have a function, certainly not a central locking system.

Short of hacking at the fixtures herself – she was almost ready to do it – she needed a locksmith, urgently. She stood by the stairs, looking into the refurbished stone *caves*, conscious once more of the appalling stench. Luc's world stared silently back at her. Whatever trouble he was in, whatever he was concealing, he was not going to hand it over without a struggle.

Clarisse expressed only mild surprise at the idea that Luc had kept all his files squirrelled away, while both Claude and Matty shook their heads in puzzlement. Neither knew anything of the whereabouts of another set of keys, but Claude could assist with the phone number of a local *serrurier*. However, before they called in the locksmith, Matty instructed Arnaud to have a go. No damage, insisted Jane. The Lefèvre son glowered at the locks. Unless he used a crowbar and wrenched the doors open, there was nothing he could do. It needed a professional. He offered to have a shot at finding the source of the appalling smell. Jane prayed it would not, after all, be the dog as Arnaud went down to rummage for the stinking carcass, armed with a torch, sack and gloves. Without success.

She thanked him for his trouble and for the kind sentiments he and his brother had expressed when Luc had died. He stared at her with his habitual discomfort and disappeared out of the kitchen door.

The following morning, the growl of a battered white Renault drawing to a halt outside the kitchen door delivered the locksmith, Monsieur Tassigny, a stocky middle-aged man, with a handlebar moustache and cropped hair the colour of flecked tobacco. He wore a black beret, a red kerchief knotted about his throat, a faded blue shirt, scuffed boots and bright yellow socks. His trousers were held up at his thickening waist by braces and a leather belt. He shook Jane's hand vigorously, almost crushing her fingers.

After rooting about in the cellars to assess the work involved, while Jane watched over him, fearing for Luc's material as he slapped, banged and harried at cupboards and cabinets, he announced in his strong Provençal accent, 'It'll cost you eleven hundred and fifty euros.'

Jane was speechless. He smiled, crow's feet cracking about his brown eyes. 'This is *hors taxes*,' he pointed out. A cash price, best offer. 'There's the *déplacement* to consider, the skilled work involved, a fair few hours of drilling . . . a variety of locks to accommodate. The one key would never open all. If Madame requires a written *devis*, another twenty per cent must be added to the total.'

Jane was reluctant to accept his estimate. It was an outrageous amount and her personal funds were running low. Until the London flat was sold, she needed to budget carefully – and even then money would be tight. On the other hand, she was loath to force the locks but determined to get beyond the hold-up.

Matty quietly suggested to Jane that she wait. 'Let Claude ring some other locksmiths from further afield. It's Madame Cambon's estate so he's trying to rook you.'

But Jane was bent on uncovering whatever lay behind those sealed cupboards. She wouldn't rest until she found answers. Her quest was becoming an obsession. The sooner the studio was opened, the sooner she could clear this up and get on with her life, although she couldn't picture what that life might look like. 'But will the other quotes be any kinder?'

Matty sighed. 'She's made herself so unpopular.'

Jane nodded her silent agreement to the locksmith, promising to go to the bank before the day was out. *Monsieur le serrurier*, satisfied, stroked his stupendous facial hair, trudged back up the stone stairs to the rear of his car and drew out a scuffed black leather bag, rather like a house-to-house doctor would have carried in the olden days. Next came a large drill and various other formidable tools, such as a jemmy and a crowbar. Matty went in search of an extension lead, shaking her head in disgust, muttering to the fellow in their Provençal tongue.

'No damage,' reiterated Jane. She left him to his work, drove to the bank and returned to wait in the narrow corridor beyond the pantry while the man underground drilled and hammered. His first bullseye was the discovery of a small decaying corpse in the second catacomb. The rodent had breathed its last behind a tall metal cabinet. Tassigny wrapped it in one of his greasy rags, climbed the stairs and thumped it down in the small pantry. Not Walnut, thank God. Matty was definitely not pleased: she swiped the hateful thing off her chopping space and disposed of it outside in one of the dustbins. 'When his lordship's done, Claude will put some poison down there for you.'

It took the locksmith the best part of the morning to get himself organized, jotting notes, measuring, calculating. He then departed for his lunch, to return two hours later. Eventually, as Matty was setting off to close Arnaud's chickens back into their coop after their day in the yard, all doors and drawers stood open. Jane counted out the euro notes, showed Monsieur Tassigny out and returned to the basement alone.

Luc's life was hanging open all around her. She stood still, afraid to take one step further, and then, heart hammering, hands shaking, she made a start.

The top desk drawer to the right contained cheque books – Barclays, Camden Town, and their French bank in the village; Luc had opened his accounts when Jane had opened hers. A navy-blue leather-bound King James Bible. Curious, with Luc's atheism. Jane opened it and read the dedication, '*Pour Luc, merci beaucoup*', in what might have been a child's handwriting. No signature. She riffled through the pages, found nothing else and replaced it. Opening the drawer to its full extent, she found a white cotton pillowcase. It was one of the big square ones from a set for their bed upstairs. Within it, a box, and within that a nickel-plated gun with walnut grip, 'Colt 1911' engraved on the barrel. Jane stared at it. What was Luc doing with this lethal *thing*? Cautiously she lifted out the weapon. She turned it over in her right hand. It was in good condition, only occasionally used by the look of it, but not modern. It was surprisingly heavy. Was it loaded? She had never handled a firearm before so she decided not to fiddle with it to find out. Claude or Arnaud would know. She examined its box, which was a little scruffy, one corner dented, as though it had travelled distances. A serial number was printed on a sticker on the lid: 285, 03 . . . The remaining numbers or letters had faded and were no longer legible.

She was amazed that Luc had known how to operate a gun, let alone owned one. As a boy, of course, he would have learned to hunt. Did he have a licence for this? It certainly didn't look like any hunting gun she'd ever seen. Was it a means of self-defence? Why would Luc be in possession of a second-hand gun? Had his life been threatened? Detective Inspector Roussel had raised that possibility in the days following the accident but it had been dismissed.

She placed it on the desk alongside its box and sat down staring at it. Her attention returned to the Bible. Both were items that, in their life together, she would never have guessed Luc would need. She picked up the cheque books and flipped through the stubs. Phone bill, subscription fees for professional magazines, membership fees, film unions, Air France, Visa, AmEx . . . Nothing to suggest massive expenditure, nothing to raise alarm.

Except the gun.

Had Luc been contemplating suicide? Was the Bible to give him courage? In those last weeks when she and Luc were not together, had he been facing such financial hell that he had planned to take his own life? If the car had not run off the road, might he have returned here after Christmas and put the gun to his head?

Such an image . . . It was too shocking. She had to get out of the cellars.

She locked up the workspace, leaving it as it was, and hurried back upstairs to make coffee. She needed a break. Fresh air. Her head was swimming. She had to think, clear her mind. She felt unable to continue her search. She would continue, but not immediately. She had to set her thoughts in order. A gun and a Bible. Might they have been props for a scene in his film? It seemed unlikely.

The coffee was percolating.

She slid her iPad from out of her handbag, left open on the breakfast-room table, and typed in the information she had for the gun: Colt 1911, she described the look of it and found 'post-war .45 ACP nickel finish'. The model had been manufactured in 1960. There was a list of such pistols, collectors' items, offered for sale on eBay and one or two other sites. Was it really so easy to acquire a gun? Where had Luc bought it? Had there been a sales ticket in the box, a receipt? She hadn't noticed one.

The presence of a gun among Luc's possessions was disquieting.

She put through a call to Robert in London. He was in a meeting but acted on her message before the coffee had even brewed.

'I was just going to ring you,' was his opening gambit. 'Good news. We received an asking-price offer on your property this morning.'

'That was quick.' A surge of panic rose within her. Her home was going. It was a reality.

'And, even better, they would like to complete before the sixteenth of July. I'll push hard to get it wrapped up sooner rather than later. The mortgage company will jump up and down with delight. How are you getting on?'

'Robert, did Luc leave instructions about what to do with his film stock and research materials?'

'Nothing in particular, no.'

'Was he in some kind of trouble?'

Pause.

'Was he?'

'Jane, we had this conversation over lunch. His debts were driving him to bankruptcy and they were beginning to encroach on other areas of his life.'

'What do you mean? Which other areas?'

He sounded exasperated. 'The problems were wearing him down, Jane, and may well have caused the accident. Lack of concentration, exhaustion . . .'

She was trying to recall the allusion Roussel had made to Luc killing himself. 'Aside from the money, was there anything else, any other difficulties?'

She heard him breathing. Was he deliberating, mulling over what to divulge?

'Robert, was there anything else? I have to know.'

'Nothing he shared with me, Jane. How's the weather there?'

'Might Luc have been contemplating suicide?'

She heard him laugh. Too loudly? 'Jane, please don't allow your loss to get the upper hand. I realize the situation you're in is not –'

'Did he ever say to you that suicide was the only way out of the hole he was in?'

'Of course not. He was far too resilient. Try to make some time for yourself, Jane, go to the beach. It's easy for me to say, I know.'

'Thank you for the news about the flat.' She hung up.

She tapped the home screen again on her iPad, accessed the calendar, clicked 15 July and typed: 'Move out of Lady Margaret.'

She had to remain calm.

She pulled out her pen. On a sheet of paper that bore the heading *Things to Do*, she wrote, hand shaking, 'Find a London removal firm.'

And then what? she asked herself. What's next?

Could Luc have contemplated suicide, *suicide*, in preference to confiding his troubles in his wife, his lifelong friend? She lowered herself into a chair and laid her head on her arms on the table. What was to become of her alone, without Luc, without her refuge in London?

Why did Luc have to die, and for what reason had he left her in such a predicament? A flash of anger took hold. She sat up, steadied herself, exhaling slowly, attempting to regain her composure, but the anger returned, boiling within her. 'Damn you, Luc, for deserting me, for leaving me in this hellish mess. And for not saying a bloody thing about it!'

She would send their furniture to auction, most of it, or donate it to charity shops. The little that remained could go into storage.

Always in times of difficulty it had been to Luc she'd turned. Now there was no one, besides her father. For the past six months Jane had been battling to stay afloat, struggling with each day as it came. Shock, numbness had, ironically, kept her semi-capable, forcing her to stay in the present in a robotic fashion. Now the future was looming, and it was shapeless and terrifying, accelerating towards her at a speed she couldn't handle.

5

Three centuries earlier, Les Cigales and its extensive holdings had been a Benedictine stronghold. Here, on land rising from the shores of the Mediterranean, the monks had tended their vineyards and produced exceptional vintages from shale soil. The gentle Mediterranean climate and the warm winds coming in off the water had nurtured grapes that were perfect for fermentation. In an era when the Midi was not renowned for its wines, the monks grew wealthy and reinvested, purchasing land to extend their acreage. On the outskirts of the abbey's vast grounds towards the western perimeters of what today was the domain of Les Cigales, stood a two-storey house. The limestone building, rather like a vast shoebox, had been constructed to offer a place of education for the offspring of the labouring families from the valleys and villages thereabouts. It was designated the Malaz Benedictine School House, although it was some distance by foot from Malaz.

Today, the old stone shoebox, School House, was the residence of Claude and Mathilde Lefèvre. It was one of the sturdiest of the domain's farmhouses, spacious and better equipped in that it possessed decent plumbing, electricity, a kitchen and a bathroom. Round the front of it was a porch that looked out in the direction of the sea, although you couldn't see the water from there, masked as it was by sloping fields of orchards and ripening vineyards.

It had been years since Jane had stepped inside their home. On the last occasion, they had occupied a more modest cottage further inland on the estate. At some point during Jane's teenage years, after she had become estranged from Les Cigales, Clarisse and Isabelle had offered the larger, outlying property to their caretakers because Matty had given birth to a third child. Long after Matty's twin sons were born, she and Claude had been blessed with their baby girl, Annie.

Jane drew her car to a halt beneath the shade of a spreading mulberry tree. Across the backyard, she caught sight of Arnaud. He was bent forwards on one knee, banging and nailing wood. It looked as though he was assembling a small shed or coop. All about him, domestic fowl rummaged and pecked, honking, hooting and crowing. His two hunting dogs, lean black-and-white pointers, were dozing in the sun. Arnaud, in blue shirt and overalls, glanced up from his chore, laid down his hammer and ambled over to greet Jane. He was a slow-minded but well-meaning fellow, built like a tractor, with shoulders broad as beams, well designed for carrying goats and sheep. A shy, solitary man, who seemed happiest herding livestock or alone with a rifle slung across his back, roaming the Alps, he lacked most social skills, had never married, had never left home.

Jane had often asked herself whether he might have suffered from being in the shadow of Pierre, his non-identical and more extrovert twin, who was living in the Camargue, caretaker of a splendid equestrian farm, and married to a pretty woman of gypsy heritage, who had given him two gorgeous children. It occurred to Jane now, as she stood watching Arnaud, his head bowed low, that she knew very little about the family's personal circumstances, even though they were the backbone of the estate. She wondered at the difficulties they must be facing with only one day's paid employment a week to sustain all three of them. Arnaud drove into the hills to lend a few of the livestock farmers a hand with the slaughtering of their pigs, but it was occasional employment, not regular. A little poaching in the months when hunting was not allowed would bring the family illicit game, but there could be little else to keep the kitchen stocked. Did Arnaud pay for the few grams of tobacco he needed by logging illegally in the nature reserve or the pine forests? Even the estate's kitchen garden was bare of produce to sell at one of the local markets. By all appearances, the Lefèvres were facing bleak days.

'What are you building there?' She smiled as he held out his hand to her. Huge calloused hands, broad and leathery as cabbage leaves. Their flesh was burgundy-hued. Hunter's hands. She had seen him skin whole beasts, wild boars, chamois, with the dexterity of one peeling an apple.

A winter's afternoon, in the early years of her marriage, flashed out of her memory. Arnaud had come striding triumphantly into the yard, with a limp red deer slung over his shoulders, shot hours earlier, the corpse still warm. *Une biche*, a female, with shocked eyes, frozen like glacial lakes. The hunter had tossed the lifeless creature across an outdoor table and drawn out a knife from one of the many pockets in his trekking pants. Pierre, Annie, Jane and Luc had stood huddled alongside one another, glued to the spot as Arnaud slit the ruminant apart. Inserting the curled tip of the glinting knife below its stomach, drawing it upwards in short pushing movements, he had unzipped the creature.

Jane watched, horrified yet mesmerized, as he opened the deer. She had glanced about her, expecting to see the same revulsion on the faces of her husband and companions, but no. In the season, hunting was an essential pastime to these people and the kill provided food for their tables. The deer's ruby blood had flowed, globules at first, then spluttering and gushing into a zinc bath positioned on the ground beneath it. To this day, Jane could recall the sound of that blood plopping, then pouring against the metal while Arnaud drew out the young deer's stomach, bulging with recently eaten grasses, and threw it victoriously onto the ground where it split and stank to high Heaven.

Jane had been mildly discomforted by his presence ever since. The hint of savagery. His relish in the mastery of killing.

'Beehives. Claude's gone to town,' he informed her now. Arnaud never offered his cheek or attempted the conventional three kisses. He was too ill at ease and withdrawn.

'Is your mother home?'

He nodded, awkwardly pointing the way to the back door. He had blood on his fingers.

Jane knocked gently on the semi-open door. Flies were circling above where she stood on the step. A bucket on the ground contained pinkish water and dishcloths; droplets of blood stained the step. Arnaud must have decapitated a chicken for their dinner.

'Who is it?'

As Jane had expected, Matty was in the kitchen. She was rolling pastry. A metal colander holding freshly shelled peas lay on the draining board. A bunch of purple asters stood tall in a Bonne Maman jam jar on the windowsill. Same design as the jars that adorned Luc's grave. So, it was Matty leaving the flowers, probably when she went to Mass. Matty and her two sons, who had loved Luc as one of their own. It reinforced her desire to do all that she could for this family.

'Matty, may I come in?'

'*Mon Dieu*, what a surprise.'

Matty wiped her hands on her wrapover floral apron. She

hurried to usher Jane in. The room was exceptionally dark with only two small windows to access the light. They exchanged kisses and the older woman steered Jane through the kitchen to the sitting room, which was cool and also dark. Here there were larger windows but the shutters were bolted closed. This would have been the main schoolroom. It was long and narrow, with only one fireplace, and must be hell to keep warm in winter. It was furnished in two parts, to create sitting and dining areas.

'What a surprise,' the housekeeper repeated.

'Forgive me for turning up unannounced.'

'Coffee or a cool drink?'

Jane shook her head. She had not considered the possibility that her visit might cause embarrassment or confusion. 'May I sit down?'

'Of course, make yourself at home.'

Jane lowered herself onto a sofa while Matty hovered close by her. She was suddenly lost for words, feeling herself an intruder.

'Claude's gone to town,' said Matty, as though to explain away her perplexity.

'Yes, Arnaud told me. I could have phoned you but, well, I thought it better to drop by. I probably should have called first. I came on impulse to discuss something.'

'We like to think of you as family, Jane. Please, don't apologize.'

'Clarisse mentioned to me that she is, well, she . . . The wine business is a bit slow and the estate's finances are not the brightest . . .'

Matty lowered herself into a chair. Dread tightened her features. 'Claude's gone to look for rented accommodation for us in town. As soon as he's found somewhere, we'll . . .'

'Oh, Matty, no. That won't be necessary and please don't

look so concerned. I'm not a bailiff, not here as Clarisse's representative to deliver further bad news.'

The older woman let out a tremulous sigh. 'I thought for a moment you'd been sent to ask us to leave the house. We're very aware, Jane, that the residence comes free with the foreman's job, as the law states, but one day a week, well, it doesn't justify giving us a home, does it? Our time is up, we can see that.' She lowered her head.

Jane feared tears.

As her eyes adjusted to the shadowy light, she noticed a series of photos in plain-cut wooden frames lined up on the stone mantelpiece. The subjects of the pictures were indistinct. Family snaps, a wedding, groups of smiling people huddled together. Memorable days in the lives of the Lefèvre clan. At none of which had Jane been present.

'We're under a lot of strain, what with no work. We'll have to sign up for *chomage* if we don't find another situation fast as we're still a bit young for our pensions.'

'Well, that's my reason for dropping by. There's no need to sign up for unemployment benefits because . . . Well, I've been thinking . . . As there is so much material in Luc's studio to log, pack up and donate, I've decided . . . well, that I need to stay on.'

'Marvellous! Oh, that's marvellous news.'

'It'll only be for a short while. I've spoken to Clarisse,' she lied, 'and we both agree that, no matter how dire the estate finances might be at present, we can't manage without you and Claude. The old farmlands will grind to a standstill without you both and that's the fact of the matter.' Jane attempted a laugh to substantiate her deception. It rang hollow in her ears. 'I hope you'll agree to return to work with us, starting as soon as would suit you both.'

Matty lifted her eyes. Her brow was drawn. She was pale

and weary. Her hands, still clasped in her lap, looked as though they had been boiled, like old rags, then boiled again. She wore no jewellery save for a thin silver wedding band around which the flesh had expanded.

'Claude'll be pleased to hear you're staying. We've both been hoping, praying. I mean, who's left to run the place, make the decisions?' There was a long pause. 'It's a complicated situation, without Luc to keep things on an even keel . . . He was so very generous to us all.'

'He valued you highly, both of you and Arnaud too. You will say yes, won't you, Matty?'

'I haven't been sleeping nights, tossing and turning, worrying about what lies ahead for our family. Who could have foreseen this turn of events, eh? I felt sure that Clarisse wanted us gone . . .'

'Why on earth would she want you gone?'

'Madame Cambon's not the easiest. We feared she might have grown resentful, full of regrets now that she's lost her only boy.'

'Resentful? I don't understand.'

Matty, whose attention had been focused on a carved wooden coffee-table where several more framed photographs were displayed, lifted her gaze back to Jane. Her eyes, oval as almonds, registered surprise. She looked hard at Jane, as though scouring her thoughts.

'Full of regrets about what, Matty?'

Matty continued to stare at the younger woman and then a penny seemed to drop. 'Oh, my Lord!'

'What, Matty?'

'I've – I've left the oven on. Pastry's burning. Excuse me.' She scrambled to her feet and heaved her bulky frame to the kitchen, abandoning Jane.

Jane was at a loss. She stood up, remaining where she was.

Her mind was replaying the conversation. Had she missed something? She bent to the coffee-table and picked up one of the photographs. Three youngsters in swimming costumes on the beach. Arnaud and Pierre, two strapping teenage boys, and their tiny sister, Annie. She replaced the photo mechanically, still trying to unravel the exchange that had just taken place. She went into the kitchen and found Matty leaning over the sink, crying.

'Matty! Have I upset you? I'm so sorry if I have.'

'No, no, of course not. I'm a foolish old thing, don't pay no attention to me.'

Jane moved up behind the bulky woman, who smelt of onions, and hesitantly wrapped her arms about Matty's heaving shoulders, pressing her head hard into the broad back. 'You will stay, won't you, Matty?'

Matty nodded, and her entire body juddered like a mini earthquake. 'Course we will. We haven't got anywhere else to go.'

'You don't need anywhere else. This is your home.'

'If Master Luc were here . . .'

'It's almost unbearable, isn't it, Matty? The way we all miss Luc,' whispered Jane, head still buried in ample flesh clothed in damp cotton. 'There are days when I think I can't go on without him. I just can't keep going. And it's *for ever*, Matty. Luc's never coming back. That's what I can't come to terms with. I keep waiting for him, expecting him, listening for his step, his voice, his laughter. I don't want to take my next breath without him and I pray so hard that the air won't come, but it always does and I'm still here and I don't know what to do with myself. Thank you for staying, *merci beaucoup*.'

Jane slid out of the door and ran fast to her car. Tears were blinding her. A guinea fowl in her path caused her to stumble. She sat in the sticky driver's seat under the mulberry tree with the trunk that had divided and split and crept along the ground. They were still growing, those new trunks, seeking out new directions, sinking down new root systems, surviving.

Why would Clarisse want to discharge the Lefèvre family? She surely couldn't harbour doubts about their qualities as employees? About employing them in the first place? And how did she intend to manage without them? The place needed physical strength and direction.

What if Jane could make a temporary life here, search for her next step from this territory she knew so well? Was that what Luc had wanted? Was Clarisse telling her a truth that Luc had never expressed? Or was his mother trying to trick her, to manipulate her? Jane's head was spinning with so many convolutions, she thought she might go mad.

She pressed her hands against her face and screamed, sobbing hard. She threw the car into gear and reversed at speed, sending up whorls of small stones. Two geese honked and flapped.

Arnaud, from a distance, watched her retreat.

6

An empty coach was parked outside the wine-pressing block. Its driver, in sunglasses, was leaning against the bodywork, smoking, idling. Clarisse was in her office combing her hair, fixing her make-up. She was dressed in an old black-and-white Chanel suit. Jane was drawn up short by the pearl necklace she was wearing. It was the one her mother-in-law had worn on the day they had first met. She suddenly pictured her father, charming, young and virile, arriving here, pitching for employment, and all that had ensued . . .

'Clarisse, may I have a word with you, please?'

'Can't you see I'm busy? There are clients waiting, potential buyers. Japanese tourists on a wine-tasting excursion. They have money to spend.'

'It's about Claude and Matty.'

'Oh, God, what about them?'

Jane could hear laughter through the open doors, and the incomprehensible drift of Japanese being spoken. Corks were being drawn. The clinking of glasses. Clarisse was hovering impatiently by the open door, keen to be on the move. 'Well, what is it?'

Jane spoke quickly: 'I have reinstated them, put them back on full salary. God knows it's a pittance, Clarisse, you cannot leave th–'

'How dare you? They have a large, comfortable house, all bills paid, and you had no bloody right to go against my decision.'

'For as long as I'm here, I'll need their help. You owe them for their loyalty. For Heaven's sake, Clarisse, have you no heart? They have nowhere to go, no income.'

'I owe them NOTHING!'

'Clarisse, they're here for you.'

'Mind your own damn business. You said you were leaving, so go! I'm the one who's left with nothing. I have nobody. With Luc gone, I have no one.'

'They have given their lives to you, to Isabelle and this estate.'

'Spare me the heartache.'

'Fine. Then I'll pay their wages. For as long as I can. The funds will come out of my earnings and the proceeds of the sale of the London flat, unless you agree to pay them from the estate.'

Clarisse sighed loudly. A voice from the tasting room called to her, 'Madame Cambon?'

'Claude and I can clear up the vegetable garden and he can sell the produce at market, bring in a little extra cash for you all.'

Clarisse scoffed at such a suggestion. 'Does that mean you're staying on?'

'There's far more in the cellars to clear out than I'd . . . It's going to take me a while.'

Someone called again for Madame Cambon. In haste, or for whatever reason, she agreed grudgingly that the estate would, for the foreseeable future, meet the cost of the couple's salary. 'And from now on, you keep out of my affairs. You're just like my headstrong son. You don't know what you're meddling in.'

Armed with a bottle of mineral water, her iPad and a torch, Jane closed the pantry door and turned the key, locking herself in on the cellar side to prevent anyone – who might she be wary of? – disturbing her. Descending gingerly into the bowels of the house, she was already rattled by what she might find, intimidated by the prospect of further unsettling disclosures about Luc. Luc, who was revealing himself to have been quite another man from the one she had loved and married.

The rancid odour had gone and Matty had washed and disinfected the floors. Another, more chemical, smell had superseded the previous one. Claude had scattered lurid pink poison pellets on saucers and spread them here and there to keep any further trespassing creatures at bay. Mousetraps were set under filing cabinets. And there was another scent, a lingering, sweet yet fetid odour of old wine or decaying apples, soaked into the walls over centuries.

She began by locking the drawer that held the Colt and the Bible, promising herself that, for this day's search at least, she would not root in there again. She was here to list professional data. Nothing else. Then she would contact a film institute, or Dan perhaps. He must be back by now from his location work on the feature film. *Call Dan*, she scribbled, in a previously unused exercise book she had found down here.

Many of the cupboards were stacked high with paperwork. Each of Luc's films – twelve in total, excluding his last unfinished one – had been allocated large, labelled boxes. Each box contained the preparatory work: shooting scripts, budgets, stills, research material, interviews. The documentation was meticulous, the process fascinating to follow. She had never fully appreciated all that was involved in the construction of a film. She glanced to and fro, wondering where he'd stored the boxes for his latest project. Where were the scripts? The transcribed interviews he and Dan had been working on in Marseille?

She came across an outmoded 8mm film projector. Was

there a screen? Film stock? Yes, she had noticed 8mm film reels the first time she'd been down here. She spun about, trying to recall where she had spied them. There was such a wealth of data and it was getting dustier and wrapped in cobwebs. In no other area of his life was Luc a hoarder but here nothing appeared to have been thrown out. Where were the films? She was making notes on her iPad and back-up notes in the exercise book, using a black-ink ballpoint biro that had belonged to Luc and seemed polished by his grip. For such booty, the basic utensils seemed more appropriate, easier to get an overview, a perspective. Room one, room two and so forth.

She turned her attention to a stack of circular canisters containing spools of celluloid film. They stood in a corner like giant silver coins. She lifted the top one off the pile. The label, in Luc's black-ink handwriting, read: '*Mum and Aunt Isa. Cannes 1966.*'

It would have been filmed three or four years after their flight from Algeria. Jane thought it would be intriguing to watch a film of Luc's mother shot during a happier, more carefree era. She discovered that the spool was Super 8mm stock and was not compatible with the 8mm camera, or the camera was jammed, broken, dusty. Who knew? She couldn't marry them, couldn't play the film. In any case, it probably needed a projector and a projection screen. A pity. It would have been fascinating to see how Clarisse had looked and behaved back then. A swift forage through the canister pile suggested that these were all personal films. She logged them under *To Keep*, promising herself she'd find a way to watch them later.

She eased herself onto a stool to reach into a cupboard drilled high into the wall. As she did so, she was asking herself whether Luc had been the cameraman on all these films. If so, his film-making instincts had been seeded at a very early age. She drew open the cupboard. It was stuffed to bursting with disintegrating green and orange paper wallets. Each read 'Kodak' or 'Fuji'. Many of the photographs within them were almost sepia with age, brown and curling. She rummaged and then lifted out the first few. Isabelle and Clarisse in summer dresses with full skirts, Luc between them, so young he could barely stand on his chubby legs. Palm trees, hot clear sky. Behind them a shiny black Citroën. Jane flipped the photo over: 'Algeria 1960'. Within the folder there were several more postcard-size shots of the two women on the same occasion. No others with Luc, but all with the Citroën DS. They seemed to be showing off their new car. Clarisse couldn't have been more than mid-twenties back then in Algeria. Nothing in the images suggested the ravages of war, although in 1960 the war had been under way for six years. Jane remembered the car. Clarisse had kept it locked in one of the old stables. Luc and she had sat in it once as kids, Luc at the steering-wheel, pretending to drive, the car spotless, all burgundy leather and polished.

'It's a Safari Wagon. We escaped from Algeria in it,' he'd told her.

Jane wondered whether the car remained on the estate or whether it had been sold. She set the photos aside and reached into the cupboard for another handful. That caused a miniature avalanche of letters, photos and postcards to pour out from the two shelves, spilling over her and onto the stone floor. They looked as though they hadn't been opened or glanced at for years. Luc's past tumbling out of the walls around her. Jane crouched on her haunches and began to shuffle through them.

A face stared up at her, a black-and-white, head-and-shoulders photograph of a lean unsmiling man. He appeared to be in khakis. Dark hair, moustache, tanned skin, thirty or thirty-five, perhaps. She turned the image over and read: 'Adrien 1960'.

He must be Luc's father. Jane studied it carefully, trying to find Luc in him. 'Adrien' was certainly handsome but, in this photo at least, he was very serious, lacking warmth. She laid the picture aside. At the centre of the stack was a more recent offering. A single photograph. It stood out because it was larger than most of the others, A4 size. Its image was of the rear of a slender woman walking outdoors, wearing a black coat, collar turned up against the weather, a black woollen hat pulled low over her head. No hair visible. The image was chopped at the waist. The female was carrying a small child, a boy, two years old perhaps, whose chubby face over her shoulder was looking in the direction of the lens. Dribbling and frowning, the infant's pouting gaze was fixed on the photographer. It was a winter scene. Stark. The cameraman would have been walking directly behind the mother and child. Jane scrutinized the image. Where had it been taken? The location was a town or city. Slick-wet wide street, zebra crossing ahead. In the direction the woman and child were headed, on the right side of the lane, there was a *boulangerie* and a series of cafés and restaurants. Further along, Jane saw an M for Métro. It was possibly somewhere in the suburbs of Paris. A northern metropolis, almost certainly. It couldn't be Luc with Clarisse because they were still living in Algeria when he was the same age as this small boy. Had the French built a Métro system in Algiers? Jane swung the picture onto its back and read in bold script in French: *Missing you when you're away, Luc. We love you. A . . . x*

She stared at the words, unable to take them in. She needed to sit down. Her legs were giving beneath her.

Missing you when you're away, Luc. We love you. A . . . x

A?

'A' as one half of A and P? A and P whose lives had been irrevocably changed by Luc's death? No, A and P were Matty's boys.

The photograph was undated.

Jane settled the snapshot on Luc's desk. Sickness swirled in her gut. Had Luc been the cameraman? Who was this A who had signed the photograph? Was Jane facing the possibility of a mistress?

7

She wasn't wearing her watch, had forgotten her phone and there was no clock in the windowless environment with no natural light, so it was impossible to gauge how much time had passed. How long had she been staring in disbelief at the stub from the Crédit Agricole chequebook? She pushed it aside finally, still in a state of shock. Deep-rooted misgivings were taking hold as one more piece of a disturbing jigsaw fell into place.

Were they all building to the same picture? Or was she jumping ahead?

A thousand euros written in ink on a cheque stub, an account Jane had not previously been aware of, paid '*pour Annabelle*'. Luc's writing.

Was the A in the photograph 'Annabelle'? Was the boy her son? Was the chubby boy Luc's son? A second family?

She peered hard at the child. Did he resemble Luc? She pulled over the pictures from Algeria, shuffled for the only one of Luc aged two. Was there a similarity between the two small boys? A little bit, yes. Or was she superimposing her emotions on the image? She couldn't say. Her mind was playing tricks. Please let Annabelle be a staff member on Luc's payroll, not connected to the photo of mother and child. But if that were the case, why would the cheque to Annabelle have been paid from a private account? An account whose existence Luc had kept from Jane.

She stood up shakily. A landslide of photographs surfed over her shoes. She kicked lightly with her toe, pushing them to and fro. A quick glance without bending down offered nothing else of that mother and child. In any case, she had lost the will to continue. She felt dizzy, weak. There was an ache, a pulsing, in her chest that was threatening to choke her.

Had Luc been leading a double life that included a second family? A duplicitous existence that had led him into debt and possibly cost him his life? How many payments had he made to Annabelle?

Was Clarisse aware of the existence of another woman? Her mother-in-law had seemed genuinely surprised when Jane had disclosed details of Luc's financial troubles. So, probably not.

Was anyone else aware of the hidden family, if that was what this evidence suggested? Robert Piper had denied any knowledge of anything untoward. But had he been too quick to do so? What about Dan? Why hadn't he kept in touch? Or was she misinterpreting everything, allowing her reasoning to lose control? Were grief and loneliness driving her round the bend?

She needed to get out of the cellars before her head exploded. She left everything more or less as it was, took her iPad and beat a retreat, but halfway up the narrow wooden stairs the doubts pushed her into reverse, drawing her back to the photographs, the evidence of undisclosed moments in Luc's life. Had Luc sired that woman's child?

The idea caused a tsunami within her. She couldn't face the possibility that another woman had delivered to Luc the child she and he had so passionately longed for, whom she had failed to produce. She took hold of the photo again, staring hard at it, searching for a clue, a fashion accessory, a hoarding, anything to date it. To fix a point where she might begin.

There had to be another explanation. One that was not about to demolish the twenty years of marriage she and Luc had shared, all that she had held as true. But if this was the reality, the *real reality*, the sky above her would split wide open, she would be blasted into a thousand pieces and the fragments would never come together again. She was trembling, grasping for a line, a logical thought. Jealousy and insecurity were seeding themselves.

She would return to London on the first available flight, hang the expense, organize the removal of her belongings from the flat, put into storage everything she wanted to keep, vacate the premises immediately, hand the keys to Robert Piper and draw a final line under that period of her life. Then she would return here. Clarisse would surely make no objection. Until then she would steer clear of this hateful studio. Once the sale of the London flat had been completed, once her horizon was uncluttered, she would face these revelations head on. It was more than she was capable of at this juncture. Practicality and logical thinking had to be her path forward. One step at a time.

8

There was no one Jane could turn to, no one to confide in. No friend she felt able to share her black doubts with. If he were in his right mind, what would her father have said to all this? But all conversation and intimacy, their father-daughter bond, had long been denied to her. In any case, confiding in her father, even if he had been in full health, was a nonsensical idea. Had she not disturbed him in Clarisse's embrace? Her father, she had learned before her mother's death, had enjoyed a string of mistresses. Clarisse had not been the only one. She had not been singled out as special. Yet now, it seemed, he remembered only Vivienne. No other.

If she was to return to France for any length of time, what was to become of him? Could he be moved from the home? When Jane met with the director of the nursing home, to inform him of her extended absence, he counselled against Clarisse's suggestion of bringing him to Les Cigales. 'We wouldn't recommend it. Unfamiliar surroundings will disorientate him further.'

'He knew the estate well when he was younger,' Jane argued. 'I thought it would be nice for him to be near me, to have him close.'

'Are you intending to move to France permanently?'

She lifted her hands out of her lap and let them drop again. She was exhausted, hadn't been sleeping. She had no answers, only a Ferris wheel of questions turning in her head.

'Whether he is moved or stays here, he needs trained care and that will become more critical as his illness progresses.

Any move will cause disorientation, which could trigger periods of wandering, sleeplessness, physical falls, and changes in his eating habits. Are you planning to be away long?'

Jane sat in the director's antiseptic office listening to voices along the corridor, a clock ticking on the wall above the closed door behind her. Time passing. She looked out of the window. In the grounds of Garden Park, a man on a four-wheel tractor was mowing the garden while a few elderly patients were sitting huddled together on benches on the sidelines, watching him and clapping, as though a cricket match were in play. One old codger in a woolly hat darted forward onto the lawn, gathered up handfuls of the mown grass and began throwing them like snowballs.

'I have no idea,' she admitted eventually. 'My husband was killed in a road accident. I have matters abroad to . . . contend with.'

Dr Eath offered his condolences. He had heard of it from several members of his staff. If there was anything he could do . . . Would she like a cup of tea?

Jane lowered her head. How could she divulge even to this man of medicine, of supposed healing powers, the depth of the uncertainties she was facing? The abyss. The distress. The grief.

'If I may offer a word of advice, Mrs Cambon? Relocating a patient with dementia, Alzheimer's in your father's case, involves challenges. There are risks. My observation of the situation has always shown that you are a caring daughter. Don't feel guilty about Peter. He's in good hands here, and can't share your burden or your bereavement. He's no longer able to respond to the emotions that are hurting you now. Unless you're unhappy with the care we're offering him – and that is quite another matter – my advice is that you should do what you need to do and we will take care of your father. Leave us all contact details, please, and keep in touch with us regularly, as we will with you, but please put yourself first, Mrs Cambon.'

'I don't want him to think I've abandoned him.'

'He won't. You know yourself that dates, periods of time elude him. If he grows anxious and feels isolated or abandoned, I'll be in touch with you immediately. Does that offer you some peace of mind?'

Peace of mind . . .

Jane nodded. She had been given the physician's blessing. Even so . . .

'If you would like me to suggest someone for *you* to talk to, please don't hesitate to give me a ring. If I may venture into territory that is not directly mine, you need to heal yourself now, Mrs Cambon. Please take care of your health. Look to the future.'

What future remained for her? England was the country she had so stubbornly clung to during her married life and now her stake in it was being sold from under her feet. She perched on a sealed crate in her living room, which was cluttered with boxes, books and jettisoned coat-hangers, and punched out the number for Cherry Tree Lodge.

'Hello, Clarisse?'

'Why would I object to your return? I expect you back, I insist you return. You owe me,' Clarisse reiterated crisply. As Jane had been so cavalier as to reinstate the Lefèvres, she went on, it was her duty to be on the domain to set them to work, to keep them occupied, earning their living. 'I expect you to supervise. And Luc would have expected no less.'

It had been only the previous autumn that Clarisse had accused Jane of lacking all management skills, but Jane did not remind her of this. 'Shall I suggest to Claude that we begin with the kitchen garden?'

'And the rest. The estate needs regular injections of cash. That means harvests. When can I expect you?'

Less than forty-eight hours later, Jane watched the small removal van chug away and disappear beyond the bend in the junction. She walked the empty rooms, her echoing footsteps on bare wooden floors, and then she walked them again, recalling conversations, precious moments, lovemaking, laughter, arguments, sometimes foolish ones, arrivals home, departures. Where had he been going on all those occasions when she had waved him *au revoir* from here? Was it credible that the man who had so vitalized her years in this home had been double-dealing her? No. No. Grief and financial instability had caused her to overreact. She was sure of it. How could he, Luc, who was so full of kindness and integrity, betray everything she believed had belonged exclusively to him and her? To Luc and Jane.

He hadn't.

The previous afternoon she had found a note, shoved at the back of the drawer of her habitually cluttered bedside table. He must have written it and hidden it there, leaving it for her to find during one of his absences – and somehow it had got pushed, unopened, behind nail varnishes, scissors, tissues and never seen the light of day till now as she packed up the flat. Sealed in an envelope, crumpled and squashed, a plain white card: *Tender are the nights by your side. Whatever happens, I will always love you. Lucx*

In the earlier days of their marriage they had frequently stashed notes for one another in luggage or books or wallets. It had become a treasure hunt they played to sweeten their separations. That note, discovered only now, was far more recent: he had used one of the hand-printed Mode de Paris cards from Quill stationery she had bought for his birthday in August the year before.

She walked to the front door, opened it, hauled outside the belongings that hadn't been loaded into the van for storage, and pulled it shut. For the very last time.

Typically it was raining, a late-spring steady downpour, as she closed and Chubb-locked the door. Struggling with an umbrella, surrounded by bags and cases, she hovered on the step at the foot of her empty home, with its high ceilings, naked light bulbs, the ghostly marks on the walls where paintings and mirrors had hung since she and Luc had taken possession. They had spent a weekend climbing over boxes, listening to the Stones on the stereo, jiving on the unmade bed, eating fish and chips out of paper, while happily bickering over the where-shall-we-hang-this decisions.

This was yet another farewell hurdle to be faced. Another moment of 'moving on'. Wheeling her suitcases, struggling with the brolly hooked now under her chin, she proceeded down the leafy street she had trodden so frequently, in all seasons, with and without Luc, its plane trees growing alongside the kerb, its snug corner shop, which reeked of washing powder, newsprint and spices, with its overpriced cartons of milk. Mr Patel, who had occasionally agreed to look after her door keys when she was out and someone needed access to the flat, was outside, gathering up a display of brushes he had hung out earlier before the rain had started. She nodded a good morning to him and strode on past without a further glance. 'Off on holiday, Mrs Cambon?' he called after her. 'Fleeing our British weather? Very wise.' Round the corner, down towards the high street, she waited for a taxi but none passed, so eventually she climbed aboard a C2 bus heading for Oxford Circus. From there she went to Piccadilly, to

Robert Piper's offices, where she deposited three sets of keys with his receptionist.

'Robert has my number if he needs me,' she reassured the young woman.

To save her dwindling funds, she travelled with her two suitcases on the Piccadilly line to Heathrow. From there, a British Airways flight back to Nice.

Claude collected her at the airport. She would buy herself an old run-around at some point, she promised him, if she stayed for any length of time. She was determined to project an optimistic frame of mind, a foreseeable, tangible future.

'I thought we might attack the kitchen garden.' She laughed. 'It's late in the season for planting, I know, but once the beds have been cleared and dug, you and I could decide together what is still growable. It's a hell of a jungle, but we can't leave it idle.'

'I made a start during your absence. Yes, it's late for planting so I thought it'd be best not to waste these precious days. The weather's been kind. I've put in some tomatoes, about a hundred plants of various varieties, and a couple of rows of courgettes and aubergines. It's too late for strawberries. When you've got a moment, perhaps you'll take a look.'

'Of course. I'll reimburse you for the plants. What condition are the greenhouses in now?'

'More broken windows than glass.'

Isabelle had ordered the construction of a quartet of greenhouses, originally for the reproduction of the wine stocks, but then she had tracked down a family-run nursery in the Var, near the town of Gaillane, and it had proved more cost effective and less time-consuming to buy the grape seedlings. So from that day onwards, the greenhouses had been given over to winter tomatoes, strawberries, and a few half-hearted attempts at more exotic fruits until they fell into total neglect. According to Claude, rats had set up home there.

'Shall we take a look and calculate the cost of repairing them?'

'Not cheap, I'd say. If you order the cut panes, I can glaze them in. It'll cost a fair bit in time, but I can do it.'

'It would provide food for the winter, so perhaps worth a try.'

'Matty and I were thinking, if the idea appeals to you, that I could take you on a tour of the whole estate. Not all at once, of course. We can do it a few hectares at a time. You know the layout and have been more or less everywhere, but I don't suppose you've looked at it from the perspective of wine production. What do you say?'

She hadn't seen Claude so chirpy in years and his mood rubbed off on her.

'I tell you what,' she replied, with a smile, 'why don't I allocate my mornings to emptying out Luc's cellars and doing my translation work, and if the afternoons suit you, we could dedicate them to my learning the business of wine-making. Is that a good plan?'

'And not forgetting the olive groves.' He winked.

'Not forgetting the olive groves.'

She hadn't visited the olive groves since she and Luc had played there as kids and, on one or two occasions, helped with the harvests. Carefree memories. She looked forward to spending time among those trees again, to washing herself in joy remembered. As she waved her thanks to Claude from the door of the big house, she felt a rush of excitement. She was allowing herself to believe that what lay below in the cellars was just a bad dream, that reality was a happier story.

9

It was the beginning of June. The summer solstice was but slender weeks away. The sun rose early, bursting into the bedroom, shedding a golden light that was warm and clear. Blossom abounded, green shoots flanked the pathways, and Jane felt drawn into the season's radiance. It was hard not to feel buoyant. There was a mood of optimism about the flower-filled grounds, of renewed activity, regeneration. She threw open all the windows of the manor house and slept with the shutters latched back, allowing the blessed mornings to creep into her room. It was a visual alarm call to accompany the cockerel's and the distant bray of donkeys. Within a matter of days she was sleeping better than she had in weeks. Hard work and long hours in the fresh air were the remedies.

She asked Claude if he could do anything with the stagnant emerald-green swimming-pool or if it required emptying, scrubbing and refilling: an expense beyond any of their budgets.

'The broken tiles and the leak will have to wait, but I can get it scrubbed up for you,' he promised. 'Give me a few days and I'll have it looking spick and span.'

On her first morning back, when she went down to the empty kitchen, she found a pot of coffee on the boil, three fresh eggs in a small *faience* dish and one of Matty's homemade loaves awaiting her. A discreet expression of the caretakers' gratitude.

Over coffee, Jane set herself some resolutions. She would

begin each day with a swim. There would be exercise, walks along the beach. No moping. No grieving the loss of her London home. The more profound loss of Luc was more than sufficient. She and Clarisse must find a *modus vivendi*, even if it was simply to live their lives separately on the same estate. As Luc had pointed out last year, Clarisse was not far off her eightieth birthday and Les Cigales was a challenging responsibility. Jane must show her kindness, whatever inner turbulence it cost her.

While Claude gave an hour or two of his time pouring ghastly chemicals into the pool and lifting from it, day by day, the deepening layers of algae and rotting leaves, Jane forced herself to return to the cellars. She sat at Luc's desk and gathered up the photograph she had found the last time she had been down there. While she had been in London packing up their home, she had determined to destroy it, rip it to shreds. She had persuaded herself that it was nothing. But now that she was looking A's boy directly in the face, her resolve wavered. The doubts came flooding back. She had allowed herself to be lulled into a state of denial, but the face was real. This mother and child existed. And she had no idea who they were or what role they had played in Luc's life.

She plucked a red rose from the garden and took it to Luc's grave. There were always flowers standing upright in jars on his earthy dwelling. Today there were gentians and aromatic lavender. She slipped the rose among them and sat at his side on the freshly grown grass, the sun on her face, watching bees and other pollinators feeding off the hedges and plants, listening to the occasional aircraft overhead dipping its way to the coast. She brushed her fingers against an invisible shadow where she imagined his arm might be.

'Tender are the nights by your side.' They were, Luc. No

words can describe how much I miss the warmth of you . . . but I have to move on. Not from you, of course not, but it's essential I find a way forward without you. I need your strength. I'm earning a little money, translating books and enjoying the work. The sale on Lady Margaret will soon be completed so I'll be handling the debts. I'll clear out your workspace, be sure your material ends up where it needs to, but that face, Luc, that boy with his mother. If there was someone else . . . another family . . . don't let me find it. Please, Luc, don't take everything from me.

One of Jane's favourite spots in the past had always been the little-frequented beach known as the Cove of Illusions. It lay almost directly south of the property beyond the winding coast road that led from St Tropez to Cannes. By car, it was barely ten minutes from the manor but Jane preferred to cycle. Out of the main gates, along the A road, then second left, heading seawards, hair flying behind her, through lanes flanked by vineyards and olive groves where occasionally she spotted families of goats chewing freshly blooming wild flowers. Walnut used to delight in haranguing those poor goats.

It had been Luc who had first taken her to these secluded shores when she was a girl. Since then, the cove had become her place of escape, a solace and refuge, a gently sloping bank of shingle surrounded by colossal arms of blood-red boulders. Here, birds were her only companions. Flotsam and garlands of seaweed interspersed with discarded plastic bottles were the sole signs of man's occupancy on earth and, occasionally, cinders from a late-night beach party. The water was clear and clean – even during the months of heavy tourism – ideal for paddling and lazy swimming. She left the bike on the grass bank at the edge of the coastal path and descended the dishevelled weedy track. Slender, finger-sized lizards fled at her footfall. She bent to a pair of Swallowtails fluttering about a willowy milk parsley, with its tight droplet heads. Swallowtails had been the subject of Luc's debut film. The first stone of his success as a film-maker. She lifted a finger to the plant's umbel, watching them playing, flirting. These creamy-based beauties with their fine black stripes she could identify. Years earlier she and Luc had come across a fat green caterpillar with two orange horns secreted in a fennel plant in the kitchen garden. 'They never stop eating.' He'd laughed. 'Chomp away for months until they burst out as glorious Swallowtail butterflies and then they only live a few weeks.'

She had been saddened by the brevity of their lives. But Luc had assured her that they spent their entire adult existence making love and sipping nectar. 'From the first hour beyond their caterpillar state, as soon as their wings are strong, they seek out their mate. Hundreds of them together. I'll take you and show you. It's a rare and magnificent sight to see.'

It was still early. The light had a pearly quality, pale rose in colour. She slid on down to the shore, let fall her shorts and T-shirt, kicked off her sandals and stepped carefully across the stones. The slap of the waves licking the patches of damp sand, then the drag and pull of the tumbling pebbles were inviting. A cleansing sound. A baptism. Gentle and appeasing. It was early in the season and the water had not yet warmed up. It nipped at her toes, her feet, her calves before she plunged fully into it and began to breast-stroke fast, out beyond the limits of the bay into deeper water. Gulls overhead squawked and circled. A fishing boat was sketched against the horizon, a marriage of blues. She heard a dog barking and turned on her back, kicking to stay afloat, peering to see who was there: an early-morning walker out with his companion, a graceful English Setter. A pang of longing for Walnut overcame her – the desire to pat his warm head, stroke his astrakhan ears. It leached the fragile cord of joy out of her. Tears sprang forth and rolled down her face. She was alone at sea. There was no one.

She was heaving mouthfuls of salt water. She was a strong swimmer – learned from Luc – but she seemed out of synch with her limbs. Kicking and spluttering. Was she going to drown? Should she let herself drown? Why not? In Paris after Christmas, she had shied from climbing the railings and plunging into the Seine because it had been her duty to bury Luc. She had owed it to him, but look at the legacy he had left her. Look at the disarray she was facing. And there was no one, not a soul, to hold out a hand to her. Why not let go? Why not sink to the seabed?

Eventually her breathing calmed, grew more rhythmic, and she regained her equilibrium, managing to splash back to the shore. Only then did she realize she had forgotten to bring a towel and was obliged to tug her clothes back on over her wet bikini.

She was in the stables, storing the bike, hair dripping salt water onto her shoulders, still shaken by her morning's panic. A quick shower, another coffee and then the cellars. Her dungeon. As she exited and bolted the wooden door, Claude was passing behind the house with a wheelbarrow stacked high with plants, shovels and digging utensils resting across the handles. Jane waved and hollered a greeting but he didn't see or hear her. She called again, but he was too distant now. Perhaps his hearing was less acute than it had been. He strolled on towards the walled garden, whistling, oblivious to her presence. He was in his element, possibly talking to the plants as he and Matty used to do when she was a child.

Jane felt herself begin to slide again. She wouldn't set foot inside the cellars this morning. She wouldn't look at that child's face again, not yet. She refused to let 'Annabelle' gain power over her. Luc had loved Jane, his wife. She was getting better. She needed to heal herself, as Peter's specialist had advised.

After a hasty shower and change of clothes, she jogged to the kitchen garden. Claude was alone there, digging and rooting. He straightened his back and gave a wave when he heard her cry.

'I counted the broken panes in the greenhouses,' he said, as she drew near. 'It'd be a challenge for any bank account.'

'How about I help you finish planting all these and then we begin our tour?'

'What about the cellars and your work?'

'Foolish not to enjoy this fine weather. I can clear out all those cupboards in the evenings.'

Claude handed her a trowel. 'Do you want to visit the greenhouses after?'

'No, let's get going on the vineyards.'

The weed piles had grown into sizeable hillocks and the earth embedded beneath her nails would be hard to winkle out. She was perspiring, flushed from the arduous digging, back aching from extracting stumps and loose rocks. She fell into the passenger seat as Claude pulled away in the estate's battered Renault van. He passed Jane an apple from his lunchbox, bit hard into one himself, its juice spraying like miniature stars as he crunched, and began to talk through the cycle of grape-growing in their southern region.

'A little less than five moons,' he said, 'the grapes grow on the vines. From the fruit's set, it's approximately one hundred and forty days until it's harvested.'

'The fruit's set is flowers to berries, is that correct?'

He nodded, shifting up to third gear. As they ascended the gentle incline towards the estate's hinterland, the car growled and bucked.

'I don't think I'd realized that vines produce flowers.'

'It's one of the best seasons of the year, Jane, and it does the heart good to see it.'

She smiled at this. Her decision to return here had been a sane one. 'Spring flowers?'

He nodded. 'And we have hectares of them here. It's a splendid display.'

It occurred to Jane as she listened that she had never been there in March. As a child she had visited in the summer months during her school holidays and once or twice during autumn half-term. Since Isabelle's death, she and Luc had also spent Christmas and New Year at Les Cigales, until the last tragic one. Still, there were several months of the year she had never experienced here. The changing colours of the leaves, the patterns of growth. 'Do they have any perfume, these grape flowers?'

'Each variety has its own scent when it blossoms. The differences are subtle, so delicate, but an attuned nose can identify them.'

Jane marvelled at his words. Not for the first time, she remarked that when many of these Provençal people spoke of the land, they did so eloquently, using language that was elegant, almost a poetry of the earth.

'Can you tell the difference?'

Claude let out a hearty laugh. 'Blindfold me, Jane, and lead me on a chase and I swear I could pinpoint where in the

South of France we are and which variety of grape is growing at my feet. I wouldn't know the varieties from the north, mind, Bordeaux and Burgundy, not those, but all along the Midi, I could pretty much identify them.'

'That's amazing. I'm very impressed.'

'It's not a great skill, but it adds up to a fair old portion of my life.'

Jane grinned. She was looking out of the window, kept closed due to the dust rising around the rolling wheels. Beyond the track, in either direction, there were acres of overgrown vineyards, pendulous with young green bunches of hard grapes. She wondered why they had been left to grow wild like this. Clarisse, the estate, needed the harvests to survive. They were driving inland. Clarisse's chestnut mare, Rêve, was cantering free in one of the fields. Did she still ride the horse? It was years since Jane had seen her on it. High in the distance ahead of them the mountains soared towards a cloudless blue sky. Claude must be what age? Not quite retirement, Matty had said, but surely he was more than sixty-two. He was a native Provençal, born not too many kilometres from where they were now, soon after the end of the Second World War. She knew his parents had owned or rented a couple of acres of land and had managed a small *tabac*, where he had been brought up, living above their shop in his village about twenty miles from Les Cigales, and that he had met Matty on the estate. Aside from those few facts, she knew next to nothing about him or his wife.

During the last war, this region had been unoccupied territory, the free zone, but there had been a very active resistance movement operating down here in the south. Had Claude's father or any of his relatives been members of *la Résistance*? Or might they have discreetly given their allegiance to the Vichy government? She hoped not, but she had no idea where he and Matty stood. She assumed they were socialists, but didn't know for sure.

Who knew the secrets people held buried from their past? She sure as hell didn't.

Claude drew the Renault to a halt, switched off the engine and stepped out onto the dusty track. A blast of heat hit her as she followed. The air smelt sweet, of wild flowers and aromatic herbs. A whistling overhead drew her attention. She looked up, squinting into the sunlight.

'It's a pair of Short-toed Eagles,' he told her, as he scrunched his eyes to follow her gaze. 'They nest all over these parts. Fewer now than there used to be.'

When she and Luc were youngsters, they had explored, tracked, mapped, taken notes and made hundreds of nature discoveries all around here. She remembered the eagles, although she had forgotten about them till now. Luc had taught Jane almost everything she had ever learned about nature and the environment, and the discoveries had always been thrilling, but she had not pursued the passion as Luc had. Luc had been on a path of innovation all his life whereas she had been happy with the way things were . . .

Was that why he had required another life, the secret existence he had kept hidden? Had he been unable to settle to the conventional routines she and he had known? Had he always been impelled to go further, to challenge himself with the next experience? The next relationship? Unearthing new directions? She pushed the confusion and doubt from her mind. They were scratching at her wounds. She resolved to remain in the present, here in the sunshine with Claude, miles from anywhere or anyone. Miles from Luc's cellars.

Her guide had crossed the track now and penetrated a field of vine stock. He was barely visible within the overgrown rows, each out of alignment and scruffy. No pruning had taken place this year. The weeds shooting up in the alleys between the vines would soon be as tall as the fruit-bearers themselves. They were threatening to strangle the grapes. Denied sunlight, the fruit of their future harvest would fail to develop or ripen. If there was no opportunity for air to circulate, diseases such as mould and leaf rot would set in. Even to her inexperienced eye all this was evident. She could see the warning signs, the dangers.

Jane crossed the track to the edge of the field where Claude was bent low, probing with his fingers around thick roots, nosing like a truffle dog, picking off leaves and rubbing at them, surveying stems, studying and assessing. She stepped in among the foliage, nudging branches aside to approach him.

'They are suffering,' he said. The comment was not addressed to her, more to the land itself.

'Will we lose our crop?' she asked, surprising herself. *We*. *Our* crop.

Did she have a responsibility to these acres that she had never acknowledged before, let alone taken on board? 'These fields need serious work, eh?'

'I'll say. Usually in March, after the winter's growth and the spurt of early spring weeds, we clean all these grounds up. We begin back here with the terraced fruit and then we move down towards the sea, beyond the road, to the flat soil fields. After the weeds have been dug out, the earth between the rows is ploughed. That makes the soil looser and lighter, enabling the plants to breathe, better to produce. Our method is labour intensive, bloody hard work, in fact, and expensive, but it paves the way for the finest vintages. Everything that can be achieved by hand is done so. The estate is organic. No pesticides. Luc and Madame Isabelle instigated that change themselves and he was proud of it.' Claude fell silent. Then: 'That boy'd turn in his grave if he saw the wretched mess we're in.'

They dropped their heads, remembering him.

'Why didn't the work get done this year, Claude?'

He rubbed his lips and chin with the palm of his hand, but made no response.

She became aware of the bush crickets and grasshoppers, dozens and dozens of jumping creatures buried among the crops, all trilling away in the heat. 'Surely *you* could've over-seen the programme even without Luc. And the others, the local men who are always here to lend a hand with the harvest: Jean Dupont, Michel Lonsaud and Arnaud, of course. And there are others living in the villages all about here. They know what needs to be done.'

'I'll say they do. We taught those two women everything. Isabelle was willing but . . .' He shook his head.

'There's no shortage of experienced hands and I bet more than a few of them would be very glad of the work.'

Claude let out a long sigh. 'She . . .' He coughed and began again. 'Madame Cambon said there's no money in the kitty to pay anyone. Said the loss of the crop last year –'

'Oh, come on!'

'As well as the poor yield . . . She says it's done for the estate.'

'I don't –'

'Anyway, that's what she says. Who am I to argue?'

'And now we have nothing. The fruit will be choked and diseased, right? It's a tragedy.'

'Listen to me, Jane,' his tone grew more insistent, 'we could still save a few parcels of the fruit and set ourselves on course for a vintage. It'll be a lean one, but look at the growth everywhere. We'd need to begin clearing the fields now. *Right now*, Jane.'

'Otherwise how will anyone get in here to do the picking?'

He nodded gravely, but was there a glint of trickery in his eye? Did he know how susceptible she was? How she craved a guiding hand, the certainty of the seasons, the rhythms of nature and the oblivion of punishing physical labour if she were to start to heal? And might he be using that to win her over?

Jane spun a slow circle in the sunlight. The heat was agreeable, not yet raging, and the song of the grasshoppers was pleasing. Her gaze reached far in all directions, over carpets of young-leafed fields and tall flowering weeds. In the distance, clinging at angles to the stony slopes, the silver-hued olive groves were visible. Beyond them, there was fragrant scrubland, with its sea of wild thyme, rosemary, sage and briar roses growing alongside dozens of other soft-leaved shrubs Jane could not identify. These were the ground-cover for the mountains, climbing to the altitudinous pines. God's own southern belt beneath a sky that stretched for ever and kept secrets beneath its canopy.

'And another thing. Without wanting to worry or frighten you –'

'What's that, Claude?'

'The fire risk in the overgrown fields and groves is very serious indeed. Once the heat sets in . . .'

She cast her eyes from left to right.

'You've never been down here during a forest fire, have you, Jane?'

She shook her head.

'Nor would you want to be. It can be terrifying and very distressing to see the charcoaled wildlife. Do you know that further over in the Var, the Hermann's tortoise, a rare breed, has become almost extinct because its habitat was burned out by the fires? It's the law here to keep the vegetation cut back and safe. We have to manage the land with respect.

That's what Luc always drilled into us. It's what we taught him when he was a kid.' He chuckled. 'Even if we didn't give a whistle for the vines and the crops, the maintenance of the grounds is another matter altogether. And there are heavy fines levied against those who don't.'

This was no job for an amateur. It needed dedication, devotion and some serious investment. Was this why Claude had suggested the tour? Had he and Matty discussed their fading prospects at home in their kitchen, at table with Arnaud? Were they gambling on the fact that when Jane was faced with all this disarray, with what was at stake, with the dangers and loss, that for Luc's sake, Luc's memory, she would be unable to turn her back? They were calling on her sense of responsibility towards the estate, and towards them, its caretakers. This was their livelihood. Their retirement prospects. If all this went to Hell, they had everything to lose.

But where did Jane's future lie within all of this?

'Why would Clarisse tolerate such an asset falling into ruin? There must be another reason besides her financial predicament, surely.'

'She has passed the responsibility to no one, Jane. She refuses to. All this would have been Luc's if he'd lived, but without him . . . It's as if she wants it all to rot rather than entrust it to others, as if she's punishing us or herself or Lord knows who for the past. Matty says grief and loss have done her in. The loss of Luc has brought the past flooding back in on her.'

The eagles were still circling overhead, spiralling higher without effort on the slipstream until they were floating flecks of brown feathers against a silken sheet of cobalt. Their haunting whistle reverberated, an eerie cry echoing into the hot silence. It was like a phantom from on high beckoning to her. Or forewarning her.

'She's all knotted up with regret and grieving, Matty says. When people suffer too much, they get mean and they behave ugly. Something dies in them and they resent others enjoying life. So Matty, with her church ways, says. Our local *curé*, he says the same. Loss is eating at her innards.'

The loss of Luc has brought the past flooding back in on her.

Jane listened, measuring Claude's words. 'Aside from Luc, what else is Clarisse grieving for, Claude?'

The old gardener's head hung low. He made no response. Jane thought he hadn't heard her and repeated the question.

'No use asking me. I've never fathomed women. Them's all Matty's opinions, not mine. All I know about is out here on the land, the ploughing and the digging and the picking. I live by the seasons. Women's troubles are beyond me.'

What in Clarisse's past had come flooding back? Was Claude keeping something from her?

He picked off a vine leaf and scratched at its petiole, at a black pebbled disease or collection of minuscule flies on the stalk as though trying to remove the rot, as though avoiding Jane's question. 'All I know is that after all these years of building this domain up into something to be proud of, after all Isabelle's hard work and Luc's and ours, it's a bloody tragedy to let it go. That's my opinion.'

Later, reflecting on her conversation with Claude, Jane concluded that he must have been referring to the Cambon family's flight from war-torn Algeria. Clarisse cited it frequently. They had never been welcomed here. Their relocation had involved much sacrifice. They had bartered their home for freedom. They had been obliged to abandon their magnificent estate, a vast property that had been in Luc's father's family for four generations. It included lucrative vineyards from which, every autumn, they had loaded thousands of tons of grapes onto tankers bound for southern France for winemaking. All had been planted by Luc's great-grandfather. Clarisse must have grieved for the loss of such wealth, of her privileged colonial existence, as well as the death of her husband, Luc's father, Adrien. Luc had been Clarisse's final thread to the life she had left behind. Those must have been the sorrows that Clarisse had hidden deep and was still grieving for.

But Jane couldn't know for sure.

10

Later, towards evening after a hard but invigorating day on the land, followed by several hours of translating a rather dry medical-research text, Jane returned to the cellars. She was standing on a chair, rummaging through cupboards and drawers, when she fell upon a cardboard box containing a trove of old pictures, including some Polaroids. Here were stored joyful souvenirs, uplifting memories from their early married life and courting days. Luc, one eye closed, operating a movie camera, his cigarette smoke clouding the image. She had taken that shot of him in Rome, days before or after their wedding. On the reverse he had written, *On honeymoon with J. Promised her I'll be the next Truffaut!*

Jane in the Cambons' old family fishing boat in a bathing costume, grinning proudly while displaying her catch of one sardine no larger than a pinkie finger. Luc in the same boat drinking beer, wearing flippers and swimming trunks, smoking. They had made love in that boat, offshore, awkward and uncomfortable yet passionate, giggling as he removed the flippers, rocking wildly, diving overboard afterwards, playing naked in the water together. She sat and idled through the entire batch, reliving those days of unadulterated bliss, days when no lonely destiny loomed, when doubts were not tearing her to shreds, when she and Luc had had prospects and a secure future together.

As she was sliding the box back onto its shelf, she dislodged an unmarked pale blue folder that had been pushed to the rear of the cupboard. It fell to the table, like a fan unfolding, foolscap pages spreading: a tenancy agreement for a two-bedroom *appartement* in avenue de la Dame Blanche, close to Bois de Vincennes. It had been drawn up in the name of Luc Cambon, his address given as Les Cigales, not London, and countersigned by a property letting agency in the fifth *arrondissement* in Paris. The date of the contract was 10 October two years previous. The duration of French agreements was usually three years, renewable. So, a little over fifteen months was left to run on the first term. Unless it had been cancelled when Luc died. Jane shuffled through the pages in increasing turmoil. She was searching for the bank from which the sum of 1,800 euros per month was paid by direct debit. When she found the clause it confirmed her worst fears. The flat's monthly rental and charges were collected from the same Crédit Agricole account Luc had used to pay a thousand euros to 'Annabelle'.

Luc's fatal accident had occurred east of Paris, north-east of the suburban town of Vincennes, close to Bois de Vincennes. Wasn't that the information Roussel had given her? The three missing hours had never been filled in. The last time she had spoken to her husband, he had been battling through foggy, snowy conditions somewhere a little north of Beaune. His direction had been to Paris but not towards the motorway for Calais. He was intending to make a stop, to deliver papers. Wasn't that what he'd said? Jane fought to recall their conversation, to drag it from her damaged memory. His voice had been weary with exhaustion.

'If I put my foot down and the roads stay clear, I might just manage the last Shuttle,' he had told her. 'If not, I'll check into a B-and-B somewhere in Calais and board the first one in the morning.'

But there was more. He had said more.

'I have one brief stop to make outside Paris.'

'Oh, really, what for?' had been her reply.

'Some paperwork, research material to deliver.'

'Couldn't you have emailed it across?'

Pause.

'Luc?'

'It won't take long.'

'Luc, it's Christmas.'

Outside Paris? To the address on the rental agreement? He must have left the rented flat, driven north and, in no time, had hit the tree. Had he been cunningly attempting to celebrate two Christmases? A Christmas stopover with gifts for the boy and the boy's mother – his mistress? – before speeding onwards to his wife, a woman kept in ignorance?

What if Jane had agreed to spend the holidays in the south with Clarisse? How would Luc have played that? Excused himself, driven north to 'outside Paris' for a swift pre-Christmas 'business meeting'?

Fuck you, Luc! I'm forced to sell our home for this?

Luc, so honest. A man respected for his professional integrity . . . How could this be? Since when had he been negotiating this double existence? Weaving such a hateful tapestry of lies.

'I told you I didn't want to know!' Was she, 'A', the last person he'd seen?

She flung the contract onto the desk.

No, there *had* to be another explanation.

A sealed envelope slipped from a pocket in the folder. It was addressed in Luc's black-inked writing, his elegant, slightly forward-slanting script, to 'Madame Clarisse Cambon – In case of my untimely death'.

Had he been expecting an untimely death? The Colt in the drawer. Suicide, or under threat? Or was he simply being cautious? What had Roussel said? The OAS had sympathizers today and there had been concerns for Luc's safety?

Jane, shaking with anger, tears streaming down her face, held the unopened envelope at arm's length, as though it might contain a bomb. It was addressed to her mother-in-law. She should deliver it to Clarisse. It was her duty to deliver it to Clarisse. She ripped the flap open and tugged out the letter.

Chère Maman,

By the time you read this, either you will already have acknowledged our responsibility towards Annabelle's son or I will have reached an untimely end and someone else will hand you this missive. If the latter, this will make you cognizant of the situation and it expresses my wishes.

My intention is that I will find a quiet moment to talk this through with you myself, rather than you read it here.

Whichever, and no matter how you feel about Patrick's existence, when the inevitable date arrives, it is only right that he inherits the estate.

Annabelle and Patrick . . . not Arnaud and Pierre.

She had been punched in the gut. She sucked in breath but was fighting for oxygen. So violent was her inability to breathe that she was barely able to continue reading.

According to French inheritance legislation, once you and I have passed on, Patrick is the rightful heir to Les Cigales, so please let us not be at odds over this matter. Over time, I have come to accept, grudgingly I must honestly state, that for your own reasons – lack of courage or cold-heartedness? – Annabelle has no claim on Les Cigales, but you cannot deny her son's rights. Patrick is your grandson, your flesh and blood, and I will not tolerate your rejection of him and his right to inherit the Cambon estate.

No one else needs to be told of our decision at this stage, but when the day comes, if I am not in a fit condition to institute the legacy, I beg you to behave with decency.

My wish is that our property and estate assets are bequeathed to Patrick. Second, you and Jane are not easy in one another's company – another fact that I have been forced to resign myself to. I must accept some responsibility in that I have failed to change this deadlock even if I have never understood its genesis. Nonetheless, although by law Jane will not inherit my share of the estate, she is entitled to a home with us. Before anyone else, Jane has the legal right to inhabit the manor house for the duration of her life. If she wishes to remain at Les Cigales, that is, and as a member of our family. I hope she will accept this. She is my wife. She is a Cambon. If I go first, I would like to think that she will step into my shoes and enjoy the pleasures of Les Cigales.

I hope, as well, that she might come to accept Patrick.

Dearest Maman, please be just and loving in your dealings with all this.

I love you.

Your loyal son,
Luc Cambon

Jane read the letter again, then three times more. She could barely get her head round the words she had read.

Patrick is your grandson, your flesh and blood . . .

Her worst fears, the fears she had been denying with every breath she took, had been substantiated. Luc had had a child by another woman. Annabelle. Jane had fought with all her being to resist, to deny this reality.

'I don't want to know,' she wailed. 'I loved you. I've always loved you. I would have done anything for you and now you leave me with nothing . . .'

A and P.

A and P, whose lives would never be the same after Luc's death.

And what of her own life? It would certainly never be the same ever again.

Luc was providing a home for Patrick and Annabelle, the *mother of his son.* As well, he was taking steps to safeguard and secure the boy's future. Why else would he have accepted responsibility for a flat with two bedrooms on the outskirts of Paris? Two bedrooms, one for the mother (with Luc when he was in town?), the other for the boy. Jane Googled the *agence d'immobilier* and found their telephone number. She lifted the phone and tapped in the ten digits. It was ten to seven in the evening. Most offices in Paris closed at seven. With luck, they'd still be open.

Jane was in luck: a woman answered. *'Agence du Quartier Latin, bonsoir?'*

What to say? Which questions to ask? There were so many. Had Luc accompanied 'A' to the agency? Had they gone together as a family of three? Would the estate agent or receptionist at the other end of the line in Paris remember Luc? Would she have recognized him as the film director? Probably not. Documentary film-making did not create celebrity status.

'Allo?'

'Yes, *bonjour*! I understand you represent a two-room, no, excuse me, sorry, a two-bedroom flat in Vincennes?' Jane's voice was husky – even her French felt uncertain.

'We have several properties in that district, Madame, how can I help you?'

'I was wondering if the monthly payments have ceased or are still being honoured?'

The representative at the other end of the phone sighed. 'Are you ringing to enquire about an advertisement you've seen?' She sounded impatient.

'No.'

'Well, Madame, what do you want, *s'il vous plaît*?' Parisian curt.

'To know whether a contract drawn up by you is still valid.'

'I am sorry, we don't release such information over the phone. Who are you?'

Jane panicked. She should have foreseen this. 'There has been an accident. Someone died . . . I may . . . may need on their behalf to terminate the contract. If the lawyer has not already contacted you.'

'And you are?'

'I – I am the lawyer's assistant. Yes, Monsieur Piper's assistant.' She panicked again, her sweaty palm gripping the receiver. There was a possibility that Robert Piper had lied to her. He was working for Luc and he was Luc's long-time buddy, not hers. Robert's loyalty lay with Luc. Perhaps he had negotiated the terms of the rental agreement. She should have thought this through more carefully before picking up the phone.

'Give me the full address, please, and if possible the contract number. This is a little irregular.'

Jane read out the details.

'Just a moment, please.' The woman coughed. Jane heard the flick of a lighter as the woman called, '*Bonsoir, à demain*,' to a colleague in her office. She heard fingers tapping a keyboard. The estate agent must be scrolling down her computer screen. 'Hello? I have found it. Yes, I can confirm that this is a current contract, Madame.'

'But Monsieur Cambon is deceased.'

Pause. 'I am sorry. Let me look at the notes here.' An exhalation. 'Hello?'

'Yes?'

'It seems that we were notified of the death. All is in order.'

'And?'

'Madame Cambon chose to take over the lease herself. This was acceptable to us under the circumstances. An addendum has, I believe, already been drawn up and signed.'

Madame Cambon?

Was Clarisse in on this? Jane very much doubted it. According to Luc's letter to his mother, there was a *froideur* between the two women.

Jane hit the End button on her phone.

Was Annabelle masquerading as Luc's wife?

11

The following morning Claude drove them to the foot of the Alps where the most distant of the estate's vineyards were situated, overhung by their olive groves. 'During autumn and winter, after the harvest, the land lies dormant. This is when we fertilize. We let it seep in nicely, into the sleeping earth. We buy our organic fertilizer from the small pig and goat farmers in the higher regions close to the national park. The meat from around those parts is rather fine, too. Matty always insists I come back with a few kilos of sausages. Mineral fertilizers and natural compost are what we use.'

The earth was red and the fruit a startling green. After a sleepless night, Jane was bleary, puffy-eyed. She had tossed and turned, tense and wakeful throughout long bleak hours. Too exhausted, she had skipped her dawn cycle ride to the beach for a swim, as well as her trip to Luc's grave, the first day she had failed to do either since her return. Her heart was beginning to swell within her, pumped by a black despair that threatened to strangle her.

Should she fly to Paris, pay a visit to the rented flat and challenge 'Madame Cambon' face to face. Was this so-called 'Madame Cambon' even aware of Jane's existence? If Luc had kept such a dark secret from Jane, might he have lied also to his mistress?

'In spring, we prune the vines by hand, cutting each plant individually. This takes time and expertise. We take a great deal of care in order that we don't harm the stems. It's painstaking work, Jane, for so many hectares. Arnaud is employed with me full-time during that season, along with Jean and Michel. If our other boy, Pierre, is able to take some holiday from the horse farm he manages, he comes back for a couple of weeks to give us a hand as well. He brings the grandchildren, which pleases Matty. Otherwise Clarisse, Madame Cambon, I should say, gets me to hire in a few fellows from the villages roundabout. We tend to prune a little earlier than the larger estates further west so we can nab the good hands first, those who have the skills and the knowledge. If we don't grab them, they hire themselves out to the established domains in the Var. Because of this, it's vital that they know they can count on us, that every spring they'll find employment with us. That loyalty saves costs, saves us dedicating time to explaining to newly hireds. This year, we have dropped the stitch. Now they will be looking elsewhere for employment. We are losing their allegiance. So, next year, if there should be a next year for us all here, we'll have to scratch about for labourers.'

Jane was struggling to concentrate, to keep abreast. She lifted her face heavenwards. The morning was hot and sunny. A few clouds peppered the sky, puffy and white as cotton-wool balls. Her skin was stinging from crying. Yes, she would go to Paris. As soon as Claude delivered her back to the manor house, she would book a flight for the following day. She had considered asking Clarisse about Luc's private affairs but she knew that would yield no results. She would always be loyal to her only child. There was no alternative but to find out the truth for herself.

'So, when we've pruned back all the vines, the alleys are free of foliage and the spring rains can more easily penetrate the soil. Oh, and you haven't yet seen how they bleed sap when we cut them. You'll be amazed by it next spring, I promise you. As I said, once the weeds are all gone, the bare soil can absorb the early spring rain, guzzle it up. All that goodness, the nutrients, goes into the vine stock, to process and feed its growth. It drinks in all Nature's gifts, morning dews, early warm sun. The plants are preparing themselves for their flowering and then to give birth to the fruit.'

Jane said nothing. The old man's enthusiasm and passion for the earth were almost heart-breaking under the circumstances.

'Once you've seen the cycle of growth, Jane, you'll look forward to each season. It puts a spring in your step to see old Mother Nature at work.'

'Claude, I have to leave.'

'Leave, but I –'

'I need to go to Paris.' She saw the shock, the disappointment in his wrinkled face. 'We can continue when I return.'

'Will you be gone for long? Matty and I, we'd been hoping . . .'

'No, no, of course not. Not long. There's something I . . . need to complete for Luc. It's unavoidable.'

'But what about the weeding, the clearing of all the vineyards?' He sounded as though the rest of his life depended on her response. After a fashion, it did, and she had given him and Matty reason to put their hope in the future. Now, it looked as though she might not be able to guarantee anything. Clarisse had chastised her for interfering. Perhaps she should have been more cautious. Charging in, making promises she might never keep.

'If we dither for even a day longer, Jane, we're done for. Why don't I call the men in and get it all cleaned up? We can start while you're away. We need to think of the crops and the risk of fires.'

He couldn't know how in one night such a sea change had taken place within her. What would the investment he was asking for cost her? The total number of man hours? If she agreed, could she finance it? The funds from the flat were not hers yet, completion still a month away. Anything could happen. But she had received a nice little sum from the publishers of the guide books and they had emailed her a contract for three more. Why not agree with Claude that he could go ahead and enlist the men to clear the vineyards? She felt connected here – as Luc had once described his own relationship to Les Cigales; she enjoyed the prospect of the work that lay ahead and the changing face of Nature yet to come. But what if she discovered a truth so unpalatable in Paris that she couldn't return?

'It had better wait, Claude. I think it needs Madame Cambon's authorization to –'

'But she won't agree, Jane. She's holding out on us on purpose. And it will all go to ruin or up in smoke. That's what she wants. Despair is eating her. And what's destroyed in one year can't be picked up as easily in the next. It'll set us back much more than one year.'

'Claude, I – I can't offer the commitment yet. Not yet. Surely two or three days won't make such a difference. It will have to wait. I'm sorry.'

The old man shook his head, baggy eyes downcast. Common sense and Jane's adamant tone warned him that, for the moment, he was beaten. They walked on in silence, the mountains soaring up behind them. It was a couple of degrees cooler here, so close to the mountains, or was she shivering with uncertainty?

'Would you be willing to drive me to the airport? If it's not convenient, I could take the old car and leave it there, but you might need it while I'm gone.'

'Of course I will. If there's anything we can do, Jane, to . . .'

She shook her head violently. 'Do you mind if we drive back to the house now? Then I can confirm the time of the flight and let you know when I'll need to leave. If possible, I'd like to set off this evening.'

Back at the empty house she had a few undisturbed hours to prepare herself. For what, she didn't know. Her life, as she had known it, was being dismantled. And she was about to face the woman who was responsible. The woman with whom Luc had spent the last hours of his life.

12

Line One to Métro station Château de Vincennes, the last stop. The terminus. A fifteen-minute walk in a surprisingly attractive suburb. Her journey had been city-hot, sticky, dusty, but once she was out in the fresh air, it was a fine early-summer day east of central Paris. The château, a large and imposing fourteenth-century castle, was across the street. Jane stayed on the opposite pavement and continued towards the Bois de Vincennes. Young women were sauntering in short sleeves with babies in prams, drinking in the sunshine. A couple of men, one black, one Arab, were drilling a cordoned-off section of a small crossroads. A waiter was placing two or three tables with accompanying chairs outside a modest eatery, preparing for the lunchtime trade. There was a pleasing choice of cafés, bars and restaurants along the way, catering, she supposed, for the tourists who had travelled to visit the castle, where Charles V had been born.

Jane glanced at the app on her phone to confirm her route to avenue de la Dame Blanche, 94300 Vincennes. It stated twelve minutes from the Métro station. She had no notion what she would do when she arrived. Knock? Press a buzzer? Stand across the street, like a stalker or private detective, waiting for 'Annabelle' to appear? What if she was away or at work? Or if the address was a block of flats with a steady stream of inhabitants coming and going. How was she to recognize 'Madame Cambon'?

When she reached the avenue, cutting through a wooded path to arrive at its starting point, she found herself in a calm, leafy setting. It was an elegant street facing directly on to the famous Vincennes woodland. There were buildings only on one side of the avenue. Fine conifers and spreading Cedars of Lebanon grew in the manicured gardens and at the park's edge. Several of the properties were four-, five- or even six-storey art-deco apartment blocks. Iron gates and railings. All were well maintained. Why hadn't Luc housed his mistress and child in a less upmarket neighbourhood? Why gamble their London home for this?

A few rather lovely red-roofed *maisons bourgeois* with white façades clinched this as a very affluent district. They were possibly also divided into flats, maisonettes discreetly set back from the avenue in private grounds. If 'Madame Cambon' inhabited a floor in one of these she would be harder to catch sight of. There could be a back alley for residents' exclusive use, to avoid the main thoroughfare. A gated entrance opened by a code that led out onto a narrow, rarely frequented lane. Jane would have to make a tour of the entire block to find such a path. She wandered back and forth on the woodland side of the street, one tiny stretch of the perimeter of what had once been royal hunting grounds.

Jane was looking for number sixty. She glanced at her watch. It was a quarter to one. Her prey – she was feeling very much like a stalker now – would either be making herself some lunch in her kitchen (the boy would be at school), out at work or possibly lunching with a girlfriend. The fact was, the woman could be anywhere. The possibilities were multitudinous. The chance of her being at home at this time of day was slim. Jane might need to hang around till evening, when the son returned home from school.

And then it occurred to her that it was Wednesday. French schools were closed all day on Wednesdays. Mother and son could be out on an excursion. Museums, swimming-pools, football pitches, dentist, library or walking in these magnificent woods . . . This was an insane expedition, utter foolishness. Even should she track the woman down, what was she intending to say to her? Her opening gambit: *Bonjour, are you Madame Cambon? Well, how about that? So am I. I believe your son's father is my husband. Oh, is he your husband as well? He is. Well, that complicates matters.*

There was no social etiquette for such a scenario. Even Luc would be hard pushed to write the script.

Jane had not until that moment seriously entertained the possibility that Luc might have been a bigamist. The plot grew more grotesque with every twist and turn.

She was now standing directly outside number sixty, facing the building. It was one of the art-deco blocks, six storeys high, with a pale rose and white façade. Each apartment, or those facing the street, at least, enjoyed a road view via a semi-circular balcony. Six storeys meant a minimum of six flats, six sets of occupiers. She shuffled up to the gate, trying not to behave in a manner that could be perceived as conspicuous or shifty. There was a code box for access to the grounds. She pressed a button beneath the digits in the hope that during daylight hours the code was not required. It remained locked. She searched briefly for a set of buzzers. Yes, to the left of the gate. She scanned the list of names. Cambon was not among them. She fingered down the list again. Abbé. Nicolas. Beaulac. Manéval. Therlault. Palomer (interesting: Palomer was a Provençal name, meaning pigeon-keeper). Guinard.

Definitely no Cambon. Seven names, not six. Seven residents, or was one the concierge? Jane ran her finger back up and down the list to see whether there was a note beside any, stating that it was the concierge's bell. Aside from ringing all of them, which she was not intending to do, not yet anyway, what was her next step? Her options?

A dog in the grounds or in a ground floor flat began to bark. She glanced up, still deep in thought. Bolting from out of a side-door entrance and now running wildly about the grass, tugging and worrying at a tea-towel he must have stolen, was Walnut.

Walnut. *Oh, my God.* Was this some delirious dream?

In all Jane's imaginings, enactments played out over and over in her mind, nightmare storylines that had threatened to swamp or suffocate her, this scene had never been in the play. She called the spaniel's name and immediately he scampered towards the iron fence, tongue hanging out, as he had done so often when chasing along, panting, at her side. 'Walnut, it's Jane.' He barked a greeting. 'Do you recognize me?' She glanced about her. There was no one watching her. The dog was leaping back and forth playfully. He dropped the cloth and turned a circle, overexcited.

'Yes, you do, *viens içi*!' She scanned the length of the railings. How could she access the dog? If she could lean over, reach down and lift him up, she'd take him, but the spiked iron fence was too high. Anger shot through Jane. Walnut was wagging his tail, waiting for his mistress to throw a ball and a game to begin. 'Whoever you are, you have even stolen our dog,' she said aloud. She wanted to shout all the names she had just read on the doorbells, to rain down a torrent of threats and blasphemies.

She crouched on her haunches and slipped a hand through the railings. 'Come here,' she encouraged. Walnut approached and licked her hand. She stroked his muzzle, patted his black head and his tail began to wag, like an overwound clock. He yapped and puffed and jumped. 'You remember me. Of course you do.'

'Walnut! Walnut, *viens içi*.'

Her voice calling the dog from inside. Jane leaped

hurriedly away from the fence, almost tumbling backwards as she rose, teetering to her feet, burying herself within the shadows of a tall Lebanon cedar.

She held her breath as though, in spite of the traffic, the honking of horns and a crane grinding several streets away, she might be heard. The spaniel turned and ran back to the caller, its new mistress, disappearing through a door set to the side of the ground-floor balcony. Jane heard the gentle thud as the door was closed, securing the animal inside.

She had to think. She was incensed, outraged. *You stole my husband and now you have our dog.* She had to think. Her reflections, convictions were fragmented. After disjointed minutes, she decided to return to the long street of cafés and bars between this spot and the Métro station where she had seen a waiter setting up tables outside a pizzeria. She needed a drink. She had to think. Nothing was as she had played it out in her mind.

Walnut, *here.* If she had not seen Luc's body, had not identified that blue-cold face herself, she might almost be convinced that he had upped and left her and was living here, that he had chosen this other life – a complete family – over the one he had shared for so many years with her.

Madness set in and began to spin its web. Had the corpse been real? Had she been tricked into believing her husband was dead, into identifying him, when in fact he was still alive? You read of such scenarios in newspapers, or in *films noirs.* An insurance fraud and a tricky woman. An insurance fraud to raise funds. Might that be the story here? A crooked method for salvaging Luc's financial catastrophe. Bodies switched. A corpse replacing Luc from the car's wreckage. She would call Roussel. She pulled her phone from her handbag and began scrolling for the detective's number. No, stop. Stop. She was out of control, tipping over the edge. She had to calm down. Breathe deeply. Get that drink.

Luc was dead. But Walnut was here.

The prospect that Luc might have preferred spending time with this other 'Madame Cambon', with her and their son and the dog, broke Jane's resolve. Without any control over what she was doing she collapsed to the kerb, her overnight bag at her side, and began to sob. She cried with such force that the retching and gulping threatened to empty her of her innards, of all volition and strength.

Luc was dead and he had betrayed her. Their long life together had been a sham; it had meant nothing. Luc, her friend since she was a kid. Had any of it been real?

She sat hunched at the pavement's edge, staring blindly at the traffic. To throw herself under a car seemed the easiest option. For a third time, she was looking her own death in the face, staring at it down the barrel of a gun. One lunge and it would be over, wheels crushing the life out of her, but she withdrew. Impossible to identify which fraying thread kept her clinging to life. The thirst for revenge? The desire to kill the other woman? Cowardice?

A troop of horses clopped by, each with a child in the saddle. Their cheeks were flushed from exertion, from the pleasure of their activity. They had been riding in the woods and were obviously making their way back towards their stables, trotting two by two. Jane, from ground level, watched the handsome beasts. Luc had loved to ride. He and Clarisse used to gallop around the estate for hours. Clarisse had taken pleasure in the fact that Jane was not very comfortable on a horse and had never accompanied them. Had Luc taught his son, Patrick, to ride? Here, at these stables?

Who knew about his clandestine life? How was she, Jane, ever to get beyond this? *We must talk*, he'd said to her before Christmas. Had he been intending to come clean, to put an end to the duplicity, request a divorce over the duck and

Haut Médoc, move in here with his dog – their dog – and this other family?

Slowly, she lifted herself to her feet and picked up her bag. She needed a coffee or a cognac or both. To reassess, to draw up a game plan for her next move. She stepped, on heavy feet, towards the woodland track that led to the road where the château reigned.

The pizzeria was crowded. No tables were available. In any case, Jane could not face even a morsel of food although she had not eaten that day. Instead she installed herself in a *café-tabac* situated on a corner further along the same street. It was a poky, fuggy little joint, its wooden floor littered with discarded game cards and strips of cellophane peeled from cigarette packets. The customers with their drawn, sallow faces were drinking beer or staring at an overhead TV screen relaying horse-racing. Here she drank two cups of strong *espresso* and a brandy and sat staring out of the window, biting her fingernails, a habit she had never before indulged in. It was then she spotted Walnut. The boy, who was perhaps eleven, had the spaniel on a lead and was loping in the direction of the Métro station, carrying a rucksack over his shoulder. She leaped to her feet, grabbed her overnight bag and ran to the door, pushing it open with a fierce urgency. Immediately, the proprietor behind the bar yelled after her, 'Hey, lady, you haven't settled your bill. Eleven euros fifty, if you don't mind.' Heads turned, accusatory or disinterested gazes. Jane was fumbling for her purse, dropping keys, desperate not to lose the trail of the child. She had only caught a brief glance of his profile. She might not recognize him again. It was the dog, Walnut, she had to follow. *Her* dog. She tossed a twenty-euro note onto the zinc bar and ran, twisting and staggering as she hurtled along the street towards the entrance to the station. No boy or dog was anywhere to be seen. She clumped down the stairs to the ticket barrier, scanning all about her, returning to street level, perspiration breaking out on her forehead, heart palpitating.

Had he crossed this main road? She ran to the traffic lights, which were green. Halt for pedestrians. Cars flying by. Parisian cyclists on rented bikes. The lights were changing, traffic slowing. She stepped out. He could be anywhere. Was there another park nearby? Was he intent on dog-walking? No, he would have crossed his own avenue and headed into the woods. He'd been carrying a holdall. Was he going to play football, on his way to a gym, the riding school? But not with an animal surely.

Damn it.

He had disappeared. A driver was honking. Others followed. She was floundering in the road. The lights had turned green. She retreated to the pavement once more. There was no alternative but to retrace her steps to the apartment block and face 'Madame Cambon' or whatever other name the woman was parading under and have it out. Luc's boy, Luc's dog. For all that was worth living for, she prayed this was not Luc's wife. The mystery had to be resolved before she went mad. She knew for sure now that the woman lived on the ground floor. The piece of luck Jane needed was access to the building. From there she could wait in the corridor or the garden by the front door to the apartment and pounce. But how to gain access to the block's interior? She could wait by the iron gate until the return of the boy and accost him, insisting that he let her in to talk with his mother. Did Luc's son know the truth?

What was the truth?

A telephone was ringing. It took a moment before she cottoned on that it was hers.

'Jane, Robert Piper here.'

'Yes?'

'You sound a bit stressed.'

'I'm fine. I . . .' She was moving along the street, more crowded now: the bars and cafés were emptying as people began their return to work. A flock of Japanese were following a woman holding high a small flag. Faces whirled and chattered about her. She was pacing up and down, still desperately searching for the boy, trying to construct a plan, a sequence of actions.

'Your buyers have been on the phone.'

Her heart sank.

'It seems the chain they were in has dropped a link.'

'What does that mean?' She pulled back, attempting not to snap.

'The couple who were buying from them have been refused a mortgage.'

'Oh.'

'Yours are still dead keen, but they've requested a delayed completion date to help them find a replacement. They're cash buyers but don't want to take a bridging loan.'

Oh, shit.

'No, I – I can't agree to that. I need to get this over with, Robert.'

'You want me to call the agents and put the flat back on the market?' He didn't sound over-enamoured of the prospect. 'This won't go down well with the creditors.'

'Do whatever you think is best. I have to go.' She snapped the phone closed.

While in conversation with Robert she had set herself in the direction of the avenue. She was peering down lanes, looking for an alleyway that might lead to a back entrance to the block, when her phone rang again. 'I've spoken to them and they'll respect your wishes. They'll go ahead with a bridging loan. And it gets better. As they're not now waiting on their own sale, they can move whenever you're ready.'

'I'm ready. You have the keys.'

'Yes, we do. I'll get this wrapped up for you as soon as I can, Jane. Take care of yourself.'

'Thank you.'

'More soon.'

'Oh, Robert, before you go, I was wondering about Patrick . . .' She let the name slip down the phone, and waited.

The silence roared back at her. She could all but hear Robert's brain ticking over. 'Patrick?' he repeated eventually.

Her casual tone was a winning performance. 'Yes, wondering whether Luc had drawn up any legal documents regarding him?'

'He never mentioned any Patrick to me. I'll try for a completion date next week. I'll let you know.' The line was dead.

It was after six in the evening. Jane was still loitering, leaning against a tall oak tree on the edge of the Bois de Vincennes, across the street from number sixty, avenue de la Dame Blanche. Many had come and many had gone but no boy and no dog had returned. There must be another access that she had overlooked somewhere. What was she to do? Find a hotel in the vicinity? Press all the buzzers? She was tired and thirsty, dizzy from hunger. A headache threatened, kicked off by brandy and strong coffee on an empty stomach. Her feet were torture from standing around all afternoon and her mind buzzed, like a wasp trapped in a jar, with the single-mindedness of her task. Had she slipped up, lost concentration and missed a coming or going?

She was on the point of giving up, for that day at least, when from the front door of the art-deco building a woman appeared. A handsome woman in her thirties, with a fine, strong figure, in khaki pants and Converse sneakers. Her hair was long and wild, a mass of auburn, like a spill of syrup. She was laughing, talking animatedly on a mobile, hiking the strap of her bag onto her shoulder. She switched off the phone, pressed it into a pocket and jogged to the gate. Jane watched her, speechless. It couldn't be. An image flashed into her memory of Matty's daughter, Annie, gatecrashing the wedding dinner Clarisse and Isabelle had laid on for Luc and Jane so many years ago. The child Clarisse had chided and sent packing. The woman standing alongside Matty at Luc's funeral.

Matty's daughter.

Matty's daughter, whom Isabelle had said worshipped Luc when she was a girl.

Luc had a son with Matty's daughter?

Jane watched silently, pressing herself back into invisibility as Annie Lefèvre hurried out of the gate, half turned towards her, almost making eye contact. There was a nanosecond's pause, as though she was about to change course and approach Jane, but she strode off fast in the direction of the Métro station, digging her phone out of her pocket.

Jane didn't follow. She was too stunned.

Were Matty and Claude aware of this situation? Annie and Patrick had both been present at Luc's funeral, but that was normal. As the offspring of family retainers, it was to be expected. Jane would not have recognized the boy, not from the fleeting glimpse of him this afternoon, but Annie? Yes, she was sure of the identity of this woman who was parading as Madame Cambon. One thing was certain: this imposter was fully aware of Jane's existence. Hadn't she gatecrashed their wedding party?

13

When Jane pulled up outside School House, no one was about. She had not contacted Claude to ask him to pick her up at the airport but had taken a bus instead, then walked from the town. It had been arduous. The summer was getting into gear. Why had she not called Claude? Why put herself to such inconvenience? She was confused, uncertain about what the caretakers knew of their daughter's city existence and whom she could now trust. She parked the car alongside a trio of fig trees near a disused stable block, strode to the back door and beat on the glass. No one responded.

She waited, listened. All was still. She made her way, over stones and soil, no pathway, to the front door where she lifted the knocker and rapped. Her rat-tat disturbed two chickens on the veranda. One, pure white, was perched on the back of Claude's old wooden rocking chair. A speckled companion was on the ground, trying to lay an egg. Aside from the fowl, the place appeared lifeless. A broom leaned against the wall. A pair of slippers lay by the entrance.

She called Matty's name. No response. She retreated to her car. On the way, she paused to scan the barnyard. The Lefèvres' Deux Chevaux was not in sight and there was no sign of Arnaud either. Jane returned to the back door and knocked once more. Gingerly, she closed her palm over the handle and turned it. As she had expected, the door was unlocked. She pushed gently and set one foot inside the kitchen. It smelt warm, of food and domesticity. 'Matty?' A clock ticked. A washing-machine was turning.

Jane hovered, half in, half out, on the threshold, then dared to enter, closing the door behind her. As an afterthought, she turned and opened it again, leaving it ajar. Her heart was racing at this transgression. She had no right to be there, to trespass, to meddle or pry. She had not driven here with any such intention. Her desire had been to talk to Matty, woman to woman, to find out what Annie's mother knew, but it was early afternoon and the housekeeper was out. Claude was most probably in the vineyards or the vegetable garden. Matty could be anywhere. She had not been cleaning up at the manor house when Jane had arrived back from Paris.

Now that she was standing in Matty's kitchen, what was she intending to do? What was she looking for? Proof, evidence, a rebuttal, assurance that this was all a ghastly misunderstanding, a misinterpretation of facts? She glanced about the old-fashioned Provençal kitchen, spacious but cluttered with wooden cupboards, a dresser and an impressive oven. The square porcelain sink was gleaming and empty. She could smell a recent brewing of coffee but the percolator had been washed out, cups returned to the pine dresser. This was a pristine environment, spotless, with swags of dried herbs and copper pots suspended from metal rails and butchers' hooks hanging from the ceiling. There were no photographs on the kitchen walls. There was little spare space. A calendar from the Malaz fire brigade was pinned to a cupboard door. Certain dates had been marked with Xs in pencil. On the oak kitchen table there were a couple of open letters, bills, resting on their torn envelopes. A sugar bowl covered with a vintage beaded doily, pepper and salt pots, a pencil and a half-consumed bottle of dark red wine, the cork replaced. Above the table, hanging from the wall, was a large framed picture of the Virgin Mary, blue veil, hand raised in blessing. Little else. Floral printed cushions on the chairs.

Jane crossed the kitchen to a door that opened onto a dark, narrow corridor. A bundle of winter coats hung from a wall rack and wellingtons stood on the floor in an otherwise empty hallway that dissected the lower half of the house, leading from the front door to the stairs at the back. From there into the school room, converted now into a sitting and dining space. As it had been on her recent visit, it was dark and cool with the shutters closed. She lingered on the threshold waiting for her sight to acclimatize. The collection of framed photographs on the mantelpiece came into view and she picked her way carefully towards them. She needed light but resisted switching on the overhead bulbs. In the crepuscular glow she glanced about for a table lamp but could not see one.

She had reached the fireplace. There must have been a dozen framed pictures on display. The first she picked up was an old-fashioned image. Claude or Matty's parents, perhaps, standing in a village street outside a shop. A wedding, wartime. Their *tabac*? The woman was pretty with a dimple in her chin and a small flower arrangement in her shoulder-length dark, wavy hair. He had cropped hair and a neat suit. Yes, the parents of Matty or Claude, surely, on their wedding day. Jane replaced the frame and took up the next. Matty with her newborn twin sons. A younger, far more slender edition of Matty than the woman of today. Handsome, strong-boned. Jane reconsidered the first photo and decided these were probably the housekeeper's parents, not Claude's. There was a likeness between mother and daughter.

She reset the newborn boys with their mother on the mantelpiece and glanced over the others until her attention fell upon a set of rosary beads placed in front of a picture of Luc. Luc with a small girl standing in front of him. Luc and Annie. The girl could not have been more than eight at the time and he in his twenties. Jane picked up the picture. How she had fussed all those years back over the seven-year difference that had existed between her and her dead husband.

She turned from the fireplace and moved to the centre of the room, where she had recently sat talking with Matty. She remembered the photo she had gathered up from the coffee-table of the three offspring. The twins and Annie. Alongside was another of Annie, younger, early twenties perhaps, holding a new-born child. Patrick? In the background of the shot, behind Annie, there was an unsmiling man possibly about the same age, slightly out of focus, not one of her brothers. A stranger to Jane.

A car door slammed. Jane was abruptly shaken from her absorption. She had completely forgotten that she was trespassing, spying on others' lives. It was becoming an uncomfortable habit. She slammed the framed picture back onto the table nervously and, in the act, knocked over two others. One flopped flat onto the low table while the other tumbled to the stone floor. Its glass cracked and splintered.

'Oh, God!' She was at a loss and fumbling, all guilty fingers and thumbs. She snatched up the casing without looking at it and laid it face down on the table. Droplets of glass bled from it. How frequently Luc had warned her that these Occitanian people had no truck with busybodies. A rule of thumb in these parts, he'd drilled into her, was, 'Don't busy into others' business.'

Well, given his life, no wonder his advice.

'Allô?' Arnaud was at the back door. She had left it ajar. She prayed that Matty was with him or even Claude. If she had to be caught red-handed, please let it be by someone to whom she could explain herself. What in God's name had possessed her to do this? Arnaud must have seen the estate

Renault. He would have deduced that someone was in the house. In any case, where could she hide?

'Papa?' He was approaching.

She heard him clear his throat as he exited the kitchen and crossed the hall. The light went on. Arnaud was standing at the sitting-room door. He stared at her with surprise. She had cut her finger on the broken glass, she realized now.

'*Bonjour*, Arnaud. I was – am waiting for your mother.'

He was frowning, puzzling, brow creased, glancing about him uncertainly, like a badger sniffing for danger before entering its sett. He travelled a few steps into the room. Jane saw then that he was filthy, sweat-stained with a day's unshaven growth, and had been working at something physical. He was in his socks. Matty, not surprisingly, must insist that work boots were left at the back door. Arnaud's blue overalls were stained with oil and dirt. He was staring at the broken glass on the floor, the damaged photograph, and then his eyes moved upwards, locking onto Jane. He noticed her bleeding finger.

'I let myself in,' she explained stupidly.

'Your finger's bleeding.'

'I knocked it against – Apologies. Careless.'

'Shall I find you a plaster?'

She shook her head vehemently, wanting no fuss, wanting to disappear, to be thin air.

Then a thought must have crossed his mind because his face grew darker, troubled. Outrage brewing. 'What do you want?' he demanded curtly.

Did he know that she had offered to help his family, and then when his father had requested permission to hire the men she had fled, reneging on her word? Did they judge her as harshly as they judged Clarisse? Did the local men know that she had not kept her promise?

He bent to the broken glass and touched it without clearing it up. He leaned down to the photographs and lifted the one lying on its face, the one now protected only by loose shards of glass. Jane hadn't looked at it. It was of Annie, a wedding portrait. She was standing alongside the figure Jane had seen in the previous snapshot, the one with the small child, the baby Patrick. Arnaud held it towards his broad chest and stared at it lovingly, clearly heartbroken.

Jane watched him, curious. 'Your sister,' she dared.

He raised his eyes. There was anger in them, and pain. 'Did you break this?'

'It was an accident. I'm very sorry. I came in here to – to sit in the cool and – and wait for Matty and I must've – knocked it with my skirt,' she lied. 'Let me take it with me and I'll have the glass replaced.' She stretched out her hand with the bleeding finger to recover the photograph but he spun it away from her. An act that was both protective and aggressive.

'What do you want here?'

'I've already explained to you, Arnaud. I wanted to have a chat with Matty but it's really not so important. It can wait till another time and I'm sorry I intruded. Why not let me take your sister's photograph and have the glass replaced?'

He held it fast, like a stubborn, awkward child. 'She's not . . .'

'Arnaud!'

Both swung round at the sound of the voice. It was Matty's, forceful and sharp. Her eyes were burning. Neither of the occupants in the room had heard her entry.

'Matty!' Jane crossed the room in a flurry of relief, eager to be gone, desperate to explain herself, to ward off reproach. 'Matty, I let myself in. Apologies if I shouldn't have done.'

Matty's attention was not on Jane. She was focused on her son across the room. He had remained where he was, head bent. 'Why don't you go and clean yourself up, Arnaud?' she said to him, in a softer tone. 'And give me whatever has been damaged as you go.'

Arnaud obeyed, handing the portrait to his mother before he strode from the room without a word. Matty glanced at the likeness held firmly between both hands. 'You've been in Paris.' She sighed. It was not a question.

'Yes, I had some . . . some business of Luc's to wrap up.'

'Annie saw you there.'

'Sorry?'

Matty crossed the room and began to gather up the broken glass, scooping the shards into the palm of her leathery hand. 'She saw you waiting in the street across from her flat.'

Jane was speechless. So Annie had recognized her and, in that moment's hesitation, had decided not to confront her.

'You'd better tell me what you want with us, what you know.'

'Could I have a glass of water, please, Matty?'

'I'll make you some tea.'

The two women returned to the kitchen. Jane ran her finger under the cold tap and it stopped bleeding but she couldn't control the trembling. Her spine seemed to be clenched, rock hard yet quivering. Matty was at the stove, heating water for the teapot. Her expression appeared sterner, less forthcoming than Jane had ever seen it. She had no notion of whether Claude and Matty knew that their daughter had been involved with Luc, that their grandson had been fathered by her own deceased husband. How could she disclose to Matty all that she knew without risking the destruction of their equanimity, their family bond, the loss of their respect for everybody's beloved Luc? The indignity and disgrace.

The washing-machine bleeped, its cycle completed. The

room grew quiet. The clock ticked; timbers shifted and groaned. Footsteps above them: Arnaud crossing a room.

'The photograph in the broken frame is of Annie and Raymond on their wedding day,' said Matty, now over by the fridge and lifting out a jug of milk. 'You still take milk with your tea, don't you?'

Jane nodded. An English habit she had never eschewed.

'It'll be steeped in a few moments. Do you want me to get you a plaster?'

Jane shook her head. She was still shivering.

'If you were still a girl, I'd tell you you'd got what you deserved for poking about in others' affairs. You had no business coming in here nosing about. There's no respect in that for other folks' privacy, Jane, but I still think of you as family and you're a bit old for such scolding. You'd better sit down.'

Jane hovered by a chair. Matty had never spoken to her in such a manner before. It was true that she'd had no business creeping in here like a thief but, under the circumstances, what would anyone have done?

'Annie was champing at the bit to get away from here, to get on with her own life. The result was she jumped into a relationship with the first man who made eyes at her. Foolish girl. I saw it coming and told her so – I told Claude as well – but she wouldn't listen to me. Raymond was the wrong man for her. They were no good for one another and he hurt her. It ended badly. The marriage didn't last any time at all. Ever since she's been fending for herself. Or she was till Luc stepped in.'

Jane lowered herself into one of the pine chairs at the table. Matty placed a floral-design china cup and saucer from the household's best set in front of her guest, drew the sugar bowl close to it and returned to the stove to await the tea.

'We thought you knew it all. We thought you'd returned to Les Cigales to set things in order here, close the doors on the past and get this place moving and operating again. That was what Claude understood, at least.'

'I came back to clear out Luc's cellar, his workspace. Staying on permanently had not been my intention, not at first, but the nature, the surroundings sort of drew me in. But then I found . . . the rental agreement for Annie's flat, and I . . . Thank you.'

The pot of tea was in front of her now. Matty settled herself alongside her visitor and rested her thick arms on the table, fists bunched together.

'I rang the agency, but I needed to find out for myself –'

'Jane, you don't need to know everything, every detail. What's done is done and there's no going back on it. We've all got skeletons of one sort or another.'

'But?'

'You can rest assured that Annie knows her place. Her marriage was a mistake, yes, but she's a decent girl, brought up right, even if I say so myself, and she's not trying to grab anything from the estate, not even for Patrick, although he has rights that none could contest. My advice to you is to close your eyes to what's gone before and look forward. We're all grieving for Luc, each of us for our own different reasons, but no amount of sorrowing or heartache will bring him back, Jane. Hear me, for what it's worth, and look to the future. Build yourself a life. Claude and me, we've been hoping it might be here, that you'd be willing to forgive the transgressions.'

'Forgive the trangressions? It's not that simple, Matty.'

'She was a young woman and lonely. She meant no ill and she didn't intend to hurt anyone. The child came along unexpected. It's not easy in these parts. People talk. Surely you can understand that.'

'No, Matty, I can't!'

'Jane, be bigger than you've been. Forgiveness, that's the Lord's way. Step into Clarisse's shoes, see it from her point of view. Take over the responsibility and get this place back on its feet because God knows, and God give peace to her troubled heart, Clarisse is barely capable of it now.'

'Matty, what you're asking of me is too much –'

'Well, if you can't or won't forgive, can't put aside what's on your mind, what you've found out, you'd better go, forget us, leave us all with our crosses to bear.'

Jane was sipping the tea, too hot but sweet and calming. 'You're asking me to simply forget, to forgive? Not to judge Luc for keeping such a secret from me?'

'I suspect he thought you couldn't handle it, Jane. Your relationship with Clarisse has always been so . . . delicate, shall we say? Your role here never committed. I'm not saying Luc discussed any of this with Claude or me, by the way. He didn't, not in any direct fashion, but I expect his thinking was that what you didn't know couldn't hurt you.'

'But, Matty, how could it not hurt me? I'm astonished. You're a practising Catholic, a God-fearing woman who goes to church every Sunday. Could you forgive Claude such a lie? Could you just look to the future and pretend all this had never happened?'

'Things die and things grow, Jane. Life turns. We can't change what's done. We cannot undo the past. And Luc has gone now.'

'If only I could bring him back, to help me –'

Matty laid her hand over Jane's. 'But you can't, girl, and that's a fact. No one foresaw his accident, losing his life so young, least of all Clarisse, who's suffering bad from it, from the emptiness, but his death is a fact and there is no point in wasting your energies, or whatever time remains to any of us, on the past. Build a future, that's my advice. You think all this hasn't pained me too? It has. Deeply. I did what I believed was right by Annie.' She paused, reflecting, rubbing her fingers together, brushing aside a tear from her cheek. 'And now, if you don't mind, I'd prefer not to discuss it further. It cuts deep, and I don't want to be churning it all up again. I'm going upstairs to see to Arnaud. Stay and finish your tea and I'll see you up at the manor tomorrow. We hope you'll decide to stay.'

'Matty, wait, please –'

'I'll see you in the morning.'

Jane sat in the failing light, staring out at the darkening landscape. The cries of children, released from school, playing football on the beach, rose up into the evening. Doves cooed and crickets chirped. She was listening to the distant barking of dogs in the valley and thinking about Walnut. The air smelt sweet, of falling blossoms, of wild lavender, but her heart was raw.

She was numbed by all that Matty had said to her, by the chiding and the intransigence. For a short while back there, Jane had thought, prayed, that Patrick might have been the son of Raymond, Annie's ex-husband, but always her mind returned to Luc's letter to his mother: *Patrick is your flesh and blood, your grandson* . . . She could not brush the facts under the carpet. And she wasn't capable of laying them to one side, as Matty advised.

Her mind was running in circles. She was exhausted, too befuddled to untangle her options. She could walk away from this estate, this weight of misery, this evening or tomorrow morning, but where was she to go? Withdrawing her flat from sale was not an option. In fact, advancing its completion would be her smartest move.

She hastened to the table in the breakfast room and tapped out an email to Robert Piper, confirming that he should push for the soonest available completion date. If, as he had suggested, it could take place within a week, she would stay on here at the manor house. Whatever funds remained after the mortgage debt had been settled would be transferred to her account. Then she would be free to do as she pleased. In the meantime, she would work with Claude on the land and bury herself in the effort. Later she would address the torment and suffering of Luc's betrayal that were throttling her love for him. For the time being she would force herself to set aside her emotions. She would operate on automatic pilot. She would log Luc's material in the cellars as she had prepared to do all along; anything she found that was personal, she would burn without reading it. Claude and Matty, who had always been Luc's loyal supporters, allies, were now accomplices in an act of duplicity, but she was determined not to allow herself to become the victim. As for Clarisse, Jane would not let on that she had uncovered Luc's hidden life and his child or mention her visit to Paris. Luc's letter addressed to Clarisse still lay in the file along with the rental agreement. No one knew of its existence except her. She should hand it over to her mother-in-law, but not yet. The old woman mocked her with the words *There seems to be quite a bit he never shared with you.*

In the days that followed, Jane worked furiously. She emailed the rather dull medical text she had translated, along with her invoice, and began on the next guide book. It was the fourth in a series written by a Frenchman on cities of Europe. She rather enjoyed the armchair travelling they offered, a respite from her melancholia.

Because she could no longer bear to hang out in the cellars, she decided to vacate them, to move Luc's film material into the smallest of the drawing rooms, known as *le petit salon.* It would be a more convivial atmosphere to work in.

She hated spending time underground. More so now than ever. So she began to box up books, manuscripts, scripts, notebooks and then, in spite of dust and tiredness, she lugged them up the stairs. She noted everything in a solid, old-fashioned accounts ledger she had come across. The Colt and the Bible were also removed from their drawer and placed on the sideboard in the *salon*, which she kept locked.

The daylight hours she spent outside, digging and weeding the vegetable beds. The days were sunny and the outdoor chores were restorative. If not yet a path to healing – that was beyond sight in the distance – the physical exertion kept her trauma and isolation under cover. From the stable block she carried a ladder to the walled kitchen gardens, where she fastened and resecured the espaliered apple trees against the east-facing stone wall. She made a fair job of it, alone with the nails and a hammer. She rested in the sun on a bench beneath one of the fig trees, munching two nectarines, while she watched a pair of golden orioles in a cherry tree, both males, screeching and squabbling as they filched the remaining fruit. Then she set to clipping and weeding around the lemon verbena bushes, the chamomile and bergamot plants: the Tea Garden. It would always be the last on Claude's list: he had little interest in tisanes, herbal remedies or natural healing.

She slept from sheer exhaustion, rose early and, after her morning swim in the sea, she unfurled hosepipes, crunched her way across the stone paths and irrigated all the newly planted vegetables and the areas she was clearing and preparing. Would she be here to see the results of her labours? It didn't matter. The tidying of the land was a spiritual exercise as much as physical.

Claude found her on her knees, sweating and exhausted, covered in dirt, digging with a trowel and sowing frenziedly.

He offered to help, but she shook her head, adamant that these were chores she preferred to achieve singlehandedly.

'Let me know when you're ready to continue with our land tour,' he said, watching uncertainly while she pummelled the earth. Without a glance upwards, Jane nodded that she would. Robert Piper had set the date for completion on the flat's sale, and freedom was round the corner. She could be on her way as soon as she wished, but where to? Walk away, leave Luc and his family to the 'crosses they must bear'?

Leave Luc.

She drew an invisible boundary between Claude, Matty, Clarisse and herself, but from time to time she bumped into Matty in the kitchen. At every opportunity, the housekeeper asked after her health and on one occasion remarked that she was pleased Jane had decided to stay on. 'You seem to be keeping yourself well occupied.'

Jane always responded calmly that she was taking each day at a time and would do so until the answers became clear to her. This seemed to satisfy Matty, or at least quelled her curiosity.

'Oh, and, Matty, I'm working in the *petit salon* on the west side of the house, so please don't bother to clean in there. In fact, the door is locked.'

Matty frowned, keeping her opinion to herself. But late one morning, Jane found a freshly baked cherry tart on the dresser in the kitchen, and one afternoon, a pork casserole.

It hurt Jane to dissemble, to deceive Matty, who in bygone summers had been almost a surrogate mother to her and who was clearly attempting to make amends. Still, the fact was, Matty and Claude had masked truths from her, leaving her, once again, the outsider.

14

Early one morning while Jane was drinking her breakfast tea and quietly reading in the shade of the fig trees, Claude came looking for her. 'We're due a visit to the coastal vineyards,' he announced.

'Not this morning, thank you, Claude.' She did not lift her eyes from the page.

'Let's get going.' His tone was firm, determined. She stared up at him in surprise. He stood, waiting. His broad outline cast a shadow over the table and her Kindle. He was not budging.

'Give me five minutes then.' She slipped on her sneakers, collected her phone and followed him to the van.

They passed orchards of soft fruits: apricots, peaches, nectarines. Most were not yet ripe, not quite blushed, but their plenitude weighed down the thick-trunked trees. The sky was cobalt, the light clear and dry. A perfect early-summer morning. As they approached the coastal fields, Claude began to talk through the pre-harvest considerations. She wound down the window and inhaled the briny air. The springs of the old Renault creaked and bounced as they drove over furrowed, rutted paths leading to pastures and groves. Even so close to the water's edge, the earth was rich and blood-red. It pulsated with goodness. Its warmth rose up to greet her.

'Towards the third week of August and into early September, tension mounts and Madame Clarisse starts getting edgy. Well, we all do, if I'm honest. It's understandable. Our year's work hangs in the balance as we prepare to sample the grapes. From here on, we're keeping a daily eye on the plants, deciding precisely when to harvest. There's no outsider called in to measure the grapes' sugar levels. We select the right moment ourselves. In the past, Madame Isabelle always had the last say-so. After she passed on, it was down to Luc . . .'

Jane stared out of the window and listened in silence. Her heart was hurt and hard, but even the mention of Luc's name stung sharply. She hadn't been to his grave for several days.

'At this stage while we're waiting for the sugar level in the fruit to be just how we want it, we're also keeping a hawk's eye on the weather patterns. Our prayer is that we'll have a marriage of a clear run of fine weather – unlike last year when you were out with us – and good healthy fruit, ripe and mature, ready to be clipped from the stocks. As you know, we pick each vine by hand, one after another, bunch by bunch, fingers and secateurs. We use no machinery. Commencing with the varieties up behind the main house, we work solidly until those hectares have been picked clean and then we hit these fields, these lower lands, the seaside crops, where the salt that blows in off the water gives a special personality to the vines. You will know, Jane, that our first culling takes place while the bunches are on the bushes. We leave the bunches we can't use as food for the birds. For example, if the fruit is damaged or under-nourished. Well, you know all this. You've learned that bit.'

They parked and stepped out, feet against dust. The brittle stillness inland was broken by a breeze coming in off the Mediterranean. The air was hot and salted. It dragged and drew against her flesh. A pleasing sensation. The incessant cicadas and drifting cries from tourists on the beaches cut through the heat. They picked their way through forests of weeds. It was tough going. The vines were choked. Out on the water, a small flotilla of sailing ships was ploughing a path towards St Tropez. A local regatta, perhaps. Once upon a time an adolescent Luc had dreamed of building his own boat and sailing back to Algeria in search of his past. Who would complete that film now? Did Dan still have the rushes he and Luc had shot in Marseille? If only she had the aptitude. She wondered again, fleetingly, why Luc had changed tack and given up on his family story in favour of exposing the OAS. Would he be alive now if he hadn't? Had his life really been at risk?

All Luc's energies gone to waste.

Like this estate.

She couldn't wrap up his film for him, but she could assist with the land.

If I go first, I would like to think that she will step into my shoes . . .

Her world had been smashed apart. She had to gather threads of optimism from somewhere, cling to them.

'If you brought the men in now and cleared all these fields, might they agree to work for a share of the crop?'

Claude frowned.

'In other words, take the risk along with the estate.'

'We've never worked that way in the past.'

'What about with the olive crop?'

He nodded. 'In bygone days, when I was a boy, the farms brought in *les journaliers*, day workers. Some were *paysans*, others travelling bands, who moved between one fruit crop and the next, often working in Spain as well as along this Occitanian coast, living in tents or stables. If the farmers didn't have the cash to pay them, yes, the families, groups, individuals were given a roof over their heads, fed three square meals a day and a percentage of what they'd gathered. The accumulated francs were doled out to them as they packed up and moved on.'

'So it's not unknown in these parts?'

'It's totally out of date, Jane. I'm talking forty and more years ago. You're trying to turn back the clock.'

'But we're not the only estate in crisis. Even if our situation is more critical. If it were the only way to clear these vineyards and preserve some of the wine harvest, would your compatriots consider it?'

Claude shrugged. His personal opinion was that the notion was preposterous.

'Will you mull it over and see what you can propose to the men? If we're starting afresh, we have to begin somewhere and, as you know, the estate lacks funds, according to Clarisse.'

He glanced round at her, following him through the fields. Walking abreast was impossible. Weeds had choked most of the alley space. The landscape would be a jungle if something wasn't done soon. Harvest or none, the estate needed rescuing, but Claude wouldn't beg favours of his boyhood chums. They already despised Clarisse, for her airs and graces and where her money had come from. They might have reconsidered their position for Luc, but for another woman, another foreigner . . . Fat chance.

Jane pulled off her sneakers and socks. Sand scattered on the kitchen floor. The cool tiles against her swollen feet were a comfort after the swelter and dust. She was about to climb the stairs to take a shower before she began the daily late-afternoon task of sorting Luc's material. Hand on banister, she changed her mind, swung about and made for the breakfast room. There, she picked up the telephone. The call was on the off-chance. Once again there was an answer-machine. 'Dan, it's Jane Cambon. Maybe you're still away on location. I'm at Les Cigales, going through Luc's papers, his film documents. I was wondering whether there are files, rushes or stock here that you can use. Or maybe you could help me place it. And what happened to the material for the Algerian film? I can't find it. Too many questions! It would be great to catch up. Give me a ring at the estate.'

Too many questions . . .

The following morning, when Jane and Claude arrived at the wine-pressing plant, Clarisse was not in her office. One of the two permanent labourers, who was unloading a consignment of barrels, said she hadn't phoned in or mentioned anything about arriving later. He hadn't seen her since the previous lunchtime.

Claude frowned.

'I'm signing this load in myself,' the hired hand explained to the gardener, who glanced at the delivery note, counted the barrels and nodded his approval.

'Usually everything that takes places here comes under Clarisse's supervision,' Claude said, 'sales, marketing, stock orders. Much of it was handled by the estate manager but as we haven't had one since soon after Isabelle died, Clarisse takes charge, after a fashion.' He smiled. 'Let me show you around. Curious she hasn't shown her face, though I hadn't told her we'd be dropping by. These are hewn from young oak,' he explained to Jane, as they stood watching the barrels being eased down from the lorry. 'They're delivered from a cooperage in Toulouse. We've been purchasing from the same company for years now. Isabelle did a deal with them and we've used their supplies ever since. The quality is top.'

'It had never occurred to me that you would need to change the barrels, not unless they were rotten or leaking.'

'The wood flavours the wine. This young oak gives a specific tang to our red. Let's go inside. If we don't have a harvest, though, we won't need the order. I don't know why it wasn't cancelled. Clarisse must've overlooked it.' He shook his head. 'The old lady's losing her grip, good and proper.'

Jane was beginning to get a fuller picture of the lack of direction. Luc had remarked almost a year earlier that Clarisse had no perspective on stock levels. Since his death, her grasp seemed to have slipped entirely. 'Let's go inside.'

They began their tour of the interior block.

She followed the gardener into a chilly, windowless space, a temperature-controlled wine cellar. 'Eighteen degrees,' confirmed Claude, as he checked a thermometer and nodded. Two rows of eight gleaming stainless-steel tanks were standing vertical on tiny legs.

'Sixteen cylindrical tanks made and shipped in from Italy. Each vat containing . . . Well, any idea, Jane, how much rosé is here in front of you?'

She shook her head. This was impressive. The austere tranquillity and the spotless environment were a surprising and, yes, impressive sight, reminding her of a pipe organ in a cathedral. And then, out of the blue, an evening of long ago crept back. She and Luc had been leaving the Louvre. He had led her by the hand to the church of Saint-Germain l'Auxerrois to listen to an early-evening recital, a low-key public performance. What was remarkable was the programme on offer: Queen's *A Night at the Opera* performed on the organ. Luc and Jane had sat close, shoulders touching, in the packed pew, absorbing the hard rock compositions rising like dulcet poetry from the pipes of the church instrument. 'Bohemian Rhapsody' floated high above the religious icons. Incongruous, and yet entirely in harmony with its surroundings. Amazing. Who else but Luc would have ferreted out such an unlikely recital? At a later date, when she was at university in London and writing to him regularly, he had replied with a postcard of Claude Monet's painting of the church of Saint-Germain l'Auxerrois. He had scribbled only three words on the back: *My Sweet Lady x*.

She must still have the card somewhere, packed in a box, stored, slipped inside a book. Moments frozen, in boxes. Why had there been no organ music at Luc's funeral? She would have included that long-ago rendition of 'Bohemian Rhapsody'. Luc had loved her, she was sure of it. This other secret life, the betrayal was, well, impossible for Jane to get her head around, to accept, even while it was breaking her heart.

Claude was still talking. She had lost the thread.

'So, we press the rosé slowly, allowing the tint from the fruit's skins to seep into the liquid.' He paused, glancing at her. 'Each vat when full contains one thousand litres, so sixteen thousand litres, which amounts to close to twenty-two thousand bottles of *cru classé* rosé. Plus there's the red, of which there is far less, but it is mighty fine and sells at between twelve and fifteen euros a bottle.'

Jane was taken aback. 'And the rosé?'

'Eleven, twelve euros a bottle.'

'Are these vats full?'

Claude struck the side of one repeatedly, as though he were giving a saucy slap to a woman's buttocks. It reverberated hollow. 'The juice is way down this year. And it's too young to sell yet.'

Jane had always been aware that Luc's family landholding operated as a lucrative business, but she had not understood to what extent. Who would want to see all this go under? Clarisse's negativity was bewildering. Even if the dedication and energy required to keep it all afloat was far more taxing than Jane had envisaged. Too much for anyone approaching eighty.

'A mighty shame to let all this fall into ruin, Jane.'

Was Claude fighting for Patrick's future, calibrating his grandson's inheritance, which would be nothing but walls and unruly hectares if someone did not take the entire proposition in hand? Did he and Matty know that Luc had been intending Patrick to inherit all this? Or was Jane the only living soul who knew of Luc's designs for his son?

Might he also have addressed postcards to Annie, his 'sweet lady'? The thought almost immobilized her. 'Yes, yes, it's certainly quite an investment,' she murmured. How could she even for a moment contemplate remaining here? Luc's betrayal, the devastation it was causing her, was not going to heal while she remained surrounded by his world.

'These gleaming casks replaced a cellar full of cement storage tanks the two Cambon women inherited when they bought the property. It was before my time, but Madame Isabelle took one look and declared them old-fashioned. Several were cracked. They'd been here since the nineteenth century, she said. She also believed the cement was leaking unacceptable quantities of iron into the wine.

'She organized their replacement with these stainless-steel beauties. They cost a heck of a sum, plus the installation, but the improvement to the wine has been marked and upped our standards no end. We use stainless-steel vats and oak barrels, a different settling system according to the wine. Our top reds are fermenting in wood in the old cellars. The white and our rosé – our biggest crop – are in these, at controlled temperatures. Shorter wait time for them before the wine goes on the market. Hence swifter return.'

Their voices echoed as they passed along brick and stone corridors, the floors laid with vintage octagonal tiles. This building was as old as any on the entire estate. They were in mid-conversation.

'Yes, we produce and bottle here so we are a domain wine, estate wines.'

Jane shook herself back into the here and now. 'It's really a boutique outfit, isn't it?'

'Spot on. Clarisse would like that as a sales angle. Les Deux Soeurs boutique wines. You should discuss it with her. I'm surprised no one's come up with it before.' Claude was now entering a crushing room, Jane on his heels. The air was potent with the heavy winey odour.

'So, this is where the alchemy gets under way. Once the *comportes*, the full baskets, arrive here at the vinification plant the grapes undergo another standard control. And this one's vigorous because it is the last opportunity to discard any fruit that might lower the calibre of the wine. Anything in the crushing tanks that does not meet our quality standards is chucked out. What we are left with are top grapes, those that are the basis of the wine. And bloody good wine it is too.'

Jane had never visited the settling tanks before, the stainless-steel vats, or the crushing tanks. One day all this would belong to Patrick, Luc's son. Luc had stated in his letter to Clarisse that he hoped Jane would come to accept Patrick. How could he expect such forgiveness, when her own son had been lost? If she could contact Dan, she would ask him to accept responsibility for the dispersal of Luc's material. Then her obligations would be at an end.

'You have to hand it to them. *Les deux Madames Cambons* put this property and, along with it, our tiny *quartier* back on the agricultural map. Madame Isabelle managed the wine and olive-oil production – all extra virgin – while Clarisse took the reins of the marketing and sales operations. Together, they founded a profitable and highly regarded business. Your father was their outlet to Britain and he proved himself a sharp and persuasive salesman. Madame

Clarisse had been hoping he'd extend their reach into Germany and the Netherlands. But, as you know, more exciting opportunities came your father's way.'

Jane wondered silently whether Claude and Matty had ever known about her father's liaison with Clarisse. Clarisse must have excused his abrupt disappearance with some fabricated story: an offer of better-paid employment elsewhere. Or some such.

They took a break for lunch, perching side by side on a stone wall facing an overgrown but rather attractive meadow, wild with lipstick-red poppies, blue borage, white daisies, and beyond to soft-fruit orchards. Matty had prepared them a basket. Chunks of her own dark bread, cloves of garlic, which Claude peeled and ate raw between slices of sausage he shaved off with his pocket knife, cracked olives, dried figs, hard cheese. He took his food seriously, washing the mouthfuls down with gulps of the estate's cheaper wine. A chilled, slightly sharp white today.

They spoke infrequently or not at all, passing morsels to and fro. Casual conversation did not come easily to the gardener, and Jane's heart was too heavy, her appetite less robust. Claude's sole comment, aside from grunts about the merits of his wife's kitchen, was to reiterate his concerns regarding the excessive growth on the land.

When they strode back to the pressing unit, there was still no sign of Clarisse. The two men working in the crushing plant said there had been no news from their *patron* and that it was most unusual for her not to put in an appearance. Claude remarked as an aside to Jane that Clarisse had been skipping the odd day here and there since Luc's death. Matty had said she believed she was suffering. Jane suggested that Claude continue with whatever chores he needed to be getting on with – they could pick up their tour another time – while she whizzed over to Cherry Tree Lodge to call in on her mother-in-law.

She drove along the rutted paths under a silky blue sky, bumping through jungly vineyards and orchards in the vehicle, which was now coated across its dashboard and seats with red dust. Wilderness was sweeping over the great wide spaces. The bright colours from the wild flowers and the rich yellow sunlight were almost blinding. She hurtled by a tractor standing idle, abandoned. Who knew that it was out here? Shouldn't it be in a barn somewhere? High-investment agricultural equipment going to rot. From beyond a wooden fence, Clarisse's chestnut mare stared at her with startled eyes, as though she had forgotten there was life beyond the lonely paddock. Who was caring for her, feeding her? Jane made a mental note to ask Claude.

Upon arrival, Jane's knock received no response. 'Clarisse!' she called, and called again, then waited. It was chillingly silent. A pair of cream butterflies fluttered by the window where the curtains were drawn. Swallowtails. Wherever they were, Jane fancied the spirit of Luc was too. Jane rapped on the glass. Eventually, she lifted the latch and let herself in. The air in the room was dank and close. Acrid. Every window shut. Flies buzzed and circled, caged within the stifling interior. The ashtray was overflowing with butts. Clarisse was on the flagstone floor at the foot of the stairs, crumpled as though she had tumbled and rolled down them. Jane ran to her and lifted her up, leaning her against her own crouched body. The old woman's pale face was cut and bruised, motionless, mask-like, but she was breathing – Jane caught faint sour whiffs.

Upstairs by the bed, Jane had found an almost empty bottle of Gordon's. Dr Beauchene diagnosed Clarisse's condition as alcohol poisoning, which had precipitated the fall. If Jane had not stopped by when she had, Clarisse's life would have been in danger. Clarisse was ferried in Beauchene's car to the *bastide* and from there by ambulance to the hospital in Saint-Raphaël. Jane accompanied her and stayed at her bedside, listening to the incessant overhead fans whirring hot air from one place to another, breathing in the less than pleasant odours of the hospital: old flesh, deodorant, air-freshener, *eau de Javel.* Every one of them reminded her of the loss of Luc and those weeks in Paris.

When the old woman came to, a tube was in her arm, her skin was sallow and greasy, her eyes drugged and milky. No longer nettle green, more a bleached mint. Her voice was reedy and slurred, as though she had suffered a mild stroke, and she had difficulty recognizing who was at her side. She tossed her head back and forth against the white pillows, her hair sweaty and matted, hanging like lengths of red-brown seaweed.

'Annabelle? Is it you at last?' she muttered.

Jane was roused from her reading. 'Clarisse, Clarisse, it's . . . You want Annabelle?' Jane was deliberating. Could she play the imposter?

Clarisse murmured incomprehensible nothings, then drifted back to sleep or semi-consciousness.

Why was she asking for Annabelle? Jane had understood from Luc's letter to his mother that the women were estranged. She must have disapproved of Luc's adulterous involvement with her. Surely Clarisse hadn't been fighting Jane's corner. That would be ironic.

All the while as Jane sat reading, watching over her mother-in-law, the woman's features lacked peace, her mind troubled. When Clarisse was capable of speech, of coherence, she was disgruntled, aggravated, vexed to find herself where she was. She demanded to be transported back to her home instantly. The doctor on duty vacillated, warning Jane, out of his patient's earshot, that Clarisse's blood alcohol level had read troublingly high. She had been drinking for some time, possibly on an empty stomach, and the anti-inflammatory tablets she had been taking to ease the arthritis in her hands and hip had caused a mild stomach ulcer. Spirits and smoking had exacerbated her problems. 'Who is her next of kin? You?'

Jane was flummoxed. Was she Clarisse's next of kin? Who else was there to claim the role, besides her grandson, Patrick?

'She needs rest and nourishment or her system will cave in and she'll suffer more serious consequences. It was fortunate you found her. I would prefer she stays here for another day or two.'

Clarisse growled, beating her fists against the sheets, insisting on being released 'this minute'.

The doctor, who had more urgent matters to deal with than one difficult patient, acquiesced and prescribed medication to protect the lining of Clarisse's stomach, strenuously warning her against alcohol. Jane collected the drugs from the *pharmacie* on their way out.

Was Clarisse safe to be on her own in the lodge, at such a distance from others? Logically not, but she wouldn't hear of being moved to the manor house, not even for a brief recuperation period. She became angry and threatening: a spark of her former self.

Jane managed to haul her up the narrow stairs and into her own bed, promising to call in again later with provisions. Before she left, she checked the cupboards for alcohol. They were pathetically depleted of all foodstuffs. The bottles of estate wine Jane found, she discreetly removed. As far as she was aware, there were no spirits stashed away, or at least she found none.

When she returned later in the afternoon with a bag of shopping, Clarisse was downstairs in her living room in a pale turquoise dressing-gown with a grey wool shawl wrapped around her shoulders, smoking. Jane had entered without knocking, expecting her to be asleep.

Clarisse was spoiling for a fight. 'Have you been through my cupboards?' she barked.

Jane went into the small kitchen and began to deposit the purchases. 'I thought I'd make you some vegetable soup.' She was attempting a breezy air. 'There's nothing much growing in the garden yet, but I –'

'I'm not hungry.'

'How about a bowl of pasta?'

'Fuck off.'

The unloading of the shopping continued in silence.

'You were asking for Annabelle.'

No reply.

'I think you mistook me for her in the hospital, when I was at your bedside.'

A stubborn lack of response ensued. The unwrapping of plastic packaging and the gentle whoosh of the fridge door closing were the only sounds.

Jane folded the bags, left them in a drawer and returned to where Clarisse was seated with her feet up, bare legs blue with veins. She was lighting a cigarette from the tip of the dying one.

'Aside from the level of gin detected in your system, you smoke too much.'

'Yes, well, maybe I'm trying to get the hell out of here. What business is it of yours and do you give a shit either way?'

Jane sat down and studied Luc's mother. Without make-up

and her habitually well-cared-for presentation, she looked drawn, as old as the limestone hills behind her property. Her facial skin was marbled, hair greying at the roots. She had grown frail, as though she might disintegrate at the first touch; she was a desiccated, vulnerable shadow of her former self and it was hard to hate her. 'Will you tell me about Annabelle?'

Clarisse made a show of inhaling the smoke from her cigarette and fussed with her dressing-gown. 'I don't have a clue who you're talking about.'

'I really would like to know.'

Pause.

'You mentioned her name several times.'

'I must've been dreaming.'

'No.'

'Some things are best left alone, best not spoken about.'

'What things? What do you mean?'

'You wouldn't want to hear it.'

'Of course I do.'

Silence, but for Clarisse inhaling and exhaling smoke, wheezing. Her eyes were screwed closed.

'Clarisse?'

'She's your sister.'

'Clarisse, I'm serious.'

'So am I. Your father's other daughter. His second girl.'

15

Jane sucked in her breath as though someone had just kicked her in the stomach.

Clarisse roared, triumphantly or bitterly, 'Ha! Happy? That's shut you up, hasn't it? Did you remove my gin and the wine bottles from this house? I want a drink and I don't remember signing over my power of attorney or decision-making to you.'

'My father's other daughter? Are you telling me that you and Dad –'

'Oh, don't sound so fucking self-righteous. I really don't know how my son tolerated you.'

'Shut up, Clarisse! Shut up.' Jane was on her feet. 'I've had it with your opinions about Luc and me. TELL ME ABOUT ANNABELLE.'

'You've just told me to shut up.'

'Who is Annabelle? Where is she?' Jane was screaming now. Her eyes a cauldron of fury.

Clarisse shrugged. 'Annabelle is your sister.'

'That's not possible. What are you talking about? Does my father know of her existence?' Anger spewed out of her, like oil from a geyser. A plume of hot savagery. 'I can't believe this.' Jane was pacing, trying to gain control, to rearrange her thoughts, to make sense of what had been thrown at her.

'Peter never knew.' A deflated delivery.

'You had a child with my father and he never knew?'

'You got it. Where's my gin?'

But Annabelle was Annie, wasn't she? Or so Jane had

supposed when she'd seen her in Paris. Matty's daughter, not Clarisse's. This made no sense. Had Luc known that he had a half-sister? In the letter Jane had found, he spoke of Annabelle, not Annie. He never referred to her as his sister. Did Luc know that Annabelle was his half-sister? He'd had a child with his half-sister? Was Clarisse concocting nonsense, confusing facts? Losing her mind? Or was she playing a macabre game?

Jane swung back towards her mother-in-law, who had heaved herself from her seat and was hobbling towards a sideboard set in a shadowed corner in a rear recess of the room. She yanked open a lower door and dragged out a full bottle of Bombay Sapphire gin.

'Leave it!' bellowed Jane.

'Who are you to give me orders? If you don't like what you see or hear, then get out of here.'

'Give me that bottle.' Jane lunged towards Clarisse, almost toppling the woman, attempting to confiscate the liquor, but somehow Clarisse deftly out-manoeuvred her and shuffled to the hatch that separated kitchen and living quarters where wine glasses hung on stalks from overhead hooks. She clambered, stretching, reaching, bucking Jane off her back and shoulders. They tussled. The bottle fell and smashed on the flagstones, spilling the clear liquid everywhere. Clarisse crumpled onto her hands and knees, splayed like an injured lizard.

'Get up – get up. Mind your arms!' Jane leaned in to her, attempting to lift her, to protect her from the glistening shards of blue glass. Clarisse shrugged her off. Both women were wild, demented, out of control. Decades of hatred, of mistrust had broken loose. Jane was insane with half-formed information. The pungent vapours of juniper rose into the air about them, burning into their nostrils. Jane was the taller, the stronger, the fitter and younger, but Clarisse fought with a trapped vixen's fury, tearing into the fleshy topside of Jane's hand, drawing blood. Jane let out a howl and recoiled, leaving Clarisse free to crawl to her chair, spent. Blood trailed after. The underside of her arm from wrist to elbow had been lacerated on the broken glass.

Both were damaged, done for, lying in the emotional cinders.

16

Day was breaking with a warm flaxen light. The early-morning sky was veined, a variegated pearl and salmon pink. Overhead, the moon was receding, bleached to a distant white ghost hanging high. All was still. Jane, motionless, hands in her lap, sat contemplating the dawn, waiting for the day. The sun was breaking now, gilding the vineyards, turning the vines' dark unruly forms into an aureate display, a torrential river of gold. The morning promised fresh summer. An early-in-the-season day, not yet humid, not yet burdened by the debilitating heat of late July or August's sultry extremes. A bird overhead was warbling, flitting from branch to branch in the cherry tree. It chirruped and whistled with such unencumbered merriment Jane might have thought the tree itself was in song. Luc would have been able to identify the little soloist, but Jane had no clue. The sounds, longer or shorter whistles, were more or less the same to her.

Beyond the fence along the lane, a fox came stalking, russet and lean, hungry-looking, pointed head wheeling from left to right. In front of the closed gate it froze, one front paw drawn cautiously off the ground, leg crooked, sniffing. It had caught a whiff of human scent. Then, reassured, it continued on its way. Jane was in a wicker chair she had carried out from indoors and placed on the grass between cottage and cherry tree, her knees pressed tight against her chest, Clarisse's bloodied shawl knotted about her shoulders to keep out the chill. Clarisse was upstairs in her bed, sleeping, snoring, sedated. Jane had called in Beauchene, who had dressed the gashed arm – fortunately no arteries had been severed – and administered a potion to calm Madame, to take the edge off her anxiety.

'Go on, drug the shit out of me,' she had rasped, but had eventually submitted to his reassuring tones, too spent not to let go.

After Beauchene had cleaned and plastered Jane's hand, she had agreed to stay over at the lodge. The second bedroom was a storeroom, stacked from floor to ceiling with the Lord knew what; it was impenetrable. Jane had curled up on the sofa, from which she listened out for her mother-in-law directly above. The old woman had not stirred. The sedative had worked its magic, while Jane had barely closed her eyes. Tossing and turning, her mind working overtime, her neck was cricked, her back ached. Dark and terrible emotions, jealousy and fury, were wrestling within her. Rage tussled with reason, against incredulity. What if this was not true? What if Clarisse had lied, taunting her with the unlikely yarn that she had given birth to a child by Peter? But if it was true, where had the infant been born? Was there a record of the birth? Where would she find it? In the ledgers at the Malaz church?

Jane had lain on the sofa, contorted and uncomfortable, going back over dates to bring logic and order to the jigsaw puzzle. Had Clarisse been pregnant on the night Jane had interrupted her father's adulterous tryst? Had Peter been aware of an illegitimate second daughter? Clarisse had claimed not, but was she lying, fantasizing? Was the entire story fantasy? While she was giving birth - if she had given birth – Jane's mother had been wasting away, heartbroken, dying of cancer. And if Peter had known, what choice would he have made? Would he have left home and settled here with Clarisse and Annabelle?

And then the sudden implausible possibility that Jane had

a sister, a half-sister. And a nephew . . . The actuality of a family. A sibling. That she was not alone. But a sibling of Clarisse's making, with Clarisse's genes. Her father's too. What freaked her more than any other thought was Luc's role in this scenario, Luc's relationship to Annabelle and Annabelle's son, Patrick.

Who was Patrick's father? Annie was his mother, wasn't she? Patrick was Annie's boy, Matty's family. It was a maze, a minefield, it made no sense . . .

Jane was tired, befuddled, drained. Logic was evading her. She had half risen from the sofa, deciding to return to the manor house, to Luc's hoard, to reread the letter he had penned to Clarisse, to reconsider it in the light of all that she had discovered that night. Luc's gun lying on the sideboard. Its hidden presence had returned to her during the night. If he had discovered he'd fathered a child with his half-sister . . . The complexity of such an existence might have driven any sane man to contemplate an act of suicide. Suicide as his last remaining solution. The car driven off the road. End of it.

It was urgent that Jane complete the discharging of his professional affairs. Bring the remainder of the material upstairs, store it all in *the petit salon*. There, in comfort and tranquillity, she could sort through Luc's life. Or pass it all over to Dan, if he would accept the task. She could pay Arnaud to carry the heaviest of the boxes and files, the old film stock, up from the cellars and place them all in the one room. From there she would work, executing the task as efficiently and swiftly as possible.

And what of Luc's gun? Might she give it to Arnaud? If not, who else?

The coffee brewing in the kitchen began to gurgle. Jane yawned, covering her mouth with the palm of her hand, rose, rubbed her face, bringing it to life, and padded inside to pour a large mugful. The ground floor still reeked of gin. It sickened her empty stomach. Clarisse, overhead, was groaning or muttering in her sleep. Even so she must have been disturbed by Jane's entry into the house, a presence below, for now she was calling, yelling for Jane, who turned and climbed the stairs. Her feelings towards her mother-in-law were fuelled by the woman's perfidious act. She hovered at the threshold of the room, uncertain that she would be able to form any words. By what twist of fate had it come about that she should find herself the carer of this creature towards whom she felt murderous?

'If looks could kill . . . I smell coffee. Bring me up a cup, will you?' Clarisse's arm, bound from wrist to beyond elbow, hung loosely from the bed, her ringed fingers almost brushing the carpet. Morning sunlight bled through the beige muslin curtains and streamed into the room. The sun's brilliance haloed the cherry tree, as though it had been plugged in or possessed a supernatural transparency. Jane gazed at it and beyond to an endless sea of vineyards, lit up as though consumed by flames, before she plodded back down the stairs and returned with two full mugs.

'Put it on the night table and sit down. I've been thinking about how similar we are. Both of us with our broken hearts.'

Jane placed the coffee on the white wood bedside table and waited, standing.

'You don't believe me, do you?'

Jane shrugged. She was bone-tired and had no idea what to believe.

'Annabelle was born in the January, six months after you and your father hot-footed it from here.'

'How can you be sure that she was his?'

'She *is* his. There was no one else. I was pretty smitten with Peter. The only man I loved after Luc's father.'

'Luc's father, the inspiration for Luc's film?'

'Ugh! Adrien? He was a bastard. A cruel individual. I hoped Luc would never find out the depths to which his father had sunk.' Clarisse turned her head towards the window, the veiled sunshine, then closed her eyes. 'I'd foolishly hoped Peter and I might have a future together, a different life, but you put paid to that.'

Jane ignored this declaration of love. 'Tell me about Annabelle.'

Clarisse lay silent. Then: 'Pass my cigarettes.'

'What happened, Clarisse?'

'Cigarettes!'

Jane handed the packet and lighter across the bed and waited.

'It was unthinkable that I could keep her, not here in this community. Isa and I were hated right from the outset. Pieds-Noirs from Africa, that's how they judged us. These Provençaux villagers are narrow-minded and jealous, living in tight-knit little factions. Back then, more than forty years ago, they even perceived the inhabitants of their neighbouring villages as foreigners, and they did not, still don't, take kindly to outsiders coming in, buying up the best land, giving the orders. We were two women with no men. Two women and one small boy living in a society of superstitious Catholics, Communists and misogynists. No one wanted us here, no one trusted us. We were excluded, walled out. How could I rear and educate an illegitimate child under such circumstances? Imagine her days at the local school. And what was I going to tell my son when he returned from university in Paris? "Guess what, you have a sister"?'

'So?'

'I gave her away.'

'Gave her away? You mean Matty adopted her?'

'I did a deal. She was less than a day old. Quiet little thing, hardly bawled at all. Slipped into this world like a petite ballet dancer and lay there sleeping at my side. But I knew she had to go. I'd steeled myself.'

'And the doctor? What did he say? Was it Beauchene? No, not Beauchene, surely. A midwife, then.'

'She was born up at the manor house. In the room you and Luc have shared these last five years. No doctor, no midwife. No one to leak the family secret.'

Jane was now perched on the foot of the bed. 'You gave birth to her alone? Or was Isabelle . . . ?'

'Matty. Matty was with me. She delivered her. When she took her first look at the little girl, she began to weep. More than anything in the world Matty had wanted a girl. It seemed as if it was meant to be. Matty took her, and when I was stronger we signed a contract. Isa drew it up. Matty, Claude and I signed it. One copy only.'

'Did you destroy it?'

'It's in my safe.' Clarisse began to cough again, a hacking that racked her. Jane plumped up her pillows and the wizened woman sank deep into them. 'I need to sleep,' she whined. 'Pass me my pills and the coffee, then leave me be.'

Jane handed her mother-in-law her sleeping pills and a glass of water. She stroked the old woman's head. Clarisse shrugged her off, but Jane understood now, finally, after all these years, the sacrifice Clarisse had made. She had lost Peter and given up her daughter. Her bitterness made sense now. 'I'm sorry if, as an angry girl, I forced that sacrifice upon you.'

'You?' Clarisse slurred. 'You wrecked my bid for happiness, but that wasn't the sacrifice. Now leave me be.'

17

'What sort of a contract was it, Matty?'

Matty was stewing chick-peas for their midday *bajane*. Steam clouded the kitchen, fogging the windows. 'At that time, we judged it a fair one, more or less. I brought Annie home that very day in a bundle of bedclothes. Just like that, Clarisse passed her over to me from beneath the sheets as though she were handing over a blouse she wouldn't be wearing again. I was taken aback, speechless, but I took the little love in my arms and she didn't make a sound. Into our lives she came. No resistance. I never even consulted Claude because I knew he'd be over the moon to have her.' Matty's face softened with the memory. Crow's feet appeared, like corrugated sheeting, around her eyes. 'In return, we were obliged to keep Clarisse's secret. Not a soul was to know.'

'No money was exchanged?'

'Lord, no. She and Madame Isabelle moved us here to School House, so that we had a bigger home to raise the girl in along with the boys. Annie, whom Clarisse had intended to christen Annabelle, was baptised "Annie", along with our family name up at the local church and she was registered at the *mairie* with our names as parents. Annie Lefèvre. In return, the girl, when she grew up, could make no claims whatsoever against the estate or any of its household members, most especially Luc, who stood to inherit everything. Clarisse also requested that Annie move away from the estate altogether when she reached eighteen – she wanted no reminders – but Isabelle felt that was harsh. I don't remember if it's in the signed paper or not. We were sworn to secrecy. The girl was ours and that was the end of the matter. She was never to know her true heritage. There was nothing to trace Annie back to Clarisse.'

'Except the contract. Do you have a copy of it?'

Matty shook her head. 'There was just the one. The madames kept it. They said we had no need of it.'

'Were you informed who Annie's father was?'

Matty shook her head. 'I had my eyes, my suspicions, but no one ever confirmed anything. I never asked and I was never told. Prying is not my way. We were over the moon to have our own daughter, and that was enough for us. I never thought I'd done wrong. Better Annie was brought up here, we'd thought, close to her biological mother, but Clarisse would have nothing to do with her. She showed no interest in her or affection towards her. Quite the opposite. She seemed to hate the sight of her and sometimes was even unnecessarily cruel towards her. Arnaud hates Madame Clarisse to this day for the way she treated his sister. Occasionally, I noticed resentment towards me as well, but that came later and has grown over the years, worsening since our dear Luc died.'

'Cruel in what way?'

'As a child, Annie was forbidden to play up at the main house and in the surrounding grounds, forbidden to show her face. She and the boys were afraid of Madame's sharp tongue. They kept their distance, and knew their lowly place. If they ever wandered too far, they were scolded. Clarisse discovered Annie in the stables with her horses one afternoon. The girl had gone up there when the mistress was out riding. She loved the horses and would have liked to learn to ride. She got a right whipping for that. Well, you remember the night of your wedding party?'

Jane nodded.

'Arnaud, in particular, has suffered from Clarisse's harshness. He's particularly fond of his sister.' Matty fell silent, her face closed off. From outside came the insistent thwack of a hammer. Arnaud was repairing a rabbit trap. His two hunting dogs had been at his side when Jane pulled up. He had watched her arrival with suspicion. Since his discovery of her in their home, he had shown no warmth towards her.

'Do your sons know the truth?'

'They do now. All three were told the Christmas just before Annie turned seventeen. I broke it to them myself. Claude was with me. We sat together as a family by the fire in the sitting room and I spilled it all out.'

'Why did you violate the agreement?'

'It was their business to know. It wasn't right of us to hide it from them. I think the revelation was what sent Annie off the rails for a while. She wanted to leave home immediately, she couldn't bear to be here, and the first fellow that came along . . . Well, you know the rest.'

'And Luc? Was Luc also let in on the secret, Matty?'

Matty frowned. 'I thought you knew all this. The reason for your trip to Paris . . . It was Annie who told Luc. The pair of them had always got on well. She looked up to him, and when she learned of her true heritage, she spoke to him over Christmas. He was shocked, of course, but being Luc took it in his stride. I think it quite chuffed him, the thought of a little sister.'

Jane dropped her head. 'So, Patrick is whose child?'

'Raymond's, of course. Raymond Palomer. Annie's ex-husband. For what he's worth. The boy doesn't see much of his father, who's never contributed to his son's upbringing. Luc stepped in for all of that. Whose son would he be? Take your pick.'

Jane burst into tears. The deliverance.

'Whatever's up, lass?'

She shook her head. 'Sorry, Matty, I'm so relieved that it's . . . it's out in the open, for all our sakes.' She was too ashamed to voice the doubts that had diseased her these past months and the judgements she had levied against her innocent dead husband.

18

It was the last week of June. The wings of midsummer were unfolding and shimmering with a fluted incandescence. The days were long, scented, luxurious, the evenings caressed with their warmth. Lavender perfumed the air, its blossom buzzing with honey bees, Swallowtails and Hummingbird Hawk Moths. Swallows abounded, swooping to the pool, skimming its surface as though it were a helterskelter ride. Martins were nesting in the eaves of several disused properties on the estate. Butterflies were everywhere on the wing.

Before the heat rose, after breakfast and a swim, Jane hiked to Malaz, going up through the village, passing the old men in worn hats playing *boules* in shirtsleeves or vests in the dappled *place*. She waved a shy greeting to them and to the priest, Père Simon, who had said the Requiem Mass for Luc's funeral. He was seated at one of the outdoor cafés in the shade opposite the fountain, enjoying a glass of refreshment with the commune's mayor, well-heeled Monsieur Romerio, who owned a caravan site, a thriving tourist business, in a neighbouring canton set back from the sea. The pair watched her walking by and nodded a greeting.

Beyond the square, she strode, climbing the stone steps carved into the cliffside to the ramparts beyond which the church was situated, to Luc's grave. She was carrying an armful of burnt-orange and creamy-white roses gathered from the garden in the hour before she had set off. Their scent was rich with notes of cinnamon. The mid-morning call to weekday Mass was chiming from the tower as she stepped onto the pathway that led to the main church entrance. These days, it was sparsely attended.

The petals in her bouquet had begun to wilt after her long hike and she drenched the cut stems with water from a tap in the holy grounds, splashing her face and hands as well. Then she carried the flowers, dripping, to Luc's graveside.

'The flat has sold,' she told him. 'It's gone. Not ours any more. Robert completed yesterday. Best of all, the debts have been transferred to the various parties. We owe nothing. You can rest in peace now.'

A warbler or similar small passerine broke into song. She watched it chirruping, perched atop a row of hawthorn bushes that had been trained as a hedge along the south-eastern stone wall of the cemetery, from which, on a clear, crisp day, you could see all the way to Italy. Luc would have instantly identified the Sardinian warbler, a common enough sight in these parts. Its tune was melodious, lighthearted, befitting Jane's mood. Lighthearted, yes, in part, although her loved one's absence continued to tear at her. She carried her grief as a murmuring ache buried within her, unquiet, always present. There was so much that had been left unsaid. Each time she visited here, she was bewildered by where to begin.

'I wonder why you never felt able to confide in me. Was it because of Clarisse? Were you ashamed of your mother's behaviour, or did you think it would entrench deeper my feelings against her? I wish I knew. I wish I understood. Annie's my half-sister too, did you know? Patrick is my nephew. My father's grandchild. It feels weird and quite wonderful too.'

Jane wanted to reassure Luc that she would honour the hand he had held out to Annie, the generosity he had shown to Matty's daughter and to Patrick, even if his financial problems had cost her greatly and she was not able to afford the same assistance. She had delivered his letter to Clarisse, who had read it, guffawed and tossed it to the floor at her bedside. 'Always the foolish romantic, my boy. So unlike his father. Thank God.'

Clarisse was growing weak and less and less reasonable, displaying streaks of cruelty towards poor Matty, who in return was patient always, bestowing care and attention upon her.

Jane recounted some titbits of news. 'I'm going to stay on, for a while at least, see how it goes. I'll help out, as you wanted. It's so glorious here now, Luc. These young summer days. The golden orioles have been feeding on the soft fruits and Claude is bad-tempered about it. "One of the few crops we have at present and I haven't managed to keep them away. They nab the lot with their thieving beaks," he moaned to me yesterday.' Jane had attempted to mimic Claude's accent. There was no one else visiting the cemetery to observe her talking to herself, waving her arms about, warming to her narration. 'Arnaud discovered a swarm of bees up near the courtyard at the manor house. He said they'd fled their colony and were scouting for a new home.'

The swarm had clustered and hung, like a giant chocolate egg, beneath the eaves of the newly converted stables, she told Luc. 'I watched as he collected them – the whole bee community all at once – and settled them in a box in the back of his truck. He's housed them now in one of his newly constructed hives. Their queen was among them, so soon the estate will have its own honey, Luc. Honey to accompany our morning croissants . . .' She bowed her head, knowing that they would never again share this small delight together.

Tender is the night at your side. And the awakening. Oh, Luc, if only . . .

A tear fell and sank fast to her chin, then another. She rubbed her face with the back of her hand.

'What else? *Je t'aime.* The place lacks a rudder, Luc, a motor. It lacks *you.* Clarisse is giving up on it entirely. Her poor health and mood swings, her increasingly unhinged mind mean that she's more or less housebound and she's not very good-tempered about that either. She says the farm is my responsibility. And I don't know where to begin, whether I should begin at all or whether I should pack my bags and disappear, though I don't know where. So, what now for me, Luc? Give me a sign, please. Tell me what you think is best for me. Wherever I end up, please stay beside me.'

That evening, Jane sat alone on the terrace with a glass of chilled white wine, watching evening fall slowly and flocks of birds silently cross the sky to their feeding sites. In the distance, the sun was sinking behind ragged rows of trees in the unruly orchards. The sky grew red, like a rosary of fireballs hovering over the Mediterranean Sea. Slowly, as twilight paled into darkness, the silhouettes of the trees grew black. Venus rose. The moon appeared like a circle of muslin and began its languid trajectory. The darkness was thick and velvety. Jane felt at peace within it, her pain lying quiet, assuaged by the beauty.

A text message pinged on her phone. It was from Dan. It read: *Evening J, good to hear from you. Am back from a LONG shoot in West Australia, Prince Regent, Kimberlies. Delighted all getting resolved. Will call soon, Dx*

It lifted her heart to hear from Dan after so long, even if he was still far away. Beyond the loss of Luc, Dan was continuing to build his career, which both pleased and saddened her. She looked forward to hearing one day about the film he'd been shooting. She was surprised, though, by his comment about 'all getting resolved'. Was he referring to Luc's archives? Was he intending to help her? She hoped so.

That night, before going to sleep, she considered her position, her options, her solitude. She felt less alone here, even while regretting that she couldn't turn back the clock to share her new life with Luc in the light of all she now knew. She lay staring at the ceiling. The first ceiling that baby Annabelle, her *sister*, had ever set eyes on. Imagine that: *she had a sister.* She lay pondering sisterly activities. Bike rides together, blackberry picking. Borrowing one another's clothes. Visiting her dad, their dad. Peter had a daughter and a grandson but would never know about them. That saddened her.

Did Annie know they were related? Did Annie have any inkling of the identity of her father? Had Luc known that his half-sister was also his wife's half-sister? Had he been protecting her and her father? Was that why he had kept silent? Should she make contact with Annie?

The possibilities were boundless.

Tomorrow, she resolved, she would sanction the recruitment of workers to assist Claude. A squad making a concerted effort to set the estate back on track. She would remain here till the grape harvest had been brought in and possibly the olive harvest too. Beyond that? Well, she could decide her future later. Her gifts to Les Cigales, in memory of Luc, would be to clear out all that remained in the cellars, register Luc's film archives with the various institutes and participate in the restoration of the domain. All before she deliberated over the building of her own future.

She closed her eyes. She should contact Annie, of course she should. Excitement washed through her. It had been a long while since she had felt so alive.

19

Eleven were booked, behatted and taciturn. Claude had been hoping for a few more and would have been able to rope in an extra three or four if Clarisse had not embargoed the employment of Arabs on the estate. Arabs, especially Maghrebians, many of whom were Berbers, from north Africa, were the cheap workforce in these southern districts of France. They weren't popular with the Provençaux. *Au contraire*, they were despised and mistrusted by many, but they came in handy for labouring purposes. Frequently, they worked, *au noir*, for cash, at lower than legal rates, and they kept themselves to themselves, respected *salat* – their five sets of daily prayers – and shied away from alcohol. Many small enterprises hired them for the manual grind, but that made no odds to Clarisse. She had always refused to employ them. She feared them, she said.

Jane argued that she was being ridiculous.

The Cambon family had fought against them in Africa and Clarisse feared their revenge.

Jane overrode this nonsense and Claude found three willing Arabs to join the team.

So, finally the roll-call was fourteen. Or sixteen, if you included Claude and Arnaud. Claude had offered the men *le SMIC*, the *salaire minimum de croissance*, the minimum wage, increased marginally at the beginning of the year by ten centimes to 9.53 euros an hour gross. It was a modest rate but a legal and declared wage. They would also be given their meals and a rough bed, if they preferred to stay over. He had told

Jane that not a man among them had agreed to employment in return for a share in the upcoming harvest – 'Too uncertain,' he had explained. The truth of the matter was that he had never presented the proposition to his cronies. Times were hard down there in the south, and unemployment figures were on the increase all over France. *La crise viticole* was biting. Still, a man deserved a wage for a decent day's graft.

The rural workforce had their rights and demanded respect, which Clarisse was rarely willing to acknowledge. The men had been employed at Jane's bidding on behalf of the estate. So the estate could dig deep and find the funds. It was Clarisse's fault that the place was on the decline, no one else's. Claude was ignorant of the fact that Jane was advancing the cash out of her own pocket.

He and Matty were both living under the illusion that Clarisse or the estate, which boiled down to the same thing as far as they were concerned, had capital stashed away, no matter her pleas of poverty. He might have been a little more flexible if Jane had confided that the funds were coming out of her own earnings.

When Claude placed his hand-scribbled calculations on the breakfast table, Jane swallowed hard and sat down, seated stiffly against a straight-back chair.

'We're looking at a layout of fifteen weekly pay packets.' Claude was already employed by the estate so his salary was not included, but Arnaud's was. 'So, it amounts to a little over five thousand euros per week. The national working week is thirty-five hours, a measure brought in by our socialist prime minister, Lionel Jospin, in 2000, and hotly ranted against by Clarisse. Beyond the thirty-five, the men are on overtime, Jane, and their hourly rate increases.'

Jane nodded, staring at Claude's sheet of paper torn from an exercise book. She sipped her coffee. This was going to gobble up all her savings and all that she had earned and put aside this year. She prayed it would not eat into the small lump sum she had been paid from the flat sale. It was summer, long days, and the urgently required work was enough to give her and her bank account nightmares. 'How many weeks are we looking at?'

'It depends how far you want to take this, how thorough you want to be. Back when Madame Isabelle was alive, the regular land crew counted eight, plus me as foreman. To get this place to where it was when she was running it will possibly mean work for a dozen employees for a year.'

'A year? Lord, let's see what we can achieve in a fortnight.' Jane laughed brightly. She was putting on a brave, undeterred front.

Claude nodded. 'We'll doubtless need longer, Jane. You'd better relate the facts to Madame, but I'll tell the men to be ready to start the day after tomorrow. Tomorrow Arnaud and I will service the machines we own and we'll drive to the *cooperative* to hire those we don't. How does that sound?'

Jane nodded. She dared not ask the tariff for machine rentals.

'Any thoughts on how you want to go about the clearing?'

Jane shook her head. 'I'm counting on you to organize it, Claude. And while we're about it, let's get the tractor back under cover if you're not going to be using it.'

'Arnaud's already towed it in. He's preparing it for oil changes and it needs new brake linings. We're sorting it.'

'Good.'

'Right, then. What I'll do is this. I'll break us up into four small teams of four men each, with me flitting between all of them, keeping an eye, as will Arnaud, but no matter how hard or thoroughly we work, Jane, we won't be able to resuscitate all the vineyards. You're clear on that, aren't you? I'm not promising miracles here.'

Again, she nodded.

'We'll tidy up as many fields and groves as we can manage and strim the highest-risk growth elsewhere. The days are getting longer and hotter. The region's on red alert in terms of fire. The commune's sent out leaflets to all the larger holdings, including us, warning that there'll be hefty fines if we don't clear back responsibly. When the tourists get here – it's July so any day now they'll start descending in droves – with their sloppy land ways, their disrespect for the environment, their selfish disregard for us working farmers. And if there's one whiff of a mistral, the fires could flare up in a second. One thoughtless match, that's all it takes. Or arson. Then the flames rage and spread at speeds that beggar figures. The estate should never have fallen into this decline, but it has.' Claude was clearly thankful that Jane was finally giving him the go-ahead to cut and prune.

'It's in your hands, Claude.'

That oniony scent of felled vegetation: weeds, wild flowers and grasses levelled. It was an exhilarating perfume. The buzz and thrum of machines firing in every direction. There was an unexpected splendour, a grace, in the sight and motion of the men hard at work. Figures squatting in the shade of the *pins parasols* for refreshment breaks, labouring in fields amid the sun-blasted yellows of Van Gogh, the delicate tones of Paul Cézanne, and even, in the pre-dawn light, if she were out of bed to ride with the crew, a hint of Millet's *The Angelus*.

Distant pines reaching for the sky, bleached-out vegetation, sea and mountains with only heat and crickets to remind Jane that there was life born of this ancient rock-solid stillness. Rural panoramas were being stripped and reconfigured by the muscular labourers with their chainsaws and cutting machines, their strong hands as rough and hirsute as giant spiders. Jane accompanied Claude on several of his morning or afternoon reconnoitres. Ahead of and encircling them lay semi-jungled fields, groves, vineyards climbing towards the purple-blue mountains. In each, where a quartet of men had set to strimming or uprooting the wild greenery and blossoms, there was orchestrated movement. Nothing appeared to be haphazard. Without a word spoken, a signal given, they worked in harmony, like dancers in a troupe. And before Jane's eyes, as she watched, the landscape was transformed.

She wished Luc and Dan had been present to film the metamorphosis. Layers of vibrantly pigmented growth were being peeled away, chiselled to the bone. Shafts of light were revealed through the empty spaces, a deep-blushed rose was the earth's hue when revealed, while flurries of multi-coloured blossoms were settling, one on top of another, like a kaleidoscope of expiring butterflies. The contours of the terrain were being laid bare, exposed. Here was the most dramatic change. Where the sloping land was *en restanque*, a Provençal term for drystone or mortarless terracing, the eye was suddenly drawn to the chunks, the slabs, of magnificent limestone, orange-toned from having been embedded for centuries in the roseate soil, hewn from these Mediterranean mountains, to the medieval craftsmanship of the walls and to the powerful imagery of the hills.

And the land made no complaint. *Au contraire*, the liberation seemed to give it voice. Higher inland towards the base of the mountain, the olive groves, all planted on ancient terraces, were also being cut back, but there the men left great swathes of the wild vegetation to continue to grow freely. The visual result was an enchanting patchwork of colour and height alongside razored yellowing grass. They docked and cut the swards, shaving circles round the feet of the silvery trees, revealing felled daisies and knobbly, snakelike olive roots, grey as elephants' trunks, burrowing across the surface of the pebbled calcareous soil.

'By late 1962 when the Cambons took possession of this domain, Les Cigales was a bankrupt affair. The women drove a hard bargain and purchased it for a good price. No one locally had the funds to step in. In those early days, the olives picked during the estate's harvests were trussed up into hessian sacks and transported to a local co-operative set on a craggy slope west of Malaz, where they were pressed into peppery green oil, bottled and sold locally.'

As she stood on dried earth and stone, listening to Claude with his head raised upwards towards the mountainside, the sight of the gnarled groves spoke to Jane's soul.

'How many olive trees have we on the farm?'

'Three hundred centenarians and close to seventeen hundred younger ones, planted by our two French-Algerian women during the 1990s, the decade when European Union subsidies had looked favourably upon French olive businesses. The fruit is harvested by us and then Arnaud drives it in that old truck to one of several mills hereabouts where it's pressed into oil. Only a few kilos of our fruit are cured for table olives.'

'Any particular reason?'

'Our variety, the *cailletier* cultivar, is particularly fine for oil. We produce some of the best oil in France.'

Jane recalled the disused mill near Cherry Tree Lodge from her childhood expeditions with Luc, and its burbling stream that in high summer dwindled to a trickle. It was rated number seven on his list of 'Les Cigales' Top Sixteen Hiding Places'. The stream water was clear as glass, *eau potable*, quenching their thirst after their long hike to that hinterland spot. They had wiled away many contented hours at the old mill while Luc took photos and made sketches of how it might have looked and operated, and Jane watched, weaving daisy chains or jotting down the French names of the flowers in a sketchbook Luc had given her.

She often wondered why Luc spent so much of his time with her and not with the twin sons of Claude and Matty who, a little older than she, were closer to his age. 'They have to work when they're not learning,' Luc had replied. 'In any case, I like to pretend you're my kid sister. I would have liked a sister.' It had saddened her back then that he had thought of her as a small sister when her passion for him was on fire.

And now they both had a sister. Annie.

'I remember the water mill up behind Clarisse's lodge.'

'Oh, Lord.' Claude laughed, and his brown face puckered into a dried fruit. 'That place has long since fallen into disrepair, Jane. Not for a century have olives been pressed on this estate.'

'Why are they leaving so many pockets of grass overgrown and not strimming the entire grove?' she asked. He was tearing morsels off a baguette with his teeth and chewing them with a lump of hard cheese. He'd been up since four and this was his second snatched breakfast.

'Habitat for nature's creatures, Jane. Pollen for the honeybees and every other pollinator, all of whom *entretien* the grounds and do their bit towards keeping the earth healthy. That in turn helps keep the dratted olive fly at bay. Even so, it'll be a poor olive crop this year in spite of all those good-looking fruit fattening on the branches. I fear we'll lose the lot. It's a bloody shame.'

'Are all these olives no good, then?'

'Without looking closely, I'd guess that about sixty per cent of them have already been infested with fly larvae. We didn't clear the groves and burn the fallen diseased drupes at the end of the harvest last year. We were going to do it after Christmas when Luc got back from London . . .' Claude fell silent, picked a crumb off his unshaven chin. The strimmers droned on insistently. Only the cicadas answered back. For one moment their zinging was like the wailing of women at a wake.

'Fallen olives rotting on the ground are home to the hibernating olive flies, where the little blighters winter, ready to rise up in the early summer and lay their eggs for larvae in the next season's fruit. It's the same problem here as with the vineyards, Jane, land management. It all comes down to land management. Without the clearing and cleaning of the grounds, we're asking for trouble, for disease, fire and undernourished crops.'

She swung on the soles of her boots and turned to face south. The sun was full on her face; the noise of the machines buzzed on the hillsides behind her. The view to the distant glimmering sea was spectacular, as though the entire country was spreadeagled at her feet, sweeping to the distant blue ocean. Jane had not visited the olive trees for years. She had forgotten their beauty. Then a memory crept back from these groves, of climbing in the gnarled old trees with Luc. It must have been that joyous first summer, so full of wonder and discoveries, or perhaps her second here. She had never climbed a tree before. Luc had led her by the hand and together they had scaled towards the upper branches, perched on their wooden thrones within touching distance of the endless blue sky.

'When I die I want to come back as an olive tree,' Luc had declared, roosting high in his branch, drinking in the view, scanning the sky for birds.

'Why?'

'Because they live for centuries and then you don't have to keep on dying and coming back again. You can be the same tree for a thousand years.'

She smiled at the memory, taking heart that Luc was present here somewhere, watching over her.

20

It was raining. One of those almighty South of France summer storms when the gods go to war and the sky's imaginary platelets crash and collide against one another, causing lightning and deluges of water, irrigating the baked earth, feeding, saturating the fruit of the land, dampening all talk of potential summer fires.

It was Friday, late afternoon, 4 July, Independence Day in the United States and always an occasion for celebrations along this South of France coastline; it was when the US Mediterranean navy, its Sixth Fleet based in Naples, anchored offshore and extravagant firework displays illuminated the beaches at the major resort towns. With all Claude's warnings about fires spinning out of control in areas where the land was desiccated and unruly, Jane had been fearing the worst, so the rain was a blessing. They were two days into the land clearance. The dramatic change in the atmospheric conditions might halt the proceedings for a day or two but it had eased off the fire threat. And it was the weekend, so the cutters could rest and she wouldn't be obliged to pay them overtime.

Jane was alone in the house and for the first time since Luc's death she had music playing. His iPod plugged in, she was listening to Pablo Casals. She had just replaced the receiver on a call to Peter's care home.

'He's been asking for you. He's getting a little fretful,' Frances had told her. 'He's not been going out in the garden as much as he used to, though I know one of the nurses always puts her head in and offers to have a stroll with him. It's a shame because the days have been quite warm. "I best not go now, dear," he says to the nurse. "My Jane's on her way. She's running a bit late. It's the traffic." I popped up to see him myself, to remind him that you're away and will be back soon. His face lit up as though a switch had gone on. He told me then that you were on location with Luc in Algeria.'

Jane felt her heart split. She had been neglectful. It was almost two months since she had seen her father. In spite of his dementia, he had observed the passage of time more acutely than she. A trip was beckoning. 'Thanks for telling me, Frances. Can you put me through to him, please?'

Jane waited, listening to the extension ringing in his first-floor room. Trilling and trilling. Was he staring out of the window, his back to the phone on the table, its flashing light not visible to him? His hearing was poor, and he was blithely unaware of the urgency with which she wished to hear his voice.

'Hello?'

'Dad! Dad, it's Jane.'

'Hello, love.' There was a long pause.

The lump in Jane's throat was almost choking her. *I have a sister, your daughter*, she was thinking.

'Luc's been in, but I haven't seen Jane. Is she away?' His voice was weak, insubstantial.

'Dad, this is Jane. Dad? I'll be there soon, I promise.' After a few more incoherent exchanges, she replaced the receiver and stared out at the trees waving in the summer storm, blossoms blown from their flowerheads flying everywhere. She was feeling melancholy. And then she smiled, remembering how Peter used occasionally to sing to her, 'My Melancholy Baby'. Calling to his 'favourite' girl to come to him.

'I'm on my way, Dad.'

When the knock came, a rap on the back door, Jane had

already placed the plate from her solitary early-evening supper in the dishwasher and was considering a nightcap – a little premature, perhaps. She wasn't expecting anyone. She was at her computer, at her temporary desk – the breakfast-room table – going through her accounts, firing off invoices for three translation contracts she had managed to complete during these turbulent weeks. Importantly, she had just finalized her booking for a flight to London and was feeling rather excited at the prospect of stepping back into England and seeing her father again. Her bank account was showing a credit for the first time in a long while. Robert was nagging her to let him invest the capital sitting in her current statement unless she had plans to purchase a property immediately, which she hadn't. Whichever, a trip to London was essential, most urgently to see her dear father, then to discuss her options with Robert and to move her funds somewhere sensible. She wasn't intending to let him know that she was shelling out her hard-earned income and personal savings for the upkeep of Luc's family estate.

Matty had promised to take good care of Clarisse during Jane's brief absence. Bless dear Matty, who was getting it in the neck on a daily basis from Clarisse, foul-mouthed and ungrateful. Every time Matty drove over to change the sheets, clean the house, bring the patient hot homemade food, loathsome bile greeted her, recriminations about the theft of Clarisse's child.

'It's painful, I can't deny it,' confided Matty to Jane, 'but she's never had the sweetest tongue, we all know that.'

'It happens,' the duty specialist told Jane when, desperate to put an end to this behaviour, she had rung the hospital.

'Is there nothing you can prescribe?'

'Ask her GP to up the level of sedative,' was his response. 'I wouldn't worry greatly, Madame Cambon. Your mother will probably pass through this phase. They usually do.'

Mother!

The knock on the back door was repeated, a little more firmly this time. Jane frowned, glanced at the time on her phone: seven forty-seven. She definitely wasn't expecting anyone. She rose and crossed through the pantry to the back door, running her hands through her unbrushed hair, tired and ready for a warm bath rather than a bracing starlit swim in the rain. She frowned, thinking she'd heard a dog barking. Arnaud? Was it Arnaud with his hunting hounds? Christ, she hoped not.

She released the latch.

It was Annie, sopping wet in yellow wellingtons and a hooded yellow rain jacket. 'Don't say it, I look like Paddington Bear.'

The two women stood facing one another in silence. In Jane's head ran the message she'd seen on the flowers: *Our lives will never be the same again without you.*

'May I come in?' Behind Annie, the rain was falling in solid sheets.

'Yes, of course.'

Charging about in the yard was a very muddy and almost demented Walnut. 'Walnut, oh, *viens içi*! I've missed you.' Jane drew open the door and shuffled backwards to allow Annie to pass. She bent low and clapped her hands for the dog. The arrival of such an unexpected guest was a little overwhelming, the last caller she had expected.

Annie shucked off her boots, threw the coat to the floor where it settled, like melting butter, in a pool of water, and headed in stockinged feet directly through to the table where Jane had been working, as though she instinctively knew the pulse of the house. Puddles spread across Matty's clean tiles in her wake. Jane waited for the dog.

'I brought wine.' Annie grinned perhaps a little over emphatically, drawing a bottle of red from a shoulder bag with a wink. '*Un peu* crazy, but I didn't feel I ought to raid the house cellars. I thought a glass or two would break the ice. You do drink, don't you?'

Jane nodded, fazed, remaining where she was. Annie returned to the kitchen to collect a corkscrew. 'You don't mind if the hound comes in, do you? He's very wet, I'm afraid.'

'No, I want him to – I called him.' Surely Annie knew that Walnut was *her* dog.

Annie was back at the scullery door whistling for the spaniel, who bolted inside and began jumping frenziedly against the hem of Jane's skirt, smearing her legs and feet with mud. She laughed loudly and ruffled his warm black head, hugged him hard, filthying herself, and crossed to the dresser where the everyday china was stored. She pulled out a low-rimmed bowl and filled it with water. He slurped thirstily and splashed even more dribbles all over the floor with an energy that was almost alarming. She bent to his side and stroked his ears as he gulped. 'Take it easy, boy.'

'He's excited,' observed Annie.

Glad to be home, thought Jane, while deliberating about whether she could ask for the dog back or was that too unkind, too selfish? Had Luc given Walnut to his half-sister and nephew?

'Are you all right?'

'I was wondering about the dog, about why –'

'Oh, Lord, do you want me to chuck him back outside? I never fuss about the mess he makes at our place but maybe you or Mum object.'

Mum? Jane raised her eyes and looked Annie full in the face.

'I meant Matty,' Annie said softly. 'Matty's my mother, whatever else . . . you know.'

'And what about Luc?'

'He's . . . he was my friend, best friend and big brother.' Annie strode past Jane to the dresser and drew out two long-stemmed glasses. She sloshed a good serving of red Shiraz into each. 'It's Aussie wine. I hope that's fine with you. Not as grand as the estate homegrown stuff here but cheaper.' She laughed nervously. 'Let's go and sit down, shall we? You look a bit . . .'

'What?'

'Green.'

'Green?'

'Sick. Freaked, maybe? At the sight of me. A golden vision in sopping plastic.' Annie let out a small chuckle. She had Peter's eyes, indubitably, and a little of his brash, swaggering style too. Jane's heart swelled with warmth.

The urchin and the princess. On that long-ago night of her wedding party, what if she had known, guessed, that the little girl, the intruder, this woman, was her half-sister? Such a deft hand of Fate.

'Do you mind?'

'Sorry, what?'

'I hope I haven't barged in?'

Jane shook her head. 'I'd thought of calling you.'

'I'm down for a few days to see Mum and Dad and I thought we should talk, you know, you and me. Mum said you and she had had a bit of a chat.' Annie was calling over her shoulder as she led the way, glasses and bottle in her hands, through to the breakfast room, sipping at a glass as she travelled.

Jane followed. 'Apologies, it's a bit of a mess. I've been working. Why don't we go through to the library?'

'Mess doesn't bother me, but we can, if you like. After you, then. The only time I've been in those front rooms was for Luc's funeral. I was never allowed up here.'

Jane entered the room first, followed by Walnut, who settled his dripping self, coat reeking of drowned dog, on the mat by the fireplace, which had been decorated for the summer with pine cones and dry olive logs. He was panting and comfortable, tail thumping. He was home. Jane stood and looked towards the window, to the rain beyond. It hadn't rained like this, as far as she was aware, since the day of Luc's burial.

'How is it that you have our dog?' she asked, as Annie placed the bottle on the small table between them, then slid a glass towards Jane. Jane gathered up a box of matches from the fireside and lit two candles in tall tulip-shaped glass holders. The glow softened the light in the room.

'Yes, Walnut belongs here, I know that. *À la tienne.* It's good to meet you properly at last. Luc spoke of you so frequently.'

'Cheers, *à la tienne.* Did he? He never mentioned you or Patrick to me, ever. I seem to have been kept in the dark about quite a lot of . . . rather vital information.'

'I know and I'm sorry, truly.' Annie lifted her glass and took a sip. It was already close to half empty, Jane noticed, while she cradled hers, untouched, at chest level. 'Please sit.' A formality, stiffness, had overtaken her and she seemed unable to shake it off. She was unsure whether she should throw her arms around Annie and hail her immediately as her sister or be angry with her for not coming forward sooner, for stealing the dog, for the debts, for so many resentments Jane had built up against the unknown woman who, thank God, had not been Luc's mistress.

Annie, seated, picked up on Jane's discomfort and it tempered her initial approachability. 'Walnut is yours,' the younger woman confessed. 'Luc left him with us for Christmas and then . . . and then when we heard the news and the awfulness of everything, I couldn't bear to part with him, for Pat's sake as much as mine. Pat loved Luc like a father. His own dad is, well, he's a bit of a shit, to be honest.'

'Yes, Matty told me . . .'

'If Luc hadn't stepped in and helped us . . . well, I don't know what would have become of me. I'd've been back living with Mum and Dad, bringing Pat up here, where everyone would gossip about my divorce.' She shuddered. 'Village life. Give me big-city anonymity. How's the wine? It's OK, isn't it? Not plonk.'

Jane hadn't tasted it. She was still standing, still trying to get a handle on Annie's arrival.

'I'll leave Walnut here when I head home next week. I shouldn't have kept him, should've given him back months ago. Sorry, big-time. It was really selfish, but I couldn't bear to deal Pat another blow. The loss of Luc . . . Pat's taken it very badly.'

'Where is he now?' Jane finally sat, sinking into the sofa opposite Annie. She sipped the wine and placed her glass on the table. 'It's rather good, this Australian Shiraz.'

'Yeah, I like it too. I buy it at my local Carrefour. He's doing a few days sleepover with school pals in our neighbourhood in Vincennes before they break up for the summer holidays. They all go horse-riding in the park. He's a great kid. You'll love him.'

The two women looked at one another, then smiled, and uncertain laughter broke out between them. Jane was thinking how beautiful Annie was, radiant. She seemed to have inherited the best features from both Clarisse and Peter. The eyes from her father, Clarisse's magnificent mane of auburn hair, the hour-glass figure she had so seductively flaunted when she was younger.

'Have you been to see Clarisse yet?'

Annie shook her head and raked a hand through her long locks. 'Nor do I intend to. We don't speak, I'm afraid.'

'She was asking after you, after Annabelle, when she was hospitalized recently.'

Annie shrugged. 'I'm not Annabelle and nor have I been since, well, literally since day one, although Luc often called me by that name in deference to his mother.'

'Are you not on speaking terms because she gave you away?'

'The good news is I got Matty and Dad in exchange. I lucked out there. It was a terrific piece of good fortune. No, not because she gave me away – I can sort of understand that, although I'm bringing Pat up as a single parent – but because she always kept me at arm's length, never let me play or hang out anywhere near her or Luc or the main parts of the property, as though I was a contamination, a nobody. My existence was completely denied. I thought I was rubbish – very bad for a growing girl's self-esteem, because I didn't know the story back then. And because she insisted Mum sign a paper swearing her to secrecy. I would never have known the truth about myself, my origins, if Mum, Matty, had held fast to the contract. When I eventually found out that I had been adopted, I contacted Clarisse and tried to arrange to talk to her, but she refused to see me, put the phone down on me. So, no, I won't be paying her a visit.'

'She's quite ill.'

'Mum'll help her. She always does. Always has done. Even so, until you came back, she would have kicked my parents out – she'd taken their jobs away. She's got no heart.'

Jane wondered whether Annie's observation was true. Everybody has a heart, but whether Clarisse's had grown cold for reasons unknown to those around her, Jane couldn't say. She must have suffered deeply when Peter and Jane had disappeared, knowing she'd lost someone she loved and that she was pregnant. Had she been intending to reveal to Peter that she was having his baby, hoping to persuade him to leave Vivienne? Who knows what the future might have held if Jane had not discovered them together and not blurted out the facts, baldly, to her innocent mother, who had taken it so badly.

'Penny for them?'

'Do you know the identity of your father?'

Annie shook her head and took a sizeable gulp of wine. 'Claude's been a great dad to me. He's my dad, but my biological father . . . I would guess some local toff, high-ranking official or other, probably with a family so he couldn't marry Clarisse. I don't know and I don't want to know. I'm not even *un petit peu* interested in Clarisse's past. Do you mind if I have a cigarette?'

Jane was not fond of smoking, particularly indoors, but she nodded that it was fine. 'I'll have to find an ashtray.' She was about to rise in search of one – since Luc's death, the ashtrays had been in cupboards – but Annie said, 'Don't worry, I'll just chuck it in the fireplace. Or maybe I won't light up. Don't go. Let's just sit and listen to the rain and talk, maybe get a bit sloshed together.'

Jane resettled herself. On the floor by the fireplace there was an old coal bucket. 'Why not use that?' she offered.

'Thanks. I smoke and drink too much. Luc was always on at me about it. Mind you, he smoked plenty. Jeez, I miss him.'

Annie spoke of Luc with such affection, such intimacy. It was painful to hear. She would not appreciate the comparison, but in certain aspects, her gestures, mannerisms, she took after Clarisse. Jane longed to chat about Luc, to magic him into the room with them, conjure him up and have him present at their serendipitous tête-à-tête. It was wonderful to sit of an evening and have someone to talk to, particularly about Luc, but there was also a frisson of jealousy. The world that Annie and Luc had shared with Patrick, and their communal lives, she had been barred from. Excluded by their choice, never hers. If the truth had been divulged, would she have accepted to be a member of their select little family?

Yes, like a shot. Whose decision had it been to preclude her from all knowledge of Annie and Patrick's blood relationship to Luc? Had it been Luc's, because of her father? Who knew that Peter was Annie's father? It was conceivable that Clarisse had never confessed it to Luc.

Annie was lighting a cigarette and dragging on it. Her hands were shaking. She's more nervous than she's letting on, thought Jane. The smoke rose into the warm humid evening. It was still raining hard: Jane could hear rolling claps of distant thunder, the falling drops hitting the garden tiles and sodden earth. Occasionally the room was lit by a flash of lightning. Annie leaned forward to refill their glasses.

'What do you do?' asked Jane.

'You mean as in how do I earn my living? And how pathetic am I at it, that Luc was subsidizing us?'

'Well, I –'

'I write music. I write it but I'm not yet selling a whole heap. It certainly doesn't keep the bills paid, the wolf from the door. I wonder where that expression came from.'

Annie wrote music!

What shall we sing next, Dad?

What would you like to sing? You choose, Janey. Or how about 'The Bells Are Ringing For Me And My Gal' or 'My Melancholy Baby'?

I don't know those songs, Dad.

No, you weren't born when they were written.

Let's sing one that you wrote then . . . Yours are the best.

'You OK? You look a bit green again. Does it freak you having me here?'

Jane shook her head.

'Are you angry because Luc never told you about us?'

'Why didn't he? Why keep such a huge secret from me?'

'He felt Clarisse behaved very badly towards me. He knew you and she didn't get on, which hurt him, and he didn't want you to carry any further gripe against her. He wanted to tell you, I know that. He felt you should know that he'd been, well, more or less keeping us.'

Jane lowered her head, wondering whether this was the subject Luc had alluded to when he'd said they must talk. 'It was all a bit of a shock. On top of everything else.'

Annie sipped from her glass. 'I'm glad it's out in the open.'

They sat a while in silence, both lost in their own memories.

'I wrote the soundtrack for one of Luc's films. He was really cool about it and encouraging. He said to work on it and not give up, but he didn't use it. I didn't study music or anything, didn't attend the Conservatoire. I would've liked to go to college, but when I found out about my background . . . I went a bit loopy. Music helped. It seems to come naturally, an easy way to express myself.' She paused, dragged on her cigarette. Jane kept silent. Annie shrugged, looking embarrassed. 'I talk too much, smoke, drink. I'm full of nervous energy but when I'm with my music, I feel at peace. Songs. I like penning songs best. Jazz, ballads.'

'Your father was a musician.'

'Sorry?' Annie's face, with a light brush of freckles, clouded with confusion.

'Peter was a musician. He doesn't play much now, strums a few bars for his own pleasure. He has Alzheimer's and, well, that's it really.' Tears had sprung from nowhere and were falling down Jane's face, rolling off the end of her chin and landing on her T-shirt. She wiped her cheeks with the back of her hand, sniffed and stared into the empty fireplace. 'Chimneys in summer are *triste*, aren't they? Lacking purpose. I must remember to get them swept.'

'Are you talking about your dad, or whose dad? Sorry to hear he's got Alzheimer's.'

'Clarisse had an affair with my father. It was the summer

of 1980. I found them together. Sunday, the eleventh of July. She was already pregnant with you, as I understand it. I was a little upset, to say the least, and Peter, my father, and I left the following morning. I never came back here until I returned as Luc's wife ten years later. You gatecrashed our wedding supper, remember?'

Annie nodded, mouth open, silenced.

'According to Clarisse, you were born six months after I found her in the throes of . . . with my father.'

'January the tenth, 1981, that's my birthday. I think we need more wine. Maybe Clarisse was sleeping with someone else. Or had been before your dad came on the scene.'

'She claims Peter is your father and that she was, well, in love with him.'

'Wait, are you telling me that . . .'

'That we're sisters, half-sisters. Yes.'

'Holy Moses, Jane, that's amazing. We do need more wine. We need champagne.'

'Luc didn't know. You're sure?'

Annie shook her head. 'Definitely not. *Wow!* This is extraordinary.' Annie jumped up and began to pace the room. Jane watched her. 'It's like being born again.' She was punching her arms above her head as though dancing to music. 'You and I are sisters?'

Jane grinned. 'Half-sisters.' She lifted her glass. 'Cheers. I've never had a sister before. I've been thinking about what sisters do.'

'Me neither. Awesome. Fucking fantastic. We should run out in the rain and shout it to the heavens.' Annie held out her hand. 'Come on, let's go.'

'Are you serious? It's lashing down.'

'How many times in your life do you meet your big sister for the first time?'

Jane stood up. 'Kid sister in my case.' She took Annie's hand. They cantered through into the kitchen where the door was still open and the rain was settling on the mat.

Annie stepped out first. She lifted her face into the rain. 'Come on, Jane, don't be wet!' She burst out laughing and Jane joined in.

Jane ventured outside, hunching her shoulders against the downpour. 'This is madness. We've got no shoes on!'

'Too right. Feet sinking into mud! Give me a hug. I'm going to write a song about this moment. It'll be a huge hit.'

Come on, Janey, let's sing. She heard her father's voice, so clearly he might have been at her side, and lifted her fingers to her face. 'Oh, Annie, I wish I could share this moment with Peter.' They were dripping, both of them sopping wet. Walnut had padded through into the kitchen and stood at the door inside watching them, his head turned to one side, a habit he had when he was curious or puzzled.

'Look at him!' laughed Annie. 'He's such a cute thing. I will miss him. I wonder if my mum knows. Or maybe best not to say anything. Our secret. It's AWESOME.' Annie was yelling now, arms spread out either side of her.

'I think Matty has a fair idea. Come on, let's go in.'

They ran through to the library, squelching as they went. Annie was shaking her head, raindrops spinning about her. She was pouring the last of the wine into her glass and topping up Jane's, even though it was hardly touched. 'So Clarisse, cold-hearted and bitchy, fell in love and got hurt. How about that? Hey!' Annie swung about and hurried across the room to Jane, who was pulling off her T-shirt and using it as a towel to dry her hair. She hugged Jane tightly.

'I'm completely blown away by this. Hi, sis.'

21

The summer gale raged on for another day and night. By Monday, calm had returned, leaving just one tree uprooted. A dead soldier straddling two terraces. There was little other damage. They had been fortunate. The television news was showing footage of floods further west into the Var. Homes destroyed, roofs, tiles, dustbins and cars floating down streets transformed into mucky rivers. At Les Cigales, the bright summer sun reappeared. One of the hired hands sawed up the fallen pine, stored the logs in the woodshed, and it was as though the storm had never passed that way, except that the grounds had been well and truly irrigated and, for the next week or so, the fire risk was non-existent.

By Tuesday, the men had resumed their land-clearance tasks and Jane set off for London. Annie drove her to the airport. The two sisters had agreed between them that Annie and Patrick would come back at the end of the school term to spend their summer on the farm.

'I don't think Clarisse will be too thrilled when she finds out,' declared Annie, as Jane was closing the car door.

'She's bedridden. It's unlikely she'll know you're with us.'

'But she's not going to be confined to her house for ever, is she? She's not terminally ill or anything. She'll be up and about again at some point. And if she should catch sight of me or Patrick strolling about the place, she'll be fit to kill.'

'We'll deal with that problem when it arises. See you soon. Have a safe trip back to Paris and tell Patrick his aunt looks forward to meeting him.'

They smiled at one another and hugged tightly.

'On one of your trips to London, maybe I could tag along. I'd like to, you know, meet your father. My father. Well, Claude's my dad and always will be, but . . .'

'He won't know you, Annie. Even if I try to explain to him who you are.'

'It doesn't matter. It would just be good to see him. Take a look at where I came from. Those musical genes.'

Jane nodded, careful not to make a promise, uncertain as to whether this would be a good idea for Peter. 'Let's talk about it at the end of the summer.'

A tailback of vehicles queuing behind them was growing impatient. One or two drivers were hooting. A head poked out of one of the windows and shouted impatient abuse.

'See you soon.' They embraced again and Jane was on her way, back to London, running with a spring in her step that she hardly recognized, that she hadn't known in a while. Nothing and no one could replace Luc, but for the first time in months she felt less alone, less abandoned. She felt the embrace of family.

The worst of all tragedies had befallen her, the loss of her husband, childhood friend and sweetheart, the man she had loved all her life, and she was still here. She had not killed herself, although her own annihilation had been what she had craved. Life would move her forward gently and it would be kinder to her from now on.

As she was about to enter the terminal, she turned her head and swung round. Annie had pulled the car over and stepped out. She was jumping and waving, like a demented creature. 'Bring me back a photo of Prince Harry.'

Jane's face broke into a broad grin. She stuck out her arms and gave her sister a double thumbs-up.

PART THREE

Second Harvest

France

I

The days of summer were slipping away and the drowsy mellowness of autumn was rolling in. The vine leaves were growing burnished, claret-toned and yellow. The few shrivelled grapes that remained on the stems beyond Les Cigales' modest wine harvest had been left as fodder for the birds and scavengers. The air was redolent with all the scents and portents of a year drawing ineluctably to its close. Bonfires burning; beads of morning dew on the plants; squirrels foraging; mulch underfoot along the wooded pathways; leaves drifting to land, decorating the lawns; long fine threads from spiders' webs glistening in the sharp, clear sunlight; the setting forth of flocks of swallows borne on gentle winds. The cicadas had gone underground, but the long-bodied wasps were still droning, gorging on the overripe figs that had split open and were bleeding red, resinous seeds all along the pathways.

There was a serenity yet a finality about the shift in the seasons.

Mother Nature was turning the great wheel, resolute in what she was about.

Claude, with Arnaud, was arranging logs for the *bastide* for winter. The woodshed was almost stocked to bursting.

Due to a bout of pneumonia and a perpetually troubled mind, Jane had relocated Clarisse, almost kicking and screaming, to one of the spare rooms on the first floor at the *bastide*. After her return from London, she had replaced Matty in the regular ministrations to her mother-in-law. It was essential. Clarisse's behaviour towards her housekeeper had grown unsettling and aggressive. However, the twice-daily excursions to and from Cherry Tree Lodge had proved debilitating during the preparations for the *vendange* and the grape crushing. Jane was exhausted by Clarisse's mood swings and demands. Still, she was coping, and while her mother-in-law was close by her, she could care for and keep a wary eye on her. Aside from flying to London one weekend in every three to spend precious hours with her father, and occasionally snatching lunch in town with Robert or a girlfriend from the old days, Jane remained on Luc's family estate. This rural existence, she was discovering, brought a structure to her days, and the lifestyle was therapeutic. She enjoyed rising early, working hard, sharing al fresco packed lunches with Claude and *les mains embauchés*. And when the day was drawing in, the sun setting, she looked forward to solitude, time alone to be with her memories and the spirit of Luc, to deliver the farm's news to him. Or she would sit reading peacefully, sipping wine, enjoying the musical accompaniment of frogs at twilight, playing long-forgotten CDs, while glancing at the swooping excursions of the bats.

Before Luc's death she had been one creature, and at some point she would become another, though she had no urge yet to shed her cocoon. She was too timid to fly. This life stage seemed to be a necessary process and a protection. Her dead husband was spinning a web about her, holding onto her, embracing her.

Was grief redefining her?

She had no urge to return and buy a small flat in London. Aside from proximity to her father, and the few cherished hours in his fading company, England held no draw for her now. It represented the past. She was discovering that she was more at home in France and she regretted painfully that she had been so resistant to the move during Luc's lifetime. Her stubborn resistance to Clarisse shamed her now.

Jane's money had been invested but she was not quite ready to turn her mind to where she might put down permanent roots. Possibly, at some future date, in the springtime perhaps, she might lean towards Paris: the City of Lights, the city of sweet memories and the city she felt had belonged to her and Luc. The added bonus would be that she would be close to Annie and to her nephew, Patrick. Wherever it was to be, whatever her next move, she trusted that Luc would give her a sign, that he would guide her forward.

It was more than a full year since Jane had led the grape harvest for that one nightmarish day. It might as well have been a lifetime ago for all that she had lived through since, although the loss of Luc, now ten months gone, tore into her as sharply as it had at its first hook. Time will heal, was proving to be a preposterous lie.

Led by Claude, who had risen to the occasion like a newly appointed adjutant heading up the battalion, they had achieved this year's *vendange* a month ago and the wines were now in their settling tanks. The regular smattering of *les villageois*, hired country folk, had assisted, but no foreign labour, not this year. A turbulent, humid summer climatically and the tardy tidying up of the vineyards had, as Claude had predicted, blighted much of their crop. The result was an 8,000-litre vintage, a paltry quantity by this domain's habitual production standards but, once sold, the returns would bring in sufficient revenue to keep the estate afloat for possibly another season. The end-of-year land and *habitation* taxes, plus the arrears, had all been paid – a whopping sum – and the books were showing a very modest positive balance. Jane was satisfied. At some point she would hand her temporary, self-appointed responsibilities to Claude or Annie or conceivably back to Clarisse, if she rallied from her health problems. (Jane's own small investment of three weeks' pay for the men to partially clear the land, she had chosen to see as a gift.) One day she would leave, move on. But not yet, not just yet. She felt no urge to go anywhere yet. She intended to mark the anniversary of Luc's accident, his departure, here alongside him, and she had promised herself she would not walk away and leave Matty to care for Clarisse. In time, Jane supposed, Annie and her biological mother would be reconciled, then Jane's work here would be at an end.

For the present, they were enjoying Indian-summer days and preparations for the olive harvest were afoot, which, in spite of Claude's misgivings, promised to be far more bounteous than he had predicted. This revelation caused an uplift in spirits, a certain merriment. As a tiny team, they had achieved the bringing in and pressing of the grapes, and now they were moving on, heads held high, to the next challenge.

Elsewhere, chainsaws were striking up like instruments in a rehearsal orchestra, whirring across the valleys, anticipating the slow creak and crack of felled trunks as they thudded, like shot beasts, to the earth.

The starlings had arrived. Jane drank her morning coffee in the courtyard sunshine while Walnut twitched and snored at her side. She tilted her head skywards and played audience to the high-flying pyrotechnics of the murmurations, swooping and wheeling playfully – until, in one united dip, they bee-lined for the olives. The movement of their wings – how many thousands of wings? – was like the tinkling of tiny bells; a caravan whizzing across the sky. Most farmers hated them, perceived them as predators. Some spoke of trapping them or laying down poison for them, but wouldn't that kill all other birds as well and put the dogs at risk? At Les Cigales, Claude's decision was not to go with the chemicals, not to kill or trap, but to move the date of the olive harvest forward, to gather in the semi-purple drupes before they were gobbled from the branches.

For the last couple of years, a majority of the olive mills had started to open several weeks earlier than had been the centuries-old tradition. Due to a perceptible shift in seasonal weather conditions, farmers were picking earlier. The Cambons' habitual choice of mill, *le moulin de la famille Bonnard*, had already set its wheels turning, which meant that Les Cigales was at liberty to press as soon as they had collected their first batches of fruit.

'Before our groves are wiped clean, what say we get those drupes off the trees? This bout of late-summer weather could bring out the olive flies again and we'll stand to lose the lot. Between the flies and the starlings, our olives are a sitting target.'

Jane concurred and Claude set the upcoming Monday as the launch date for the harvest. This put them two weeks ahead of their projected schedule. Arnaud, due to the change in programme, would not be available. He was departing *en vacances*. Claude shook his head and said that it was a drawback, and that the boy should stay. Arnaud stood his ground. He was going hunting. End of the discussion.

Life shifted into top gear.

It was half-term. Annie and Patrick had returned south for the week and were staying with Matty and Claude. Habitually, it was Arnaud who serviced and drove the Citroën truck, ferrying the dozens of crates – *les cageots* – brimming with purply olives to and from the mill. As an apology for his upcoming absence, he was working day and night to make the old transport roadworthy before his departure.

A radio on the ground was blasting out Coldplay. Arnaud's

head was buried in the bonnet of the vehicle, which he had towed out into the barnyard from one of the outbuildings where it had been on blocks since the previous year's olive harvest. He was bleeding oil, servicing the filters, cleaning or replacing spark plugs, changing tyres, balancing wrenches handed to him by his newly appointed assistant, his nephew, Patrick. Annie was nearby, engaging in lighthearted banter with her brother and son while hosepiping the *cageots* as well as cleaning out the *bidons*. The *bidons*, Claude explained to Jane, were the stainless-steel containers that kept the newly pressed oil stable while it settled in cool dark corners of the cellars no longer dedicated to Luc's film enterprises.

Claude, with perennial collaborators, Michel and Jean, was in the groves, laying the nets around the base of each of the trees' trunks, both young and old. The wives of the two regular employees had also pitched up to lend a hand. These countrywomen were no strangers to olive harvests and knew the process of net-laying as well as any male (some thought better).

Once the nets, used to catch the falling fruit, were in place – red nets, white nets, green nets, like dozens of Italian flags draped over the ancient stone terraces, reaching from one tree to the next – the signal was given to call in the crew. Claude estimated that the picking of the two thousand trees would take them *une bonne semaine*, a good week. They needed to work fast and not every one of the younger plants was offering olives. So, yes, it was agreed that *une bonne semaine*, eight or nine days at the outside, should do it.

Late on a Sunday morning in the last week of October, the team, with their family members, assembled around two iron tables, dragged into the courtyard for the purposes of meetings, coffee breaks and slices of Matty's almond and ginger cakes. A slant of sunlight bled across a bowl of purple grapes and apples set in the centre of one of the tables. Fallen fig leaves lay like a mosaic underfoot as Claude talked through the schedule. Each day Jane was impressed by the ease with which their caretaker had assumed so much of the responsibility. He was in his element. Clarisse should promote him to estate manager, she was thinking, as she listened to him, but Clarisse was still sick and was showing no signs of recovery. As he spoke, in his sing-song Provençal accent, Claude was gesticulating theatrically, emphasizing the points with his hands, as so many from these parts did, hands as hairy as bacon rinds.

'We'll start out as the sun rises and we'll pick until we lose daylight, which I estimate will be around five thirty to six. So, be ready for long days.'

At the end of each day, the fruit and crew were to be driven back – the estate tractor and trailer would be used for the journey – to this courtyard area where two other hired helpers, who usually worked with Clarisse at the wine-pressing unit, would sort and select the fruit by hand. While the others slept, they would work through the night till dawn, jettisoning the silvery leaves, the debris, every mountain stone, twig, broken stick or tiny clod of earth that had been hastily gathered up with the olives as they were poured into the crates. The sorted olives would be loaded onto the truck and driven to the mill at first light.

'But without Arnaud who will drive the temperamental old lorry?' quizzed one of the team.

In every previous autumn this had been strong-muscled Arnaud's role – everyone referred to the vehicle as 'Arnaud's truck' even though it officially belonged to the estate. But the hunting season was well under way and he had set off that bright Sunday morning for the national park with a couple of his chums on a shooting expedition. The trip had been arranged before Claude had rejigged the timetable, bringing forward the opening of the *récolte*. Arnaud was happier over-nighting in a tent and spending his days in the Parc de la Mercantour at high altitude where only chamois and booted men with rifles climbed; it had proved a waste of Claude's breath to try to persuade his son to cancel his much anticipated shooting party. So, they were one man short and the position of chauffeur fell to Jane. 'Me? No, not me.' But there really was no one else, unless they hired another assistant, which budget constraints prohibited. She had never been at the wheel of even a Transit van before, and certainly nothing as ancient or treacherous as Arnaud's heap.

Claude would brook no objections and the role was designated hers. 'It will be the men who work the trees,' he decided. 'You will scale the wooden ladders.' They would stretch and pick by hand, filling baskets suspended from their shoulders, like satchels, or sending the olives directly to the earth. Showers of fruit. The women would gather on hands and knees from the nets below. No sticks were to be used to beat the drupes from the branches – 'It bruises them and our extra-virgin label matters to us,' Claude reminded the team, who nodded silently, each knowing the business as well as he.

Matty would keep the meals coming, as she was doing with the cakes right now. 'There'll be no disappointments on that score,' promised Claude, with a rheumy-eyed wink. 'All will be up to my dear wife's usual magnificent standards. She'll be working from the manor-house kitchen, loading up the pantries, as is her usual routine.'

The difference this year was that Clarisse had been installed in one of the upstairs bedrooms. She remained bedridden and barely aware of the endeavours in progress, and Jane was a little concerned that the disturbances created by the comings and goings would unsettle and upset her, but returning her to her cottage was out of the question. Aside from playing chauffeur to hundreds of kilos of olives and running to the local shops for fresh provisions not available from the land, Jane intended to keep a watchful eye on her mother-in-law as well as being generally available to deal with any unexpected estate emergencies.

The programme was set. Each knew his role.

The following morning at the hour before dawn, when the birds are beginning their song, the team assembled, bleary-eyed, and the annual *récolte* was inaugurated in the stables at Les Cigales with a vast breakfast, baptized with several litres of a gentle estate red. Everyone, including Annie and Patrick, was present, save for Arnaud and Clarisse.

The kitchen was a hub of enticing aromas and activity. Matty was at her perennial task of keeping the soldiers nourished, while Claude was doing his surprisingly fine best at running the show. While the adults were out gathering the olives, their sons and daughters or grandchildren, nieces and nephews, offspring of the pickers, chums of the offspring, all on mid-term break from their local schools, had assembled into a band, like so many chirruping starlings on the estate. Led by young Patrick, with a Trojan's energy, they disappeared en masse, shouting and jumping, immersing themselves within the copses and the pine forests. The raucous tribe was on the hunt for mushrooms, particularly the fleshy *cêpes*, *Boletus edulis*, also known in these parts by their Italian name: *porcini*. As well they kept their eyes peeled for the more delicate chanterelles, morels and the modest whites, returning to base, the courtyard, hours later, their arms laden, twigs in their hair, jumpers torn and boots soiled. They were breaking the law, of course, but who was to uphold it on this vast fertile tract of private land? They should have been collecting in wicker baskets to allow the spores to fall out as they were carried and thus aid propagation. The stipes should have been cut with knives, but no one was in a hurry to give their offspring such a potentially dangerous tool. One or two of the older adolescent boys carried their own pocket knives and they were responsible for the protection of the mycelia. The children had grown up with this annual field and wood recreation and there was little fear they would return to Matty with poisonous fungi. They could identify the edible choices instantly.

Others, predominantly the girls, were collecting green acorns and removing them carefully from their tiny chaliced cups or, higher inland, shiny chestnuts. All for the red squirrels whose bronze tails were turning black as they prepared to go into hibernation for the colder months. The children amassed neat hillocks of food beneath the fig trees on the large, yellowing leaves that lay like serrated plates across the lawn, hoping that the animals would help themselves to a few future meals before they disappeared into their dreys to sleep winter away.

'How sad that they miss Christmas,' remarked one small girl. 'If we knew where they were, we could take them presents.'

Shouts, cries of joy, could be heard rising in the distance, from across fields, groves and hills, when a bounty had been discovered and hoarded, or when an elated, frolicking Walnut had charged through the hard work and sent the acorns flying.

While the pickers were collecting sufficient crate-loads for Jane's first trip to the mill, she busied herself in the small salon where Luc's possessions were now almost entirely piled. She was packing up boxes of his written materials and archives to be posted off to the CNC in Paris. She had promised all this to them weeks ago. It was long overdue. The collections of old family films, the homemade movies, she had catalogued and stored in the library. She dreamed that she and Annie might sit and watch them together. The pistol lay on a side table. Its presence continued to mystify her and she was uncertain how best to dispose of it. When he returned from the mountains, she would ask Arnaud whether he could find a use for it. The Bible had been a gift from Patrick to his uncle and she was intending to return it to him before he went back to Paris.

She was gathering up the old photos she'd found a while back of Clarisse and Isabelle posing in front of their Citroën in Algeria – 1960, two years before the war's end. She thought she might paste them into an album for Clarisse, and for Patrick in years to come. Between her fingers was the head-and-shoulders shot of Adrien Cambon, Luc's father. Should it be included with the family history? Clarisse had spoken so negatively about him . . .

The telephone rang in the breakfast room – the house line. Jane cleared aside the scissors she had been using to cut lengths of string, to make space for the photos on the table. Then she hurried across the hall. She had left the key in the lock of the small salon for she always kept the room firmly closed, chock-a-block as it was with Luc's life, as well as many souvenirs of her own. Now, in her haste to reach the phone before it went dead, she omitted to close the door and remove the key.

It was the miller's wife, Madame Bonnard, returning Jane's unanswered calls of earlier that morning.

'*Ah, bonjour, Madame Bonnard, merci pour me rappeler.*' Jane perched herself on the window ledge, catching sight of her reflection in the open glass, refracted by the sunshine streaming in. She brushed her fingers through her hair. She needed a trim and was mentally calculating how long it had been since she had last visited a hairdresser. She was negotiating dates, times, rates with Madame Bonnard, while listening through the open windows to the exuberance of the youngsters. It made her heart sing to hear such vibrant life about the place. Walnut was scampering, barking, hugging Patrick's heels. Patrick, who reminded her of Luc, of the adolescent Luc, when she had first met him. Patrick, who lacked Luc's finesse, was a rougher cut of his uncle but certain lights and certain angles – a turn of the head, a smile, a question, a spoken thought, his boundless energy and curiosity – took her back years to their precious days among the trees, on the beaches, questing and growing, running side by side with the same exuberance beneath a wide blue sky. She and Luc: partners in the heady business of discovering life, of growing up. She sighed, replacing the receiver after securing their first mill booking of the season for the following day, finding herself once more yearning to turn back the clock and pushing aside all thoughts of what the future, which on some days she dreaded, held in store for her. Today, though, she was content and she was occupied, surrounded by this rustic life and bustling activity.

Clarisse yelling her name broke into her reverie. She scribbled the rendezvous details into her notebook, tossed her pen onto the table and darted up the stairs, her work on Luc's boxes and memorabilia temporarily forgotten.

From one of the first-floor-landing windows, she noticed two figures bending and working in the walled garden. She stuck her head out, waved and shouted, 'Coo-ee!' Annie straightened and returned the greeting with her broad smile. She lifted one of the few remaining tomatoes still growing on the vines and waved it high for Jane to see. There were no more salads now but a handful of deep ruby aubergines, skins still shiny, offered themselves. Annie and Matty gathered up whatever was edible for the pickers' lunch. Golden grapefruit and lemons were hanging in abundance from the trees while the bitter oranges used for marmalade and orange wine were green bullets only, slowly ripening. They would be a post-Christmas harvest.

Jane gave Annie a thumbs-up and sped along the corridor.

'Who were you calling to?' There were magazines spread all over the bed and floor. Clarisse's make-up bag had spilt its contents over the duvet cover. Face powder stained the pillows. Cold tea sat in a mug, untouched. A cloying perfume hung low in the air.

'Matty in the garden.'

'That woman is a witch.' And Clarisse began reiterating her invective, to curse, to verbally tear poor Matty limb from limb.

'Clarisse, you were calling me. Is there something you need?'

'What's going on? It's so noisy. There are a lot of people shouting and yelling. I can't rest.'

'We're starting the olive harvest.'

'With children? It sounds like children. Who's here?'

'I invited the pickers to bring their young. I've sent them off with Pa– to play on the estate. Why not try to sleep?' Jane was gathering up the lipsticks and creams and stuffing them back into their pouch. She was tidying the magazines into piles on one of two bedside tables. Foolish. She had almost let slip the fact of Patrick's presence.

'You just want me out of the way. Who's running all this? Surely not you. You made a mess of the grapes last year. I need to get up. Someone's got to –'

'Your blood pressure, Clarisse.'

'I don't want this place overrun with village children tearing up the grass and I don't want that bitch who stole my daughter – Where's your father? He should be here.' She was getting het up, throwing off the bedcovers, kicking her way out of the bed and was on her feet, gaunt and unsteady. Her jewellery was all that had not shrunk and the rings seemed grossly oversized on her wrinkled fingers.

'Please, get back into bed, Clarisse.'

'Stop ordering me about!'

They tussled as Jane attempted to stop the patient in her nightdress making for the door. A glass of water on the bedside table went over, spilling across the magazines Jane had just arranged there. She grabbed the frail but surprisingly strong old woman by the shoulders and began forcibly to lead her backwards towards the bed. Clarisse resisted and slapped out, elbowing Jane in the bosom.

'Oh, for – I said get back into bed! Or I'll have to call Dr Beauchene.'

Was it time perhaps to find a safer residence for Clarisse? Jane recalled how difficult that decision had been with Peter. Still, heartbreaking as it had been, placing him in a care home had proved the best conclusion in the long run. Jane would not be here for ever; Clarisse was not her relative; the task could not be left to Matty; Annie had cut the cord. When the harvest had been completed, Jane would sit down with Dr Beauchene – and Annie? – and talk through Clarisse's options. What would Luc say if he were alive? She was mopping up the water with a face towel from the bathroom and pouring a fresh glass of Badoit. Clarisse, scowling, had returned to her cave of sheets, coughing, muttering incomprehensibly, drained by her outburst.

'If your father was here, he'd care for me.'

'Here, swallow this. I'll pop in a little later, bring you a cup of tea. Sleep now.'

*

Downstairs at the kitchen door, Matty was laughing and shaking her head with incredulity as she took charge of the armfuls of earthy mushrooms from the excited boys and girls clamouring to hand over their booty. As remuneration, she was serving them multi-coloured plastic beakers of home-made fizzy lemonade and bowls of her grapefruit sorbet 'to be consumed outside, mind. No muddy feet in here, please. Oh, and the mistress is upstairs and unwell so keep the racket down. No screaming and shouting in the courtyard.'

'She's riled and restless. I've given her one of the tranquillizers Beauchene prescribed. I'm off to buy cheese. I'll see you shortly. Where's Annie?' Jane patted Matty's back and skipped out of the door.

'Claude took her off to the groves to join the pickers,' Matty called after her. 'See you later.'

Once the hordes of children were settled, drinking and slurping outside in the autumn sunshine, Matty set to preparing a prodigious pot of pumpkin and mushroom soup for the labourers. She'd take a bowl up to the obstreperous Clarisse too.

Jane reversed and gunned the accelerator on her way inland to a herder's highland farm to buy *crottins* of dried cheese and a fresh round wheel of Tomme, made from goat's milk, ripening in chestnut leaves. As she wrestled with the corkscrew bends in the estate's almost clapped-out van, fretting about how she was ever going to manage the loaded truck, she was climbing through forests of evergreens or deep-red and orange deciduous trees. This startling beauty brought her back to the present, overriding her petty concerns and duties.

Columns of blue smoke rose skywards and hung, like a celestial carpet, across the hillsides and over the valleys. The bonfires were fuelled with vegetation pruned back during the summer months, when lighting fires was illegal along this coast, and end-of-season vine and olive clippings. The rural homes she drove past were stone rectangles perched precariously on cliffsides. The perfumed smoke gave off scents of thyme and rosemary, cindered oak and olive stumps.

Jane wound down the window, a manual operation in the old banger, and put her head out to inhale the perfumed hinterland air, crisp at that altitude. Even though she was anxious to be back with the cheeses for the lunchtime spread, she slackened her pace to savour the moment and the alpine view that swept all the way to the sea. Her deceleration was a blessing. A black saloon, as yet out of sight, was hurtling down the mountainside. It took the bend at a ferocious speed. By a hair's breadth the driver, who was spinning close to the edge of the rocky ascent, swerved to avoid her van but clipped her wing mirror. Glass splintered, while the offending vehicle slewed and zigzagged, roaring and skidding, millimetres from the precipice. Jane slammed on her brakes as the Audi fired off down the winding road, disappearing out of sight, leaving her shaken.

She found a spot scooped out of the rock for overtaking and pulled over, stepped out and crossed unsteadily to the edge of the scarp. It was a leafy drop of some four hundred metres. If there had been a collision and the van had been thrust over the side, she would have been killed. She recalled Luc and his last minutes of life. After having wrestled with so many earlier thoughts of suicide and surmounting them, she might so easily have joined him today. She found herself laughing, a little insanely, and realized how glad she was to be alive.

2

Annie was assisting with the olive-picking, an occupation she had never been allowed to participate in before due to the *froideur* between Clarisse and herself. This year, for the first time, she was heading up the women's team and revelling in every minute of it. She was acquainted with these country ladies: they had been a part of her family life since her childhood. It felt empowering to be back in their company, out in the cold fresh air, breathing in the pungent scent of freshly picked olives, fingers blackened. Without Clarisse's oppressive presence, Annie was growing less wary about showing her face, about joining in with the estate's enterprises. She was more confident, careless, perhaps. She had a rightful role on the land, but she was not intending openly to flout Clarisse's written demands. The women sang as they collected the olives, French songs, country ditties, all the while watching the mountains of fruit swell impressively. Each day, while the workers were surpassing the previous day's loads, Jane, aided by the two fellows who were responsible for the sorting and sifting, cranked up the Citroën truck and set forth soon after dawn into the misty hills. It was a first for her too, to captain the pressing.

Backwards and forwards on a daily basis she commuted, scaling the heights expertly, even if her recent lucky escape had caused her to be extra cautious. She was a little jittery but she also believed that the arm of Luc had protected her. Still, those expeditions were hazardous. The old truck belched clouds of black smoke from its rusty exhaust, screeched at her gear shifts and balked at the winding ascents with the will of an overburdened stubborn donkey. At every swing, at every bend, the hundreds of kilos of olives rolled and rumbled, transiting their red plastic crates. It was her responsibility to make sure that the results of the team's labours arrived at the mill in the same impeccable condition they had left the estate. There was to be no damage caused by any jerky movements, no bruised fruits to oxidize the oil, Claude had instructed.

Upon arrival at the mill, François Bonnard, the younger, lame brother of Stefan Bonnard, the miller, was hanging about in the yard waiting to greet her. In the chilly autumn morning, his breath rose like smoke. In a neighbouring garden, a family of butter-yellow caged cockatoos screeched their respects. Farmers tipped their hats and eyed her calibratingly. As a rule, each diehard farmer unloaded his own harvest, but François appeared all too ready to lend her a hand with the shunting and weighing of her *cageots*. It crossed her mind that he might have taken a shine to her, or perhaps it was simply that Les Cigales, with two thousand *oliviers*, was a valued client. Whichever, she was grateful for his kindness because it was back-breaking labour. Jane was ferrying on average thirty-five to forty crates a day. Each crate contained twenty-five kilos of olives. So, on a daily basis, Jane carried consignments that approximated a ton of fruit.

Stefan suggested that she might want to set down her freight and leave it with them, once they had all agreed the weight. The olives could be pressed in her absence. There was no need for her to hang around in the frigid pressing-room temperatures. He suggested she collect her full cans when she delivered the next charge and that she deliver less regularly – perhaps two or three visits throughout the harvesting – but Jane had learned from Luc years earlier that the best oil is produced from yields that are pressed directly after they have been removed from the trees. And theirs was organic fruit so she was keen to oversee the entire process, to be assured that their single-estate pressing was respected, not mixed with others of a poorer quality or tainted with traces of chemicals. In any case, it was a vain hope that Arnaud's poor old truck would make the ascent with three or even two tons of crop aboard. So, for several reasons, she had no real choice in the matter. Up before dawn, the journey was a daily one, and stressful.

Clarisse never failed to remind Jane that she had let the wine harvesters down the previous year. Consequently, this time, as temporary *châtelaine* of the estate, she was determined not to botch her commitments. It meant hours of hanging about while the olives were washed, conveyed on moving belts through to the grinding machines, then crushed, the paste turned and pressed, before the final stage when the oil and water were separated. She spent the time, when not watching the olives, reading through material booked for translation. She was rather chuffed to be receiving more contracts than ever these days. Finally, the joy of the gurgling arrival of the velvety green oil, still warm from its transmutation. And the cautious drive back down the hillsides in the falling late-autumn light, hungry as a horse, chilled and stiff as the sun sank from view, empty crates and sloshing *bidons* in the back of the truck.

Each evening when she eventually chugged into the stableyard and pulled on the handbrake, exhausted, but relieved to have made it safely back to base, the pickers were already done for the day. They were relaxing and in a convivial frame of mind. In readiness for Jane's arrival, Matty had laid out chunks of her dark bread. The steel containers were dragged off the truck in the dusk light and transported directly into cool storage quarters while one – usually the last to have been charged because it was frequently not quite full – was kept back and conveyed by one of the labourers to Matty, who, hair falling loose, was in the kitchen sweating, stirring, muttering commands to scalding pots.

Faces flushed from hours in the fresh air and from imbibing rosé by an open fire, each man and woman was swigging the next mouthful of chilled wine. While they hunkered down comfortably with their legs outstretched to ease their aching limbs, booted foot over booted foot, soles steaming in front of the warmth of the open fire, chuckling at the prospect of a hearty meal, Jane jogged into the house for a hasty shower and to throw on some clean clothes.

Matty decanted a jugful of the freshly pressed, sharp, peppery oil and carried it ceremoniously out of the back door, crunching her way across the pebbled yard to the stable block, where Annie and Patrick had laid the dining-table, and Claude was stoking the open fire with a pair of sturdy seasoned logs.

Everyone cheered. Tired to their bones, they still couldn't resist rising and shuffling to the table to press their noses to the porcelain jug, to sniff, to inhale, to eye the miracle liquid, viscous and green. Before any meal began, each of the pickers served themselves a few drops of oil onto their plate and dunked a chunk of bread into it. Sucking, dribbling, munching, they relished, extolled and applauded the oil, born of the fruit of their labours. Oil that by their toil belonged in comradeship to each and every one of them. These were hallowed moments during which many opinions were pronounced, often with a poetic turn of phrase. This was their grace.

'Better yesterday.'

'Nonsense, it's the finest we've harvested.'

'Perfectly peppery.'

'Easy on the throat.'

'It's a fine vintage.'

'Like spun silk.'

'No land produces better.'

'*Cher Claude, tu est un maître.*'

The tradition, many millennia old, of the tasting ceremony was played out while stomachs growled in anticipation of the steaming plates of food soon to be devoured. Matty and Annie were carrying through the piping-hot dishes now to rounds of applause and rising cheers.

Jane could hear their ebullience from upstairs in the house. A glance round the door of Clarisse's room showed that the patient was sound asleep. Jane let out a sigh of relief. On other evenings, she had found Clarisse restless, angry, champing at the bit to be let out of bed, to resume her role as lady of the manor, lording it over the staff. On those occasions, Jane was obliged to take the time to quieten the woman's tormented mind, to settle her.

'How many are down there? How many are we feeding? I can't afford it.'

'Go to sleep, Clarisse, please don't fret. It's the same gang as always.'

'It sounds like an army. Oh, I'm so weary of it all. How much longer?'

'It will be finished in two days.'

'And then what?'

'Sssh, go to sleep.'

'Don't fucking patronize me! Are you staying or what?'

She had meant to care for Luc's mother. She had promised herself that she would, that she would resolve the rift, for Luc's sake, but not even Jane had read the depths to which her mother-in-law's grief, frustration and despair were driving her. Everybody was active, busy, high on the daily results of their labours and delighted to be a member of the team, which at its heart was a family affair.

And Clarisse should have been its materfamilias.

But the once-elegant beauty was declining, riddled with pain, and the seeds of the impending tragedy had been sown far too long ago.

At sunset on those days, Jane was tired. She was longing to skip back downstairs and share in the camaraderie, the laughter and lightheartedness of unwinding with family and neighbours. The olive squad. She was grateful for the distraction.

Perhaps Clarisse sensed that she was not wanted, was redundant, no longer the centre of attention. The estate was getting back onto its feet, slowly, without her . . .

But that evening, when Jane popped her head round the door, Clarisse was lightly snoring. Their evening would be untroubled. It was only as she gathered up a fallen box of paper tissues that Jane noticed, half buried beneath Clarisse's pillow, her own framed photo of her father. She frowned and crossed to the bed, intending to remove it. Clarisse must have gone into her and Luc's room. She must have taken it from the dressing-table. Jane stood for a moment, observing the sleeping Clarisse, a bag of angry bones. The wrinkled flesh, the once lustrous skeins of hair brittle and greying, the make-up spotted and uneven. Of all the objects in the room she might have filched, including one of several photographs of Luc, Clarisse had chosen the picture of Peter. *I was pretty smitten with your father.*

Was it possible that the old woman, long widowed, had genuinely carried a candle for him through so many years? That there lay a well-concealed core of vulnerability in a marble heart? Jane felt a wave of compassion rise within her. She wouldn't want to be in Clarisse's shoes. To have lost so much, a child and a lover. If the adoption of Clarisse's only daughter had not been 'the sacrifice', then, Jane asked herself, what could have been greater? The loss of their life in Algeria? Her husband, Adrien, whom she had described as cruel?

Jane left the picture where it was and returned downstairs to join the party.

The following afternoon when she returned from the mill, the photograph had been restored to its rightful place.

The Indian-summer days smiled on and there was no sign of the weather breaking. The harvesting was blessed, for so many reasons. It was a special joy. Families were bonding, not least Jane's own. The children were active, making the most of their holiday from school. Patrick was a natural leader and one day, if Luc's wishes were implemented, he would make a first-rate squire at Les Cigales. Jane and Annie watched him with pride, then smiled silently at one another. No one else, besides Clarisse, was party to their secret, except perhaps Matty. The gift of sisterhood enriched, invigorated Jane and she looked forward to the evenings with a new sense of perspective.

Jane was exhausted in a contented way, and satisfied that the season was winding down towards its successful conclusion. The following Friday she would be flying to Gatwick for a weekend visit with her father. And she was contemplating returning via Paris, spending a few days in the city, a brief sojourn with Annie, a time to consider her future . . .

After the end-of-harvest party.

Annie suggested that the pickers' closing dinner should be held outside in the courtyard. 'Let's make it a sumptuous starlit affair.'

The late autumn was so mild that there seemed no good

reason not to hold the celebrations beneath the stars and there would be less disturbance to Clarisse; the proposition was cheered by all.

'We'll invite everyone, from the local shepherds to the mayor. Les Cigales is having an end-of-harvest party! They don't have to be let in on our secret, to know all that we're celebrating.' Jane winked at her sister.

The pickers had completed their gathering in the groves the day before the party – the last of the drupes were off the trees. Two thousand *oliviers* picked clean.

'We've done better than the starlings,' joshed Claude.

Nonetheless, the men and women had returned that morning to assist their chief with the lifting of the nets, clogged now with clods of earth and tufts of grass and the odd mountain stone. Before they were rolled up and stored until next year, they needed to be cleaned, washed and left to dry. Then there were the ladders, clippers, secateurs, which were packed away in a natural limestone cave conveniently located not far from the groves. They would be required again within a few weeks for the pruning. The housekeeping chores were time-consuming but eight were at work and in high spirits. Soon, they would be paid and tonight they would be fed and well watered. Every Provençal loves a party and this one promised to be exceptional.

Back in the yard, Annie and Patrick busied themselves with cleaning the plastic garden tables and chairs stored in the stables. While Patrick arranged the seating, Annie delivered from the laundry room the linen tablecloths and then the cutlery. Matty offered to do it. More prudent, she said, for Annie not to be found wandering about the house when Clarisse was upstairs, but Annie shrugged, told her mum not to fuss and said everything was fine. Matty knew the old woman's temper. Annie didn't, but her adoptive mother kept quiet, not wanting to scotch the mood.

Annie and her boy set the table placings. From the kitchen could be heard regular thuds. Matty was cracking green olives with a small mallet, to store them in jars for the winter months to come. They were ideal for accompanying a good apéritif. A few jars of olives in brine from last year's *récolte* remained in the larder. She was intending to set them out in dishes for tonight's bash.

There were the lanterns and coloured lights still to be hung and, oh, a million other tasks waiting to make this crowning party go with a swing. But no one was in a rush. They were taking their time, enjoying the tasks and one another's company.

Arnaud was back from the mountains. 'You timed it well,' remarked Claude, when he caught sight of his son pulling up in his van, unshaven, at first light. Arnaud was back to rig up the barbecue in the courtyard. He laid his hunting rifle and bags down in the *bastide* kitchen where Matty, up since before daybreak, was flushed and baking.

Constructed from disused ironmongery, including the half shell of a heating tank, which performed as its grate, the handmade brazier was a curious marvel to behold. Its purpose for that evening was to barbecue a whole wild boar Arnaud had bagged on a Sunday hunt a few weeks previously, skinned and hung to cure in anticipation of the harvest festivities. It would be ample to feed the gathered assembly, even the large turnout Jane was counting on.

'Let's cater for a hundred,' she had warned Matty, who had beamed at the prospect: if the mistress had been up and about, no such extravagance would ever have been sanctioned.

To keep every child occupied and out of mischief, for this

was the last day of their school break and energies were riding high, they had also been allocated assignments. The boys were employed as Arnaud's assistants. Throughout the warm, sunny morning, substantial quantities of chopped logs and kindling were being transported, cradled in arms or wheelbarrows, from various storehouses and open-air stacks across the land to be piled neatly at the ready alongside the hunter's great old iron spit, beneath which Arnaud was laying the fire. Meanwhile the small girls were at the dining-table in the stables, kneeling on chairs, elbows on bare wood, designing labels for Matty's sumptuous dishes with dozens of multi-coloured crayons.

'How do you spell "venison tart"?'

'And "feasant". Is that right?'

Arnaud struck a match and held it to the screwed-up balls of *Nice Matin* tucked beneath kindling sticks and logs expertly arranged in the iron base of his barbecue. The roaring as the flames began to spread was like the sound of someone beating a broad cymbal.

Jane was leaving for the mill. Mug of coffee in one hand, she was running late. She knew she should get going, but the buzz of activity in the kitchen and Arnaud's blazing fire outside put a spell on her. The dead boar was prostrate on a bloodied cloth on the kitchen chopping block. Jane had never before been witness to the preparations for such an impressive roast. She slung her bag into the pantry and grabbed a chopping knife.

'Fifteen minutes of dicing vegetables and then I'll get on the road. I want to see this fellow launched.'

Arnaud stepped into the kitchen, his huge hands blackened from the fire-making. 'Right,' he said, slapping the pig on the haunch before downing a half-full glass of wine from the draining-board. It was not yet eight in the morning.

'How much does it weigh?' Jane wanted to know.

'Sixty to seventy kilos. This lad'll more than feed us all.'

Matty and Annie were already hard at work with the vegetable dicing, their fingers glistening and moist. The high-spirited mood was affecting all. The stuffing of the pig – a fully grown, hefty male, possibly three or four years old – required an entire vegetable garden, it seemed. Arnaud had slit the creature's stomach before hanging it. Matty passed a heavy dish of tomatoes to Jane. 'If you're staying, get chopping. And then there's the onions to do.'

Placed in dishes at the ready were swags of herbs from the garden, branches of bay leaves picked at dawn and scented with dew – a saline Mediterranean dew that blessed all that grew in those quarters – entire rose-tinted garlic bulbs and sufficient sacks of estate potatoes to sink a ship. Once the pig's cavernous stomach had been upholstered with food, Arnaud, aided by his mother and sister, closed the flesh flaps and sewed them together with thread almost as thick as string. Then the hefty pig was slung over its slayer's shoulder and hauled to the barbecue, where its trotters were attached securely, two by two, to the turning spit. Using swags of bay leaves, Matty sprinkled it lightly with last year's olive oil. The new vintage was far too precious for the job of basting.

Jane watched the flames spread and then she set off for the mill to deliver the last cargo of the season, before the final shipment home of their liquid booty.

And party time.

3

Party time

Tired, scruffy, starving, Jane swung in through the gated entrance to Les Cigales and chugged up the cedar-banked driveway in third gear. Even from down the way, she caught the winking of multi-hued lanterns through the trees. The temperamental old truck had made it and she was safely home. The last pressing had been bounteous and the return of oil to olives had been exceptional. In three months, or a little later, the litres available for sale would inject a vital boost into the estate's coffers. She was delighted, and a teeny bit proud. Tonight's celebrations would be the icing on the cake. She might even make a speech, a short one. Or should she offer that opportunity to Annie? No, too soon to hand the limelight to her. So elated was she that she was considering escorting Clarisse from her bed to the party, perhaps for a quarter of an hour. She remained, after all, the estate's mistress, even if her grasp was fading. Ironically Jane was beginning to feel sorry for her, a tiny bit affectionate towards her, aware now of the years of loneliness she had endured.

Jane had insisted that the Provençaux employed for the olive *récolte* invite their families to this celebratory repast not only because she wanted to honour the harvest but, more importantly, to offer the hand of friendship to their neighbours and others in the locality. She wanted the word spread that the proprietors of Les Cigales were approachable and that they could be counted upon as a vital thread within the community. It was time, long overdue, to quell the fires of gossip that she remembered from as far back as her first visit here with her father. Judgements and opinions that had been passed on to the younger generations. The superstitions, the resentments, Jane intended them to be brushed aside, for the slate to be wiped clean. She dreamed of sowing seeds, of breaking the spell of mistrust. This domain, which should have been handed on to Luc, needed to be spiritually and emotionally, as well as physically, rebuilt. Its perpetuation required the goodwill of the community, not their resentment. Jane wanted to return it to what it might have been when the Benedictine monks had built it and farmed here, a guiding light, a place of succour, an opportunity for fair employment. When she finally disappeared, she hoped that Annie and Patrick, who would inherit the title deeds if she had her way, would run the estate within an ambiance of harmony and wisdom.

In memory of Luc.

Jane locked the handbrake, hooted for the men to begin to unload the oil and tossed the keys to Arnaud, who would return the vehicle, once emptied, to School House. She bounded inside, up the stairs, and ran a bath, pouring in a good dose of lavender bath salts. Then she strode along the corridor to her mother-in-law's room. Clarisse was lying with her eyes closed and for a moment Jane assumed she was sleeping and was about to close the door again.

'It sounds like a fucking demonstration downstairs.'

'We're gearing up for the pickers' party, Clarisse. The harvest is complete and the olives pressed. You'll be pleased to hear we've had a good season. I'm going to get cleaned up and change.'

'And what about me? I'm the owner here, remember? Or have you forgotten your place, Jane? Pushing me further into the corner day by day. Usurping my role.'

'Do you want to join us for a little while? Come and say hello to everyone?'

'I don't think I need you to invite me.' Her voice was reedy, the sentiment combative, but there was little punch behind it.

'I'll be back in ten minutes. Think about it. If you feel like it, you can tell me and I'll help you get dressed.'

In her exuberance, Jane had overlooked the fact that Annie and Patrick would be present at the festivities. Patrick, surrounded by a gaggle of other vibrant children, moving about like tadpoles in water, might not catch Clarisse's attention, but Annie surely would. Jane cursed her thoughtlessness. She should have discussed this with Annie first.

Damn it! She could hardly uninvite her mother-in-law now.

She hastily dragged on some clothes, too concerned to give her appearance due care, then sprayed herself with Chanel, and she was acceptable. She jogged along the corridor, returning for Clarisse, but when she swung round the open door, the covers were peeled back and the bed bare.

'Clarisse? Shall I help you?' Jane popped her head round the door of Clarisse's bathroom. Medicine-cabinet door open. Pills spilled into the washbasin; caps off their containers. What concoction had she swallowed? She must have gone on alone. She hadn't even dressed. Jane pelted back along the corridor and down the stairs. She stuck her head inside the open doors of one of the two larger drawing rooms, where Matty had lit fires in the unlikely event of rain. Matty was in the red room, on her haunches in a fine black velvet dress with buttons and lace collar, working with a pair of bellows to boost the flames.

'You look terrific. Have you seen Clarisse?'

Matty frowned and shook her head. 'Not in her room?'

'Unfortunately not.' Jane turned and ran to the other room across the hall. No one. Then she spotted that the door to the *petit salon*, the one she was using as a storeroom for Luc's affairs, was wide open. The key was in the lock. Had she, during the harvest, forgotten to turn it and put the key into her bag where she had been keeping it? She stepped inside. Papers had been moved, shoved to the ground. A box fallen on its side. It looked looted. Was anything missing? There was such a wealth of material that it was impossible to gauge immediately what, if anything, had been removed. She cursed her own negligence.

It must have been Clarisse. Who else? Jane turned on her heels, closed the door, pocketed the key and went through to the breakfast room. Empty. Noises from outside, voices. Corks drawn, popping. The party was getting under way. Jane deliberated. If she stepped out of doors now, she would find herself caught up among others in the flutter of the festive mood. She should make one last search for her mother-in-law first. The library. If she didn't find her, she'd seek out Dr Beauchene, if he'd arrived for the party.

The library was still, books and empty chairs. Clarisse must be outside. In her nightdress? She'd catch a chill. Jane was getting alarmed. How could she have so misjudged this? Stupid of her to invite Clarisse before she was ready to accompany her.

But Matty would surely have found her by now.

Matty, surprisingly, was not in the kitchen, where the table was autumn-toned, groaning with luscious plates of vegetables: roast potatoes, grilled aubergines, a stuffed cabbage dish, earthenware bowls of her own tapenade. All to accompany the roasting pig. Succulent scents wafted in from the yard, the crisply browning beast on the spit. Outside there was firelight, candlelight, lanterns. The courtyard was dense with shadows, silhouettes holding glasses, convivial chatter, laughter. *Monsieur le curé*, the Catholic priest, was in conversation with the barber, who was in a suit, his wife at his side draped in a purple feather boa. Even his drinking chum, the mayor, had put in an appearance. Droves of villagers, guests. The invitations had been accepted. Jane's heart swelled with pride. But where was Clarisse? So small and frail, it would be easy for her to disappear among the throng. Jane, at the kitchen steps, scanned the spectacle, hoping to spy her, or even the doctor. A neighbour pushed forward and wished her good evening. Jane accepted his greeting and engaged in a few words of conversation, 'Yes, the harvest was *très bonne*,' torn between politeness and concern. She spied Matty beside the spit with Arnaud. She was bending and rising, face flushed from the flames, basting the boar. Jane excused herself and pushed her way through the crush.

'Where's Annie?' she called, as she approached mother and son.

'In the stable dining room collecting more wine. What a turnout. I hope we have sufficient to feed everyone.'

'Of course we have. Did you catch sight of Clarisse?'

Matty frowned. 'Are you sure she's not in her bed? She's not down here.'

Jane didn't wait to explain. A sickening prescience was taking hold. In her mind's eye, she was picturing the room where Luc's possessions were stored. She had worked out the item that was missing. Not that she had noted its absence when she was there, but an image was flashing, like a warning signal, in her mind, and it was alarming her.

She had to find Clarisse.

Clarisse was in her slippers and a short-sleeved nightdress, shivering with the chill. She was stumbling about the forecourt, past the palm trees, bouncing from parked car to parked car, her head pounding. Something heavy was weighing her down. A gun, her gun, Adrien's Colt pistol. She'd thought she had misplaced it after keeping it hidden for all these years. Luc had confiscated it – he'd admitted as much – and forbidden her to go near a firearm ever again. She had seen it in the room with all the boxes, picked it up and taken it. Then, unable to face the congregation of people in the stables courtyard, she had slipped out by the front door. Lanterns everywhere. Flickering lights, blinding and confusing her. Raised voices, laughter. Parked cars surrounded her. She wove her way in and about them, her head swimming.

Long ago in Algeria, on hot summer nights, guests had gathered – evening after evening of dancing on the terraces surrounding their swimming-pool – when she was married. Her blissful life in Algeria. Before Luc was born. Days before the war. Days before the killings and massacres. Days before the birth of the OAS. Then there had been the black years, Adrien never at home. The bombings. She, terrified of the repercussions.

Finally, her escape. With Isa and Luc.

Where was Luc? Who were all these people? Guests. She must go and welcome them. She was the hostess. Was this her party?

'Clarisse!'

Who was calling her? She recognized the voice. Isa – was it Isa? Isa, who had stuck by her, never betrayed her.

'Clarisse, where are you?'

No, not Isa. Jane. Yes, Jane. This was her daughter-in-law's party. Not hers or Luc's. Jane was taking control of her property, moving herself in, sidling, gaining the upper hand. Where was Luc? He must put a stop to this. At once. Clarisse spun unsteadily on her slippered feet, almost losing her balance before tottering towards the rear, the south face of the house, following the direction of lights and music.

The sounds were deafening. Heavy percussion. Not sweet dancing notes. Voices raised. The courtyard was crushed with bodies. A troupe of excited children rose up from nowhere and raced past her. One, a big boy – was it Luc? – knocked against her shoulder, then another, sending her flying.

'Luc! Luc, come back here!'

They barely noticed her. Sped off, gone. Clarisse had almost fallen over, a rag doll. She sucked in a breath. She was dizzy, heavy-headed, drugged, shuffling onwards towards a bank of backs and shoulders. Men and women animated by conversation, guffawing, holding glasses aloft. A figure, female, in sleek black trousers and shiny blouse was easing through the group, bearing two wine bottles, beaming, chattering. She was pouring wine – Clarisse's wine, her estate label, Les Deux Soeurs – refilling glasses, chatting, sharing laughter as she socialized. Her face was lovely, lively, freckled, wholesome. Peter's eyes.

Annabelle. It was Annabelle. She had no right to be here. What did she think she was doing?

Clarisse raised her hand to her brow, confused. It was heavy. Something metal gripped between her fingers. She had to think.

'Clarisse! Clarisse!'

A voice from behind her. Not Annabelle's. Heads turned at the sharply raised cry.

Jane hurried towards Clarisse but stopped short when she caught sight of the light glimmering on the nickel-plated pistol. She moved cautiously now. A voice from somewhere behind them warned, 'She's got a gun.'

'It's the witch.'

News spread, like a rolling wave, until those further

towards the stable block by the barbecue had learned it. 'The old woman, that old bag Madame Cambon, is here with a firearm.'

Arnaud, sweating and flushed from the fire's heat and a couple of beers, raised himself from his haunches with the tightly sprung instincts of an animal that smells danger, blood. He stepped warily backwards and into the kitchen, snatching up his rifle from where it had stood since dawn. Still loaded. He pulled back the rifle's hammer and retraced his way through the crowds, muzzle trained safely downwards. Trigger finger ready but clear of the trigger, he ploughed through the mass of people, head lowered, pressing forward, a bull ready to gore.

Matty raised her arm to stay him. He knew nothing. His mother followed him.

'Arnaud, stay back,' she called.

Panic, more frozen than in motion, was setting in among the guests.

Annie handed the wine bottles to a mystified onlooker. Still, she held her ground, uncertain.

Inching forward, Jane approached her mother-in-law.

Behind her, Annie drew towards the woman who was her mother. 'Madame Cambon?'

Clarisse was perplexed. Two women closing in on her, one from her rear, the other ahead. These women were not her friends. Annabelle had never come near her throughout her sickness, and Jane was after the property. She lifted the Colt and trained it on Jane, both hands gripping it to keep it steady. It was years since she had pulled this trigger, since she had killed with it. The pressure of the wobbling firearm, the haunting memories were making her dizzy, nauseous. She had no control, her wrists weak.

Jane stood her ground, still as a post. 'Give me the gun,

Clarisse. It's not loaded.' She was bluffing. Jane had no clue as to whether or not the Colt had bullets in its chamber.

Annie was advancing on the woman she had never known, frail as a bird in a nightdress, preposterously waving a firearm at her half-sister. Jane's attention shifted from her mother-in-law to Annie. Clarisse sensed it and swung about, gun still in her grip. Arnaud had broken through the wall of partymakers, followed by Matty. Others were closing in. Clarisse was still holding the gun at arm's length, pointing it now at Annie. It was weighing her down. She was feeling faint.

Before she knew it, someone, Jane, was upon her. Matty gripped her son's arm. A shot rang out, exploding into the night. A woman's cry. People were gibbering and screaming, running like frightened hens. Clarisse hit the deck.

4

Regeneration

Clarisse passed away in the early days of December. Jane was at her mother-in-law's bedside. At the end, the old woman seemed relaxed, eyes closed, lids flickering, as though she were a dog dreaming. She no longer recognized Jane, who sat reading or working alongside her, watching over her. She talked a great deal, streams of sentences, many incomprehensible. The subjects ranged from war to gunshots, the OAS, Isa, Annabelle. And, in the latter days, Luc. She called for Luc incessantly. She grew distressed. When Jane tried to pacify her, she gripped Jane's fingers and held on, vice-like. She begged Luc not to make his film. She warned him of the repercussions. She repeated, 'Adrien', her husband's name, over and over. Sometimes she seemed to be weeping. 'It was necessary,' she murmured.

Jane could follow precious little of the crazed monologue, even when the words were entire and coherent.

And then Clarisse fell silent. Occasionally her eyes opened and she glared at Jane in a troubled fashion, but without recognition.

All that was left during the last days was the laboured breathing and then the death rattle before the eternal silence. Jane remained where she was. Seated, staring at an old shrew's corpse. Clarisse dead. The anger and pain silenced. Her face, smooth as a peach, resembling an innocent child's.

Jane recalled sharply how, only a little less than a year ago, the blueness of Luc's immobile face had bitten into her. She missed him, ached for him. She always would. She regretted deeply that he had not lived beyond his mother, that he had not been witness to the joy she and Annie were finding in one another's company. Their half-sisterhood. He would be waiting somewhere now to usher his mother onwards to her resting place, where she might discover the first peace she had enjoyed in decades.

And what of Luc? As Jane sat gazing at the motionless body of the woman who had caused her so much misery, such heartache, she wondered about Luc's peace, his resting place. Was she, Jane, holding him back? Was he patiently waiting for her to let him go? The possibility decimated her. She couldn't bear to let him go.

When the door opened softly, Dr Beauchene found her, head bent over her knees, in tears.

Back in November, the days following the party had remained bright but had grown cooler. The colour of the mountains in the distance had changed daily from purple-blue to white. Somewhere, not too far away, snow was falling and reupholstering the caps of the Alps. Its chill snapped at the air. Gunshots were forever resounding across the valleys. Yet more unsuspecting beasts had met their fate. Some fortunate kitchens would soon be steaming with the simmering meat.

But not Matty's. Not Arnaud's rifle. Matty was in shock, recuperating, tended by Claude. She had pushed through the crush of people, cannoning forward, knocking her son's arm, as Arnaud had lifted his weapon. Her action had caused his rifle to explode. The bullet shot skywards, thankfully trained on no one. At almost the same moment, Jane had wrested the gun from her mother-in-law and Clarisse had crumpled, as though the pistol had been holding her up, not the other way around. According to Beauchene, who was on hand, Clarisse Cambon had suffered a severe myocardial infarction, a massive heart attack.

The evening had ended in disaster. The entire community had been witness to their family drama.

The following day, two of the local *gendarmerie* – two of his hunting chums – had paid Arnaud a visit and escorted him to the police station. There wasn't one in Malaz – crime was almost non-existent there – so they had driven him to the nearest town to interview him. Before they set off, Claude had given the men a couple of hens. 'Good layers, the pair of them,' he told the officers, then slapped his son on the shoulder. '*Courage, mon brave*,' he muttered to him.

Arnaud was obliged to give a statement. To state clearly what had been the nature of his intentions. He was a man of few words and failed to explain himself. He had been among a crowd of people with a loaded rifle, the hunting chums' senior officer pointed out to him. Arnaud had believed his sister's life was in danger: that was his explanation.

Arnaud was not charged. Instead he was ferried home. Witnesses would be called and proceedings would be decided upon.

'We'll carry on as best we can.' Claude's firm words to Matty.

Clarisse was laid to rest on 3 December in the family plot alongside her sister-in-law and close to her son, who had gone ahead of her almost twelve months earlier. Two women and one son lying in peace together. Jane lowered into the open grave a branch from the cherry tree in her mother-in-law's garden. Its woody length lacked the early buds of spring, but when the spring came round again and the flowers were full upon the tree, Jane would return with a bowl of white-pink petals to scatter on the grave. She silently gave Clarisse her promise of this. She had also discreetly placed within Clarisse's coffin a dog-eared passport photograph of Peter. Out of respect to her own mother, she couldn't bring herself to include the larger, framed likeness.

Annie had flown down from Paris. She and Jane prepared the funeral meal side by side and laid it in the silent dining room where Luc's reception had taken place. There were few to attend the proceedings. Unlike Luc, Clarisse had not amassed crowds of friends and caring souls about her. Hers had been an embittered, isolated existence. She had been despised by the *villageois*. Nonetheless, a handful turned up, hats pressed against their breasts, as a mark of respect to the folk still residing at the grand estate.

'Peter should be present.' Annie smiled.

Jane had contemplated the possibility but such a journey was far too arduous an undertaking for him. In any case, he continued to have no memory of Les Cigales or of Clarisse. And he had not been told that Clarisse had borne him a second daughter.

'I would like to meet him one day, though. My father.'

It was not the first time Annie had made this request.

'My next trip to England, we could go together, but you must be prepared for . . .'

'I just want to touch him, look at him, hold his hand, to know that just once I met my father.'

'Then we'll do it.'

The winter nights were exquisite, no clouds, starlit, unrelentingly chilly. During the short hours of daylight, the sky was a starched blue, hard as ceramic but clear and sun-filled. Berries hung heavy on the bushes. Birds gorged.

Jane spent her time alone, gazing at the flames in the hearth as they galloped over last year's pruned olive branches. The hatred, fear and violence that had crippled her and Clarisse were melting away, softening within her . . . As Claude had taught her in the vineyards, after the bleak, leafless months of winter, we pull out the weeds and dig the ground until it has been cleared. Then we till the soil, turning it, loosening it, making it easier for the earth to breathe, to feed the vines. But first, essentially, we must pluck out all that grows wild and chokes the good growth. It's important to keep the vines' root systems healthy, well-drained. Important to root out the poisons that choke them.

Can a person's life be shaped, its direction altered, by an early trauma? We start out one way and then life changes us? Even if the answer was affirmative, redemption was surely a possibility? Regeneration. It was Nature's smartest trick. We damage the soil with toxins, burn it, poison the plants . . . Still, Nature will find her way back through the earth, will reshoot vigorously, rarely defeated. There is no reason, thought Jane, why we should not be the same. Why should we not follow this universal DNA pattern?

'Who doesn't have blood on their hands? We all have. Including you, Jane,' her mother-in-law had once barked at her.

After the loss of Peter, the door to Clarisse's heart must have finally snapped shut, or had that already taken place before Jane had met her? Might Peter have been Clarisse's redemption and Jane, full of adolescent self-righteousness, have derailed a journey of love? Jane would never know the answers. To so many questions, she would never know the answers.

'I couldn't keep the girl. How would it have been possible in this region of prejudice? Imagine for one moment

Annabelle's life at the local school. She would have been ostracized, without friends, judged. What I did, I did for her sake, and I never told your father of Annabelle's existence. I never forced his hand. All my life the *paysans* here have hated and despised me for being a colonial from Algeria. They will never know the sacrifice I made. No one knows. Only Isa. She was there.'

Clarisse had spoken these words to Jane during her fading days.

When Jane began to empty Clarisse's house – yet another house clearance – she had found her mother-in-law's safe tucked away in her wardrobe, hidden by glittering evening dresses and more pairs of dancing shoes than Jane had owned in her entire life. Clothes and furs and outfits that must have dated back to her Algerian days. She called in the bearded locksmith, Monsieur Tassigny, to unlock the safe. There was not a great deal within it, apart from some rather valuable jewellery and a few large envelopes. In the envelopes she found the details of several bank accounts, mainly in France for the estate, and one – a jackpot – in Switzerland, which had been opened by Monsieur Adrien Luc Cambon, Clarisse's long-deceased husband. Within it sat a fortune that had been accumulating interest for more than half a century; a deep, untouched pot of money that Clarisse had hoarded or hidden or, Jane preferred to think, that in her dotage she had simply forgotten about. Either way, the funds would be withdrawn, the accounts closed and the cash would be fed into the estate.

Along with the bank accounts there was a folded, disintegrating, yellowed newspaper cutting displaying a black-and-white photograph. It was the same snap but full-length of the lean young Adrien Cambon Jane had found among Luc's belongings. In this fuller shot, Jane saw he was posing in high leather boots and khakis, one foot on the running board of a sleek Citroën. The family Citroën. The vehicle that had ferried Clarisse and Luc to France. Dark hair, moustache, tanned skin, thirty or thirty-five, perhaps. A cigarette was smoking between his fingers and he was carrying a pistol. The same Colt Jane had found in Luc's drawer? Jane examined Luc's father's face, with its air of arrogance. There was a resemblance. Luc had spoken so rarely of him. Jane wondered what had become of him. The newsprint beneath the photograph was in Arabic. Jane would post it to one of her linguist chums and ask them to translate it for her.

From a fraying white envelope, she withdrew the contract Clarisse and Isabelle had signed with Matty and Claude. The gift of Annabelle to the Lefèvre couple, in return for discretion and silence. It included the clause confirming that Annabelle had no claim on the estate. There was just one copy as Matty and Clarisse had both stated. Jane took it to the fireplace, struck a match and was about to watch it go up in flames – once gone, no one would ever know that a contract had existed that barred Annie's right to Les Cigales – but then she held back. Her reflex was foolish. This and Luc's letter to his mother were the sole pieces of evidence to prove that Annie was not Matty's progeny, that both Annie and Patrick had a legitimate claim on the estate.

Without the papers Jane, bizarrely, was the last remaining family member, albeit by marriage, in line to inherit the land, all properties and all bank accounts. She smiled to herself at the arrival of such riches. Riches beyond any she would have dreamed of. She tossed the burned-out match, singeing her thumb and fingers, into the fireplace, set the matchbox on the mantelpiece and went to search Clarisse's bedroom. On hands and knees in a room that smelt foul, head shoved under the bed, she stretched and reached for Luc's letter to his mother, scrunched into a tight ball.

Back outside in the weak January sun, Jane unfolded the letter and ironed the creases against the flat of her hand pressed into her trousers.

Back at the manor house, she telephoned Annie in Paris. 'I have a surprise for you.'

Annie gave up the lease on the flat in Vincennes. Along with Patrick, who was soon to be twelve – the age Luc had been when Jane had first met him – she moved into Clarisse's cottage. The cherry blossoms were opening into tight white-pink flowers when Annie bounced along the potholed lanes in an old car packed to bursting with their possessions.

'Where's Pat?' asked Jane, puzzled.

'He'll be along shortly.'

Later, from out of the horizon of vines, another car appeared. An Espace. One of those large people carriers. It pulled up in front of the gate behind Annie's jalopy. Out stepped Patrick and Dan. Dan, sunburned and Australia-blessed, had never looked more handsome. His shy daughter, with her delicate deer-like features, was the last to emerge.

'Sissy, say *bonjour*. You haven't met Sissy, have you? It's good to see you again, Jane.'

It took some seconds for the penny to drop. When it did, she offered Annie and Dan the manor house. She would have been equally content to live in the ancient miller's abode, but Annie stubbornly resisted. 'The manor is your home. It was yours and Luc's and you must stay there. Pat and I are happy with "my mother's" house. During the brief spells when Dan's not filming and he comes to visit us, there'll be plenty of space for us all.'

When there was a moment's calm from the furniture unpacking, Jane took Dan aside and led him to the *petit salon* where Luc's work was stacked in boxes. Lying on the table was the Arabic newspaper cutting. Dan picked it up and stared at it.

'Luc's father?' Jane asked.

Dan nodded slowly. '*Sous-chef* for one of the branches of the OAS, the APP section.'

'Which was?'

'Action-Psychologique-Propagande. Psychological Warfare and Propaganda. They were renowned for their use of torture, bombings and murder. In April 1962, one month after de Gaulle had signed the Évian Accords to end the war, an Algerian school in the suburbs of Algiers was blown up. Close to two hundred Algerian children and staff were massacred. Adrien Cambon is believed to have masterminded that exercise.'

Jane closed her eyes. 'French right-wing terrorism. How utterly appalling. Did Luc know?'

'He learned it while we were filming.'

'What happened to Adrien?'

'The official report states that Cambon went into hiding at the end of the war and was never captured. Most of his comrades went to the firing squad.'

Jane frowned, lifting her eyes to Dan's. 'How do you know all this?'

'Luc and I interviewed a veteran living inland of Marseille, a Pied-Noir who'd had dealings with Cambon. The old fellow has dedicated his life to compiling a list of undeclared members of the OAS. Some of them went on to work in the French government. If the list had gone public it would have caused an outcry. Adrien Cambon's name was high on that list.'

Jane listened in silence, wondering how much Clarisse had known of this. And the shame Luc must have felt when he discovered the truth about his father, the man he had longed to cross the sea to find. 'Finish the film for him, please.'

At her side, Dan lowered his eyes and sighed slowly. 'It's incendiary, Jane. Roussel was convinced Luc's death was an assassination but his team found no proof.'

'And what do you think?'

'He was pushing himself too hard and the discovery of his father's OAS involvement nearly broke him. He shoved himself over the edge.'

'Suicide?'

'No, no, never. He was desperate to complete the film. He was exhausted. No, it was an accident.'

'In memory of Luc, finish the film, please.'

Dan shook his head. 'For Annie's sake and Pat's, I prefer to bury the past. It's already cost too much.'

Lying on her bed that night, her new family installed down at Cherry Tree Lodge, Jane replayed her conversation with Dan in her mind. Something about the story was not clicking together. Had the old man in Marseille been mistaken? Was that why Clarisse had argued so hotly against the film? Had she believed in her husband's innocence? Yet she had described him as 'cruel'.

And then Jane recalled a summer from many years earlier. She was about nine. She and Luc had been snorkelling together. Stretched out in the dunes, their hair and burned skin matted with salt, she'd asked him, 'Don't you sometimes long to go back to where you were born?'

'Only if I could bring my father here to live with us.'

'Why didn't he come with you?'

'He was shot.'

'Shot?' Jane's eyes had widened to the size of the abandoned gull's egg they had just discovered in the nearby marram and beach grasses. Luc was rolling it to and fro in the palm of his hand. 'By who?'

'It was an accident. I think. I don't know. Maman says we're never to talk about it.'

And Luc had been true to his word. Even once they were married, the loss of his father and their flight from his homeland had remained a forbidden subject.

5

Two women and a boy

Jane took a flight to Geneva to meet with the director of Crédit Suisse where the Cambon estate deeds and bank account were held. She learned that over several decades until 1962 large sums of money had been transferred from Algiers. The account had been held in the Cambon family name since its inception in the 1920s. Madame and Madame Cambon, once their French property had been purchased from the invested Swiss francs, had never touched their capital or its interest again. Clarisse Cambon, the last to survive, had written to the bank stating that she had no further use for the money and requested that the account be closed. The bank had responded that, without the lodged monies being withdrawn, the account could not be closed. The director confirmed that Crédit Suisse had never received a response.

Jane signed the forms to close the account. The bulk of the funds were to be transferred to a recipient whose identity she would furnish at the first possible opportunity.

She and Annie chose not to touch the capital but to keep a portion of the interest that had accrued over the decades since Les Cigales had been purchased. It was more than sufficient for the estate's needs.

They were two women and one boy to run the estate. Two 'sisters' and a son. As it had been in the days of

Clarisse, Isabelle and Luc, aided by Matty, Claude and Arnaud.

Their portion of the money from Switzerland was transferred to an estate account, to be managed by Jane. The greater sum, close to sixteen million euros, was transferred to Marseille to inaugurate a private initiative foundation for the construction of the Luc Cambon Film School, which would specialize in regional documentary-making. Any sums remaining were to be invested to offer scholarships for underprivileged students. All Luc's professional files and films were destined for the film school's library.

'I hope he'd be proud,' mused Jane, brushing a photo of Luc as a small boy. She and Annie were in the small salon, kneeling beside one another on the floor, sifting through the stacks of family albums, tears of laughter or sadness, cries of surprise, accompanying their discoveries.

'We'll have to persuade Dan to set up these old 8mm movies and we can have cinema evenings.'

Annie laid her arm round Jane's shoulders. 'There's something I've been wondering if I should tell you . . .'

'What?' Jane felt herself stiffen.

'That last evening when Luc was hurrying to be with you for Christmas, it was getting late for the last crossing and Pat was delaying him, not wanting him to leave, begging him to read him another story. Luc bent down, hugged him tight at the door and offered him Walnut. "He can keep you company till after the holidays when I return," he said. Then he hastily embraced me. He was dashing as always. As he left, his last words called back to us were how much he was looking forward to getting home. "I'm off to see my sweet lady." He laughed as he ran down the path. He always called you that. "My sweet lady". He really loved you, Jane.'

*

Claude hired a dozen men, offering them a year's employment and a decent wage. Jean Dupont was taken on as foreman and Claude was promoted to estate manager.

'We'll give this domain the spring cleaning it's lacked in decades.'

They needed new water systems. Glass for the greenhouses. Every one of the estate's outbuildings was in a sorry state of disrepair: leaking roofs, musty, uninhabitable. They included two stone cottages, one of which had been where Jane and her parents had stayed once during the seven years Peter had been employed by Clarisse. Ever since it had remained unoccupied. The other had been the original residence of Claude and Matty when they had taken on their role as caretakers.

'Agrotourism.' Annie winked. 'We'll get them renovated. Arnaud can do most of the work and he can call in some of his hunting mates, who are plumbers and electricians. If he starts now, we'll have them ready to rent out for summer.'

Arnaud had been called in the dark month of December to answer for his actions on the evening of the harvest party, but not a single guest had had a word to say against him. The case was dismissed.

Funds aplenty were withdrawn to buy piping for the irrigation, a thousand and more panes of glass for the greenhouses, stones, tiles, kitchens, gallons of paint, all that was required to refurbish the dilapidated properties and set in motion the small agrotourism business Annie had set her sights on managing.

The seasons turn. The land regenerates. And spring returns.

The scent of cedar resin and jasmine imbued the warm spring days. They had work to do, much to occupy them. It was a family affair – two women and a boy – with many mouths to feed from the vineyards, rich with the young lime-green leaves, and silvery olive groves that promised yet another year of generous harvests.

When Dan was among them, he spent his days foraging through Luc's film stock, archives and notes. Jane had desperately wanted him to complete Luc's film, but she knew that if he continued with the project, he could be risking his life. She had no right to ask it of him. He was a terrific father figure to Patrick and he cared deeply for Annie. He had taken over Luc's responsibilities in those areas. It was time to let Luc's film go.

Was it also time to let Luc go?

Jane set out one morning to walk, hiking inland until she reached a raised spot, a leafy hillock, where she and Luc had frequently come to hide. She could no longer remember which number it was on his list of 'great hiding places' but it was wondrous for quite another reason: it was where the scarce Swallowtails came to mate. Dozens, dozens of dozens, of the males fluttering and congregating, awaiting their virgin females.

'They live short lives, love intensely,' he had told her, 'and then they are gone. One month of life and they disappear for ever.'

When she reached the low-lying hilltop, the butterflies were there, hundreds of winged adults, spinning and dancing, some in courtship, some already locked together in their consummating embrace. She stepped among them and lifted her head towards the rich blue sky speckled with their fluttering cream bodies. They barely noticed her presence. The joy of the butterflies, their breeding energy, heartened her.

She stayed with them, feeling their touch against her face, knowing that Luc was alongside her too. It was time to let him go, to set him free on his journey. She wept and wept, and begged him not to disappear for ever, to return from time to time to love her intensely. His spirit, she felt sure, would find its resting place in the olive trees. Wherever you are, she told him, I will always love you.

She opened her mouth and sucked in the fresh spring air. She stood still while the oxygen sank and circled in her lungs. Wings flapped and fluttered against her flesh. A light breeze ruffled her hair and left a strand out of place, striping her face. She reached up a hand to release it. And then, without knowing why, she lifted both arms high into the air, embracing the day while the butterflies fluttered and swooped about her, and she felt the power of wings lifting her from the ground, and cried out, 'I love you, Luc. *Je t'aime.*'

Her voice carried on the slipstream, echoing on the waves of the morning. She was alive and she was strong. She was a girl and she was a woman. She felt Luc's energy soaring like a comet about her, rising high, returning and then, *whoosh*, departing. And she waited quietly in the sunshine, amid the confetti of fluttering life. Tired, saddened, yet joyous. She had no notion of what lay ahead for her, but to accept life for what it is, there lies contentment. She would remain on this hot southern land, with her sister and nephew. Les Cigales was her home now. Together, they would weather the losses along with the bountiful. And they would bring up the boy, Patrick. They would forge a path forward as a family. Two women and a boy. Accompanied along their way by the silent inspiration of Luc.

EPILOGUE

The Forgotten Summer, 1962

Flight from Algeria

The house was so still, it was unnerving. It was too early for his family to be awake. Even so, the stillness seemed terrifying. It crept towards him and settled all around him as though ready to snatch him up and steal him away. Luc Cambon was in his room, lying in his bed in the semi-darkness. Horizontal bars of low sunlight were filtering through the slatted shutters, creeping in his direction. He had no idea what time it was. Early, that was for sure. He hadn't learned to read a clock yet. He knew the big hands, but was often confused by the small ones. His father had promised to go through it with him again as soon as the fighting had calmed down and France had secured its colony.

His father . . . The boy let out a deep moan. He lay rigid, toes pointed, like the big black hand on the Comtoise grandfather clock in the hall downstairs. He could not move. His limbs felt as heavy as the oars on his granddad's fishing boat. He held his arms stiffly, pressing his bitten fingernails tightly up against his naked torso. He was a small soldier, keeping watch, green eyes wide open, sharply alert to the possibilities of danger, to the possibilities of further horridness and bloodshed.

Had he dreamed all that about his father? Had it been a nightmare or had they really put him in the ground with a towel over his face? Luc let his eyes close for an instant, and then he promised himself he would open them again. He would be brave. He knew he had to keep watch – 'Be on your guard at all times, my son,' his father's mantra, 'or they'll knife you in the back' – but he yearned to blot out the scene from yesterday.

The screams. His mother's chilling screams.

Two tears welled in his eyes and rolled, like boulders, down his cheeks, settling in his ears. They felt cold, itched. They tickled, but he left them where they were. It was his personal minuscule lake of misery.

His attention was drawn from his grief by a commotion taking place along the corridor beyond his bedroom. Hushed women's voices were approaching. Wafts of scent reached his nostrils, rosewater, lily-of-the-valley. His mother was out of bed and passing by his room. She was in the company of his aunt Isabelle. Outside, beyond the clamped shutters, a car engine turned over. The vehicle began to reverse, slowly inching towards the property's main entrance. The crunch of gravel under tyres. It drew to a halt. Once stationary, the motor idled. A car door slammed. Footsteps ascended the curved marble stairway that led to the double front doors. Someone entered. His grandmother. She was calling up the stairs to the two younger women, his mother and Aunt Isabelle. 'Clarisse, is the boy up yet?'

'Sssh.'

'Well, wake him, for Heaven's sake, and get him dressed. We should have got out yesterday.'

They *were* leaving. He knew it. It had been no bluff. Luc had no desire to flee his home. To go where? But he couldn't stay here alone without his mother. Why was she abandoning his father in the red earth beneath the jujube trees? The women had wrapped a white towel over his father's head before they had carried him out into the garden. It had resembled a turban except that it had covered Papa's face as well. Their movements had been clumsy, as though they were drugged or stupefied. All the while, his mother had been howling like one of the scrawny Arab street dogs.

Luc had not understood what had happened to his father, who was being transported by the three women of the family – all the servants had long since fled – into the lushly planted gardens where the irrigation system had left the lawn spongy. The weight of the limp body and the wet grass caused the women to stagger, lurching back and forth in their high-heeled shoes. Then his mother lost one of hers, but she continued onwards, off-balance, rocking towards his grandfather, who was standing over a newly excavated pit in the shade of the jujube trees.

Slowly, as they approached, the dry white cloth over his father's face was turning red and soggy. Luc had wanted to snatch it away. He had feared his father would suffocate.

'Don't you dare!' Clarisse had hissed at him, her eyes bulging and terrified, red from all the tears as the mascara leaked in thick stripes down her face.

The family group gathered around the oblong trench. All of them, apart from Luc, had assisted with the lowering of his father into the empty pit, one limp masculine arm dangling, the bloodied cloth beginning to unravel.

'Keep his face covered, for Christ's sake!' his mother whined. 'I can't bear to see it again.'

An acrid burning smell pervaded the air, the odour of melting flesh. Inland, flames lit up the mountains and hillsides. Entire villages, Arab and Berber *douars*, had been torched. Cinders floated like pollen. Above, a cloudless china-blue sky. No birdsong but the sharp, dissonant scratching of the cicadas. Luc turned his attention to the adults encircling the hole. His grandmother was muttering a prayer. The others, aunt, mother and grandfather, were standing solemnly with their heads bowed low, hands clasped before them. His *grandmère*'s words were incomprehensible, spoken so quickly.

'Amen.'

'Amen.'

'We have to stick together. Whatever happens . . . No one must know.' Aunt Isa speaking.

'Nothing more to be said. I did what had to be done.' His mother.

'We'll leave tomorrow,' the adults agreed in murmurs. 'At first light.' And the three women had filed away.

His grandfather had remained. He was filling in the grave with a big spade, shrouding Luc's father, while silently sobbing through eyes squeezed closed, his face in a grimace. Afterwards the old man stayed where he was, hunched over the mound of earth that now hid the pit where Luc's father lay buried. Luc, a few considerate steps distant, waited for his pal, his granddaddy. He couldn't remember ever having seen grown-ups cry before.

His mother, aunt and grandmother had returned indoors to continue the preparations for their flight.

'Granddad?'

'This is a sorry day, boy.' The old man leaned his worn hairy hands on the shovel he was gripping. 'Ever since I was a lad, I've worked here. I toiled with my father before me to build and lay out everything that is now within our sight. We built the whole damn lot, us Cambons. That's what your father was fighting for. Algeria belongs to us.'

Luc glanced about him. The Cambon house, their vineyards sloping down towards the Mediterranean, the silvery olive groves, had all been dreamed up by his great-grandfather,

Auguste Cambon, a *petit fonctionnaire*, who had crossed the glimmering sea from Nice in France to make his fortune, sailing south to Bône in 1882, which back then had been little more than a burgeoning resort town, a French colonial stake on the soft golden shores of Algeria. And make a fortune he had. Over the course of three generations, the Cambons had become the wealthiest agricultural family in this eastern vicinity of Algeria.

Outside in the garden now as Luc listened from his bed, the automatic water sprinklers burst into life. He heard them every morning as he lay warm and safe, but today they whizzed and spun, making a sound like the light clattering of clogs, keeping the lawn moist and green, the way his mother always insisted it should be. Would they be irrigating his father, soaking the earth above him? Would he drown? Would the earth be too heavy for him to move, to push himself out of the pit? Was his father lying low, in pain?

After a chaotically prepared breakfast in the morning room, yesterday's *croissants* reheated, jam and crumbs spread everywhere, stuffing the food into their mouths, everyone standing anxiously rather than seated at the table, as Luc had been drilled to do, while the adults were cramming cases, trunks overflowing with dresses, his mother's and aunt's precious ocelot coats, minks and sable stoles, wraps, snakeskin handbags, dozens of long-playing records, record player, other treasured belongings into the already overstocked boot, strapping the longcase clock onto the car's roof-rack, Luc sneaked away. Loping fast on sturdy legs through the palm grove, flying past an upended parasol, he could hear his breath, his footfall hurtling by the forgotten swimming-pool, its water already turning an emerald green, to the small stand of jujube trees. They were shading his father's grave. It was cooler this morning. He snatched and tugged swiftly, like a thief, at a handful of dried jujubes he had spotted the day before, still clinging to the spindly branches, and stuffed them into the pocket of his shorts. He stared hard at the ground. He could hear in the distance the calls of his mother and aunt: '*Luc, où est tu? Luc!*'

'Papa? Papa!' he whispered urgently. 'Please get up. Papa, we're going away.'

'Luc, where are you?' Female voices slicing the early-morning air added to his urgency.

In the far distance, a muezzin was calling the faithful to prayer. Somewhere in another direction, a ricochet of gunshots. Shootings were commonplace. The war had commenced before Luc was born. Life went on, which was why he was sure his father would rise up and continue, as they had always done in the past.

Luc got down on his knees and began to claw at the red-brown earth. Tears were falling. His father was dead. That was the only possible explanation. It would explain the gunshot of yesterday, followed by his mother's piercing screams. It was becoming clearer to him now. There had been no 'stinking native intruder, no Algerian, hell-bent on revenge and murder', as he had feared, as his father had warned him always to be vigilant against. When his father had descended the stairs in such haste, such anger, storming from the room where the women had been packing, where his parents had been arguing vociferously, yelling at one another, words batting back and forth across the room, hurled at one another over piled possessions, Luc had misread the situation. His mother had followed his father to the ground floor, skittering in high, open-toed sandals down the stairs, never ceasing her tirade. Doors were slamming. He had assumed that someone was attempting to break into his father's office and that his father was intending to defend his family as he had promised always to do. 'Shoot first, don't think. Kill the blighters. These Muslims are good for nothing.'

Luc furrowed his brow trying to recall the minutiae, the tiniest details of the events as they had unfolded the previous afternoon, even though recollecting them made him feel giddy and sick and it had all happened so fast. His memory was muddled. Who had pulled the trigger? Everybody in their household had been upstairs together, except his mother and father. Grandparents and aunt with Luc had been silently gathering their treasured possessions into one room, as though they had been preparing for an almighty bonfire. So, if the family was upstairs and his father was alone with his mother in his office, who had caused the shot? His mother?

No, no. There must have been an intruder.

'Luc, there you are! We've been calling you, looking everywhere for you. Come along with you. Nothing will be achieved here.'

The boy, still on his knees, hands muddied, fingernails packed with earth, stared hard at his mother, but did not budge. Clarisse drew close and tugged him by the arm, pinching at his clothing, yanking him to his feet. '*Viens*,' she commanded.

'*Non*.' He shrugged himself free. 'Leave me alone!'

'Luc. Don't be awkward. Please, not now. This isn't easy for any of us.'

'What about Papa?'

His mother sighed. Her softly plump, manicured fingers were now pressed against the boy's lips. She smelt of rosewater and olive-oil soap from Marseille. 'Papa wants to stay here, Luc.'

'Why? He doesn't like these people. He hates them. He always says so.'

'Hush now, we must never speak of this again.'

'Why?'

'Because Daddy prefers that. Now come along.'

Clarisse, his mother, flicked the brass clasp open on her leather box handbag and plunged her painted fingernails into it, nervously rooting until she retrieved a Colt pistol followed by an unopened tube of Spangles, which she pressed into Luc's hand. 'Here, put them in your pocket. You can suck them in the car. Let's go.' She shoved the gun back into her bag and pressed the clasp.

Reluctantly, Luc accepted the sweets and pushed them into the pocket of his shorts alongside the wrinkled jujubes. 'Where are we going?'

'On a big boat to France, *chéri*, a new adventure. Soon, this will all be over. You'll forget this summer. You must forget it.'

'What about Papa? We won't forget him, will we?'

Clarisse kissed his head, told him to cease his questions and be calm. This confused the boy because his mother showed more signs of agitation than he, and then she dragged him fast by the hand. Her open-toed sling-backs twisted and sank into the damp earth slowing their progress to the waiting car.

'Where was he?' his aunt demanded, in a raised whisper. Aunt Isabelle was all dolled up for town, her lips as vermilion as rhubarb stalks, white cotton gloves, a short-sleeved sundress and crocheted bolero. Her short dark curly hair was pushed back off her face with a thick white Alice band.

'Over by the trees. *You know where*. Let's go.'

From that moment on, the cause of his father's departure, 'the accident', was deemed taboo.

Amid the chatter and agitation, Luc was installed in the rear of the beetle-black, long-nosed Citroën, with its burgundy leather upholstery, next to the silent figure of his grandfather, who, staring directly in front of him, was cradling a rifle. His mother and aunt had stipulated that the windows were to be kept tightly shut in spite of the heat for fear of attacks by bloodthirsty natives. Nose pressed against the glass, Luc stared out. He felt a deep knot of misery in his stomach. His mother was at the wheel in her sleeveless leaf-print sundress and awkward sandals, now speckled with earth, as they descended the long, winding driveway, rolling slowly along the dappled avenue, flanked by bluish-green cedars and pencil-thin Italian cypresses, to the property's imposing black iron gates. In the distance, beyond the white city of Bône, the sun shimmered and glowed on the Mediterranean.

Although Luc loved the sea, always excitedly anticipating his Sunday fishing adventures with his grandfather, today the boy paid the view little attention. He was craning his head backwards, twisting his torso to catch for the last time, to store in his memory, the image of the shadowed mound of earth that represented his last impression of his father. On either side, beyond the procession of conifers, the clouds of dust and tiny pebbles thrown up by the tyres, the acres and acres of Cambon vineyards were heavy with ripening grapes. Who was left to harvest them? No one. On the car radio, the songwriter-singer Gilbert Bécaud's darkly brooding 'Et Maintenant'.

Yes, what now?'

Across the street, as the Citroën exited through the open gates, a young Algerian woman in cerulean blue, wearing a haphazard mix of Western and traditional dress, barefoot, hennaed hands wringing, eyes as round as hazelnuts, marked their departure. She hurled herself towards their car. Her arms, numerous silver bracelets jangling, were lifted heavenwards; her fists were clenched as though preparing to beat against their windscreen, to arrest their departure. She was screaming in Arabic, 'Murderers! Murderers!'

Clarisse spotted her. '*Merde!*' she spat, and before the girl could even cross the lane, she gunned the accelerator and the Cambon automobile swung sharply left, the gates closing behind them.

'Granddad, should we shoot her? Granddad!'

'Hush, now, boy,' commanded his grandmother.

No one said another word. Luc concentrated on the young woman's receding figure, fearing she might pull a gun and fire at them through the rear windscreen.

He held his breath as they proceeded along the lane beside the barbed-wire perimeter fence that protected the lower vineyards of their plantation while the Arab girl shrivelled to a speck that eventually disappeared from sight.

Five minutes later, two other cars joined them. Both had been waiting at the extreme point beyond the estate's furthest security post, which was no longer manned due to the abdication of all staff. The labour force had returned to their villages to fight with their own. Both of the newly arrived vehicles were transporting French families and their worldly goods, colonials from neighbouring farms more modest than the Cambons' own rolling hills, both situated a few kilometres west of the village of Mondovi, not far from St Joseph. Now they were a cortège in flight. Strength in numbers, each carrying loaded rifles. At the crossroads, they turned right. From there, the three packed automobiles dipped at a pace towards the sea. A dog barked frenziedly, then gave up, having worn itself out or lost interest.

Luc knew the way to the coast by heart. It was the same route he and his grandfather took when they went to Plage Toche to snorkel, first through the lovely port city of Bône, then habitually to the beach from which their dinghy was launched. Today, exceptionally, they were driving along the city's principal boulevard, Le Cours, descending directly to the water's edge, to the commercial port, the third largest in Algeria.

Once inside the city limits, no one within the car spoke. They were silenced by the chaos that surrounded them in the war-torn urban streets: the stop-start of traffic jamming the road; crippled soldiers begging; bedraggled revolutionaries caked in dried blood; the burned-out carcasses of French-licensed vehicles. The dregs of a traumatic war, a victory for the Algerians but far from concluded. Burned-out buildings to left and right. The heartrending cries of women mourning the thousands of bodies still to bury. Lines of military trucks transporting the wounded with their moaning, hollow-eyed faces, while the unclaimed corpses of men, women and children – Europeans, Arabs and Berbers alike – lay strewn about the pavements where no one paid them any attention. Atrocities perpetrated. Those who survived were sick to their teeth with the war, with the rotting bodies and the bloodshed.

Images engraved for ever on the boy Luc's consciousness.

'There's no law and order left in Algeria. Everyone running amok. They'll be thieving and pillaging soon, whatever they can lay their hands on,' muttered his aunt Isabelle, in the front passenger seat, beside his mother at the wheel. 'We should have boarded up the house.'

'You think it would make any difference? If they want to rob the place, they'll get in.'

'And God knows when, if ever, we'll be back. They've won the war. We Cambons will be outcasts.'

In contrast, at the port, all was eerily deserted. The tall palms shivered from time to time, as though in shock, in the non-existent wind. It was a threatening stillness, presaging a desert storm soon to blow up from the Sahara. Not a soul walked the quay. There was little activity on the water, which slicked and sucked and shifted against the land's man-made boundaries. Neither military nor commercial ships, the majestic liners the French called *paquebots*, were in dock to offer passage to the fleeing Pieds-Noirs. The President of the Fifth Republic, Charles de Gaulle, perceived as a traitor by many colonial landowners and agriculturalists, had given the order: 'No transport assistance is to be offered to the fleeing Pieds-Noirs.' The Pieds-Noirs, the black feet, were the hundreds of thousands of French citizens, French passport holders, white Europeans, born on Algerian soil, who had been the ruling majority in this French colonial state for over a hundred and fifty years but whose power was now at an end. Who found themselves little better than refugees.

'What now?'

Clarisse drew the Citroën to a halt in the shade of a towering palm, shoved the manual gearstick into neutral, but left the motor running. 'For God's sake,' she yelled, beating her fist against the wheel, causing the horn to sound. 'Why doesn't any bloody thing go our way? We have to get away.'

'Calm yourself, Clarisse,' hummed Luc's grandmother, squeezed up against the rear door directly behind her. 'Don't make matters worse.'

Isabelle ran a finger down her sister-in-law's neck but the younger woman shrugged it off. 'Come on,' she spat. 'Let's make a decision.'

The adults, save for Luc's grandfather, who stayed put, shoved at the doors and emerged from the confinement of the car to join their neighbours, clustering in a circle, a pow-wow in animated debate. The women's full summer skirts, bold flower prints against neutral backgrounds, moved gently in the early-morning air as though on springs. His mother's hourglass figure was cinched in at the waist by a thick patent red belt. The car's wireless was still on, muted, barely audible. Petula Clark was singing in French, 'Romeo', an unlikely hit in continental as well as colonial France at the beginning of that year.

'Will we go home now, Granddad?'

Luc's grandfather gave a half-hearted shrug.

Bruno Fabius, a russet-haired date farmer from the upper valley behind Mondovi, a neighbour who had regularly gone hunting with Adrien, Luc's father, broke from the group, strode towards the Cambon car and stuck his head through the automobile's open front window, filling the frame. He reeked of pastis, and his eyes were as baggy as knotted handkerchiefs. To Luc, he resembled a semi-shaved coconut.

'Sorry about your son, sir. Murderous bastards, these Muslims.'

Luc's grandfather shot a glance towards Clarisse, then lowered his gaze without a word.

Fabius waited awkwardly, the whites of his eyes marbled red, still with his head through the open window. 'The port's been taken and closed off,' he announced, as though to give purpose to his presence at the window. 'There'll be no passage for any of us from out of here. All colonials attempting to board ships along this east-coast outlet will be massacred. I've told Clarisse. We heard it on the radio on the way down here.'

Massacred?

The coconut, having delivered the bad news, returned to his car.

If they drove home, which was what Luc was hoping with all his heart, their throats would be slashed while they slept. Or so his aunt, the Cassandra of the household, forewarned as she settled back into her seat, lighting a Camel, slinging the match onto the pavement and inhaling deeply.

'There'll be no escape from this port. We have to keep going,' was his mother's determined decision. 'Fuck de Gaulle,' she yelled. Pulling out a pack of Peter Stuyvesant, she lit one with the car lighter. She dragged hard, leaving the smoking cigarette hanging from her lips, then threw herself back into her seat, pressed her sandalled foot on the accelerator and reversed at breakneck speed, almost dismantling a letterbox. 'Somehow or other,' she said, as though threatening her loved ones, 'even if I have to kill for it, we will find a passage out of here.'

'There'll be ships sailing from Algiers.'

'Let's go.'

The roads were hot, dusty and congested. All day and into the night, they kept advancing, moving west, passing through shelled, smoking villages, bodies ditched for carrion. The two younger women took turns at the wheel while the grandparents and Luc sat bunched together in the rear, crowded by the weight of possessions piled about them. It was a distance of four hundred and twenty kilometres – not a taxing journey from point A to point B, but they were forced to slow, to stop, to wait when they encountered military and FLN guerrilla roadblocks. In other areas, stretches of road had been blown up by the rebel forces, making it necessary to zigzag, to take improvised detours inland, where their lives were at greater risk on lonely rubble roads, and where finding petrol became a challenge, then a concern. When they eventually discovered a broken-down pump, manned by a dark-eyed Berber swathed in scarves, the replenishment cost them a substantial wad of their stashed-away francs.

Dusk, followed by fast-falling night, stole the landscape

from the boy's sight. Luc stared sullenly ahead into the beam of the headlights. Flying insects slapped against the windows, splotching them. A sandstorm was gaining momentum, as though they were driving directly into a swirling blanket of weather. Beaten-up vans and trucks were transporting agricultural goods, cord-secured crops of hay, tomatoes, aubergines, hillocks of food spilling into their vision, disappearing into the night.

Luc listened to his grandfather snoring gently at his side, a comforting sound, and the more alarming whispered exchanges of the two women in the front seats. He wanted them to stop: he needed to wee. He wanted to go home. He feared they might journey on for ever in the rocking vehicle.

By the time they reached the capital, the sun was rising. In spite of fatigue and hunger, they beat a path directly to the harbour, but the roads there were also clogged. The queues filed back a kilometre from the port, Algiers, where the hot desert wind was blowing grains of sand in angry whorls and closing out the daylight. It chafed their flesh, like rope burns, and stung their eyes. It lodged in their mouths and between their teeth. Three massive steamers, *les paquebots*, hugged the quay. Each was prepared, for a hefty sum, to transport the local French passport-holders who were not resident in mainland France.

'We'll find a passage here,' said Clarisse, but the boats were already spilling over with bodies, shapeless distraught masses wedged tightly together, frantic travellers, European refugees. The Cambons were too late for those sailings. No tickets available at any price. The first was preparing its departure. Low belching horns. Queues and queues of colonials were ahead of them. All fearing for their lives, waiting to escape. Luc's family joined the line. They hung on, sleeping in the Citroën, buying water, snacks at street stalls, from Berber vendors. They dared not leave the car: it would be stolen, torched, their possessions thieved. But the queues never seemed to lessen.

They lost sight of their neighbours in the other two cars. Their last link to Bône. Havoc ruled. They lacked sleep and washing facilities, and their spirits were sinking. After two days they had obtained no passage and their lives were in danger. In the eyes of the new Algerian power, the FLN, Adrien Cambon was a war criminal. A wanted man. No one knew he was a dead one.

'Enough!' yelled Clarisse, tossing the remains of a baguette and a cigarette stub to the ground, both instantly gobbled up by two squabbling black-backed gulls. 'Let's go!'

Luc closed his eyes and prayed with all his solemn might that they would return to their house, to the vineyards and his father.

Bypassing Oran, Luc's mother and aunt – both young females without men – took turns at the wheel. Foot hard against the accelerator, they traced the coastal highway into Morocco. Roads designed and engineered by the French, built with the sweat of local labour. Eight hundred kilometres to Tangier, where they were eventually herded aboard an overcrowded steamer bound for Algeciras in southern Spain. They had been on the run for six days – or was it seven? – but they were on their way out of Africa. Almost.

Au revoir to the country that had been the only homeland they had ever known.

Au revoir to the grandparents, who had decided they wouldn't be taking the boat. 'We're staying,' they announced. 'We're going back.'

'No!' wailed Luc.

'Are you crazy?' snapped Clarisse. 'They'll put you in a firing line, if they find you. No questions asked.'

'It's what we know,' confirmed Luc's grandmother.

'Take me with you,' cried Luc, arms wrapped about his grandfather's legs.

Clarisse grabbed him and wrenched him free. She embraced her in-laws, then stepped aside to give Isabelle a final moment with her parents.

'I'm further away from home than I've ever been,' wept the child Luc, still picturing his father, the risen mound in the garden, now contemplating his unexpected abandonment by his beloved grandparents.

Aboard the boat, on the slopping murky water, waiting to depart, Luc grew nauseous and fretful: the long drive, the stink of diesel and sea salt, his filthy clothes, his sadness. His mother, eyes red-rimmed, was doling out baguette sandwiches stuffed with thin strips of a bright-yellow rubbery *fromage* she had bought on the quay, but he wasn't hungry. He longed for his father. He ached for home with an unquantifiable sorrow. *La tristesse.* He rarely cried but he felt a thickening in his throat, a tightening in his chest that threatened to swamp him. Seagulls were screeching overhead. His mother was drinking gin from a bottle and appeared to be crying or snivelling, rubbing her nose as though it was itching. 'I had no choice,' she wailed. 'All our lives were in danger. I did it for Luc.'

Luc yearned to lie beside that mound of earth in the shade of the jujube trees and talk to his father. He could not grasp what was happening to him, to his life, his family, his insane mother. What lay ahead? Where were they going? Behind him, beyond the decks of the mighty ship, was land, his past, Africa, where people were milling about everywhere. Street vendors, ticket touts waving the promise of a black-market passage, food shacks, water-sellers. Arabs, Berbers, French, Christians, Muslims.

Morocco, a liberated state for the last six years.

Ahead, his future, nothing but a vast, empty sea. Beyond which, unseen, another continent: Europe. Spain and then France. The mother country, where neither he nor any other member of his family had ever set foot. The steamer's horn boomed and the giant boat began to shift, slowly tearing itself away from the quay. The eddying water looked as though it went on for ever and was hungry to suck him under.

Three hours later, along with hundreds of other refugees, Luc, his mother and aunt were disembarking, files of cars spilling out of the belly of the ship. After queuing to retrieve their now filthy Citroën, the Cambons sped north.

Blasting from the car radio, as they drove through Spain, Anglo-Saxon popular music. Dion's 'The Wanderer'. Ray Charles, Elvis Presley. Popular tunes Clarisse and Isabelle had danced to by the pool at their settler parties, their own drunken *soirées*. Like so many others of their kind, they had partied on, ignoring the war, ignoring the impending imposed dismantling of their colonial lives. They had concentrated on the good life they had always known and pretended the rest of it was not happening. The only adjustments they had allowed were weapons. They had slept with guns under their pillows. They had walked the streets armed, and if a Muslim, male or female, was following them, they stepped aside to allow the unknown silhouette to pass, fearing the stranger shadowing them, imagining that they would be gunned down or stabbed silently in the back.

'As of tomorrow, no one's going to leave us for dead on the pavement. Tomorrow we'll have reached France. Now, let's sing,' commanded his mother, crazed by exhaustion and loss. 'Sing as loud as you can. We must keep our spirits up. Come on people.' Clarisse began to croak, huskily and off-key, attempting to harmonize with the lyrics on the radio. Dion's 'The Wanderer'.

'We are roaming, no, we are escaping . . . Too right,' sighed Isabelle, lighting a cigarette that caused an explosion of coughing. 'Ugh, these Spanish fags are *dégueulasse*, disgusting, *dégoûtant*.'

Luc, tightly packed into the rear of the vehicle, remained silent. Squashed between a household of belongings, he was sleeping fitfully, his head sliding from the window. He was dreaming of his old life, of riding his new bicycle, his granddad at his side, along the coastal paths to the Cap de Garde where the pair of them would sit in the sunshine, preparing their fishing tackle, their snorkels and masks, while watching the comings and goings of the boats, sailing yachts, fishing vessels and sometimes, when they were lucky, they'd spot one of the Mediterranean tankers, preparing to drop anchor a little further along the coast, readying itself to load up with barrel after barrel of the newly discovered desert oil.

'Black gold.' His grandfather would smile to him. 'We'll have a share in that, lad. Algeria's future.'

It was after midnight, a warm starry night in not-so-peaceful Catalonia, Franco's tightly bound Spain, smelling sweetly of ripening melons, when the Citroën approached the Spanish-French border, the hard dark outlines of the unknown Pyrenees peppered with slate-roofed villages to the left and before them. Isabelle, three passports in her lap, was dozing, gently snoring. Clarisse jabbed her sister-in-law hard in the ribs with her elbow. 'Get out that sweet, red-lipped smile of yours, *chérie*. Here we go. *La France*.'

*

By September of 1962, back in Algeria, south across the Mediterranean Sea, the city of Bône, renamed Annaba by the recently installed Algerian government, was sinking into neglect. It was a decaying metropolis, its infrastructure in ruins. The richly fertile outlying farms lost to the French were being settled by bands of Bedouins. The nomads squatted on the lands, living in black, goat-hair tents and tended their flocks of sheep and goats, which fed off the planted vegetation. Those travelling tribes paid no attention to the crops tended until recently by the detested French. They drank no wine and, disinterested, left the unkempt vines to develop into jungle. On the abandoned Cambon estate, the great house was empty and forgotten. The bloodstains spattered across the walls in one of the downstairs rooms bleached in the heat to blotches of brown, then disappeared beneath galloping mildew and cobwebs. The shot fired by Clarisse Cambon that had blown open the face of Adrien Cambon, her husband, in the heat of disgust and argument, resounding through their homestead, faded to the ghost of an evocation on the coastal winds. Goats and birds drank from the swimming-pool while the grapes hung low, rotting pendulously on the boughs. A lost domain.

Meanwhile, in the Var department of south-eastern France, two young women and one small keen-eyed boy, the depleted Cambon household, were settling into their new *bastide* home. Les Cigales was a sprawling vineyard estate urgently in need of work and investment. Clarisse Cambon was its newly installed *châtelaine* and she walked its shabby floors with pride and expectation. She and her sister-in-law, Isabelle, purchased young mares and cantered the length and breadth of their new territory.

Clarisse, especially, ached to put the past behind her. She

hungered for new beginnings, new friendships, assimilation, to turn her back on the bloodshed and nightmares of war and hurt and death. To turn her back on the sacrifice she had felt obliged to make for the sake of her son. Luc would have a new life. He need never know, need never be haunted by the shame of his father's guilt.

The two women hired labour, men from the local communities, never Arabs, and set to work. The seasons turned. The land regenerated. Spring bloomed, heralding its arrival with the most delicate of almond blossoms. The scent of cedar resin, jasmine and cherry blossom imbued the warm April days. The two young women and the growing boy had much to do, challenges to occupy them, labour to blank out, to extinguish, the past. The vineyards rose forth like fluttering birds, producing lime-green leaves and exceptional wines, while the silvery olive groves promised decades of generous harvests. Yet the women remained isolated, distanced on their hillside. The past, the events of that forgotten summer, never quite let them go.

Acknowledgements

I am enormously fortunate with the team MJ, Penguin is putting around me. Maxine Hitchcock, publishing director at MJ and my editor, has shown such enthusiasm for this book. Thank you hugely, Maxine.

Thank you to my publicist, Gaby Young, copyeditor Hazel Orme and Clare Bowron, Eve Hall and Sophie Elletson.

As I am new to Penguin there will be many who will work on this book who I have not yet had an opportunity to meet, so I am thanking you all in advance! I am looking forward to our future together.

Special thanks to my splendid agent, Jonathan Lloyd at Curtis Brown, for hanging in there during the tougher days. Also at Curtis Brown, I want to thank (in no particular order) Alice Lutyens, Melissa Pimentel, Lucie Rae and Katherine Andrews. You are a wonderful team and I really appreciate all you do for me. A little thanks on the side to Sheila Crowley, also at Curtis Brown, not my agent but a powerhouse at retweeting and spreading good news.

Much love and gratitude too to Chris Brown, one of my longest-standing friends, for support and wise words.

A little shout of appreciation to Mary and Tom Alexander at Gloster House in Co. Offaly for their generosity and hospitality. Also, huge thanks to Pat Lancaster and Rhona Wells for being there when I needed that little bit of help.

As always a huge kiss to my husband, Michel, who is an inspiration and offers his love so generously. *Merci, mon amour.*